TWO ELEPHANTS IN THE MATCHBOX

TWO ELEPHANTS IN THE MATCHBOX

SATHAJANAN LUXMAN

Matador
9 Priory Business Park
Kibworth Beauchamp
Leicester LE8 0RX, UK
Tel: 0116 279 2299
Email: books@troubador.co.uk
Web: www.troubador.co.uk/matador

ISBN 978-1780880-525

British Library Cataloguing in Publication Data.
A catalogue record for this book is available from the British Library.

Typeset in Aldine401 BT Roman by Troubador Publishing Ltd, Leicester, UK
Printed and bound in the UK by TJ International, Padstow, Cornwall

Matador is an imprint of Troubador Publishing Ltd

To my God Daughter,

And

To my long lost London Bohemian Brothers
Eseh Issacs, Dawn Lanten
Where ever you are be rock and roll

And

To my dear friends Marlon Li, Dudly, Tharma,
and Tino for being there when I felt like an orphan.

The book is dedicated to my extended family and all the Tamil people of Sri Lanka, who sacrificed their life for the freedom of Tamil nation.
Tamil Ellam.

Especially to my grandparents, parents, aunts, uncles, and my beloved aunty Mary, who lost her husband, brother, sister and her children during this terrible conflict.

I salute you for your bravery and love of your country, still living somewhere, believing in a peaceful conclusion.

Finally my grand mother Mary Margaret B who named me as Luxman. This is for you. Rest in peace.

Special thanks, to Iseult Healy for editing and proof reading, Without her I would not have made it to the finish line on time.

CONTENTS

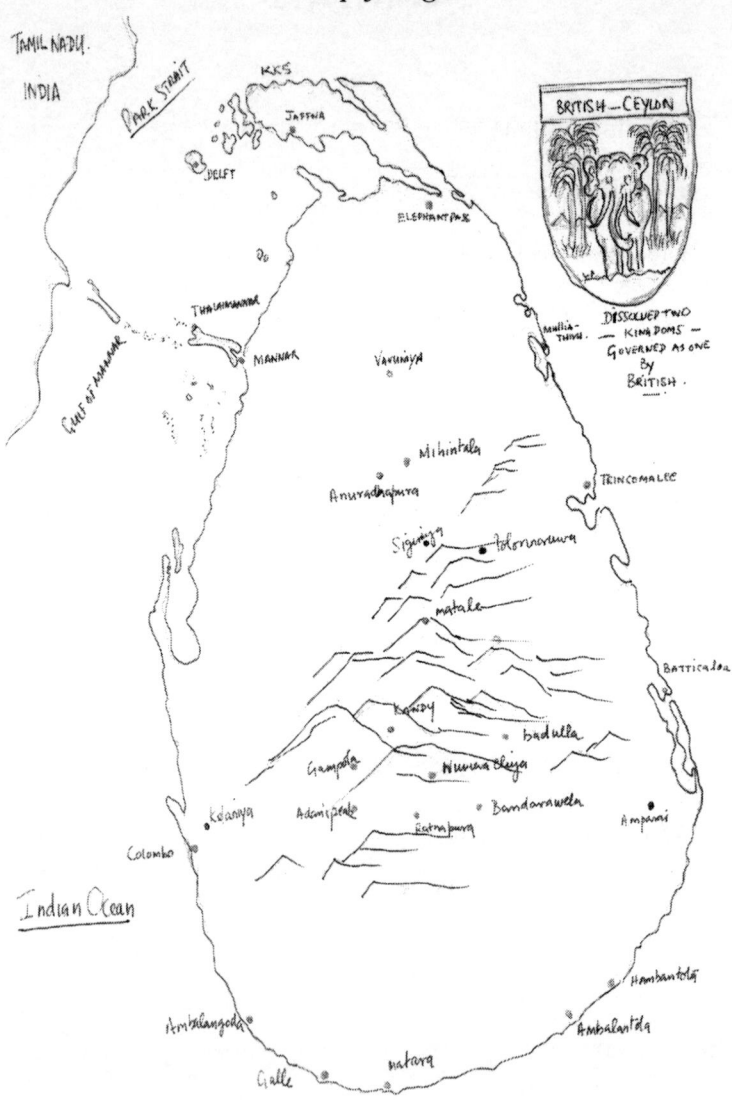

Bay of Bengal

TAMIL NADU.

INDIA

PARK STRAIT

KKS

JAFFNA

DELFT

ELEPHANT PASS

BRITISH — CEYLON

MULLIA-THIVU

DISSOLVED TWO KINGDOMS — GOVERNED AS ONE BY BRITISH.

THALAIMANNAR

MANNAR

GULF OF MANNAR

VAVUNIYA

Mihintala

Anuradhapura

TRINCOMALEE

Sigiriya

Polonnaruwa

matale

BATTICALOA

Kandy

badulla

Gampola

Nuwara Eliya

Kelaniya

Adam's Peak

Bandarawela

Ampara

Colombo

Ratnapura

Indian Ocean

Hambantota

Ambalangoda

Ambalantota

Galle

matara

CHAPTER ONE

KINGDOM OF JANA

Night fell on Beach Road. Jaffna street lights were fitted on old tree stumps painted in black wood preserver, standing tall at fifty foot. Every fifty yards, holding four high-powered thick electric cables along the roadside, they gave the light for the small dark homes which were without electricity. The cool breeze shifted in from the sea of Jaffna Gulf. The Beach Road nightlife kicks in with the Singing Fish beach volleyball team, as they begin their night game, hitting the first ball, with the bent wrist action from a sandy base line. The lines were marked by a captain, dragging his heel all the way around the pitch prior to the game. The Kurunagar outdoor stage lights were usually lit up and gave players and the locals a good view of the game from all different key corners. The stage was mainly used during the Passover to reenact the Nativity of Christ: it was named profoundly as the pass meaning the Passover. The whole city came to see that operatic show put together by the local amateur theatre group and it was very popular even among the Hindus and the Muslims. The railway line alongside the stage went criss-crossing through the shanty towns' huts made of mud and coconut leaves. It's a dirty smoked-out goods train that sounds the whistle through the Jaffna jetty at the corner of Yalta Hotel. The poor along the street have lit their kerosene oil lamps to give enough light for the night cooking. It's definitely a fried anchovies with garlic, cumin, small onions, mustard seeds with rice and dried lemon pickle smelling really fresh. The café's lit with petrol max, a pressurized stainless steel lamp with fine nylon weaved soft filament - it will burn to give enough light for six hours flat, with a few pressure pumps with your thumbs. The café manager will increase and decrease according to the business to save energy. Men going home from work pedal hard on their Dutch style Asian bikes. The loose chain strokes the mudguard, worn rubber brakes touching the wheel giving a rhythmic whistle noise from the front wheel dried with hot sandy dust which rusted the movement. It also lacked grease and service. The riders grind and creaked while pushing down the pedal by straining and sweating - they will stop for a cup of warm tea in a silver cup. Some would not stop for anything but race on the streets to get home quick for a homemade coffee brewed with roasted spices. The Beach Road Kurunagar Gym was full of occupants working out with free weights. The gym was pretty basic; open for all, four walls, roof, with three windows back and front and without doors. Free weights were made of cement rings, some on wooden poles, and some on an iron bar with the coconut fiber ropes tied either side to keep the weights from moving out of position. It was an ingenious idea worked quite effectively.   Particularly the man with dark skin, heavy set with a big moustache that curled up against his sweating face, and a small red rag tied around his forehead like a Chandian covered his left eye; a tribal headband for a rebel worn with honor. He screamed 'Achaaaa… achaaaa!' He lifted the weights up and down, up and down without any erratic movement. Then he suddenly put the heavy weights down with a big thud to the floor. The gym shook like a minor earthquake. The makeshift metal window bars vibrated. Then he sighed deeply as everybody around him looked on in amazement. The mood inside the gym was like they were preparing for a gang fight, usually down St Peter's Road and Beach Road junction. Its tribal wars erupted from time to time when a girl or boy got mixed up - loving another rival party.

The gym helpers joined and helped each other with bench press-ups, their legs knotted and also by throwing basketballs hard at the stomach. A punch bag made of canvas and wrapped around with the coconut fiber filled with rice was swinging side to side. The Elastoplast was taped around the bag where it was most punched and kicked. The dent was quite obvious on that area; a small tear had been created. There was a young Bruce Lee kicking with vigor, repeatedly saying 'yeah… huh… yeah… huh…'while breathing heavily.

'Somebody needs to stop him,' Jana muttered to himself, from a distant lookout. Somebody did stop him before he reached a point of exhaustion; he'd been on his way to losing consciousness. The rubber cycle tube holding the bag gave a little stretch and awkward returns kept the puncher alert and moving all the time. The kid was gasping for breath by now; somebody gave him a blue-edged, white enamel cup full of freshly squeezed lemon and sugar from a big bucket from the table. The big man started lifting again and again the heavy weight as everybody screamed… 'go on! Go on! Small brother - *sinna thambi* - you *Chandian* of the Beach Road.' The place erupted with cheers for the big man. They were all in a fighting mood that night. He was not really a small brother but he appreciated with a smile what they meant. He was the big brother on the Beach Road watching everybody. Looking after everybody. The man made all opponents convulse in fear. He also could take a quite a beating too. He has been in and out of Jaffna Police Station like a priest to the sacristy.

All in the gym that evening were very excited about the plan for that night.

Their excitement was disrupted by a loud bell, the bell of a *punthi vandial* - a four wheel bicycle mechanically adopted, which looked like a large glass coffin on a wooden platform, its corners made of well-polished mahogany beams. The handle made of metal enabled the vender to push or pull the cart in any direction while he worked from the rear wheel push drive. It glowed like a well-lit aquarium with a blue actinic lamp run off a small battery, enough to make those sparkling Christmas lights along the edges a real sight. The handler pushed the sweet and savory heavy cart looking side to side to avoid the potholes, all the while ringing the bell. His transistor radio also played a smooth motivational Tamil classic from M.G. Ramachadran movie songs sung by T.M. Sounderajan as he expected a good business along the Beach Road. He was also anticipating troubles with the young night crowd at Kurunagar. The punthi cart contained red orange honey horns dripping with colored sugar syrup, chocolate and coconut halves, biscuits, glucorasa chewing sweet, dark palmyra sugar, thothol with cadgunuts, roasted monkey nuts, dhal, puri, fried roasted chickpeas, mungbeans, rice crisps, prawn crackers, pappadoms, onion bhajis, pukkoras and varieties of homemade cakes with almonds called kesari, all staked and segregated according to the sweet and savory section with brown bags all rolled up like a small funnel according to the price; small paper bags on a twine through a pin hole, for easy to serve the customer quick and away during the rush orders. It all looked organized. The occasional tilt and dip or a heavy shake as a heavy lorry or a bus passed by the cart was adequately handled with ease as the vendor showed his experience of a lone long push through the potholed roads of Jaffna during the celebratory seasons. While he waited for his customers he cleanly ripped the newspapers and old exercise books in squares in order to make the disposable biodegradable paper waste. In Jaffna of the 80's, people collected papers and cans and sold them at recycling factories well before the global warming panic. The heavy brown paper was used only for the expensive gingili oil savories and kasseris to absorb the excess oil and butter. It looked a colorful and well organized moving mini bakery. Those days the best selling among the kids were the roasted monkey nuts, roasted in heavy hot sands in a barge style steel wok called *Thactchi*. The huge handle on both sides made it easier to move the wok left and right while turning the nuts without getting burned on that melting hot sandy wok. Popcorns, sweet or spicy, topped with desiccated coconut dust, were the favorite of movie-going adults. Some boys not far from home with their distinctive dark blue vest and khaki school shorts with side pockets and belt loops on their waists almost falling down from their thin and malnourished skinny bodies, began to approach the gleaming sweet chariot. Few boys wore white vests, some wore colorful cotton and nylon with thick trim around the neck with dirt and sweat marks clearly visible. Few held the loops and pulled the shorts up with one hand while he sucked the other thumb. One youth adjusted his shorts from his butt crack to avoid it cutting in between the legs and causing friction, scratched his head and was up to something when he saw the Punthiman. They mumbled secretly to each other, their heads close together, and pointed to the sweets and the savories. The boys were not happy with the surroundings for their plan; the gym, brightly lit volleyball match, busy Beach Road, the cafes. They waited and waited as the vendor began to do some business, with a smile to the passing crowd. The almighty goods train came to the rescue. It came with the loud whistle, going towards the jetty to collect shrimp. It was a season for good shrimp business exported all the way to Norway. The boys looked at each other and smiled and looked at the slow moving diesel goods train as it approached Kurunagar stadium dripping oil debris on the sleepers. It looked like a well-planned sabotage among the distracting locals. The big kid, excited with his plan, was encouraged by the others. They were excited, they approached the cart hiding behind the gathering crowd, smiling at everybody, and then suddenly two boys from the Miracle of Mary Church off Bank Street joined the cart and pretended to help the cart vender.

The cart vendor shouted with annoyance: 'Don't! Don't! Leave it. Leave it!' Then continued: 'Boy, I have it well under control thank you. Thank you, sinna puyya… small boys…'

'Go away,' said the Punthiman.

One kid from the church end said: 'Just trying to help, that's all.'

'I don't need any help,' said the Punthiman looking at the boys very angrily. 'I only need business. Are you buying something?' asked the man. 'I guess not. Just leave it out!' he screamed with tiredness and anger. 'Leave it before I get angry,' he said.

The kids took their hands off with disappointment, then

6

put them out again to annoy the man. Then took them off, put them out again. The other little group looked in disappointment as their plan was hijacked by this aggressive attitude. They watched the Punthiman and the train, one after the other, the train came almost to a standstill as some got on it while the driver screamed 'get off you dirty fools'. Then they jumped down. Everyone's attention went to the train, the few who had been sitting on the track relaxing, just stood up and let the train move by, as the driver screamed 'move, move you lazy, smelly bastards'. In the meantime, the place stank. He said the worst word, 'It stinks of fish everywhere among the fisherman tribe'. You don't dare to say that in Kurunagar. He looked around to make sure nobody heard it.

Some animals in the compartment started dropping their dung, which fell through the side of the partially opened compartment. Suddenly the place went from the dried fish smell into a farmyard collection pit. Cows and lambs together screamed at the turn of the goods train into the jetty yard. It annoyed the hell out of the lone driver, the noise and distraction, while he kept the old train on the track. Everybody for once on Beach Road pinched their noses and said *oh god, that is really a nice mixture.*

'Oh, it smells ladies, really it does,' said the old man in the hut. Then he shouted: 'Bring me that Vicks bottle, I am going to rub some under my nose. Enough is enough!'

Jana grew up in this neighborhood, so he knew all the tricks of the Kurunagar kids. It was full of cross streets and narrow lanes and houses built all different shapes and sizes and painted pink, blue and magnolia. Jaffna Lane houses also had distinctive metal gates with cultural designs ranging from Vishnu to St Anthony.

Jana spoke to Indhiran who sat next to him yawning, smelling his right forearm for his stress. Indhiran got that habit when as a kid he would wait for his mama's milk, as Aunty Rohini refused to give him milk when he was 3 years old. He would wait at the same spot smelling his arm for half an hour before giving up and walking out of the house. People have tried to grab his hand and pull it down so many times, but a few minutes later it would be back on to the spot, if he was bored. Everybody by now had given up, they all had done something but now they had stopped. Indhiran did not want to stop. He just couldn't stop it. Whenever he was quiet, thinking deeply, he just had to smell his right arm covering his face while his eyes were fixed to a point concentrating… 'hum…hum…. Jana pulled his arm and said: 'Listen, watch that little one with the Arunakodi.' *Arunakodi*, a silver charm hip bracelet worn by young boys in Jaffna.

Jana continued: 'He can't even hold his pants properly… watch what he is going to do.'

He was approaching the Punthiman. The blue and Battick sarong of the Punthiman flew up in the wind.

'He is going to pull that sarong, there is no chance, no way that's coming down, no way', said Jana.

'What?' said Indhiran.

'He's got a very tight brown leather belt over his waist.'

'It is Singalavan style,' said Indhiran. 'A belt and a knife, Kathii,' said Indhiran and took his hand down like he had just woken up from his sleep. Jana and Indhiran watched the event unfold in front of their eyes. The kid pulled the sarong, the other one opened the sliding door, one threw a few stones in front of the wheel, while the other two hid behind the tree and watched it all with excitement without participating. They just wanted a large bag of the roasted chickpeas called kadali. The vendor, with real anger, pulled the cart left and right in a hurry to the sandy gutter of the street above the gravel stones level of Jaffna Street. The man felt his waist with his hand while holding the vandal with the other hand. He made sure his money purse was secured with his business sales. It felt secure and thick. Now he was happy to deal with the boys. The boys retreated, fearing a knife would come out of his waist. One screamed, 'kathiyada!' The whole plan went up in smoke for everybody. Some elders sitting under the trees on their chairs drinking tea grappled the escaping boys and brought them to the Punthiman holding their ears. The kids roared: 'Ah! Ahhh! It hurts! It hurts!'

'Good,' said the elder, 'That's the whole idea,' as he gave the boys to the vendor. The Punthiman was used to all this drama. He grabbed the big guy and let go the little one.

'Shall I give you to the police? Do you want to eat in a nice hotel tonight, do you?' said the Punthiman. Eating in a nice hotel meant a good beating by the police, and in those days sometimes they gave left over hotel meals to the prisoners. The Punthiman tried to kick the boy on his backside hard with his leg while his slippers fell down. The boys in the gym saw that; they came out quickly:

'Hey, hey, what happened? What happened? Stop hitting the kid. What has he done?'

The vendor replied: 'He tried to derail me with stones.'

'No, I did not. All I wanted was a good portion,' said the kid.

'He is expensive and greedy,' said one of the elders and walked away; they did not want to get involved anymore.

The kid pulled out the money: 'Here, it's the money. I was going to pay,' said the kid while crying and looking with the corner of the eye. The gym crew pulled out a few rupees.

'Hey man. Come on, give the kids good portions, ok? I don't want to see you hitting the kids here at the Beach Road. Otherwise you have to face the big moustache man sitting over there,' pointing to the heavy set man. 'If he comes outside, your cart will be upside down and burning, so move on, ok? Move on.'

The kids got what they wanted - free punthi and kadalai. They walked away fighting each other for the big bag, spilling the kadalai on the sand, calling names. They screamed: 'you stinky small... small portions... [sinna kottai] small balls', to the Punthiman. The Punthi vendor spat on the streets and moved on passing the gym. He saw a few glimpses of shining metal weapons inside; he was scared for once. He pushed the cart towards the Miracle of Mary Church to get the evening service crowd. He had enough of the Beach Road drama for one evening.

Jana said: 'Always the little one don't get the nuts at the end, see.' Pointing to the big boy: 'He took his kadalai.'

The boy was crying now, they threw him back a few nuts and as he tried to catch it, it fell on the sands. Jana shook his head and repeated: 'Always the little ones haven't got the nuts at the end.'

Indhiran said: 'You got big ones!' as he tried to grab Jana's pants.

Jana said: 'you got problems man... real problems, *kambi kaka*... you.' Meaning homosexual. 'Always going for my pants. I am not sure about you anymore, Indhiran,' hesitated smiled ,Jana looking at his cousin disgustingly.

Jana sat on the Beach Road wooden bench. It was not really a bench. They were shaven tree trunks, rotten tree trunks, all lined up from the local firewood supplier. His yard was full of it, all measured and cut into two foots but dozens of piles tidied up nicely, stacked in a huge pile. The ones lined up outside would be cut to a foot but for smaller families at reduced prices. So it made a good bench for Jana and his friends in the night time; sometimes even a night bed for an over drunken dock worker who did not have the legs to walk home. Jana would come and meet Indhiran for few hours to watch the world go by at Beach Road, also to get to play with the equipment in the gym when all the big boys were out of the hall. The kids loved to hang out on Beach Road. It was an unpredictable place full of action.

Suddenly, there was a big moment at the gym. The gym crew hid their weapons in their sarongs. 'It looks like a plan of attack,' said the more experienced Indhiran.

Some men quickly got inside the parked grey Austin Somerset, and drove towards the St. David Road.

Jana was not interested in fights anymore, he was growing up, he was in his last days of the middle school at St Peter's College. He was moving into the GCE Ordinary Levels at upper school and he was looking forward to that with enthusiasm. He also wanted to captain the St Peter's Under [17] seventeen cricket team, the days of twelfth man/ water boy routine were all past history. He was also in the first [19+] eleven, and was the opening batsman. He was also nicknamed the block master.

Jana and Indhiran began to walk towards Indhiran's house. Jana stopped under the church lights and said: 'wait a minute'.

Jana read his few full scraps of paper one by one checking spelling and grammar mistakes with a carbon pencil. Indhiran finally wanted to know what he was up to. He was bored. He looked at the papers while leaning forward, trying to read with pretend.

'So, what are you reading' asked Indhiran. Jana paused as he watched that Austin Somerset car disappear in the distance from the beach road. All the men and women in that street in front of the houses and shops looked into the car while it went passed their front porch.

'Do you know where that car is going? asked Indhiran. 'You will read it in the papers tomorrow,' said Indhiran quite casually. 'Anyway forget those crazy guys. Tell me what you are reading?'

Jana turned and looked into his eyes and said: 'It is my final essay for my 9th grade exam. It is also a final paper with oral explanation of the subject matter.'

'Subject matter!' said Indhiran with a face like a cockatoo.

'I really worked hard on this English please,' said Jana. 'This is for my English teacher Miss Eve and for my dad to prove that I can do it without pressure. I am not so confident what will they think of my observation, so it's rewrite and rewrite until I get it right, also the spelling mistakes and grammar. I am terrible with that, so there you are,' said Jana. 'You know our Miss Eve?' asked Jana with the smile.

Indhiran shook his head and said 'No.'

'You know her,' said Jana frustrated. 'She lives between the 4th and the 5th cross street, right over there,' as he pointed, 'the west of Beach Road.'

Indhiran said: 'Oh yes, Miss Eve. Slim and beautiful, Miss Eve. I know, so that's why you're hanging around here, so you can get a glimpse of your fantasy English teacher. You stalker, yeah, she is lying there relaxing in her room, after a tired day in the college, cold shower, luxury soap from Colombo to her tender skin all washed and dried, just for you to go and massage her. Go on you… go on you, lover boy.'

Jana shook his head at the comment: 'Yes, yes, yes, she is

nice and beautiful but not like that man, give it a rest. I have got to hand over this to her tomorrow and that's it. She won't be teaching us anymore.'

'Why?' asked Indhiran? 'Is she getting married?'

'No, no, no,' said Jana. 'I am going to the senior school, you dummy. You are just thinking of sex all the time, nothing else.

'What else do you think? Everybody think about sex, every goddamn day and night. Do you know that Jana? You don't!' shouted Indhiran. 'You also better start thinking about that otherwise…' hesitated Indhiran. 'Anyway, it's up to you, ok? It's not my problem. It's Mr. Prahash and you.'

Jana and Indhiran stopped talking for a minute and really started thinking about it. They looked at each other without saying a word.

Jana studied English with enthusiasm, like no other subject, just because of his adolescent infatuation with the teacher who had long beautiful curly hair, all elegantly plaited, smooth legs up to her lean shoulders, beautiful brown eyes, figure like an Indian supermodel and who wore colorful floral design silk saris. She turned every head, young and old men, with effortless elegance and beauty of the wild peacock during the rain dance. She was one of a kind and mesmerizing to watch her walk down the street. Miss Eve was a dream for the school boys. They sat in the class without a single interruption and watched her and dreamed all the way through her 40 minutes class. She smiled at every one of them when they looked at her in their dreams. She was happy to make them happy. They also learned English and did the homework just to get closer to her. They never missed the class. She was also popular among the other school teachers. They all asked her how did you get that class working like this, how did you do it? She just smiled. She taught English for years, and now the time had come for Jana's class to say goodbye. They were really going to miss her. So Jana really wanted to thank her for all the hard work over the years at St. Peters by writing a great piece as a tribute to Miss Eve. He wanted that to be his greatest work ever. The inspiration was the people of Jaffna, the roads, and the lives of everyday people of Kurunagar. It was about the culture, hospitality, generosity, also violence and unsolved grievances. But to achieve this standard of prose and the writing skills, he had to thank one man, one man alone.

That was his father, Mr. Prahash, currently working away from home abroad on the Greek ships. He took a no-pay leave from his regular job to work abroad to pay off his family debt which had accumulated during his grand house building in Chundikuli, a leafy district of Jaffna, near the Old Park. It was lined with 500 year old large trunk banyans, mahogany, mango, wood apple, tamarind and purple fruit trees.

Jana began telling about his father during his absence. It was a big shock for Indhiran because they both really had a hard time with Mr. Prahash over the years. Jana said to Indhiran: 'Whatever he did to me over the years, without him I would never have studied English, like I am doing now. He really pushed me, gave me five lashes from the bamboo cane until I got it right. He really encouraged me to read and write constantly. I used to hate it. Really got wound up at times. But he kept me cool and calm, ha ha ha!' Jana laughed, 'you know Indhiran, what he used to do to me? That's something, really something,' said Jana as he shook his head. He looked up towards Indhiran with glossy eyes": 'He used to make me read the Sunday papers aloud, he would say louder, I can't hear you, louder!, while holding the cane and correcting the pronunciation, asking me questions about words and vocabulary. It was relentless,' said Jana with real gratitude and emotion. 'I used to love it sometimes but hated it most of the time. I felt sometimes the real anger and started to cry, it all depended on the article I was reading.' Then Jana smiled at Indhiran. 'I used to like the sports pages, he will redirect me to read the current affairs.' Jana laughs again. 'I am also, yeah… I also wound him up sometimes for no reason. It's my fault, too. He loved the politics, agriculture, irrigation, science and technology,' Jana paused, with tears at times, while talking with Indhiran, 'I read it, with tears; I began to get used to the pressure. He also encouraged me to say it loud, say it without hesitance, go say it to my face at the first instance, speak English without hesitance and loud. Those were his words. So I tried, sometimes I did without hesitance, sometimes hesitated, then it came into my head why I didn't say that earlier, regrets, missed opportunities. Like I always wondering why I didn't do that earlier. Then it dawned on me all what he said about the English language. I spoke broken English, but I spoke,' Jana paused, looked at Indhiran, 'eventually I began to improve. It also improved my confidence. I spoke while others laughed at my mistakes. I continued with courage and attempted with continuity, while imitating Miss Eve, actors, newsreaders, to be able to carry the conversation,' Jana paused and then said: 'Do you know who else spoke well? Richard Burton, he spoke well. Remember The Night of the Iguana? Spoke with a great diction. Liz Taylor fell for it. So I read it twice as loud when my father was not around. It meant something to me. I don't know why. It felt good. It just did,' Jana paused for a moment again. 'He also asked me to write down the article I read. Write it down what I understood. Put it in my own words. He said no pressure while swinging his cane vigorously up and down. He asked me to repeat it. Spelling and grammar was his priority. He used to say the girls really dislike the boys who can't spell. Great spelling. Lovely girls. That's right. Then he would say, now stop dreaming about girls. Write it down again.'

Indhiran laughed loudly.

'Then he would ask me to compare what I have written against the article, against my first attempt. Check your own spelling and mistakes. I hated all that mickeymouse routine. Felt repressed or some kind of punishment. Why did he hate me so much? I never understood. But I really turned the corner in my interest in the English language, soon I was picking up articles and asking questions about the politics and court cases. He really loved my sudden change of direction. I guess that was my best time ever with my father, we were like friends just on those Sundays. Just on Sundays,' Jana repeated. 'He was a Tamil Congressman. Did not like any other parties especially the *Tamil Arasu*. The spins and deceits of Tamil Arasu during the seventies elections win by the narrowest of the margin was quite obvious. Every party will try their best to rig the Jaffna election. He had great perception. He did not have great help with his English from anybody, but he spoke good English, also managed a fair bit of Sinhala for the governmental official reasons. His talent was noted by the people in Vanni. He spoke at the congress rallies during the late sixties. The elephant marches. He put me on the elephant when I was four, as he was walking along with Vanni Congress Party and G. G. Balam. Yes, he was a great character those days. Do you remember the opening of the RIO cinema? asked Jana.

'You mean the tractor scream?' said Indhiran.

'I knew that he was given a pet name *the screaming overseer,* the *kullari osear ayya.* He really had a screaming voice. No handheld microphone those days, they just screamed at home and in the public.' Jana paused for a minute. 'I can still remember that day on the Red Massey Ferguson tractor with the open low tipper.'

Tractors were used for everything imaginable; farming, harvesting, transporting building material. Especially for the river gravel, fine sand from the dunes, and most importantly, took people on trips to temples and churches. It was a real workhorse with an open top carrier, with a two foot bar keeping everyone all together safe, with a raised chassis and nut bolt and a chain. Tractors also reflected the success of the farmer, who had the paddy fields; Mr. Prahash wed his daughter from his harvest, gave to the local temple ceremonies and charities, blessed by the priest before his departure to sell his harvest on the auction market. The tractor was a sign of prosperity of the region. So it was Mr. Prahash's idea, to put this to Mr. Kathir next door, who was going to run the Rio Cinema, he was from Mallaham. They had a good deal with the Jaffna Mayor bringing entertainment to the people of Jaffna. The plan was to increase English language films. Plans to bring more tourists from Colombo to the neglected north's unspoiled beaches. There were museums, parks, beaches, hotels all nearby for the discerning couples who wanted to get away from the usual restricted environment. Mr. Prahash offered himself to be a key speaker, a promoter, stand-up comedian for the opening of the Rio cinema in Jaffna; the majority of the profits going to the municipal government improvements. The tractor was ready, all decorated with flowers, mango leaves, small banana trees uprooted and tied around the four corners on the tractor, looked really like a carnival parade vehicle. Loudspeakers invited all the people to come out of the houses into the streets. Some Tamil classical music opened the ceremony, while everybody put their heads through the gates while wearing their night gowns. The men took the mic from the sound engineer, and said, overseer aye... you ok to start? Mr. Prahash said all ready to go, son. The tractor passed the cross streets through the main road, passing the Portuguese quarter, funeral parlor, first cross street, Dutch hotel, where they stopped for the first announcement. He blew into the mic... furh... furh... and began: my dear friends, the people of Jaffna, we have got a great opportunity having a 70mm cinema near you at the top of the main street, near the police station, inside the municipal council. We have a new cinema, yes, new cinema Rio, named after the great Brazilian city of Rio de Janeiro. This theatre will encourage films of educational, intelligent nature and religious epics which you don't see in other profiteering establishments. They are just only interested in box office merits. This cinema also will create jobs and will be operated as a nonprofit organization. Money will be put back in the community, improving parks and public places and sanitation. This Rio will serve for the benefit of the people, people of Jaffna. My dear friends the first film is based on the Second World War called The Liberation, the great battle from the Russian point of view. The film shows how the war was won by the allies against the dictators of Europe. The powerful sick enemy uses methods like gassing, labor camps, the massacre of innocent civilians especially on the brave Jewish people of Europe. It also shows how people persevered through their hardships to reach their promised land. It is a great epic. There is also future re-releases of the classic Roman epics, like Ben Hur, The Robe, The Bible, The Greatest Story Ever Told, The Ten Commandments, Julius Caesar, Anthony and Cleopatra, Alexander The Great, El Cid, Henry V and many more. All the great stories of the Bible you are going to see from your own eyes with your own families on the 70mm like no other in the city. We hope to see you all on the opening day… for The Liberation it's free for all. Times will be announced at later date, see your local newspaper for details. The Liberation. The Liberation. Thank you for listening, hope to see you all for the opening. People cheered and clapped as he passed the microphone back and the music began as the tractor started to move again further down St. James Street. They turned down the music as a mark of respect prompted by Mr. Prahash. He was also a very religious and a devoted Catholic. He was happy with his opening speech. Jana sat below in the tractor and watched his father's performance with enjoyment.

'Yes, I did enjoy his speech,' said Jana to Indhiran. Jana shook his head as he looked at Indhiran. 'I don't know, I am beginning to miss him for the first time in my life. You know, after all these years I am still looking for that movie, The Liberation. I know the country of origin is Russia but not available anywhere else I guess. Whether is it a documentary, I don't know, I can't really remember. What about you?'

'I think it's Russian,' said Indhiran.

Indhiran also said it was based on true events.

But the message got through, even though they did not understand any of the drama, language or accents. They really saw the glimpse of world war and the horrific scenes. It was shocking for a quiet Jaffna which had never seen an armored vehicle or guns of that nature. The Ten Commandments and Ben Hur broke all box office records, as schools booked their matinees, teachers took their boys and girls to the cinema for the first time. Catholics and Hindus love these religious movies; there were waves of re-releases one after the other. They really believed all they saw in the films. Some praised the Lord and bowed their head with tears of joy inside the cinema. Rosary sales went up in Miracle of Mary Church.

There were industrial documentaries from Peterborough, England and the industrious railways documentary for showing during the intermission. The nature and the wild films like Born Free, Hatari, shot in real African locations, Jungle Book and the Indian Village and the little boy became the favorite of Jaffna people. Then, of course, there was of the sudden change in policy, a u-turn which Mr. Prahash really hated. They began to see the violent westerns, even though they loved the losing American Indians while they drank, it was the landscape that made them become mesmerized: the pure depth of infinity at the canyons, the vast land of America. Snow in the mountains, sun on the beach, deserts, rivers, wilderness, storms, hurricanes and twisters all were the daily lives of the United States of the wild west and the monument valley.

The red sun, guns against the samurai sword who fought for his honor, the thieving westerner with the gun was purely interested in his rewards. The spirit of the samurai changed his outlook of his life. Then The Magnificent Seven, The Searchers, 40 Guns, Who Shot Liberty Valance? Then came the Italian westerns like The Good, The Bad, The Ugly, Sabata, 100 Rifles, Take a Hard Ride, Fistful of Dollars, For a Few Dollars more, The Man with No Name, these took over their lives; that was the seventies. Changed their lives of the youth forever in Jaffna.

Jana's father asked him to stop watching violent westerns.

Jana said: 'That Terence Hill was not violent, dad. He was just a very funny guy with his mate bud.'

'Yes, I never forget that day when he said The Liberation, the moment lead to our liberation through movies.'

The town hall municipal council, Fred Dee, Jaffna mayor, new ideas, new entrepreneurship in the name of politics to fool the Jaffna people. Fred Dee was accused of betraying Tamil people by siding with the Srimavo government. There were a lot of unsolved crimes under her rule. Fred Dee was also a close relative of G.G. Balam through marriage. Jaffna marriages all mixed in there with business and politics. Tamil Arasu really did not want the congress party to exist,Because of the government back door connection. They plotted against every opponent, while Fred Dee emerged as a prospective Jaffna candidate due to the support of srimavo. Under Fred Dee, Jaffna prospered with street lights, low crime, flowers in the parks, telecommunications, clean streets, health and safety and sanitation, vaccinations and also developing the fisheries of Kurunagar, encouraging fair trade and independence. But he did come short on development of the northern farmland and villages. The Colombo office did not want to do anything with the Tamil Arasu federal areas. So his vision of Jaffna was limited by a long margin. He was accused of using public money to entertain Colombo ministers, notably the son of the madam premier. The rumors spread - only son of Madam premier is a bisexual cross dresser. Never came out of his closet or joined the priesthood, preferred partying with the innocent and vulnerable Tamil youth of both sexes. He enjoyed the company of boys and girls away from the prying eye of Colombo. Kotte newspapers wrote blatantly against the ruling families. Rightly so, because it was an interesting time for politics. People wanted to know about the ruling upper class's sleazy behavior. Srimavo would face the so-called Che Guevara Group coup d'états, Tamil Conference Massacre and drafting of the Tamil Separate State. The people were ready for the political battle. Even if it had to come to an armed conflict. People were hungry for the battle. That Fred Dee did not pay attention to the death of civilians during the Tamil Research Conference was a big mistake. He was ill-advised by his party members. No public enquiry, no justice, not even a sympathy note to the grief-stricken families, was a big mistake. The Tamil Federal Union expressed their unhappiness towards his action. The more and more militant public speakers spoke of revenge and elimination of Fred Dee. A young Leader would carry the torch, darkened by the death of Kumaran. He planned to carry out the assassination at a temple front of the ceremonies, during the Friday prayers. Fred Dee was assassinated, as planned. That was a big story in jaffna. That was the turning point in the struggle of Jaffna Tamil history in the early years. The funeral was held in Jaffna stadium in front of the Rio Cinema town hall. Mr. Prahash took Jana to the funeral. There were thousands of mourners on that day. It was a sad funeral of that kind in Jaffna. Mr. Prahash was also disappointed with all the people who worked with Fred Dee. His dirty deals all began to surface. His family[fred dee] left the country and went into exile in Far East. Mr. Prahash began to lose interest in politics, he had a family to support, that was his first priority now.

Jana read aloud the Sunday paper's obituary column of Fred Dee, to the annoyance of his father. He also made up a few lines that were not in the paper. Mr. Prahash said be nice. Be nice and give respect to the dead.

'Whether they have done good or bad,' said Jana. That

made Mr. Prahash very angry. He chased Jana around the house, screaming "someone was going to get real hurt today". That's a typical Prahash or any Sri Lankan family statement.

Jana liked to read the obituary columns. It became a hobby, like collecting paper clips. Jana's sister said collecting dead men and women stories, you are sick Jana. Jana defended himself by explaining it always told a story of a human being, from his birth, childhood, education, marriage, career, achievements, his/her dreams, popularity, the iconic status, legendary sometimes and now they are all gone. Some died of natural causes, some died of disease, some from accidents or assassinations. Shot at point blank range: Jana gave a James bond stance towards his sisters when he said that. The bigger the column, the popular or rich they were. A proud photo of stillness and regality, supported by this great big spread of true story on the national paper showed that they struggled and conquered their demons at the end by achieving their dreams with ever present danger and difficulties. Some did not make it. At least they had tried. Someone else in the family will make it. Terminal illness and road traffic accidents and murders all were the tragic stories that never ended with happy endings. A great martyrdom when they were assassinated by a lone gunman could be inspirational for the reading public. The numeracy of the dates and the facts also interested Jana, he asked the question: why... why did he die? So kept the habit of the Sunday newspapers even when his father was not around.

Jana and the family only ate meat on Sunday. Meat was expensive for the working class. Sundays were an exception. The aroma of rumba, cinnamon, garlic, shallots, coriander, mustard seed and fresh green chilies came from his mother's kitchen; nobody else was allowed in there while mum

cooked. Not even a peep. Jana began to read... it would go on
for a few hours. There was also a neighbor, Evelyn, teacher's
son who was also a loud reader, but he did it because he loved
the English language. Nobody forced him to read it. He was
a 35 years' old, Hatton National Bank Cashier looking for a
bride with a good dowry. He was only interested in fair skin,
virgin, from a middle class Vellalar caste family.

Mr. Prahash used to have a few arguments after the
Sunday Mass and the Holy Communion. One minute they
were standing next to each other saying peace be with you, at
St James' Church, then, as soon as they come out of the
churchyard, it was all kicked in with the not so loving
neighbors. They would eat each other for breakfast if they got
a chance. SO ,he read well like a news man. Mr. Prahash
would sit and listen to his sports column, then he would go
on to read letters of editors, comments from some former
congress editors-in-chiefs.

Jana also said to Indhiran that he remembered Mr.
Prahash had made him read this article on a brief history of
Sri Lanka by an advance level student observation, a
debateable essay.

'For once we both liked it. So I read it aloud. That article
inspired me to write my final middle school essay. I only read
it once, but it sticks to my memory cells like an unforgettable
dream.'

Jana remembered everybody stopped what they were doing
and started to listen Jana's reading. There were only a few in
the audience in the house. Food was coming to the table for
lunch. Jana could not resist the brown rice steamed Sri Lankan
noodles (called the string hoppers) with coconut cream, green
chilies and curry leaves all roasted gravy[sothi] sauce. This
time he ignored everything and began to read aloud:

'The Adams Peak Pedurutalegala, Totapola all stand majestically on the horizon where the Kandyan Kingdom stood, still surrounded by the rich rain forests, rivers of fine gravel and sapphire, birds of rainbow colors, wild animals like boars with the rare multicolored chocolate-like spikes. The rare wild boar protects by camouflaging himself among the dried branches and sticks. When hunted for spikes he will shake his body to let go the pricks in all directions making a deadly weapon of protection against the poachers. The ancient trees surrounded by the various varieties of anthuriums with extra large green leaves shaped like a heart, green miniature leaves and large ferns wrap the historical trees of ageless mighty. All around the streams full of ferns, some minute and green plants will fold for touch with shyness. While the predator puts the foot on the pathways, insects and green grass hoppers will jump from their camouflaged positions to the total panic of the intruder. This type of wilderness never has been seen anywhere in the world, was scripted in the Vasco De Gama, Marco Polo journeys. The tropical climate's constantly changing temperature with sharp differences during the monsoon seasons like nowhere else in the world. The north with the dry zone and the south with the wet zone both having rain over two to three meters during the rainy season annually gave the signs of prosperity. Some areas were abandoned due to wild elephants, crocodiles and even the tribal wars. Without the adequate irrigation the forests becomes a swamp regions. Malaria gripped with fever and killed thousands well before the nets came to the mosquito mangrove coast. The locals relied on smoking the leaves of the gum tree for protection. The World Health Organization gave the Sri Lankans figures not medicines. Sri Lanka survived all through these hardships and wars into the new century with the elephant as a national symbol of nature, preservation and tourism. Lion roars in the deep jungle become the flag of the Sinhalese majority nation. Even though it's criticized for the peace loving Buddhist nation as seen in its multi-coloured flag, this same flag reflected the violence. It was defended as a symbol of struggle of the whole nation representing each community in a different band of colours. In 1972 Ceylon became Sri Lanka.

The country is under a great optimism of progress. There is a great trade and from competition in the south-east seas comes further development. Sri Lanka topped in Asia in having the highest literacy in the world. The highest achieving youth are in the north and east district of Jaffna and Trincomalle. They are called the Tamils, they also had their kingdom among the great nations not that far from Bay of Bengal like Singapore, Malaysia, Taiwan, Hong Kong, Vietnam, Burma, Maldives, Nepal, Indonesia, India, Bangladesh. During this period Sri Lanka was also voted by the international communities as the most hospitable, cultural and respectable place to live in the world. It had a great extended family culture as the mother of the head of the family. Family planning passed down to the teenagers with proper education to avoid teenage pregnancies. Education was the priority, even if it was not taught in a humane manner at times. It began to reach to the young, aspiring and respectable Sri Lankans. The population is at manageable levels and we are in a great position as one of the developing countries of south-east Asia. Tea, rubber, ice, coconut, spices, gems, topaz and sapphire, were acquired by the British, for the exchange of technology and transport systems. Public transport ran on time for perfection. Irrigation and civil engineering, dams and bridge building were on a highest level. We were looking for a bright future.

The colorful culture was hijacked by the power crazed unimaginative, impressionable, not-so-well cultured or educated, incompetent politicians who wanted to create the divide among the Tamils and Sinhalese and wanted to travel back to dark ages. Discrimination of the minority, caste divisions, religion, languages, overseas plantation workers, are all perfect tools to use and abuse to retain power. Jobs were decided according to their background. Religious leaders did not do any favors to alleviate the pain of the suffering but kept their faith, custom, political preservation, and their bank balances. Physical violence towards the weak and frail increased. Human Rights lawyers were abducted and severely beaten. Some disappeared down the river of blood. Women's rights especially were repressed. The dowry system did no good to the poor and the orphans. Children witnessed violence at home and in primary schools, Jana screamed and repeated twice… then read it gently: 'physical violence at home,' and looked at Mr. Prahash without blinking an eye. Mr. Prahash was furious. The whole house anticipated the chase around the house and bamboo lashes. Surprisingly the story did touch Jana's dad… he took a moment… 'Violence is different to punishment. If you listen,' he looked around at everybody in the house including his wife… with a little smile… 'if you listen and behave there is no punishment. No persuasion… no a… yes, yes, punishment.' Then he raised his voice and said: 'If I punched your mum… ahh… that's violence, domestic violence… if your daddy punches and knocks a few teeth out of your lazy uncles who have no talent whatsoever, your granny will buy them gold teeth replacements, that creates disappointment, even an argument with your mum. It also creates violence. Reason, REASON,' he shouted in anger, 'it's the hard earned money of a widow in her sixties working in heat, making breakfast for others, that creates disappointment and very, very angry violence.'

'Dad, dad,' interrupted Jana, he just didn't want him to go in the route of grandma, while blinking his eyes with little fear, with a smile in his face. 'Dad,' he hesitated, 'how about if you throw things at people around the house in anger?' Jana looked at his mum from the corner of his eyes. Then, for a brief period, he looked at his dad, they looked at each other, eyes locked for a moment's silence.

'What is, what is that?' he laughed loudly with embarrassment. 'Well, well. Your son has spoken on behalf of the main street. Be proud of him,' said Mr. Prahash with sarcasm. 'Certain time, son, certain things have to be directed at certain people, you just have to duck and clear. That is the reason why I teach you to be alert and be a soldier. You have got to learn to duck from all the bullets, my boy. That's when you are my son.'

Jana screamed, 'ha ha ha...'

'That's enough, Jana,' said mum calmly. 'Enough reading. If you want to read go in your room and shut the door, and scream as much as you like in your room. Off you go... go on now... family of screamers,' said mum and looked at her husband. He responded with silence and respect. That was the last time he asked Jana to read an article.

Jana was by now a very voracious reader of current affairs, sports and international politics. While his father was away, mum sat at the table with the foot ruler as his sisters took turns to feel the pain in their knuckles, and then with swollen hands sat on their chairs, crying. Mum took control of the house and put everybody through the paces. Jana would disappear without telling, he would go for a run in the morning at Jaffna Central, then go to the library to read, sports star, movie magazine, Time and News Week and finally the short stories on the Reader's Digest - all came from overseas as international publications. Jana felt he wanted to get out of the house a bit more, mum's pressure at times was worse than Mr. Prahash for Jana. Even when Jana had severe beatings for his behavior, he could talk with his dad sometimes, but with mum there was no way he could express his point of view. His sisters were growing up, now three girls he had to face so he preferred Beach Road and Indhiran.

Everybody had a Dutch style pushbike. Boys and girls of Jaffna would fall into their short romances, some parents following them in distance. Some ended with marriage, some with running away, some never materialized; segregations, caste divisions always stood in their ways. The teenagers were above all that, nothing could stop the boys, they wanted their teenage years to be happy and free. So they did it all behind the cemeteries, in derelict warehouses, in fishing boats, you name it, they found a way out.

By this time Indhiran was bored and had heard enough: 'Did you make up all this... yes, you did... really your dad... did he throw things in the house? I know he is a little extreme, but not a man of that sort. Now you see, Jana,Indhiran continued, my dad will walk away, then go to grandma's house, takes a long shower with a bucket and a rope physically from the well until he pees for seven times during the process.'

'Seven times,' said Jana, 'my god, can you really do that during the shower? Poor crotons got the brunt of it, no wonder they all died even with the grandma's gentle care. I am sure she would have diverted the water to the main drain.'

'What main drain?' said Indhiran. 'There is no main drain. It all went through the fourth cross street half way to the small centre shops. The whole area knew when Nadraj is having a bath, he must have had a real argument today,'

Jana smiled, then laughed: 'Indhiran, that's right, the great generation. Can you blame them or stand up against them. You get shot or chased down the road with the well-sharpened multipurpose machete. Come on, it's enough about the greatest generation. I am starving. Let's get some tender goat and chopped roti. I only have a few rupees,' said Jana.

'Don't worry, I got a few. I did a small job at the funeral parlor,' said Indhiran.

Jana smiled.

'What? asked Indhiran.

'You just gave me the title for my essay, you are a genius.' Jana was excited, Indhiran just broke that writer's block. Jana said: 'You did it and you didn't even know it. The Greatest Generation. We got an athletic meeting tomorrow,' said Jana.

'Are you running?' asked Indhiran.

'No. This year I am on the early parade ceremony with the march past. The Bonaventure House needs to win this year. We are really fed up with coming second to Dunkan House. Next year is my year. I hope my dad is there to see it. I really want to win it for him. He thinks it's all a waste of time, athletics and cricket. We never take it up to the national level. Tamils had very little chance to get into the national teams.'

Jana and Indhiran walked through St James' churchyard, passed the bankshall street night cricket in motion under the street lights. Dr. Phil was quite busy at the main road, they had brought a few sword victims from David's Road gang fight with a heavy blood loss. They saw the tension on the streets; cops began to fly past on Triumph motorbikes up and down in front of a green Jeep with guns.

Jana and Indhiran just got to the roti specialist in the corner in time. The old man wore a white Thalapah, a head-dress of an orthodox Tamil, also with a white waisti and walking sticks and vest and double scarf over his shoulders as he stood out clean and organized in a steamy smoking café chelliah.

Indhiran said, 'Don't look at the old man, he is a white witch.'Only comes at night to this shop.

'What?' asked Jana.

'That one smiling at the small boys… he puts spells on people, either good or bad, he can do it. He lives in a secluded kottil in a corner of the seafront. People have told me stories about that place… don't look, he will smile at you, then that's it, you will follow him around.'

Jana looked down with great difficulty for a few minutes. When he looked up the old man was next to him and smiling. Jana also smiled and said, greetings sir. The old man walked past with a laugh and said, 'run boy run, run out of here for your life. You are the blessed one.' Jana smiled and listened with disbelief. He touched his head.

'Hey, did he touch you?' asks Indhiran. 'Fuck! Why did you let him do that! You stand next to me. Don't say anything.'

'He only said run, run, which I love doing. Maybe he sees me winning the gold,' said Jana.

Indhiran looked at Jana with anger. The conversation ended with big thunder as the chef in front of the flat heavy hot steel plate, dropped those tender cooked goat, green chili, fried omelette, sweated onions, sautéed green chilies, cinnamon sticks, rumba piece, and started chopping all with the double-handed blades as he shredded like a machine with rhythm. Music was playing as he moved side to side and added the ingredients one by one; finally he signaled the roti man next to him who was continuously making rotis like a machine, to put two cooked rotis in the middle of the chopped mixture. Steam came off the hot plate with great aroma, it melted the taste buds. He chopped all the roti.

'Two plates, please,' said Jana.

In the meantime, the roti man threw the mixed dough and beaten flour like a handkerchief flying in the air, then caught it, folded it back like a triangular shaped parcel, then rolled it back like a ball, then pressed it hard, then threw it hard on the wooden oily table. He repeated this action as the mixture of the dough became tender with layers when he cooked on the hot plate. The name came as a 'vettchu roti', the throwing roti, Indians called it parata. Jana and Indhiran loved the roti plate full of flavors cooked in front of them, a luxury in Jaffna.

The whole experience of having a cousin as a close friend and free to talk to about girls, family and friends with total trust and openness was a night to remember. Jana and Indhiran, they cherished those moments with total pleasure. Then they both walked down to the funeral parlor at the main road. The embalmer Malcolm was always asking for a cigarette, so they would chip in and buy him ten Rothmans or Bristol; they were his brands. He would smoke and tell us a story. He was of European decent living in Jaffna away from his up country roots. Settled in Jaffna like a native, everybody knows Malcolm the Embalmer. He was free to do anything, even the police couldn't touch him. He had been in the capital, worked close with the police and the coroners in Colombo. He just had to mention somebody's name and everybody'll be fine. He loved his job and his drinks. Malcolm would sit on the owner's Thurai table like a boss and smoke his Bristol and answer the phone. He was always dressed smart with super triple mint in his pocket and a toothbrush in his pocket. He would brush his teeth and wash his hands every hour like he suffered from a compulsive neurosis. The boss had warned him, if he ever smelt of alcohol during the arrival of any customers he would be fired. Mr. Thurai had come close to doing that, but his skillful hand with the blade when it comes to slicing up bodies kept Malcolm in the job. Malcolm was also loved by the family of Thurai so he knew he had a job for life, but he never tried to test the fate with Thurai. They had a lot of respect for each other. He also survived a few potholes in recent times.

There were no phone calls tonight. It was a quiet night at the funeral parlor. Malcolm worked on commission only. But it was the busy time for Jaffna funeral parlors. The system worked like clockwork; Malcolm would explain the details of the ceremony, and the presentation of the deceased. He spoke five languages fluently: Tamil, Sinhala, English, Hindi, Malay, the sixth one was the bad language. He also had known about cultural requirements. As soon as he did the deal, he would go down to the bar and hit a shot of brandy and get a packet of Bristol on credit. It was the natural death of an old man. As soon as the doctors and coroners paperwork is released, Malcolm would put his latex gloves on. He loved his job, he said while smelling of Martell brandy. He would prepare a table: knives, formalin, cotton sponges etc. He also had a junior assistant who would help him out during the embalming. The body would be all dressed up according to the relatives requirements, soon it would go to the deceased's house where it would lie until all the relatives arrived from all around the country or even abroad in some cases, so Malcolm had to prepare coffin accordingly.

Jana and Indhiran would stand around, learn all the details. Indhiran worked there part-time as a flower arranger and a wreath worker, made enough to have change in his pocket all the time. Malcolm also had to do the walk to the cemetery on the day of the funeral. He would put on his well-tailored suit from Singapore, black tie and Ray-ban glasses, walk in front of the stretch Mercedes Benz funeral car like a blues brother, he would shake hands with all the relatives with sympathy. They all would thank him for his wonderful job, and would look after him with the bottle at the end of the funeral.

The police would stop the procession if it had an unusually large crowd gathering, and most especially when the dead was a young man killed by the security forces. Malcolm would step in and intervene to diffuse the situation. He would talk to the boys. Sometimes it could take a wrong turn and clashes would break out. Disappointed, Malcolm would jump into the car and go straight to the cemetery. The New Orleans style band was also hired, which played by the traditional shaman drummers. It really brought the mood to the last lap of the expired. In the worst case scenario there would also be a pitched battle with police until shots were fired in the air, then all would run in every direction as the chief stood with a rifle in the middle of the main street.

People would get off their bikes, cars slow down, some pedestrians would also stop and pay respect for the dead and the gun. Mr. Thurai would walk at the back of the car with his gold rings, chains, and the Rolex with all white kit. Everybody knew who was in charge with the cars. Fresh Athyriums and lilies mixed with up country ferns and leaves decorated the coffin with big and small wreaths showing through the glass visibly. First to St. Mary's, then to the cemetery after the mass, final prayers will be said by the parish priest while the eldest of the family throws the first handful of sand on the coffin. As the coffin is lowered by the ropes slowly down, the final cry of the desperate loved ones would really bring tears to anybody but Malcolm who would stand like a professional to complete his job.

Indhiran said: 'Come, Jana. Jana, it's late, your mum is going to worry, go home, go now and don't tell her you were here hanging around with me and Malcolm at the parlor. Well, you have an essay to cover it all up, you have been studying with your mates right… right?' smiled Indhiran.

'Yes, I was around Nixon's earlier on at Beach Road, just for half an hour. He will not hint or comment on his work.'

'Why do you want to copy his ideas?' asked Indhiran.

'No, just wanted his opinion,' said Jana. 'I am not sure about my idea.'

Indhiran interrupted saying: 'It's good, it's good. Serious, you have done a good job. Go home, to be proud about your work,' Indhiran said with conviction. 'What do I know about English and politics!' he said as he looked at him from his left eye and started smelling his right hand. Jana gave him a big smile as he jumped on his Raleigh bike with shining spokes and black and gold lining around the edges on the mudguards. That was a style of the seventies in Jaffna, everybody loved gold paint lining even when they had to adopt to rations. Jana cycled past the main road while the night poster stickers were busy putting the movie posters on the seminary walls at the corner of the Temple Road and Main Road. Jana heard a big bang. It's half past midnight. He cut through the lanes, somebody somewhere was being chased by the police and shot. It couldn't be a firework, a punctured tyre maybe? It was beginning to be a dangerous place to do the midnight run in Jaffna. After the killing of Fred Dee, the police and army kept their eye on every gang in the junctions. Every mother at home prayed and worried for her son's safe return. It was like a roulette for the army, let's catch it where it lands, pick them up and throw them in the Jeep to make them informers and traitors against the Tamil movements, give them false promises in the process. Jana and Indhiran took their chances with the knowledge of the roads and narrow lanes, even dirt drains and canals provided shelter away from the cops.

Jana's Mum had sat on the chair until midnight then had given up and gone to bed. Luckily she did not put the bar on the door inside. There were no locks, just the inside bar on the Jaffna houses. The following morning, Jana woke up to face the whole family,

'We are all worried for you, leaving me and the girls alone. You will never look after us, you selfish fool,' said his angry mum. 'I was on this chair until midnight, hearing gunshot and armored car sirens. You told me you were going to Nixon's, that was at 7.30. You came home five hours later. What were you doing, Jana?'

His sisters interrupted with you must be hanging around Main Street and the Beach Road.

'There is lot going on in the town. You will get caught and beaten up you fool. Your dad is not here. Nobody will come and take you out from the police. They will teach you a good lesson, then you will learn ah… let's see your GCSE results, then we will talk. I will write your dad to come back immediately as his son is not listening or doing anything. You wait and see!' She continued screaming: 'That will really cheer him up in the high seas! Go on! Go on! I don't want to see your face today,' said his mother with anger and frustration. 'You are a bad liar and a cheat.'

Jana walked away saying: 'Yeah, just like your brothers.'

'Hey! I heard that.'

Jana said: 'Good!' while looking at his mum with disrespect; he did not like that she said he was a cheat.

Every morning Jana cycled all the way to the jetty to buy fresh fish. Fresh air from the Indian Ocean. Jana loved his trip to the jetty, that was the luxury that he would not miss out in any day. He did this every morning prior to going to school, every morning like a ritual. He would get a good deal from the big dealers of a family auctioneer. Jana was also popular due to his mum teaching in the Kurunagar girls' school at St. James. Everyone knew him as Pavalam teacher's son. She had a pet name of a flower, due to her kindness. Jana always kept the change as pocket money. Mum knew about all Jana's tricks but kept a blind eye. Jana took some real bargain that day with prawns, crabs, and sea bream straight from the nets. He also picked up some large squids which were perfect for Indhiran's family who made a great spicy recipe with a black colour left in to create a great taste and look. Jana's sister also started picking up a few tips from their mum to create a great weekend menu for Chundikuli household and visitors. Risotto and squid was her specialty with home grown lemon leaves for flavor. No wine, just coconut cream, tamarind and butter. It was rich but perfect for that heat in the Jaffna peninsula. A few hours later, after seeing all the cooking prior to going to school, he was excited: it would all be ready when he came home for the lunch break. It was only a mile cycle-ride but some would walk home for lunch. When he met his sisters for lunch, that was the only time they sat together and talked freely as no one else was in the house. They all cycled back through the midday heat. The road tar would boil and blow air like a black bubble gum. The kids would dodge the hot tar, marked with tyre grids – it would all dry up by the cool evening. But it was a beautiful sight when all the boys and girls all in white cycled through the streets with different colour ties flying over their shoulders in the wind while they held their skirts down with one hand while pedaling the bikes with real style. But this morning Jana was quietly sitting inside the college chapel at St Peter's. The rector finished the mass by saying in the name of the father and the son and the holy spirit, Amen. Students quickly sat down in the church making a clutter noise with their shoes. The rector said: 'Wait, wait,wait stand up everybody. Now, quietly, I want you to all sit down quietly without making any cluttering noise.' As they did, he said that's better. Jana sat next to Nixon.

The rector began his speech: 'This weekend we are hosting our annual Athletic meet, we have gotten quite a few old boys, families, the police chief and the chief guest who really admires our school status in the country as a whole, they will all arrive to see how we perform with our organization. We need to be on our best behavior. I want you to stay at your allocated houses. Don't get over-excited and somersaulting in the running tracks,' said pointedly as he looked at a few in the front row. The kids pointing fingers at each other and saying 'It's you, it's you!' by miming and shaking their heads. Jana looked at Nixon and smiled thinking of their early years. The rector continued: 'You will get a goody bag, yes, cakes and rolls, even a drink. So enjoy your day but please put your rubbish in the buckets provided,' he finished as he dropped his glasses and his voice. 'I don't want anything flying over the running track except the winning flag. There will be gunshots during the start, it is only a blank, nobody will get hurt but I want you to be quiet, not even a cough or a sneeze. A fault start leads to disqualification, wasted time, delays, then we all will be in the dark, that then affects the ceremony, speeches, most importantly the glory of getting the champion shield front of the school. Be an enthusiastic supporter, whether your team is winning or losing, it's participating that count. All the best on the march past, he said as he looked at the teachers and smiled for a change. I want a great opening this year. May the best team win. Now, quiet please. I want everybody to leave quietly from here in an orderly fashion in a line and no talking. No talking, I said. That means not even a whisper. He gestured for the prefects to take over. The students at the back were the last ones to go, the senior middle school. The prefects kept everybody quiet. They talked on the way to the classroom anyway, the rector was long gone to his office. The church choir sang the Hail Glorious St. Peter while they went out of the church. As they came out of the back door the rest of the school walked past the middle school corridors. There were two zones, one was Tamil zone, the other was English zone. No one talked otherwise they would have to kneel down and be punished by the prefects. The green badges were everywhere. Jana looked at the college athletic meet preparation underway. The groundsman, Thomas, tirelessly put the final touches on the staggered start at the 1500m mark. He walked towards the relay changing lanes to mark the restricted area to avoid the disqualification. Flag poles, one large and four small, stood in front of the ceremonial stand. Bonaventure, Dunkan, Mark and Lucas houses were all well allocated for their decorations. The medal podium was all put up in place with St. Peter's crest with college motto 'fight until you die' left in Latin. A champion student would open the ceremony singing Alma Mater with the speech of sport respecting regulations motto. He would also announce the arrival of the right honorable chief guest. The march past would open the ceremony with style, the strenuous efforts and the discipline of the students would make a great impact from the start. The march past was a big thing for the honorable training teachers. Sir Ratnam was Jana's teacher. He had been a big drill man in his early days.

The students were looking good when they lined up to be in attention. Ground barriers were all set up, the police would be present, not to supervise or police but to participate. The old boys' visiting clubs, like Singing Fish and Green Field would take on the police on the 4 x 100, mostly for better relationship with the local community. It was a great final event. There was a sprinter call Miskin of Russian descent from Colombo just to run in Jaffna events to promote police sporting events. He also had a weekend coaching camp in Jaffna Fort for the prospective sprinting athletes. He was well liked by a lot of kids in Jaffna. We hated the police but loved Mr. Miskin. He had a devastating turn of foot on the final leg. The police team were unbeaten for three seasons on the visitors' relay. People would just come to see him at every school. Some of the school's old boys had come close but just not good enough to beat him on the day. The team Bonaventure totally relied on the march past for points. There were points even for the decoration of the house posts. The seniors would decorate while having few bottles of toddy hidden in their decoration. Their annual graphic theme, this year's rumors say it was going to be sky, sea and ships with sari, thistles and blue balloons with hand painted Greek ruin-like columns. 'Surely we can't lose this year,' said the senior student. Sir Ratnam waited with a smooth three foot oak pole, he would begin his training after the first class at 10.00 a.m. on an early morning sun. Before that Jana had to deal with the English class essay competition between nine and ten.

'Well, we just heard that competition word from Miss Eve. Before, it was just an exam. A mini thesis.'

Jana asked Nixon again in the classroom: 'Why you never told me yesterday? Why all this secrecy? I thought you are my friend, my only intelligent friend. Go on, keep it away from me.'

'It's not a question of secrecy, it's a question of principle,' said Nixon calmly.

'You mean the Moses Joseph principal, not the principal. Principal Rector. I understand, you clever loony. I am joking, Nix,' said Jana. 'Hey, I just wanted your opinion that's all. This is our last class together do you know. You are going to do pre -medicine. I have been forced to do pre- engineering. I am going to miss you man. I was with you at the desk from the age of 5 since 1969, copied a few answers over the years. I have done the essay, handed it in. Nothing can change now, it's all done and dusted with my final big black full stop. I just wanted to do well at least on my English language, that's all. I am not an academic type like you. I know my weaknesses and limitations.'

Nixon looked at Jana's face with a smile.

Jana said, 'You will like mine, promise, go on, break your arrogant mould.' And smiled again. 'I know we not supposed to talk about it, la da la de. Ok,' said Jana.

Nixon replied finally warning Jana, 'Don't tell me yours,

ok? We are all going to know it in a few minutes and read it in front of the class. Guess mine is good, but maybe not good enough for a public read. You, you sad,' said Nixon. He took a moment with a sigh, looked at Jana and said, 'Insanity'. Jana felt the ease as he felt he was just around the final bend with Nixon.

'It sounds like mine, too,' said Jana.

Nixon is not happy, he hesitated, he regretted but wanted to say, finally he said: 'Insanity of our fathers.'

Jana was quite impressed. He said, 'It's deep, it's deep and profound. I know you will come up with something good. It's brilliant, matter of fact. You are good. Yes, you are,' he continued with praise.

'So, what's yours?' asks Nixon.

Jana replied: 'Nothing. I am not going to tell you.'

Nixon looked tricked. 'I am just winding you up. Come on, come close. It's quite simple. The Greatest Generation,' said Jana.

Nixon was quickly in competitive mood. 'Very good. Which era are you talking about?'

'Like yours, sunny. Our fathers,' replied Jana. 'I know you mean the forefathers. But this is my father's second world war generation. You know my father was 12 during the war.'

'Who?' asked Nixon.

'My father, he wasn't quite up there either. Insane.'

Nixon looked at Jana with a smile. 'Very good, Jana, really very good.'

Jana got his first compliment from a valid critique. He was just surprised and pleased. Nixon was one of the brightest in the school.

'I will buy the tea this morning during the break,' said Jana. 'You never do that you, poor fool.'

They shook each other's hand and laughed. 'No, today I

made some money by selling some Kurunagar fresh sea breams and squid to my cousins from a boat call Rathi,' a Nixon family boat named after his sister. 'Well I got to rush to the ground, you know who is waiting for us in the ground already. Sir Ratnam with the pole over there. Look,' as Jana pointed out the teacher in the ground with the full morning light from the east streaking onto the college athletic track. Nixon just realized Jana must have been to the beach and bought fish for the whole extended family by mentioning his name, and got a fair deal from the boats. He smiled as he walked away and shook his head, thinking of Jana's little games.

Jana joined the rest of the boys all in white on the grounds.

'Ok, you all warm up, please. Whatever you like, stretch, bend down, just loosen up. Some of us are still asleep. Look at this great weather. Fresh sea breeze and sunshine for the blues. Let's get on with it.'

He knew every one of us individually, where we stood, which side will face the crowd, which side will face the guests, he gave us all insight to keep us all interested and with a competitive attitude.

'Come on! Attention. No, no. I want everybody to relax first. I don't want anybody to look like they've just been electrocuted then frozen.' We know he is a physics teacher after all. 'I want the energy to pass through your limbs and the blood to flow through your heads. So be energized, look spirited and strong, that way nobody can beat us. Not just the line and keeping it on the line. Come on, let's crack on. ATTENTION!' he screamed. The whole middle school heard that. He said: 'Yeah, yeah, that's more like it.' He did the final check with the pole he was holding, he put that pole between the lines on our chest with the little taps, talking with the eye, by shaking the head left and right. Moved us in position. By this time the rector was out of his office with a few tutors supporting Sir Ratnam's enthusiasm. The poles came in between us whenever we lost concentration. Some of us could not stop laughing. 'Left right, left right, left right, left, left.' He looked at the students with a serious attitude. They also began to feel the seriousness. He said no head turning, if you're ever in doubt, just look at the person in front with your right eye, without turning your head from the person next to you. Of course the person in the front right always looked straight, even when they were in front of the pavilion. 'Come on, keep the rhythm, left right, left right, very good, very good.' They did that for 45 minutes. Sir had promised them a special treat if they won this year. They were all   excited.

Jana was in celebratory mood, he loved his running and his athletics. He talked about all the possibilities on every event with great details. He was unhappy that he had to wait until the final year to run the 1500m and the 3000m middle distance. They were all looking forward to that day with lots of argument and cheering. That was a great tradition to have college and inter college athletic meets. At St. Peter's College all the houses were named after the previous bishops and principals: Dunkan, Mark, Bonaventure and Lucas, all Irish missionaries who did a lot of improvements in Jaffna for the coastal villages. They also built churches every half mile in Jaffna town. There were eight major Catholic churches altogether in Jaffna town: St. Mary's, St. Sebastian's, St. Anthony's, Sacred Heart, St. James', St. John's, Our Lady of Miracle, Our Lady of Perpetual Help. It was a Catholic town and no doubt about that. Most of them had catholic schools attached to them. The missionaries had had a real effect on their lives, even stories that Christianity was here much earlier, before the European invasion. After all, Asia is much closer to Jerusalem than Europe. The silk trade-routes from Arabia and Africa to China operated well before the birth of Jesus Christ. Jana, thought all this looking at the mighty of St. Peter's College while walking along the corridors of the middle school after taking a tap water break after queuing up for it. He wiped his sweat with his small towel and sat down on the chair as Miss Eve looked with her great smile at her talented boys. She played the final trump card trick to take a revenge on our perverted eyes.

She marked all the essays and gave them back to everybody and said: 'You all did well. But there are three best works selected by the English panel and they will be read by the writers. Can the three who haven't been given their papers back please stand up.'

Jana, Nixon and Deva stood up confused. 'You three do not know whose work you are reading, but by reading your opponent's paper will give you the best highest mark of the year in English. No name on the top, we don't know who we are reading except Jana and Nixon know their papers.'

Now Jana understood why Nixon had hesitated all day, he was disappointed but kept his cool. He was also excited that he got there in front of a lot of talented students. He had one man to thank. That was his father. He wished he was here to see this occasion. That was the first time Jana did well in English for a long time.

Deva started with the Insanity of Our Fathers, followed by Jana reading Deva's work of Sprit that Changed the World, A Tribute to Gandhi and Non Violence. Nixon read Jana's work with great commitment, elocution and delivery. Jana

45

was really pleased that his was one of the best works with his Insanity of Our Fathers. Jana received second place. Miss Eve looked with emotion and glossy eyes, saw her hard work had finally paid off. Miss Eve loved us all. They also loved her intelligence, beauty, calm and occasionally funny, cheerful English teacher. She was one of a kind. Jana began to look back at the work that he got back from Nixon. It had a plus on top. The Greatest Generation.

The British called it Ceylon. The Tamils called it Elankai. The Sinhalese called it Lankaveh. Now we all called it Sri Lanka. It has been described by the travelers, scholars and artists as the Garden of Eden, pearl of the Indian Ocean, tear drop of India. The island of serendip. The island is 64000 square kilometers. Its most nearest eastern corner of India is a port of Rameswaram. It is separated by 30 kilometers by the Sea of Park Straight of the north west corner, where lies a city called Jaffna. The nearest port is called Head of Mannar. There is speculation and disagreement among the archeologists and treasure hunters, about the origins of Sri Lanka. There has been a great find in the northern triangle between Tamil Nadu, Jaffna and the Andaman Islands. A huge ancient civilization has been found and is still being excavated by the French under-water archeologists. These great finds created debates of these unsolved beginnings. It could have been destroyed by a great tsunami or an earthquake. It created a rise in waters, brought the annihilation of an artistic society, sea fearers and hunter-gatherers. Islanders could have traveled in shallow waters in canoes in early times. According to Mahavamsa, 543 Sinhalese arrived in Lanka. It had been a peaceful community with cemeteries, ancient burial sites, monasteries of Buddhist monks, temple gardens, irrigation systems built throughout by the kings and rulers. They were Buddhist and Hindus at the time of their reign. Sometimes they fought heavily, destroying each other's arts and historical facts to keep their dominant religion and faith of the home land. Sri Lanka had some great rulers with attitude. History was rich but dark at times. Chola kings rule brought riches, Hindu culture and fought Kalinga together with Lankans. The invasion from South East Asia was foiled by the unity of rulers and then came stability. The sea all around gave us protection. We were the proud islanders. Sri Lanka was also noted in the Roman Empire for its trade of jewels. Marco Polo visiting on one of his journeys said it was one of the best islands in the world. The Sinhala king, Vikiramabahu, finally created the kingdom of Kandy. Jaffna became the capital of the Kingdom of Tamils. Tamils and Sinhalese fought each other, and then together against the invaders for decades. All because they wanted to maintain their island tradition, culture, economics, trade, development and the honor and pride, during this transitional period.

During this difficult but challenging time they also became the victims by betraying their motherland by collaborating with the invaders against each other for the love and protection of their wealth and the country. The fertile lands were forcefully taken for foreign profiteering. Then they redistributed it to the traitors as gifts and gave praises for their obedience. Sometimes the Europeans will ask the difficult prisoner in the name of forgiveness, to run as far as he can, so he will get all the acres that he covered on his run and that will become his land. It was like Russian roulette while shooting at them to run fast for fun when they get drunk on a home brewed liqueur. The confused native thought that was his end and ran for his life. Only to find out, the horse cavaliers picked him up to give his reward. During this period some were forced, some conveniently converted themselves to Christianity. That was also a compulsory requirement to hold any high office under the Europeans. First the Portuguese in 1505, then the Dutch in 1658, finally the British in 1796 took the paradise island to ransom. Tamils and Sinhalese fought bravely and lost their lives in thousands. The Europeans stayed over 400 years, dominated

South East Asia and took all the riches and natives as slaves back to Europe. The ancient aboriginals called Vetha's, the original hunter-gatherers, were completely wiped out. Some became slaves, some found shelter with the urban communities and gave the dark complexion to a new meaning for Tamils and Sinhalese. The brave few still managed to live in the dense lion forest away from human contact.

It was an immense advantage to invade a country already divided by religion, culture and language. Traps were set to clear the path of the invading colonialists, Tamils and Sinhalese quarreled, Sri Lanka fell in the ditch. Then came occupation and discrimination in their own country. You don't have to imagine what happened if they arrived in a foreign land. Ancient artifacts, gems, sapphires, rubies, stone carvings, bronze sculptures all completely disappeared and fell into the hands of warlords like the Duke of Kinglandshire. His castle estate will become a war memorabilia museum for the western world. He even took peacocks, as many as he could, for his front garden birds of display. The missionaries of the west, constituted with different sects and beliefs, began to arrive: Anglican, Protestant, 7th Day Adventist, Jehovah Witness, French Monk, Presbyterian and Catholic, brought their bible of different versions and the plans for building seminaries, convents, retreats in every city and port in the name of Jesus Christ. Hindus and Buddhists hid their art and treasure in the caves protected by lions, snakes and deadly bees, from the prying eyes of treasure hunting missionaries called archeologists. They were even looking for Buddha for a trophy cabinet.

The British, unlike anybody else, did develop the country in the process of profiteering from tea, rubber, spices, precious stones and shipping tax for every boat or ship docked in a Sri Lankan port for refueling. Sri Lanka is situated in the strategic position of all en route ships of the Indian Ocean. The British also contributed towards the development of the existing dams and irrigation systems. They also brought the Darjing steam train, followed by diesel and electric,

English electric, locomotives. The fantastic railway network from north Khank Kesan Thurai (KKS) in Jaffna to Galle in the south then east to Trinco to up country through the mountains of Bandarawala to Ratnapura, criss-crosses the up country through the caves and mountains. The train became the ultimate way to travel to see this beautiful island in two days. The mountains of Sri Lanka give the perfect climate for a tea. It was a dark rich tea and tasted unlike any other in the world. The British were excited with joy. Their hunch was paying off in regard to Sri Lanka. Huge profits. In return they introduced the judicial and the educational systems which began to work well with the Sri Lankans. Especially with the Tamils. The British also brought Indian Tamils to work in the plantations. The British favored the Tamils for running their well oiled machines. It was quite obvious Tamils were given the opportunity to work in Burma, Malaysia, Singapore, Hong Kong, Africa, West Indies, and Guyana. It created the Tamil cultural explosion of the world. Today the Tamil language is one of the most spoken in every continent on the planet. Sri Lanka prospered with the Tamil influence. Being a minority did not stop them. Today they are the pillar of the educational middle class of home and abroad. They did their job with nobility. Senior surgeons, civil engineers, shipping magnets, agricultural revolutionaries, mechanical masterminds, teachers, nurses, farmers all contributed their skills and services for the development of this island. Tamils are also driven by progress, running hospitals, transport, local government, distribution and procurement for the beginning of a new era of the free Sri Lanka. It has mirrored the classic British officer mentality. Well organized, orientated, on-time with obedience and respect.

During the second world war, the Japanese began to dominate South East Asia. While India was neutral, Ceylon took a keen role in the war. The British anchored their royal navy ships at the strategic port of Trincomalle, a natural harbor. Captains docked their ships 100 yards *from a jetty, the water was warm, the seamen swam to the port. That was the tradition of the barmy navy. The coastal maritime ports and jetties were bombed by the Japanese unsuccessfully. It was due to the unique twisting winds of a cyclone, harsh and heavy downpour of monsoon, making it difficult to predict. The flight-path became suicidal. Many perished along the coast line. When America was victorious in Midway, the British began the push to Burma. Most of the injured were treated in Ceylon. Some never left their new found freedom. The Japanese recklessly pressed on with Pearl Harbor. They also took prisoners-of-war to Tokyo. They also held ransom and threatened to kill all prisoners, if any invasion ever occurred in Japan. America then created history with plutonium TNT bombs at Hiroshima and Nagasaki. The Japanese with morale crushed and thousands of its citizens vaporized by the bombs, took the ultimatum from the Allies seriously and surrendered. Their domination in South East Asia ended. Sri Lanka came out proud and intact. World war ended. America and Europe celebrated their victory and remembered their lost loved ones. Sri Lanka also achieved its goal and became free. In 1948 came the birth of the Democratic Republic of Ceylon (Sri Lanka). Boys became gentlemen and girls became madams and one of them was called Prime Minister. The rest is eventuality in front of your eyes. This is our greatest generation.*

Jana's essay was also honored by the middle school head teacher. Whenever Nixon mentioned Tamil or Jaffna during the read, there was a cheer from the whole class. Which was never allowed to happen in the middle school's history. Because the noise was loud. Jana was quite emotional to leave middle school as he shook the hand of Miss Eve for the first and the last time. Jana began to think about his father and the trips that he took him on when he was young.

Especially to his native island of Delft.

CHAPTER TWO

DELFT INFLUENCE

There were a few trips Mr. Prahash took with Jana when he was a very young boy. Everybody knew his dad had friends in high places. Mr. Cool, outspoken, loud and with dry sense of humor would get through security ,receptionists and private secretaries with ease. No pressure. No aggression, no, just innocent smile with conviction. He knew the right names and places to get the approval. He also made sure to remember favors with favors: flowers and cinema tickets for the girls; food for the needy; alcohol for the addicted. He always had important information to give out to the unimportant people: the police station; Chief inspector's office; the Mayor's corridors and offices; Stationmaster's quarters at Jaffna Railway Station; the Jaffna hospital's senior consultant to the embalming and coroner's office. Even the Cooperative Store at town central. He would go straight to the head of the department, like a store keeper. The man was a walking encyclopedia of current affairs, hot news and travails. The government ministers, members of parliament, he could get to anybody with somebody's help. That's how

Jana had known him as a child, even though all a little foggy and not very clear for him now. He did not understand much of all the hierarchy, business and status positions of Jaffna society - the caste, class divisions and extreme honor. Jana loved all the comradery among the white collar and national dress workers. Even if he did not understood what they were talking about, watching it all for Jana was a show, a drama and action. He kept on smiling while he sat and watched his father in action, especially when Mr. Prahash was friends of the classical musical moguls of Jaffna, the Kumarsamy family. They were the senior Karnataka singers, performers and session musicians for all the important events, openings and ceremonies in the Hindu calendar. Their extended family was also the entrepreneur of Jaffna metal and silver and water pump business. All were signature companies with local and international export portfolios. Samy's daughters were about to stage their graduation ceremony of the Dance of the Cultural Merit of Baratha Nartium. Samy's daughters were tall, beautiful with great physical elegance and ability, and they performed the great art dance to the Jaffna public with effortless serenity. Jana remembered Miss Rajeshwaran , one of the daughters of Samy, a great physical phenomenon when compared to the average population of Ceylon girls. Especially Jamuna who was world class. She moved and flowed with immense balance and suppleness on the stage of Veerasingham Tamil Cultural Hall at the Clock Tower Road. They changed costumes, saris and diamond and gold jewelry. When their legs hit the rhythm on the floor with the noise of the tiny little bells on a leather strap, it gave hearts palpitations with the music. People couldn't help tapping their feet and shaking their heads like clowns. Singers sang the classical songs with emotion and sometimes with tears.

Session musicians played their sitar, miruthangam, thablah, and the floor piano to perfection and gave a meaning to the ancient art and music of Sanskrit times. Sometimes it was so special, the moment could not be repeated anywhere in the country. The full house audience who had invitations and who had great cheers during the performances reflected the successful staging of Samy's daughters' celebratory dance. The family was thrilled and in a party mood. Jana vividly remembered his father had a backstage secret drinking session organized with Ranga Uncle. It was '... Scottish Highland Park Black Label imported good stuff,' said Mr. Prahash. He asked Jana to be with his mum while he popped into the toilet for a quick release of the nervous excitement. Due to the single malt, on the way back from the toilet break he forgot to take down his golden white westi, a celebratory sarong. He looked like a thug. When a sarong or a Westi is up, in Jaffna, it means the fight is going to start. Mr. Prahash was excited for his friend, and also he was happy to spend time with Ranga while the foreign drinks were going to keep coming his way. He asked Jana to join, knowing Jana knows that he has been drinking. He walked outside with Ranga for a cigarette break. Jana's mum was signaling him repeatedly to take his Westi down. Jana was also signaling to pull it down. He did not get the message from the distance or very close by. As usual he ignored her kindness as being vague as if a dream.

Suddenly, Ranga shouted: 'What's this Annai! Please put the Westi down.'

Mr. Prahash was embarrassed. Ranga had used a respectful closeness of expression like a brotherhood. Everybody called themselves Ayya and Annai. That was really to keep the heat down during the arguments. It really could change the mood if the tone of the voice changed from humble to anger with facial expression and few shakes of a head. A lot of language is spoken with head movement in Jaffna. Mr. Prahash was embarrassed in front of his son. He had slipped up and been told off by his best friend on a good occasion. Even though Jana was too young to understand, he felt for his father. Maybe the drinks had made him a little merry, too. He realized that just a little more than his usual weekly intake of the shining orange liquid had caused the glitch. Jana's father showed slight anger and embarrassment in front of his son, then he dropped his head waiting for Ranga to apologize.

Ranga did that without fail: 'Hey, don't get me wrong my friend, it is not personal.'

Mr. Prahash looked down at Jana and shook his head as if for the music that was going on inside. 'Good music, hah… do you like it?' as he tried to change the subject.

Ranga continued: 'Just to let you know, people are watching. You know how they are like, they like to talk, about disrespect and drunkenness on a special occasion like this, like that you know I don't mind, whatever you do at least for your family's sake.' as he burped. 'Come on, don't project your image like a drunken fool.' He did carry on a little more than usual, Ranga Uncle that night. Jana's father was really not happy. Still singing the song that was going on inside ignoring everybody, tapping his feet. Then he looked at his friend.

'Keep it cool, Ranga Annai,' said Mr. Prahash. 'In front of my son you are going on a bit. A bit too far.' He looked at him with little discomfort. 'Let's not point the finger at me Ranga Annai.'

Jana looked up innocent as a child. Then looked down.

'We all had a drink,' Mr. Prahash said. He repeated we all had a drink, Ranga Annai. 'I am not the only one here tasting the good life.'

Jana got embarrassed as his father was getting into an argument. He pulled his father's hand saying I want to go now… yes, I want to go now. He was confused, he knew his father spoke about Ranga all the time. His father always told Jana, how a good a gentleman he was. Jana began to cry.

Mr. Ranga looked down and said: 'We are not arguing, you fool. We are not having a fight,' said Ranga. 'Come on, Jana. Get him a choc ice. Come on, son, we having a usual play about.'

'No, I don't want anything,' said Jana. 'I want to go home now.'

'Ok then, you go and join your mum, ok. And please don't say anything about this to your mummy, ok?' Both Mr. Prahash and Ranga laughed.

'Good boy. Sensitive like his mother. Hey, listen, we are very good friends, we talk, we argue, that's a good sign of great friendship, son. Friendship is not all about agreeing to everything because he has bit of money and a future Minister of export living next door to him in Colombo. He is the only one I can trust on my death bed. So don't cry son,' Mr. Prahash said as he come down Jana's level and talked to him. Jana wiped his mouth and face. Mr. Prahash took his handkerchief and wiped his nose saying, 'Go on blow that nose… ahh ahh good boy… full of bogie you.'

Jana ran back. Ranga lit their cigarettes and looked at Mr. Prahash and said, 'I was impressed by the way you handled your boy. Sometimes I lack that close bond with my kids; I am too busy with my business.'

'Hey, thanks for all the good words and the hints with the smile,' said Mr. Prahash.

Jana joined his mum in the distance. Mum and son saw both men laughing and smoking.

'He is not a Delft boy, that's for sure,' said Ranga. 'He is a boy from the city of Jaffna Kurunagar. There is no doubt about that.'

'He will not farm or be a cowboy' said Mr. Prahash. Everybody laughed.

Mrs. Prahash walked up to him and said: 'Hi Ranga Annai.' Then she looked at Mr. Prahash: 'We are getting a lift from Malar Aunty so you just enjoy yourself.' As she called Mr. Prahash closer: 'Don't get carried away and get yourself blasted on the free stuff. Be at home at least by 2 a.m. Then she smiled at Ranga: 'Nice to see you. Come and visit us sometime,' said Marie Joyce. He smiled and thanked her and said it's my pleasure. She walked away giving a strong look to Mr. Prahash.

Mr. Prahash blew the Dunhill cigarette smoke up in the air as he felt real pleasure. Jana's father never came home that night. Everybody loved his company, young and old. He was an entertainer of a different kind. They drank until the early hours at Ranga's brother's house. Talked politics of Colombo, until their eyes went red, both still holding their drinks like Scottish Malt mavericks. They really wanted to continue further at a hotel somewhere as the party began to thin down, as the pressure mounted from the ladies to eat the dinner. The women succeeded and persuaded the big boys to eat. In Jaffna all eat after the drinks, not before. They like to drink on an empty stomach. It can be quite insane, the alcohol begins to hit the upper senses, all the aggression, straight talk and regrets come to the surface when the lights go down. But all will be gone at the eve of the Asian Dawn. There is a certain time alcohol can take the town into violence and a manic state. There was only a thin line between the normal and for the emergence of the manic unpredictable. Both men slumped on the table that night.

Mr. Prahash's mum, Clara, suffered from a mild form of depression. The care for the mentally ill didn't exist in Jaffna during the seventies. The families had very little understanding in regard to mental health. There was very little staff as health practitioners or to give advice and support in the community. The government had not set up any mental health governing body in the north to monitor the primary health care. Patients were abused and put in chains and shackles. The major or minor tranquilizers were not available for the public. Very few psychiatrists practiced in the northern peninsula full time. There was also a lot of superstition, and devil chasers were making money with voodoo with Neem Tree leaf bashing and arsenic cocktails until they collapsed with the effect of the drink, then chanting began in the name of the Hindu god Amman. The intention was to eradicate inhabitance of the soul by Satan. Christians practiced exorcism with priests and holy waters, all routinely done in towns and villages. 'It's all devil's work,' said the senior priest at the Amman Kovil. He began chanting Sanskrit with scarification of chicken, wild animal and milk bathing of the Amman statue to alleviate the possession of the stricken soul. Whereas the Christians took refuge at the church and bathed in holy water and drank a few cups full. Priests prayed for calm and make peace with the mentally ill. No assessment, evaluation or treatment. It was simply a clinical depression with symptoms of muteness, catatonic or manic state, all was allegedly possession by the devil. There was a place called Ancodai at KKS. Another one called Omanthai down south. We really did not know what they did there, who worked there, why people did not want to go there or talk about it. People were afraid of the word, to hear the madness. If you were to go to one of these places, it meant you were incurable, insane and outcast and you were not welcome back in the community as a human being. Mostly they were forced to live in a small shed called kottil made of mud and leaves, in the bushes in the middle of nowhere in the mangrove wilderness. Occasional travelers would give food and water. Some survived, some died of neglect and starvation. Jana was going to witness something close of that nature and it was going to affect his life forever.

Mr. Prahash took Jana to see his mother Clara at Ancodai Mental Hospital. Jana was going to see his grandmother for the first time, she had been ill for a long time. As they entered the hospital, they were greeted by Jana's grandfather, Arul. Mr. Arul went back to his slightly loose wooden rocking chair with bamboo work-like wickers slightly ripped, so worn he almost sank in the middle of it. He sat back with a smile while rocking, that turned into a laughing-like cry when we saw us. It looked quite fake, like he was not really sincere. Then he continued to laugh while shaking his head wildly. People around the hospital really wondered who was sane and who was not in that place, all looked slightly extraordinary.

Mr. Arul said: 'They have tried everything, all the treatment available… it is no use. No use,' then he laughed, 'who knows what they have done, but it looks like that's it. C'est la vie, straight to the Kottil at Delft. With an attitude of given up.' Then he turned his face serious: 'I trust them, it's the best opinion in Jaffna. Don't need the second and the third, it is all a waste of time.'

'Well, I don't,' said Mr. Prahash.

'What?' said Arul

'I don't believe that they have tried all the available

58

treatment.' Then he opened the creaking door of the confined room where they kept his mum. She looked like she was fixed to a point in a corner without any movement for a long time. It was reported they found her tearful and violently pulling her hair when they approached her. So they were compelled to confine her in the special security unit under violent category. The conditions looked dreadful, looked like a dirty derelict prison. The place stank of urine and a white slush of foam from Dettol floated around the room. As soon as she saw Jana, she turned and her eyes fixed on him and she started mumbling to everybody's surprise.

Jana said: 'There is a big black snake, yes, look, look!' pointed Jana.

Arul started to laugh again. The toilet next door gave the odor of a disinfectant, too. When Mr. Prahash leaned forward and looked, the floors and washing area looked untidy and hadn't been washed for days.

Jana asked his father: 'Why she is crying?' Jana repeated the question again. Jana's father did not say a word. He suddenly said: 'Bastards! They put her on the chains.'

This time Arul did not laugh. In the distance what looked like a snake for Jana, were heavy big chains which had cut her ankles very badly. The blood had dried on the open wound. There were no bandages or dressing on the wound. It was open and looked infected. Jana attempted to approach her. A nurse appeared suddenly from nowhere and warned them not to go close and to be careful, she can be violent, don't go close, as she stared at grandma with annoyance. Jana attempted to go again, while Mr. Prahash held his shoulders, but he had had enough.

He said to the nurse: 'Sister, for god's sake, have some respect.'

'What?' the nurse replied.

'She is a 62 year old lady with no strength to hurt anybody, you are talking nonsense, sister. After all she is my mum and I should know her well.'

The nurse replied with anger: 'If you looked after her properly in the first place she would not be in this situation, sir.'

By this time Mr. Prahash had let go Jana's shoulder. Jana quietly tiptoed and looked at the nurse and the smiling grandpa, everybody frozen for a minute expecting loud screams and mayhem. Also Jana was only 4 years old. He approached his grandma with a smile. She slowly turned, sat down and hugged her grandson. That was quite a moment for everybody even for tough men standing in front of Clara and Jana. Jana looked up, the tears came down from his grandma's face.

He said: 'You are coming home grandma?'

The nurse walked out in shame.

'Call her, call her back,' said Mr. Prahash to his father. 'I have seen enough.' He was disappointed with anger for the first time in his life. Even Jana was confused to see his father's tearful face. As for Mr. Arul, it was just fun and games as he was insanely laughing again, standing outside this time. Mr. Prahash was grey as a ghost as he looked at his father in disgust for the first time as he stopped laughing. By this time grandma had begun to mumble while hugging Jana closely: 'In dark Kaltihikodai sergeant Nuke Kano Malathi naangodai dim.' She repeated this several times while Jana smiled and was intrigued what she meant by this, but everybody understood it meant nothing but that she did not like this place and wanted to leave immediately. Mr. Prahash asked the sister to bring her medications, that he was taking her home.

Also he said to bring her possessions and release papers if any to sign regarding to her discharge. The sister put a bandage to her wound while she removed the chains and apologized for her sufferings. Madam Clara said nothing but was happy to be free to go. While Jana looked with interest during the dressing, he said 'say train, say train, grandma, it won't hurt. Yeah, I do that when I see my nurse.'

Mr. Prahash said: 'Amma Vanna, come Mum, let's go home, you are coming to Jaffna Bankshall Street. Right next to the Miracle of Mary Church. You will like that mum, I am sure.' He looked at the medications in brown packets. They were just pain killers and diuretics.

Jana's father said with disappointment: 'I don't see any medicine here for her mental illness.' This time they all laughed as they helped grandma to stand as she had no energy.

'Let's go, mum, we will eat first at a nice Hindu café with masala thosai, sambal and sambar then some rice and raisin pudding, you like that yeah mum.'

She shook her head in response and wiped her saliva, poor woman was hungry that was all. Jana sat on her lap all the way to the restaurant in the hired Morris Minor from Jaffna. Arul wanted to go through the Chunagam market as he wanted to meet his cousin who had a successful banana export business. While he stopped to talk with his cousin, Jana, his father and grandma got a nice seat near the window at a reputable vegetarian restaurant. The food was served in solid silver plates and cups. No cutlery, everyone ate with finger-picking hands without getting the palm dirty. Jana sat with crossed legs looking forward to the promised thosai and sambar. The food came in four minutes all warm with tea. Everybody began to enjoy the meal. Madam Clara began to eat fairly quickly. Mr. Prahash held her forearm, looked into her eye for moment.

'Take your time, mum. It's all yours. Nobody is going to take it away from you.'

Jana began to hide his food and looked around for that person who could possibly take it away.

'Don't rush, we got all day. I took a day off just for you. You're going to choke, slow down.'

She did slow down for a few minutes then continued to rush as Jana said: 'You like it very much, grandma. Me too,' and he dropped his sambar on his shirt. Grandpa had joined them by this time with a smile and a bunch of big ship (cappal) bananas.

'Here, Jana, all for you and your sisters.'

'Can I give one to grandma?'

'Sure you can, son,' said Mr. Prahash. Mr. Prahash asked for a water full of sembu, a small urn-shaped silver celebration water holder. He gave that to Madam Clara, she drank and settled down while looking at Jana and the bananas.

The ride home was great, it cost a few rupees for Mr. Prahash but it was well worth it. It was a great family memorable occasion to all involved.

That evening she spoke a few words with her daughter-in-law and the two little girls, Jocelyn aged four and Janine aged two, Jana's sisters. That night she slept fifteen hours flat with total exhaustion. The rest of the week she attended the church at Miracle of Mary next door. There were no further episodes all week. She quite calmly began to settle down from her depressive illness with the help of Marie Joyce. Grandma spoke softly and helped around the house, but by this time Mr. Prahash had gotten a nanny, called Miss Mahesh, to help them a little. Marie Joyce started her teaching at St James' Girls School. Grandma helped with the food preparation around the house. That was really therapeutic for her. Four months later she was fully recovered and started to help with the girls bathing and dressing. By this time Jocelyn had also started going to nursery at Holy Family Convent. Grandma Clara never missed the service during the Passover week, she even fasted for the Good Friday and never missed the Novenas. On Easter Sunday we all went to see the killing and the resurrection of Christ opera at the Kurunagar open stage, among thousands. The costumes, makeup, stage of over 100 yards, fireworks, lighting, sound, songs and storytelling with the great professional cast gave us a once-in-a-life-time opportunity to watch such a spectacle which lasted four hours. Especially the final event of the crucifixion of Jesus Christ and resurrection from the dead with clever nylon ropeworks and lighting was ahead of time. It really stuck in their psyche for a long time. It also made a major impact on our religious beliefs. People really cried, sobbing. Really cried full of tears for Jesus Christ. Amazing. Jana never forget that Passover.

Grandma settled well and was about to return to Delft due to the breakdown in her relationship with her son. Mr. Prahash was working now in the fields of Vadamaratchi near Atchuveli as an agricultural instructor. When he came home he wanted to relax with a small shot of Red Label Scotch with ice before his meals. Then he would play with Jana and the girls. Then a little later, all the old talk began to surface; the way his mum had neglected him when he was young.

Then words would be exchanged: 'You neglected me, mum. You failed me, mum. I would have been even better and more successful with my ability. You did not give me enough love and let me go to the beachfront catching fish and riding horses.'

That sort of life sounded really good to Marie Joyce. She smiled and signaled don't say anything.

'You never helped with my studies. Dad stayed away and slept at the rest house and sat in front of the porch on a rocking chair looking after everyone. You are much closer to the girls... your girls.'

Marie Joyce signaled not to say anything.

'You failed me. You failed me,' he repeated.

As Marie Joyce took the glass and the bottle away from him quickly, she said: 'That's him, a few talks of nonsense, then he is out, now the food is getting cold. He will wake up in the middle of the night and have a go at me for the food being cold. Mum, that's your son. I have to live with him for the rest of my life,' said Marie Joyce.

Mr. Prahash had fallen sleep on a stretched wicker easy-chair swing with big handles and rest bars for the feet. He finally looked relaxed and in peace. Madam Clara did not really want to give any trouble for Marie Joyce's family and wanted to go back to Delft. She wanted to die in her own home. Jana was a little disappointed, he wanted to learn more from Grandma Clara about his dad and his relationship with his mother when he was young at Delft. He was just beginning to have a relationship with his grandmother.

After years of neglect and without treatment she had a few relapses and survived for a few more years. Whatever the past history, Mr. Prahash provided care, shelter, food and clothing while she was at Bankshall Street. He even gave her a bath at times and started a plan to build a granny annex at the new land he had bought at Chundikuli. She loved all the efforts he had done to keep her at Jaffna.

She would leave Jaffna and pass away peacefully in her sleep at her own home in Delft. She was about to have a quiet but respectable funeral at her own home.

Jana had visited Delft before. He had a vague memory of the island. This time he would meet his grown up cousins and relatives for the first time.

The whole trip took half a day. First the bus from Jaffna town to Punkuduthevu at the end of the Jaffna gulf tip, passing through the tobacco fields of Velanai, paddy fields of Suruvil then the boat with the daily commuting people of the island. The most exciting part was the 5km ferry ride to the Delft Harbor through the rough ocean waters.

Jana and Mr. Prahash arrived in the early afternoon. There had been no delay. First, Jana walked straight into the rest house. Grandpa looked relaxed as usual and gave them a great smile and welcomed everybody. He asked Mr. Prahash about the plan of the new house build, how he was coping with the neighbors, politics of Jaffna town, etc. They began to walk towards the funeral house. Delft looked a lonely place with a happy and smiling few. Jana looked back at the sea, he could not see any land all around. It looked like an unspoiled haven with a people of free thinking intellectuals. Jana watched all that sea rock stacked beautifully as walls of boundaries. No cars, just cycles, Vespa scooters, horses and donkeys all passed slowly without a hurry.

Jana met Aunty Mary and gave her a big hug. She called him my big nephew. Jana was pretty shy. Everybody wanted to see this cousin from Jaffna city. People noticed Jana quickly moved with cousin Jeyanthi who showed special interest. Aunty Mary's third child, six year old Jeyanthi in Delft had all the boys circling her in her school. She was red cheeked, olive-like fair skin, big dark eyes, and a great set of small white teeth. Her long earrings jangled in the air while she jumped up in the air with her long green and blue skirt and blouse. Her dark and beautiful curls of knotted hair looked as if it might be painful if ever her mum wanted to put it in order. Jana asked questions about the place and begin to follow her around. People begin to notice them together in the vegetable patch. Jana checked the tomato and chili trees.

Suddenly Jana said to Jeyanthi: 'Don't touch that, it will burn your eyes.'

She replied: 'I am not silly. I know it's hot and burns your mouth, not eyes.'

Aunty Mary came as predicted to comb her hair. 'Jeya, come here you, your hair is in a mess.'

Girls liked their hair rough and ready. At this age though, they had to have it plaited and combed. She continued to ignore her, tried to run around the house. Aunty caught up with her eventually, grasped her hair. 'It is only going to take a few minutes, darling.' She quickly pulled it back and tidied it up gently. Her natural curls quickly turned back into position. She had small visible neck hair behind the ears. Jana began to have a crush on her. Aunty Mary put on her leg wear with tiny little bells, and said: 'Why don't you show them what have you learnt from your dance lessons. The gypsies made this challankai with fine silver. Stand still, will you,' said Aunty Mary, as Jeya looked all attentive as everybody looked upon her. Aunty Mary said: 'That's done.'

Jana watched all this as still as a mirror, like a little inspector of arts. Jeyanthi was asked to perform a little dance at the back of the house for this formal funeral crowd. When she arrived at the back, all the adult men were setting up there drinking hut, waiting for the arrival of the fresh toddy from the home grown Palmyra trees at the family land in Delft.

Aunty Mary was disappointed that the boys intended to start the waterhole early as this. Dad signaled the boys and girls to join them in that cool hut away from the main funeral house. As far as the funeral was concerned, all relatives were content with Madam Clara's loss. They understood her soul was at ease now, as she had suffered during her elderly existence. She looked in peace and the hidden smile of her nature reflected on her state in the coffin. In Jaffna they kept their dead at home prior to burial. Jana did go and watch her closely and touched her hand with the crucifix of the rosary standing out from her hand and sapphires like stones glistening on top of her fingers.

Jana said: 'She is cold. She is cold like ice, why?'

Dad said: 'Son, when you go on a deep sleep before you go to heaven, it's full of ice in heaven. They like everybody to come cold as much as they can. So they can easily settle in quickly. It is not hot like here, over there. It's only the sinners and liars have to face the heat.'

Then he looked at his dad: 'Please don't laugh, I am talking very serious here.' Both laughed as they started drinking their good home grown cool fermented toddy. People who laughed at the dead, really have to face the heat.

Jana had walked out of the hut by this time. From a small age, he had not liked the drinking environment. The men wanted to start drinking the famous Delft toddy as early as they could, due to carrying the coffin to the cemetery. Some of the relatives were scheduled to catch the last boat from Delft to Jaffna. They really didn't want any delays of the funeral burial times. The ladies sensed a little insensitiveness and worries regarding the men's behavior led by Mr. Arul and his loud obnoxious laugh. Jana went back to the house to join the prayer meeting for Madam Clara. She wore a green and red kanchipuram kurai sari which she had on her wedding day 40 years earlier, still in pristine shine with those gold threads on the borders. She also wore her own jewelry, but it would be removed prior to the burial and given back to the eldest daughter who would decide with grandpa who will get what as her inheritance. There was no will or lawyers in a close-knit cultured Tamil families, all was done with the word of honor. Most of all, the most needy in the family would get the family jewels or a piece of land to improve their lives. Family jewels or a deed of the land were the most secured assets for a loan in Jaffna from private loan sharks called Vattie men in regard to farming, house building or foreign travel. High interest with no animosity but they kept your asset until you completely paid back your borrowed money. The funeral people together, even the rival siblings, buried their hatchets and moved on as a respect for the loved ones. The stone heart, *kalnengam*, will crumble for the love of the deceased soul creating an unimaginative unity back in the big house in Delft.

Mr. Prahash avoided all the melancholy moments. He and his father liked to create drunken debates, recklessly resurfacing all the old stories. Who did what for madam Clara, who looked after her the most when she was ill? Mr. Arul liked all this when his son was around, otherwise the girls would eat him for breakfast. Arul as he got older, a man who was a strong 6'2", silver haired like an Indian chief cropped up to his neck, began to look bony around his ribcage, his clavicles began to protrude and created a little dip between the neck and his shoulders.

'Why don't you eat well?' asked Mr. Prahash, 'you look like you have been in the army camp confined to the cockroaches.'

With a smile, Mr. Arul, a man who spoke very little, replied, 'I had a bad fever, right here in the kottil, nobody to really look after me except the little ones, others all gone to work. I missed my walks, she was also ill, too. So I had a bad three weeks.'

Mr. Prahash said: 'Why don't you come and stay with us in Jaffna for a while?'

Jana said: 'Go on, granddad. I will show my new games in the house. I will also introduce some of my sporting friends from Bankshall Street.'

'Ha ha… sporting… ha ha…' laughed Grandpa Arul. 'What kind of sports, son?'

'Cricket, running around the streets of Kurunagar all the way to the beach front.'

'Just for you I am going to be there in no time, my boy,' said grandpa. By this time some relatives had brought some food for the travelling families. The funeral home doesn't cook until the burial is over. A few ladies had begun to set up a dining table in the carpentry workshop belonging to grandpa. It was like a great workhouse - anything could be fitted or repaired in there. It was a multipurpose self-sufficient carpentry with traditional tools, passed down the generations. Someone said grandpa made the coffin right here, you can still smell the fresh neem dust and the varnish. Grandpa secretly loved Madam Clara deeply, after all he was married to her for 45 years, he understood every moment of her life except the mental illness. He laughed at things when he didn't understand. That is the way he coped with the sometimes lonely Delft life.

Everybody sat down hurriedly to eat their meals and said a small prayer for Madam Clara. Mr. Prahash, as the eldest, stood up and gave a small speech before the meal.

'My mum was a great lady. She not only put up with my dad for 45 years but also she was the mother of eight children, two boys and six girls. We all did fairy well, except Mala and Tom who still remain single. The rest of us are all happily married and blessed with her grandchildren. She also enjoyed being with the kids in Jaffna, Vanni and Delft. My son really loved his grandmother. He is the first brave kid ever to approach a patient at the secure unit, sectioned and chained. She was ill, but she did not deserve that kind of treatment. Sectioned without consent. That he did at his age of 4, at Omanthai.'

The relatives looked at each other, *why he is talking about all that?* Jana smiled.

'Mary is the brightest among our family. As you all know she was a graduate from Parameswara College with honors as a teacher. She spoke better English than anybody else in the whole of Delft or even Jaffna. She was soon promoted to run a local school as the principal. All because she was the favorite of my mum's, as the eldest daughter. Mums always love their daughters better than their sons behind the seane. My sister could have gotten a better job in Jaffna with an extravagant lifestyle in town. But she chose to stay here with her mum and the locals. As for me I did not do that bad either, I got recently promoted as an agricultural instructor and have started building my own house in Jaffna Chundikuli. Tom is also having his chili farm in Visvamadu , along the rivers of Vanni, with that great soil. My other two sisters are doing well in Vanni too with their rice fields. The kids are doing well with their studies too. My mother's sprit has worked well. I am also very proud in the fact that my nephew Ragu is the first one in our family to enter into the University of Thelthenya with honours in economics. I am not sure about my son, he is insisting he wants to be a cricketer and an athlete, he reckons that will pay his meals for his kids and good luck to him.'

'Ahh…' said everybody.

Someone at the table said *leave him alone*. Jeyanthi sat next to Jana and smiled.

Mr. Prahash continued: 'There are no delinquents or depravities in our family. We all did fairly well. We have to be thankful to our parents, whatever right or wrong we thought they did in their past. We have come close as a family in recent years and should stay close as a family. Thank you, dad. God bless.'

Everybody said *God bless us all*. Mr. Prahash took out a package he had brought from Jaffna, cards printed with Miracle of Mary on the front, inside was the picture of Madam Clara and her favorite prayer, with her birth date, her funeral date and finally the 30 day date which would be the remembrance gathering. They will have a church service in Jaffna at the Miracle of Mary, where his mum recovered her illness with meditation and prayers. Mr. Prahash also invited everybody to come to his house at Bankshall Street, Kurunagar on the day of the remembrance service. Everybody said *thank you brother.*

They began to serve the food. Homemade hoppers, brown rice and string noodles with Delft dry fish, brinjalls, shallots, fennel, garlic and tomato chili sauce. Our mouths melted with the freshness of the taste and food. Everybody enjoyed the meal of great aroma with sun dried lemon pickle and dried fried chili marinated in rich yogurt. It was a custom to have those accompany the meal on special family occasions. "Morre mulakai urukai". The men quickly ate and got back to the toddy hut. They also took a plate of lamb curry for taste, while they drank. Bites (non-sauced food) are called 'Taste' in Jaffna. Jana got bored with Jeyanthi and began to ignore her. He just needed something to do. He was looking for his dad. Mr. Prahash called Jana from the chair outside the hut: 'Come here.' Jana walked over and Mr. Prahash pulled him closer. Jana said: 'You smell bad, dad.'

'Palmyra toddy kunamai kuddy,' said dad. He explained: 'If you drink the toddy with the clean heart it will bring you peace in your brain. That will bring you riches and happiness. It is like milk from the secret cow. One of the wonders of the Delft Tamil invention, my boy,' said Mr. Prahash. Somebody passed the homemade drinking plah full of toddy. 'Come here, Jana, drink some, good for your digestion. Go on, it's nice.'

Jana sipped a little.

'What's wrong? You don't like it?'

'Nope.' Jana shook his head.

Mr. Prahash said: 'Go on you to Jaffna, fool (poda, peya).

Grandfather asked: 'You don't like it, Jana?'

Jana said quietly: 'I like it but I don't want to say in front of the girls.' He suddenly laughed out loud.

Everybody asked *what, what*… he shook his head and said nothing.

Jana said: 'Let me try from your plah.' He drank some. 'That tastes better, dad.' Jana smiled at grandpa.

Mr. Prahash said: 'Listen you fool, you're going to marry her one day, so be nice to her,' as he pointed the finger at Jeyanthi. 'Yes, I will make sure of that. Everybody laughed at the seriousness of Mr. Prahash. One uncle said *she have to say yes first.*

'That's true. Boy like him with the plah in his hand at this tender age. Who is going to say no,' said Mr. Prahash. 'Here give it, who you trying to fool. Drinking all the toddy from everybody's cup.' Everybody laughed. 'We have been watching you, following her around everywhere dribbling.'

Jana shook his head, no, no embarrassed.

'Hey Jana, you got good taste son, she is beautiful, ahhhh,' said Uncle Sureshpathi. After all Jeya was his daughter. By this time Jana was annoyed with the toddy hut and Jeyanthi. Jeyanthi also felt ignored by this time and started to cry saying Jana didn't want to play with her anymore. Aunty Mary asked Jana: 'Come on, you will play with Jeyanthi won't you?' Jana said *yes.*

'My lovely, come on you two, it is all the fault of the drunken old fools who created all this nonsense.'

They screamed from the hut: *looks like she got her way and has put him to work already.*

Mr. Prahash said: 'For better or worse, in sickness and in health.' Everybody laughed. 'She is far better than all the convent girls put together in Jaffna, you fool, say yes.' Everybody lifted their drinking plah and said *cheers, cheers for the Delft beauties.* Everybody laughed. Aunty Mary said *treat the kids like kids, please. Thank you.* The hut for a moment was quiet, then all laughed. *Come on,* somebody said, *it's a funeral, for Christ's sake.* Everybody was quiet for a moment again. Yes, cousins married each other in Tamil culture, but it was nothing in the form of a forced marriage. Mostly in Sri Lanka people tried to avoid it as much as they could. But it was mainly to keep the family name intact.

Jeyanthi introduced the vegetable patch, Mr. Tomato and Miss Chili to Jana and asked him to help out with pulling weeds. Both sat down and worked with interest. Jana did what Jeyanthi said. She also explained the relationship between the vegetable couple, with great imagination.

'Mum, can I plant some flowers here?'

'Listen, I am tired of you two. Look at your clothes all dirty. Whose idea is this?' asked Aunty Mary.

Jana said nothing.

Jeyanthi said: 'Jana liked doing it, so I showed him how to weed.'

'Is that right, Jana?'

Jana said *yes* and smiled.

'Come inside you two. Do you want to play monopoly or snakes and ladders? How about some Tin Tin books?'

Jana said: 'I like the Captain Beard better than Tin Tin. He is big and fat with a beard, and he is also accident prone like me. He keeps on falling down all the time.'

They were interrupted by Mr. Prahash and company who had finally decided to leave the beloved toddy hut.

'We are going to the beach. Give us a set of clothes for them and a towel please, asked Grandpa Arul. Aunty Mary quickly provided a bag full of clothes as they all started to walk towards the beach.

Mr. Prahash said: 'Let's go for a quick swim and come back before it gets dark.'

When the night falls, the sun sets on the beaches of Delft with a multicolored reflection, mainly purple, red and yellow. People walking on the side of the beach will appear like black shadows with orange and red shine on their bodies looking like the end of a movie. Nobody is allowed to swim on the sunset in Delft. They say the sea turns wild and angry. Then it rises above the shore with huge waves changing its temperature, suddenly creating an extra twisting current. The angry mighty wave will drag you in deep in the twisters (sulli) and choke you and throw you out unconscious. Then the waves will drag you through the sharp edged crustaceans, will make you bleed and you have two minutes to revive for survival. It's normal for the locals to watch at the mystery of the dark blue ocean during this time.

'Put on your slippers you two,' said Aunty Mary.

Father, son, grandfather and cousin, three generations, walked through the Palmyra groves. They were planted close to each other so they grew by themselves and they also gave adequate shade to keep the hot sun away. They passed a few houses, coconut huts and derelict land. Jana looked back as their house disappeared in the trees. It looked very far but he could hear the ocean.

'Is it far to go, dad?'

'Not so far, Jana. Listen carefully, you can hear the ocean.'

'Yes, I know.'

Then suddenly he felt that heavy breeze from the east of Delft from the south Indian Ocean. It made a heavy clapping noise while water splashed at the dark and ancient fossilized rocks in the middle of the sandy beach. After hitting the rock it sprayed full force like a hose pipe from a fire engine. Jana was mesmerized by the sight and held the hand of grandpa, saying: 'It's unbelievable. This place, I have never seen anything like this, Grandpa.'

The beach was full of brownish white sand with shells and shaped rocks all in color from the sea. There was miles of clear blue and green sea with sand and rocks all along the coast line. Some large rocks defended against the heavy thunderous waves. The waves were gigantic, curling like pulled springs back to their shape. It could be a surfers' paradise, just nobody knew it yet. It was a totally unspoiled paradise island of Jaffna, Sri Lanka.

Now people feared for a different reason to go in the waters; Navy checkpoints, due to the tension of the Srimavo

Government. People stayed at home with closed doors in front of a beach like this. It was sheer harassment for the free people of Delft. Tourist guides took a break too, and did not want to take their chances. Some old familiar British, Dutch and the Portuguese came back to see their favorite island. Animal conservationists had still yet to arrive, for to save the cavalry horses. Early Dutch and Portuguese left their well bred horses in a hurry. It was a little memory of European occupation. They guarded Jaffna from the point of Delft. We loved the animals, looked after them like another family member. During the conflicts, they began to be neglected due to shortage of rice, millet and corn. The Suez crisis was the start. People relied on the homegrown to fight the starvation. Animals only had the leftovers.

Jana saw in the distance two horses coming their way. As they walked closer to the riders he was quite surprised. They looked young, between the ages of 10 and 12, riding bareback along the beach. Their nylon rope work was very interesting, softened around by the inner tube of a bicycle, around the face and neck of the horse, quite secure for Mr. Prahash.

'Hey, *thambi*, young brother, you are the son of Antonypillai right? You know me, son,' said Mr. Prahash.

'Yes, sir,' said the boys.

'It is your pony?'

'Yes, we caught it and fed it on millet for two months.'

'Well, you looked after them well,' he said as he stroked the horses. They looked healthy and happy. He also checked the legs.

Jana looked at his father: 'What you think, dad? Is it safe?'

Grandpa shook his head. He said: 'They have been broken well and trained to perfection. Travelers will love it. Where is your dad?' he asked of the boy.

'He is going to the funeral.'

'He missed the toddy.'

'Sorry, sir.'

'Don't worry, son. Can we borrow them for a short ride? Is it ok?'

'Sure you can, sir.'

They got down like professionals with great respect and honesty for the visitors. It did not matter who you are or where you came from, the hospitality was just equal to everybody in Delft. Mr. Prahash said: 'Jana, you jump on the black one.' Dad grasped the rope. 'Jeyanthi, come here,' as he lifted her and put her on the brown one with the white face, as he held the ropes. Gently they walked slowly for a yards.

'Hah, it's beautiful, ahhhh Jana,' said Mr. Prahash proudly. Then he said to the boys: 'Come on, jump on behind the kids, take them at a nice pace, carefully and come back ok?'

They went at a nice pace up to the breach horizon and turned back, with nice rhythm. Jana and Jeyanthi really enjoyed that moment. When they came back, the riding kids got off and gave the ropes to the adults. Mr. Prahash and grandpa jumped on the horses swiftly. They looked majestically regal in their posture. Then they took a decent gallop as the boys ran alongside cheering. The legwear of Jeyanthi gave beautiful sounds with the turn of her feet and they mingled with the thunder of the waves. The wind was making a strange noise from leafless trees. Mr. Prahash increased the tempo with a few taps to the horse. Jana was also holding the rope tight. It was something both would never forget in their lives, this event on the ocean front. Grandfather took it more slowly with Jeyanthi and watched his elder son's adrenaline rush as he came back on full speed on the magnificent black horse.

He said: 'Boys, you got a champion here,' while gasping for his breath. 'He is good. He is really a good colt. Take care of him. He will bring riches for you. Don't give or sell it to anyone.'

'Sure, sir.

'I tell you a place to hide them in troubled times, nobody will go there. Everybody knows it's haunted with the dead pilgrims.' He showed them a little cave under the rocks, camouflaged by the coconut trees. That's where I used to hide my beauties,' he said as he stroked the majestic animal.

'Thank you, sir. Nandri,' said the boys.

Mr. Prahash said: 'Wait! Here you are,' and gave the boys 10 rupees each. 'That's the best money I have spent for a long time with my son. Isn't that right, Jana?'

With excitement, Jana said: 'Yes, it's true. Dad never spent any money on me before.'

The boys jumped on the horses and rode like real Indians on the prairie.

'Did you like that, you two? Great ahhhh.'

They nodded their heads. Mr. Prahash was on a high as he remembered his younger days on the beach. He pulled out a small fiber sack, walked up and down for a moment.

'It is better than any monopoly or snakes and ladders. Come on, Jana, you promised to bring some shells and stones for your sisters and friends in Jaffna.'

Jana suddenly remembered Indhiran his cousin and grasped the bag and began to collect the shells and stones. Delft has no tortoise, crab or snail shells. It is full of limpet with purple dots and circles of Cyprian Tigris. This was the most often seen in the windowsills of the houses for luck and fortune. They lined it from small to large along the line. The fossilized grey stones felt smoother in the hand and were quickly picked up by the little ones. There was also a huge pile of colorful stones in all shapes and sizes. An ocean full of artifacts. Jana and Jeyanthi quickly picked up a bagful of crustaceans.

Jeyanthi picked up a large Sangu Stranbus Gigas, a large crustacean with orange and white colors twisting around parallel left and right in a great natural design. Grandpa quickly squatted down on the beach and told us about a secret shell of left striped gigas and right striped gigas.

He said: 'When you blow from a left thread giga it can be used as a shipman's signal during the long journey. But most endangered shell of all time was the priceless, million to one, called the *Panja Shanyam Sangu*. It was used by the Hindu gods of ancient times to bless the pilgrims of the ocean. It could be heard over a thousand miles to warn off the evil bad weather. People searched for them for years in the water, diving deep without apparatus and some never came back. Because the gods of the deep sea never let anybody take it from the ocean, only when it decides to come outside then naturally you can have it. Do you like the story?'

'Yes, but a little scary, grandpa. This sea is full of stories,' said Jana.

Jana and Jeya begin to look for those priceless gigas. They quickly picked up similar small and large shells, asking grandpa *is this the one*? By this time Mr. Prahash had begun to swim in the rough sea, going deeper and deeper. He was a natural diver in his younger days.

Jana asked: 'Is he going to look for that rare giga granddad?'

'No,' said grandpa, 'he is just having a swim.'

'Is this the one, grandpa?'

'No, Jana.'

'Is this the one, grandpa?' asked Jeya.

By now grandpa wished he hadn't told the story. The kids lost interest in the other shells and stones and started rolling in the wet sands. Grandpa Arul began to worry for his son, Prahash, as he knew he liked to go a good distance in the ocean. But he kept his cool and Mr. Prahash began to surface after a few minutes and came up with the big wave above swimming like a pro. By this time Jana was rolling on top of Jeya and he gave her a kiss on her face. The story had made them suddenly competitive, had created dislike and anger. That's the magic of the sea. Jeyanthi did not know what to do, she was still confused.

She screamed with annoyance: 'He kissed me, granddad. He kissed me.'

As the waves climbed mighty high, the sun set on the Delft beach horizon. Suddenly, Mr. Prahash surfaced, 200 yards away from the starting point. Then he began to walk towards them. There were a few marks in his body. Some cuts bleeding slightly. He dabbed some sea sand on it. Grandpa was relieved. He had been scared for his son. They hadn't been for a swim for a long time, and the mood of the bereavement made it a little anxious for a mighty Arul with history. Mr. Prahash asked for the towel to dry himself and looked back the sea.

He said: 'The suli tried to take me down. I had to fight hard this time, dad.'

Jeyanthi was still unhappy and complained to granddad. 'Jana kissed me.'

Mr. Prahash dried himself and looked above the clouds. 'Come, you two, that's enough of the kissing game. Where are the shells you collected?' asked Mr. Prahash. Then he pulled out a big left striped Giga from his loose kaki pocket to everybody's surprise.

Jeyanthi said: 'I never…' and kissed her uncle and looked at this amazing clean beautiful shell.

'That's for our new house, Jana. This will bring us luck and fortune.'

Jana looked at the smooth texture and curves with amazement. Mr. Prahash began to explain the cloud movement: 'A rapidly moving cold front with moist unstable warm air here, boys and girls. It forces the air to rise producing a cloud call cumulus which means storm is approaching.' He continued: 'The western warm front and the eastern cold wind will be going to interrupt grandma's funeral day with small rain. We'd better go home.' Suddenly he looked in a hurry.

Jana said: 'I like the rain on the beach.' He asked grandpa: 'Can we stay?'

'Sure you can, son. We will come after sending grandma to heaven. Okay now, let's go.'

Jana quickly agreed. Then grandpa laughed: 'Ha ha ha ha ha… I like the rain on the beach. You are a romantic fool you. Unlike anybody in the Delft, you and your ideas, something else, son.'

The rain came just after they buried grandma Clara. Umbrellas went up quickly. Water rushed into the grave. Mr. Prahash signaled the grave diggers to push the sand in quickly. Everybody began to walk away from the cemetery. Jana, granddad and his father stood and watched under the cemetery shelter, while everybody else left the place. The rain trickled and stopped gently. Then Mr. Prahash finally put the flowers and wreath on the grave. He sat for a moment alone and cried for his beloved mum. He looked back at Jana and his father said while shaking his head, *let's go home.* Jana's father gave something to the grave digger and said a few words. He also shook his head.

Grandpa said: 'Let's go to the port side. Jana, you are hungry? Let's go to the beach café, and have some fried dhal rings called vadai with sambol. You will like that, come on.'

'Dad, come on, let's go and eat it.'

When they approached the beach café, the tea maker lifted the silver cup above his head and poured the tea into the other cup. He continued to do that a few times for the great mixture of vanilla tea and milk to get gathered in air with bubbles. It really tasted something like no other tea. Not even from your own home. That was the secret of the tea hut success at the beach front. Not a single drop spilled outside. It tasted sensational. They took the food and the flask full of tea to the rest house. Grandpa pulled up the table and the easy chair closer to the sea front.

Mr. Prahash pointed to the coast: 'Jana, do you see that maritime coast, all the way to the place where we were earlier? People lived here self sufficiently for hundreds of years. I was born here on the famous Dutch Delft. As youngsters we lived in this port day and night. When the Japanese planes flew low, we threw stones at them. Hit them with catapults from the trees. Luckily for us there was no British navy stationed here. They were staying behind the forts of Kytes. They had plenty of camouflage with fishing nets and coconut leaves. We started a smoke with dried coconut shells and fresh leaves every morning and evening. Indians do not like to fight in the dark. The Japanese liked to come early morning between dark and light, just like the mosquitoes. Maybe that's where the name comes from for the mosquito squadron. So we smoked the place. We also had Arabian pirates from the Indian Ocean through the Gujarat region with big hand-built sailing boats. Mainly Muslim traders, they did not like the Hindus. They liked our goats for milk and meat, insisted on slicing the throat, saying for the halal reasons. We soon learned that was a religious requirement. We fought for the goat blood, roasted it on an outdoor fire with fine semolina with onions and chilies and served it with boiled eggs and curry leaves. The best breakfast ever. We used to sell it for 25 cents for half a coconut cup. That was big money then. Then we had the pilgrim season. The Saint Catcherthevu Vellankani Mary, Palithevu St. Antony, used to bring us business. We exchanged gingili oil and cloves for saris and textiles. The latest view-masters and transistor radios from Singapore were the hot properties of the seventies. During the bad weather, lost fisherman and trading ships get washed up in Delft for safe heaven. Delft saved thousands of lives over the years. One time we could not help the boat of 30 people on the way to Palaithievu. All perished including women and children. Fisherman reported they still heard the screams and cries over the waters where they drowned. They even stopped fishing around that region as a mark of respect.'

Jana looked at the black rock with RIP 1956. Jana would remember all this when he came back as an adult for the first time - including this rest house where grandpa worked for 40 years.

Jana asked suddenly: 'Does he own this place, dad? If you can get a job, he gives you wages, accommodation, happiness and leisure. You just keep it, you don't worry about the rest. Including your family. Your job becomes your enjoyment. Yeh… he owns this place now. He can stay here as much as he wants.' Jana smiled and said: 'You are the keeper of the castle.'

Grandpa laughed. 'That's right, son. One day you take over this castle and it would be yours, too.'

Jana said: 'No, you are lying.'

'No, son, you are hearing the truth, only this time, colonialists, government ministers, missionaries, opposition leaders, foreign dignitaries - when they come here I was the first one they have to greet and meet. I am the one who found them a suitable guide and a place to stay on the island. I used to encourage the politicians to look after and promote this beautiful island. When they failed, we ourselves gathered momentum and did a lot with the businessmen and the church leaders.' Mr. Arul then bent down and picked up a handful of sand, took a moment and said: 'Miraculously, we had good soil closer to the ocean. We also brought some red earth from a nearby region to fulfill certain cultivation needs. We exchanged materials and worked with other islanders. We hardly dealt with cash. There is only one phone to the nearest island. People exchanged work for a sack of rice. Roofers, carpenters, well diggers, masons all worked for materials like millet (kurakan), semolina (rava), tapioca (sovearisi), brown rice (kutharisi), Palmyra sugar (chatkarai) and purple yam (rasa velli). Plenty of drift wood and sea stones made us tables, beds and sheds. We had everything we needed except the diesel and kerosene oil. The sea was our provider and our savior. People used to bless this coast for prosperity with floating flowers and fruits. We used to dive under and eat the fruits. One thing we had in abundance, crabs, bluefin tuna, turtle, ray fish, shrimps, octopus, barracuda, gigantic red breams and many more alive and fresh. Ask your dad he will tell you.'

Mr. Prahash began to talk about his childhood at the Delft coast. 'There were eight of us. We decided to build a boat with a local carpenter boat maker. Dad, you remember, you got us our secondhand motor from Kytes. We painted it red and called it 'Rescue Delfta 8'. We provided the local volunteer service, in return for food and shelter, with search, rescue and transport of people and animals. We received gifts and money. Then we began to make real money to go to Kytes and Jaffna. I was only ten and the youngest of the crew. Number 8 was lucky for us but not for many others as the trade ships get trapped in the choppy waters through Delft. Some of our horses were also taken to the mainland to control rioters in front of a cinema hall in the 50's, when M.G.R films opened for the public. I remember when I went to see the film with the crew, called the 'Marma Yogi', the Mythical- Guru. It was a fight in front of the cinema to get tickets. But our crew of eight was unstoppable. The theatre then hired us for every new release for a week. We kept the ticket touts out, that's all. We were popular among the girls. We raised the profile of Delft. Organised beach horse races. We also had our own races in the beach,' Mr. Prahash paused. 'When they took our horses, we really hated the authority.We have to settle for the ponies. The only thing we got here now is a few horses and a good Palmyra toddy. At least the passenger boats come five times a day. This is now one of the greatest destinations in the country. Let's hope it stays that way, at least for the horses and the people.'

Jana's father never told anything about his major rescue that involved all the eight crew which saved the lives of the religious observers. They were impressed with the organized industrious youngsters, who hadn't gone to school and who had studied at home or under the street lights. All were offered apprentices and scholarships at St Antony's Kytes. Only one was keen to take that offer and that was a young Mr. Prahash. Others did not want leave the island and the boat. It is now called the 'Lucky 7 Delfta'. Young Prahash was sad to leave the lifestyle. The Lucky 7 took him in the boat to Kytes St. Antony's boarding school.

Grandfather finally got rid of his chameleon on the shoulder and was happy for his son. He was popular among the seminary boys, some who would become the parish priests of Jaffna, even bishops in Sri Lanka. He passed the G.C.E. ordinary level scoring high in English, Agriculture, fisheries, Christianity, woodwork, Sinhala and Tamil. When young Prahash saw the green of Suruvil and Vellanai paddy fields, that changed his life. He played volleyball near the cinema at Karamban. He quickly attracted the local rice farmers who were the main exporters to Colombo rice distribution. He decided to get involved in agriculture. His little humorous trickeries at St. Anthony's made him stand out as a troublemaker at the expense of some strict Obligate of Mary Immaculate priests. They quickly transferred him to St. Henry's Ilavalai north of Jaffna, where he climbed the roof at nights to scare the old retired priests as a ghost of the old church. He soon left school and pursued his agricultural diploma in Gundasalai Agricultural Institute. He succeeded in completing the course and was posted in Kytes and Survil region as an agricultural overseer. He became friends of Yohhama, Manikkam and Shunmugan families. He really loved that town and quickly learned the job of all the agricultural department - overseeing, distribution and procurement. He worked closely with ministers and local government for the improvement of the community. Some of them who knew him as a kid in the days of Delfta 8, and knew also his father Arul, had stayed at the rest house and had been looked after by the locals. He received an invite from the Yohhama family, who was Manikkam's sister, for the family ceremonial occasions. His honesty and respect quickly brought him to great heights. The man always told the truth even when he attempted to tell a lie. He was loved by all the elders of the families, he was a humble unimpressionable good listener. He also promoted schools in the area to the youngsters to take up agriculture as a career. He told stories of his friends in Delft, how they would have lived if they had enough farmland. They really loved animals, the breeding and looking after them, how people struggled with Palmyra and vegetable patch. Here he started to speak in public with conviction. He mixed and worked in the community as an agent to break barriers of caste and divisions with teachers, fishermen and landowners to promote the Naranthanai region. He raised the issue of soil and preservation, he joked about the cultural differences as he pushed the interesting aspects of agriculture. Politicians began to notice his natural talents, especially the congress party. He also met G.G. Balam, who was at that time a leading politician, with 'father' Selva of the Tamil Federal Party. He joined the rallies as congress party pro agriculture and worker of the land. During this time he met his wife, Marie Joyce, in one of the schools. Marie Joyce was teaching prior to her university to begin her teacher training in Jaffna. She also came from a big family of eight. She was also the eldest among the eight. Her mother Madam Joan brought them up alone, with the help of Marie Joyce. So she took responsibility at an early age. That attracted Mr. Prahash. He fell for her head over heels and began to follow her everywhere on the bus or on the bicycle, in a way of looking after her from the young boys. She couldn't walk on streets but would be overwhelmed with compliments for her Ava Gardner features with long hair, big eyes and full lips and a great figure. He was in love the moment he saw her. Months later he could not wait any longer. He proposed to her in front of the Kytes beach overlooking the Dutch fort. The arrangement amongst the families began a momentum to marry the eldest daughter of Madam Joan. All came through with a marriage date arranged at Jaffna St. Mary's. Mr. Prahash agreed to take no dowry. He realized he was marrying a beautiful and intelligent cultured lady from Karamban. The church wedding with white lace sari with drapes looked amazing with Jaffna tradition. Fireworks and Chinese firecrackers were followed by the church bells while they put on the rings and knotted the big gold chain with the Holy Spirit pendant around the neck of Marie Joyce. It was a quite an occasion for both the Arul and Joan families. Madam Joan gave 5000 RS. [rupees] and jewelry for her dearest eldest daughter. That was big money in 1963. Marie Joyce was in the final year at university when the marriage took place and she went on to graduate with honors. She married, had a beautiful young boy and named him after Our Lady of Perpetual Help, (Sathashaya matha) Janarthanan.

DELFT, JAPANESE TARGET
1945-

CHAPTER THREE

MOONLIGHT IN JAFFNA

Mr. and Mrs. Prahash with their first son began to appreciate the life in Jaffna; both were working for the community as government servants. That was quite respectable in Jaffna. As devout Catholics, both wanted to live near the church community. Jana was growing up fast in Jaffna; he was surrounded by a rich culture. Some positive, some was very negative. Jaffna is a coastal city. The early Silk Road route which passed through the bustling port of Jaffna was now reflected in its commerciality.

The Dutch built historical forts around the lagoon and they still stand proudly with great history and time. Jaffna Fort gave the people stability and a safe haven. The old guns still point towards the Indian Ocean. The Fort survived the invasions of the Far East, Arabian and recently, the Japanese bombardments. But in the 1990's, the Civil war and the invading Indian Army in the name of "peace keeping" force turned the guns inwards. Just before the occupation by the Indian Army, it was used as a gallows to hang rapists, pedophiles and murderers. It was a message to the criminals: there is no forgiveness in Jaffna.

Jana grew up in this town. The gallows not that far away, reminded him there was violence, murder, smuggling and prostitution all hidden beneath the good-natured Christian society.

The fort stands right next to the hilly grazing savannah; next to it stands the historical neo mogul style library with ancient scriptures of Thiravidan Tamil history. The great clock tower also nearby commemorates the visit of King Edward VII of Great Britain during 1875. Its design reflects the artistic mix of the east and west towards hope and reconciliation. The Tamils built all this with their blood and sweat. They never thought the guns at the top would fire in the wrong direction towards their houses and colleges. The Portuguese also forced the Tamils to build sailing ships, churches, cavalry quarters and ruling cultural houses. But at least they left a few Hindu temples inland for the worshipping farmer but took all the secret cows forcefully for slaughter. The Portuguese wiped out the whole herd of endangered breed which belonged to the northern peninsula's big horn cow breeders. The cows were bred on the red rice rich shavings (thavidu). The Catholicism in Jaffna took another turn of pace. But The British took an alternative keen interest in Jaffna unlike any other city in Sri Lanka. It was due to the red earth of lavish land sprouting green crops even with the short rainfall. Jaffna is a botanical research scientist's dream in all places due to the complexity of its soil. Jaffna is one of the cities blessed with that. The British concentrated first with water and upgrading of the existing irrigation and drainage systems with vast canals zigzagging through the urban area, criss-crossing via secret ancient undergrounds throughout the city. The waste was turned into farming for growth. The human waste had pit systems and by draining the excess water combined with animal bones and leaves, it provided real raw material for organic farming. Unfortunately there were certain unhealthy practices by the sanitation workers with daily changing buckets of raw feces for a clean one was difficult to watch at early mornings. This was not appreciated by certain parts of the community. But it gave jobs for people. But those people were branded as untouchables by the caste dividing old-traditionalists. Some were treated inhumanely by the upper class. The British noticed this and wanted to do something about it.

The building of the highways, schools, sports facilities, cement factories, theatres, parks and gardens, post offices and telecommunications for everybody to work and enjoy were quite a remarkable beginning for Jaffna society during the British Empire. But their greatest achievement began with the big metal 'London Electric' diesel trains and the railway network. Jaffna Railway Station was a great landmark of the British era. It gave hope to break barriers and move forward into the new century. The usual pattern of divisions such as masons, joiners, gravediggers, fishermen, road sweepers, farmers and landowners all began to change in the form of education and training for all. The good and the bad and the downright filthy all came together with the development.

In the 70's, some kids rose above all this by coming together with a student union and crossed over with mixed relationships and marriages, breaking religious and caste backgrounds. Education brought equality and opportunity. People never saw the difference except a few politicians. The Tamils wanted to change that with freedom of speech and political reform. The British Leyland blue and red Ceylon transport board-buses rode the streets of Jaffna via the main road all the way upcountry to Kandy as an express intercity service. That was one of the many jungle route services which were popular among the Tamils. Travel was affordable. Route masters, the double-deckers, were the local quick jump, short cut and small fair to the town centre. The most popular route was the No 26 to the courts (katcheri) and the main records office at Old Park. The land registry, birth records, passports, probates, death and marriages were all recorded at Old Park office near Chundikuli. The Old Park is twenty acres of greenery with ancient over 400 years' old standing with colonial buildings in the middle, housing the government agent's residence and their offices. It was quite an achievement to get to live in these family quarters among this old historical house with butlers and chefs. The government workers visited the up market Y.M.C.A. regularly during their lunch break either to play table tennis, badminton, squash or basketball. The senior management would hit the upstairs private members bar to talk about bonuses, holidays, pay rise, free first class travel warrants, finally their British classic cars all parked outside in pristine condition: Austin Cambridge, Wolsey, Hillman Minx, Austin Somerset, E-Type Jaguar, Rover 8 and the Morris Oxford were some of the favorites. The drivers kept those cars polished at all times, inside and out. It was a driver/mechanic's job those days. The officers worked in the Old Park for only three hours, after that it was all field work, supervising, passing loans, paddy fields, agricultural and civil engineering departments. It was the driver's job to get to locations on time with these officers who had the job of running the city. Some used the Morris Minor taxi, with its distinctive yellow and black color – it was affordable and reliable that time.

The Jaffna Tamils maintained those vehicles with love and affection producing modified spare parts to keep them running forever. The great love of the Austin Somerset V8 was due to the ability as a getaway car during the smugglers point at Kurunagar and Valvettithurai sea fronts. It really pulled upwards in ditches and sand dunes with great effect during the police chases. It was also the most stopped and searched car in Jaffna by the police, customs and excise. There would be no siren during the chase in Jaffna, only police fire, usually down the Beach Road, before the police gave up avoiding getting trapped in between the sea and the guns. The unfortunate few who got caught by the police, were cuffed and thrown in the green jeep. The police drove slowly, showing their catch to everybody while beating the arrested senseless while the Assistant Superintendent of Police, sitting in the front, smoked a cigarette, his hands hanging outside the Jeep, to show revenge by the police. Young Kurunaghar boys would jump on the side of the Jeep and jump off. It was all show. It was all expressed well with show and intimidation. The Inspectors sat at the back with weapons of choice. Some had their own weapons. As long as they were checked by the senior officers and stamped for approval, it was license to kill. There was nobody around to ask questions. Usually they would take the culprit, after doing the full body check, and make a few strikes at hips and heels, making a fine artwork without making any marks or bruises. The delayed effect with just internal bleeding and excruciating pain was the idea.

Jana and Indhiran used to run behind the Jeep with the Bankshall Street boys. They jumped up and put their heads inside and jumped down falling quickly, rolling on the sandy sidewalk. Batons would clang at the closed dog cage. The police shouting, *get off dirty little fools.* The road was full of cycles and carts so the police were unable to accelerate, all the while blowing their horn in order to finally get a gap to move fast. Sometimes they would brake suddenly and it would open the 'dog cage' simultaneously, making the curious kiss the boots of the policeman inside. So they kept the distance on the side, not on the back. The police would have the suspect under the seat face down, their boots on his back, one on the head, one on the shoulder, pressing hard when the suspect tried to turn and look, one officer saying *don't look up you fucking thief.*

Indhiran stopped running, he said with tiredness, bending down holding his knees:

'He deserved it, Jana, he is the one... he is the one who stole the gold chains from the Miracle of Mary Church statue.'

'No way,' said Jana with surprise.

'Stolen church property, church jewelry, he must be desperate,' said Indhiran.

'Did you see him?' asked Jana.

'No,' said Indhiran, gasping for breath. 'Only his blood,' said Indhiran, as he pointed to the road, 'which came from the back of the Jeep. That's why I stopped. What do you think!' said Indhiran angrily. 'Look at my foot, it's all bloody,' said Indhiran with disgust while rubbing it against the sandy road to take it off. 'I almost slipped.'

Jana looked in the stillness of confusion with a smirk. They never ran behind the Jeep since that day.

With sunset, the heat was beginning to drift, pushing inwards unbearably. They walked tiredly down to the Beach

Road for late evening action. Large Norwegian trawlers operated in Jaffna waters for tasty lobsters. Profits and continuity brought the development from far away Scandinavia rather than the home central Sinhalese government. Jana and Indhiran had been warned to avoid the rowdy dock-workers while they drank on Kassipu, an unlicensed local brew, and smoked opium and ganja. They looked scary with swollen red eyes with heavy bags. The cousins would go down in front of the slightly respected drunks in the beach front of the Yalta Hotel. Some Europeans preferred the first cross street hotel bars and rest houses. The blue fin tuna business was bringing more money to the city than rice. The private dancers and snake charmers were making more money discretely. An unannounced gypsy circus in front of the beach blocked all traffic with monkeys, wire walks while the pole climbing with music was quite spectacular. Lobsters were delivered daily to the senior police officers on time for dinner. Some thugs controlled certain areas of town with extortion and bribery. Everybody was referred to by their closest church or a temple street hood. Nobody complained, everybody knew their limits, except some newcomers from the south who, when they moved in, were dealt with, Jaffna style.

Trains moved out of Jaffna jetty frequently, at least twice a day, and ships docked in Kanag Kasen Thurai (KKS) Kankesanthurai port - all showing positive signs of a flourishing city.

Jana and Indhiran jumped on the train and got a free ride with the fish all the way to the main road bridge, where the train slowed down to let the traffic pass. They jumped off with a live twisting and curling lobster. The guard at the back kept an eye only on the suspicious vehicle blocking the tracks.

The kids on the train were just an extra eye for the dark diesel-smoke-faced driver with goggles. The kids along the tracks shot gravel stones with catapults at the train jumpers, the thieves who tried to grab the seats first. They were from the Chapel Street shanty towns along the canal ponds full of weaving reeds. This gave the people around the pond skills passed down the generations to make musical instruments, brooms, roofing and sleeping mats.

Jana and Indhiran, with the live lobster in their hands, avoided the bites by passing it one hand to another. They ran down the church yard to make their own lobster bisque at the back of the house. A three stone fire was set. They used a makeshift outdoor steal bucket on a stick to cook in. They cooked it with oddiyal.Dried root yam of famous northern palmyra island recipe. That tasted even better because it was stolen from the export carriage. When that was eaten with bread from Pedro's bakery it would challenge any hotel seafood buriyani chef's with Michelin stars.

Midnight was soon approaching. Under a full moonlight, customs and excise boats did their final routine checks, the coastguard standing by, while fishing boats maneuvered one by one into position for departure. They were all sizes and shapes including small canoes, speedboats, small and large trawlers, and locally built wooden barges like ferries with heavy loads with miles of fishing nets. Few sat and hand-checked every corner, every yard with orange floats before they were laid during the dark nights in deep sea at the Indian Ocean bed. All the boats were happy to leave the greenish brown murky waters full of fish waste for the seagulls and black crows who circled all day screaming with joy but who were also tired by now. Everybody waited for the final shipping report from Colombo and Tamil Nadu Chennai India. Rain or storm they have to move out and stay out for days and weeks until they come back with a good catch. Ropes and anchor ready to be pulled. Food and drinks all stocked up. Diesel fuel, radio batteries all checked and verified.

Jana and Indhiran would stand and throw with pleasure the last ropes tied to cement stumps, one by one, quickly avoiding any tangles, then go home as a ritual.

Fish traders and businessman kept their boats in rotation to keep the flow of the fish to the whole city. Seaside fish markets with live fish full of colors and varieties from the docking boats, jumping in the big reed baskets, were ready for auction. All sold in minutes with excitement to the highest bidder. There was also behind the scenes gesturing among the regular restaurateurs or hoteliers to get a fair deal. During the auctions, respect and camaraderie were priority to maintain the longevity of the business. Beach markets kept everybody happy. Traditional net men never changed their method of catching fish. Laying it first in the deep sea, then a week or a month later, pulling with two boats trapping the deep water fresh fish. Then trawlers began to move in and changed people's lives and traditions. Fish prices dropped like a heavy weight on a canvas. People preferred the small net varieties.

Mr. Prahash took his son at an early age and showed him how to look for fresh fish that would keep at least 48 hours in ice. How to get in to an early morning bidding war. He said the market was over in three hours so you got to make your mind quickly. Who is the middle man, like the man between the owner and the boat Captain. He explained how the beach market works, who is behind who and what. Who is the one you really don't want to upset. Be careful of the huge fish bones and sting rays' poison fins and tails all beneath you. It is all everywhere when they do the final quick sharp machete clean before the sale. Watch out for the ice man, carrying heavy blocks in stacks with hooks and picks hanging on his shoulder belt strap in different sizes. He will move in and out after the sale breaking ice in front of the buyer for the safe long delivery, getting hard cash on the process from every buyer. It is not really nice to see two ice men fighting for turfs. Blood does mix with the fish. Mr. Prahash laughed and improvised. The unsold fish will move to the small market at Bankshall Street. The late-arriving elderly customers while chatting to all the stall holders finally get their fish for their lunch. Jaffna children's lunch boxes full of seasoned fried fish and sauce with fresh bread were customary. Kids did not have the privilege of having crisps, chocolate and cheese and yogurt. That was a luxury at the weekends, if your family could afford it. But they sweated like carthorses after eating spicy food in high temperatures. While the gingili oil dripped from both sides of their heads, front and back of the ears. They were a funny sight for young girls. *Look at the grease ball, the gingili* (dripper/*vaddinthan*) *shining side bonds.* The girls teasing did not affect or shame the boys to the corner. Traditional gingili oil made of sesame and coconut, acted like a conditioner. Its effects are long term, said our elders.

'Good for your brain and memory,' said Mr. Prahash as he gripped Jana holding him against his chest, dabbing the oil at the centre parting of the head.

Sometimes the heat cooked our hair and roasted our skins. Sometimes smoke came from our heads. Jana hated it, but there was no way you were going to say no to Mr. Prahash.

Jaffna Tamils used various bathing ingredients, like boiled and squeezed lemon with gingili oil prior to showering. Fresh eggs, crushed flower leaves, Jasmine, Shoeflower leaves (sembarathai) gave the ladies natural fragrance. The Jaffna girls had luscious, flowing hair, and the darkest and thickest hair due to the water and the natural products. It maintained protein requirements and the softening of the scalp with adequacy. Long plaited hair appeared almost with dark blue shades when shined. They used 'Eau de Cologne' on their heads to keep the head cool and to avoid sudden shivers after a cold bath, at the centre of the head parting (utchi) where it was felt precisely. It was due to partially dried wet head that left them prone to sudden shivers and fevers. Mr. Prahash took the responsibility of drying Jana's head, by the time he came out of the towel he was spinning like a wheel without steady feet. Then he applied Johnson and Johnson talcum powder from Lever Brothers to keep him dry from cold and sweat. Everybody laughed as Jana walked in the garden white faced and legless like a cemetery ghost. The elders warned them to stay away from kullir and sudu meaning hypo- and hyper-thermia. The sudden lure of ill health would take over and attack the young and weak due to those tough humid conditions.

Ladies really showed their style: on a bicycle, hair flowing against the wind; riding along the buses; walking a short distance. Always a beautiful sight. White dresses, different color ties, chocolate and blue, red and white, red and back, yellow and black, green and gold, all were the distinctive Jaffna schools stripy ties. Everyone had a bicycle, every junction had a service and repair while you waited. People of Jaffna were practical and totally aware of their limitations. They shared their technical expertise and knowledge. Among all divides, respect was mutual. Luxuries were minimal. Like the air-conditioning, fridges, freezers were just for the affluent businessmen, hotel bars, principals' offices, the bishop's house and for the mayor's office only. The working class had plenty of ice blocks if needed for special occasions. They really did not need it. They ate fresh everything every day. They kept the small businesses running at the local high streets. Wells provided drinking water and also water for domestic usage. The heavy clay pot called kudam was burned in the making to keep it strong but it kept the water cool for long periods. Water filtration was a known pastime. Every house had a sackful of stone mixture, refined from hand, heavy sponge, cotton wool and coconut fiber all stacked on a wooden tray. Gently the boiled water poured through the filtration to the *kudam*. The kudam would stand at a 45° angle on a ring of rope to hold the base of the circle steady. The lid had a small breathing hole. A slight move with the lid, and the water would be served cool. Even though they supplied drinking water from the purified municipal tank supply tap points between seven and eight in the morning and four and six in the evening, some of their deep wells had clean drinking water. Waste water was cleverly used to grow vegetable patches, crotons from up countries. The Jasmine and Bougainvillea on every house front porch with thousands of flowers were a usual sight. Unsafe soapy water was redirected to drains to cause no harm for these up country perennials. The waste was minimal. Jaffna was environmentally conscious even when they were in the early years of over-production in the 70's. They saved everything that could be used again. Recycling was their motto before the word was even invented.

Jaffna looked great in the rainy seasons. It had the similarities of the monsoon in Malta with Palmyra trees. Farm animals were looked after properly. The cow is the sacred animal of the Hindus; it was part of the family wealth. Dogs and the cats had a bad deal. Especially the stray dogs. Pets' welfare was a little below the belt. Stray dog-catchers had a good business in Jaffna. A well-paid council job with the high risk of mad-dog bite. Animal issue was a sensitive subject. Vegans, vegetarians, Buddhists, Hindus, Muslims, Catholics all clashed in the background. Butchers had to think of everybody. There was lot of meat available including sea turtles and iguanas. It was eaten during a marriage celebration in Jaffna. Kurunagar loud speakers played songs for a few days prior and after the ceremony. The songs varied according to the occasion. The religious and motivational duets from the old black and white films were from Tamil Nadu India. More funkier colorful film songs of M.G.R. were very popular. Sometimes the sad songs from Devadas did drag on for hours. The Kurunagar boys often decided to go out to party in town with well dressed multi colored Hawaiian shirts, Ray-Ban glasses, jeans and sarongs, wallets full of notes from their hard work, which was a reflection of the good times of Jaffna's youth. Sometimes they did not look after their health, ate highly rich foods with coconut cream and rich meat of deep fried type high in cholesterol, and which brought heart conditions. Doctors like Dr. Phill and Dr. Abraham, intelligent and hardworking health practitioners, well respected in Jaffna, ran the busiest acute care units taking the pressure off the general hospital. Jaffna town region gave respect and kept these professionals very busy.

Jana's father was away at Vanni Mangulam on his second agricultural post with real responsibility. It involved, for Mr. Prahash, living alone in the jungle with a government rifle. Freedom to hunt the wild animal that disrupts agriculture was allowed under the ministry. Mr. Prahash was in his element. He had a great sense of knowledge about the jungle and had good ears and eyes. A sharp shooter with reasonable accuracy, it could only improve in time. He only had half an hour orientation from his colleague who was stationed there previously there and who was doing the handover. He carried the bolt-action British made Lee Enfield with ten rounds in the khaki canvas made especially with buckles, tied to hang on the bicycle bar safely in between his legs. This was used World War rifle weighed roughly ten pounds.People forget srilankans [Tamils and Sinhalese] volunteered to fight the first and second world wars. Still archived under 'Pathe news'.

He repeatedly practiced the safety catch until he got it totally handy. He really did not want to stand in front of a wild and angry elephant, without being completely prepared. Being an animal lover he never envisaged that situation. While he cooked and lived with a few farmers he read the Bible and prayed for his family. At the same time at home Marie Joyce also asked Jana to pray for his father's safe return before he went to bed. Jana was only three. Marie Joyce had to look after the two-year-old while pregnant with the third child. She did get help from nanny Mahesh during the day, and sister Ruby, or brother Babe would sleep over. Jana also had a few asthmatic attacks due to an allergic reaction in the form of convulsions. They had to rush him to Dr. Abraham in the middle of the night with Uncle Babe holding him in his hands. He recovered with intravenous medicines. His father was furious when he heard the story two days later. First a telegraph, then somebody had to cycle half a day to the jungle. Mr. Prahash opened it with real worry. It read:

My dear husband, your son was ill with convulsions, but

he has recovered with the treatment at Dr. Abrahams. Babe and Ruby are helping me with kids while nanny Mahesh does the cooking. Don't worry, he is doing fine. Apparently it's stress related. Your wife Marie Joyce.

Mr. Prahash was beginning to get agitated in the jungle, worrying about Marie Joyce unable to cope with the kids alone. What will he do if something happens to his kids? The following day Mr. Prahash called from the agriculture department to St. James Girl's school to speak to his wife. They spoke in detail about everything and he told her that:

'In two years I will get the transfer to Jaffna Vadamarathchi at Achuveli. Until then please be careful and stay safe. I will come and see you monthly at the weekends.'

It was a most emotional conversation during her pregnancy at the principal's office. The Rev. Sister Josephine gave Marie Joyce the rest of the week off. Marie Joyce insisted she would continue to teach, *what will the kids do without her?* The Rev. Sister reassured her she would get a replacement, the senior Advanced Level students waiting for results would be able to cover her class.

Days passed and years went pretty quick. Indhiran was born a year earlier for Aunty Rohini and uncle Nadraj. He brought all the toys when Jana was ill, kept Jana occupied. Apart from being unwell he was a child who would get on with anybody with interest. Indhiran quickly made his bond at that age with his cousin. They both went together to Montessori at St. Ignatius'. They both learned letters and numbers with songs and dance. Marie Joyce came through with her third girl called Jenine. The eldest had all the Delft features, the youngest was on the mum's side with fair skin. Jana was, as was his personality, in between. Jana always walked down to the main road after the nursery. Somebody would pick up Jana and Indhiran from the main road and they would spend a few hours until dark, then back at Bankshall Street. That gave Marie Joyce a little time alone with the girls.

Grandma Joan had a successful catering business. She supplied breakfast ingredients for small hotels. Some totally prepared, some partially, for the hotel to finish off at their own choice of time. She also did the children's parties, home ceremonies and wedding receptions. Her specialty was orange peel sponge cakes, coconut cream hoppers, tuna fish cutlets, lobster with noodles, steamed or shallow fried. But her ultimate accolade was the brown rice flour fermentation of perfection. That brought certain standards regarding to savories. Her ingredients like vanilla pods, nutmeg, golden syrup, cinnamon, fresh coconut and cloves gave the whole street an aroma to die for. Her Tamil specialties like pittu, string hoppers, idli, lentil and dhal fried rings with sauces and sambar were very popular in the rest houses.

While everybody spat on the streets when low caste members walked passed, or had bad attitude toward them or even hurled abuse directly at them. Some even went further and swept their path with a coconut spike-leaves broom to shutter the bad omen. She employed the underprivileged and trained them with reasonable wages. With monthly profit, she would provide books for the kids, saris for the ladies and sarongs for the men. She encouraged all the workers' kids to attend St. James with the help of Marie Joyce for decent education equality and reform. Grandma by now had married off three of her daughters. Uncles Regi, Mano, Raffa and Babe and finally Aunty Kavitha remained at home still relying on grandma's help in their adult years. Mr. Prahash was fond of Babe, the youngest, still in his final years in school, but

Babe was compelled to listen to Mr. Prahash's conditions and discipline.

Jana vividly remembered one day Babe cut school and was eating fish in the garden when faced by an angry Mr. Prahash with a cane. Babe took it like a man, even the big man felt ashamed and never touched him again. Their respect to each other grew.

Uncle Babe would try to work on European ships to support Grandma Joan. He was the only one among his brothers to pay his debt to Grandma Joan. Raffa was a street fighter, belonging to a small Kurunagar gang with a karate champion called Yamal. They practiced in the back of the house day in and day out and circled the burger girls (Asian and Dutch mixed Tamils) in Kurunagar. At an early age with Uncle Babe, Indhiran joined Grandma's run for the catering supplies and deliveries. Orders were beginning to come in. Grandma Joan broke a deal with the municipal council workers and the police officers to supply lunch. No delivery, as all would be picked up from main street at the corner of 3rd cross street. Jana and Indhiran would stand watch over all the preparations by the staff, tasting a few samples and getting to know the policemen who saluted to attention when they arrived at the house in the Jeep.

Grandma was proud to have the officers handy for any emergencies. It was all about influence and trust in Jaffna. In regard to her cooking, she was the master pastry chef. Every big house had its kitchen away from the main building, usually a thatched roof with clay mud ovens. For ventilation and space, a hole to take the smoke and strong aroma out through the thatched roof slowly. It was quite an organization among two or three families cooking together saving fire and wood in the process. Sometimes Jana and Indhiran had to be pulled out of the smoked kitchen with smoky eyes, having tried to taste the food while it was cooking.

Jana was growing up. He was 5 years old now. He was keenly waiting to face the school selection committee. The committee of St. Peter's made up of reverend fathers, mother superiors and senior lower school teachers. Mr. Prahash was on his final year in the Vanni region. He took a special leave to take Jana to school.

Mr. Prahash was reading the independent Tamil newspaper called Verra Kesari, while waiting for the postman. He was talking about Uncle Reggie who could not keep his job at Yarl metal, which Mr. Prahash got him from Uncle Ranga's brother. His plan was to start him there first with something then move on to do something better in Colombo. Maybe a supervisory position in manufacturing water pumps at Ranga Anna's factory. But he walked out after having an argument at his work place without even talking to Mr. Prahash. Mr. Prahash was very angry and said maybe it did not go with his status.

'Bloody fool. Can't even help an old lady. Him and his belt buckle, bellbottoms and platform shoes.' Mr. Prahash could not stand the sight of Uncle Reggie. Marie Joyce did not say anything. The postman rang the cycle bells and Mr. Prahash rushed to the gates of Bankshall Street. He opened the letter in a hurry. He looked disappointed and angry. He said:

'It's not good news. Not good news at all. I don't know what you all did while I was away. Did he do his work?' asked Mr. Prahash, looking towards Marie Joyce.

She shook her head and said: 'Yes, he did well in all his exams. I have spoken to Sr. Tharsicius, she said he passed the selection.'

Mr. Prahash said angrily: 'So it's some kind of mistake of this white coat and black sash, lying priest.'

Jana started to cry, curling his lips with tears.

'Don't cry now', said his father. 'I can't do anything until I find out what's wrong where,' Mr. Prahash said. 'Put the uniform on, Jana. Jana, put on your school uniform,' he repeated. Jana looked confused.

'I mean the blue and white one,' he said it again. Yes! 'The new blue and white.'

Mr. Prahash hurriedly brushed his teeth, put on some cologne and a vest. He picked up his favorite St Michael's shirt, dry cleaned khaki trousers with side pockets and brown thin belt, all fitted perfectly by his personal tailor Thavam at Hospital Road. Then quickly he put the polish on the brown leather shoes. He shined them with the old rag, followed by fast brushing up and down for a shine. The family never saw him clean like this. They all feared what would happen with the principal. Finally he put on his loving maroon lucky tie with two dark stripes. He looked immaculate. He dabbed a little 'old spice' around his ears and face and combed his hair. He looked like a real gentleman.

'Government officer,' said Jana. Jana watched all the detail with curiosity.

Father said: 'Let's see all your talk at the school today. Mum, can you please wipe his face and put some powder on'.

Then he got on the Dutch-Asian bike, lifted Jana and put him on the front bar:

'Come on, let's go and see,' he said while he looked around at the traffic and pedaled hard, passing the church, Leela stores, rice mills and the hotel at the corner of David Road.

Somebody called: 'Overseer ayya, what's the hurry?

Somebody annoyed this islander for no reason?'

'Ah, it's my son' shouted Mr. Prahash. 'The school admission…' and he shook his head.

'Why's your son being crying? What's the problem?' asked the passing cycling friend sympathetically.

'The lying clergy. What else!'

'It's all business. It's all Viabaram.'

'I know,' said Mr. Prahash. 'We will see about that today, see about that today. Swami marr, the priests,' he mumbled.

They reached St. Peter's about 10.30 that morning. Mr. Prahash had begun to sweat a little from the heat and the fast cycling. He took a deep breath and helped Jana to get off the bike.

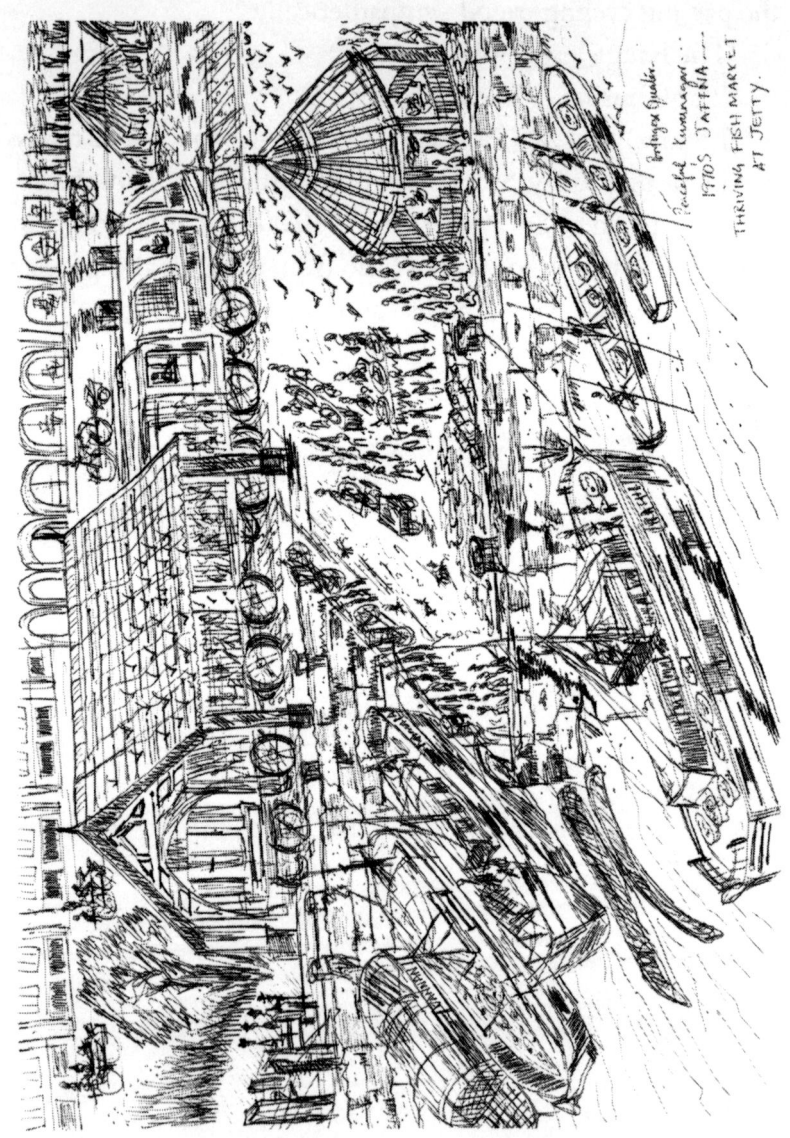

Portuguese Quarter.
Peaceful Kavanagar...
1970S JAFFNA —
THRIVING FISH MARKET
AT JETTY.

CHAPTER FOUR

WHATEVER HAPPENED TO
THE TEENAGE DREAMS

Mr. Prahash hurriedly stopped the bike in the college cycle stand, lifted Jana off, then lifted his right foot up and set the bicycle legs at position. He looked angry but kept it all under control with a calm and serious face. Grabbing Jana by the hand, he moved slowly due to the students in the class rooms in the upper college all concentrating on their lectures. He passed the immaculate chemistry lab and the not so immaculate, inevitably, student toilets. They looked in a dire and dark state with a terrible stench. That made him shake his head. Then he passed through the assembly area in the middle of the grounds and looked up. A big statue of the Virgin Mary with open arms was on a four step cement stage under the shade of six mahogany trees which stood three by three on both sides of the classrooms. They provided a cool breeze, shade and shelter from the extreme Jaffna heat. It looked like a place for contemplation. Mr. Prahash had never been there before, but he felt the calming effect of the Virgin Mary. That changed his mood into a collected discipline of a guardian. He wanted his son to study even more now after seeing the college and the students concentrating as he walked past the corridors. He never looked in the classrooms, as the students too kept their faces straight to the teacher on the class stage. At St. Peter's, the policy was if anyone looked outside, he would go and kneel outside.

He took a further six step up to enter the Principal's office under the Rembrandt print of a resurrection of Jesus Christ framed above the hallway to the Principal's office. There were a few people waiting to see the father Principal that day. But it all seemed very calm to Mr. Prahash's surprise.

Mr. Prahash asked politely: 'Are you waiting to be seen?'

The man said: 'We have already been seen, thank you'.

Mr. Prahash knocked on the door of the Principal's office.

Principal Durant dropped his glasses and said to the college clerk: 'Can you please see who is out there banging on the door.'

The clerk walked up and opened the door and asked Mr. Prahash: 'Are you ok? You need to make an appointment, sir. You can't just walk in and knock the door down. What is the matter? What's wrong?'

Mr. Prahash looked the clerk in the eyes and said: 'I have no time to make an appointment. I need to see the Principal now, sir.'

'Now?' the clerk paused, then said: 'Please sir, let me check with the Principal first, ok?'

Mr. Durant had heard the insistence of Mr. Prahash who was now pacing up and down in the waiting room. The Principal's office half glass door swung left and right enabling him to see Mr. Prahash in an agitated state. The clerk did not come back to Mr. Prahash. Fr. Durant took his time. Then said loudly: 'Come in, please. Come in. Come in. How can I help you?'

'Good morning, father, sorry to trouble you without notice. My name is Prahash. I work in Vanni agricultural department. I especially took a leave from work in order to see my son's school admission through. This is my son, Jana.'

Jana quickly said: 'Good morning, father.'

Jana looked as if he had been crying.

Fr. Durant said with a serious face: 'What can I do for you, Mr. Prahash?'

'Look at my son, father, look at him. Does he look ok to you father? He is not ok, father. He is disappointed.' He paused. 'He is very disappointed.' He paused again. 'He did not get into the school.'

The Principal looked down at Jana, then sat back in the chair with a smile.

'I want to know father, sir, what happened? What was the reason he wasn't given a place at St. Peter's? What was the reason he wasn't selected, father? His mother is also a teacher and according to her he did well enough to pass his entry exams. He was well prepared at St. Ignatius'.'

The Principal was calm, smiling at Jana and replied: 'Usually, sir, we don't give details about the reason for refusals. But, but, wait a minute. In your case I am going to make an exception because you travelled far for this. All the way from Vanni.'

Jana began to calm down.

Mr. Prahash said anxiously: 'Please father, why? Why is my son not starting school next week? He has his uniforms and books. Four sets of blue and whites. Socks, shoes and even a school bag matching the college colors. I need my son to study here, father,' he insisted with conviction. 'I really would like to know what happened. I am very disappointed for my son, father,' he said and sat down in the chair.

The college clerk brought the papers and records from the offices. A long big logbook full of names and marks appeared as the Principal took his time and looked at it thoroughly and carefully. He went down the alphabet to P for the surname.

'Ahh…' said Fr. Durant. 'I have it. Good news and bad news, sir. Your son did pass his exam.'

Jana smiled.

'Born on the 11th of February… ahh' he said and sat back and took his time. 'By a mere 11 days he was unable to get in to the highly competitive intake this year,' said Fr Durant. 'All must be born before the 31st of January.'

Mr. Prahash was fuming with anger but keeping it cool.

'That's nonsense, Fr. Principal. You know that, reverend sir. For nine days? Father, it's a feeble excuse to put a child through this disappointment. For a mere nine days you are going to waste my son's year. You have got to do something about it surely.'

Principal Durant took a moment and looked at Jana.

Mr. Prahash continued: 'We are responsible government workers. I am currently working in Vanni. You know the hardships of the Vanni people.

Fr. Durant interrupted: 'Don't you worry, I understand. I have a few acres in Kilinotchi myself. I know it all well.

'I want my son to study in a good Christian school, father. It's in your hands, father. It's in your hands.'

By this time Jana had started to cry again.

The Principal took the tobacco pipe: 'Ok, Mr. Prahash, calm down sir.' While pulling from the pipe he got up walked around and looked outside.

Mr. Prahash saw a shift in the Principal's face that gave

him a positive feeling and sat down and wiped Jana's face.

'Stop it now, that's enough.'

The Principal said: 'Jana, take a moment. Ok, you got nothing to worry about, son, sit down please.'

'Thank you, father, said Jana.

'We are going to play a little game, ok?' said Fr. Durant. 'I will ask the questions, you will tell me what it means, ok? It's easy, you know it all, Jana, I am sure.'

Jana started swinging his legs with excitement. Mr. Prahash was worried whether the priest was trying to trick him with his clever diversion. But he kept his cool.

The priest said: 'It's not a test, ok Jana? I know you are a clever boy.'

Jana smiled and looked at his father.

'Just some simple general knowledge questions,' said the priest to Mr. Prahash. He took his time again. Mr. Prahash looked outside with a still face. Jana was smiling, he liked games and competitions. He was an inquisitive kid always asking questions about everything. He looked forward to this opportunity at the Principal's office as he looked around and scanned the room quickly. He wiped his face and made ready for his questions. The Principal asked the clerk to go outside and asked everybody to be quiet. Even the secretaries stopped typing in the offices. If a pin was dropped, they would have heard the sound.

'Ok Jana,' he smiled and took a ruler and pointed to the beach front photograph which was hanging on the wall. 'Jana, what does this photo means to you, have you seen this anywhere? What do you understand from this picture?' he paused, 'take your time, Jana,' said Fr Durant.

Jana took a deep breath and looked at his father quickly, then turned with a smile. Mr. Prahash was quite anxious about Jana's answer. The priest pulled another smoke from his pipe and pointed to the picture. Puff, puff, smoke began to fill the office.

Jana shouted: 'That's Delft! That's Delft rest house. My grandfather's rest house, he lives there and worked there for a long time. Lot of important people stay there. There are also horses and boats near that place. Beautiful place father, but we have to take a boat for a long time in the big sea waves.

Mr. Prahash, with glossy eyes, said to himself: 'That's my boy. My only boy.'

The Principal smiled and looked at Mr. Prahash. 'Very good. Very good.'

Nobody saw that coming from Jana. Not even the secretaries at the back of the principal's office peeping through the keyhole. All the others were outside listening through the glass door.

Then Fr. Durant said quickly: 'What is this, Jana?' as he pointed to the telephone.

Jana answered immediately: 'This is the phone, father. I have seen this in police stations and funeral houses. People talk with this from a long, long distance. The voices go through the big long wires and pass outside the house, on the light post. Mannikappa in Suruvil have a green one. I have seen a red one in the post office. I think people like different colors. You like black father, like your waist band. Can I touch your phone father?' asked Jana as he looked at his father.

'Sure, go ahead,' said smiling Fr Durant. Jana picked it up and quickly said: 'Hello mum, I am at Fr. Principal's office.' Then he smiled and put it down and said: 'She is at school today. She is not near the phone. It's also at her principal's office at St. James'.' Jana shook his head and smiled. 'Sometimes my father calls her there from Vanni,' as he smiled at Mr. Prahash. The Principal could not believe the details of Jana's observations at the age of 5.

This was 1969.

The Principal continued: 'Jana, you are doing good. More than good. You have nothing to worry. It's your final question, Jana. It's an easy one I am sure.'

Mr. Prahash said: 'Put the phone back properly, Jana, please.'

'Don't worry, Mr. Prahash. There are no calls coming now. We stopped them all for you and Jana. How about that huh?' said Fr. Durant with excitement. He opened his first drawer, there was a pistol. He pushed it back. 'No, not that one,' said Fr. Durant. 'Ahh,' he said as he pulled open the other drawer. He took out a car. A Matchbox model car. 'What is this, Jana?'

Everybody in the room was looking at one another, even the clerks behind the doors were listening with quiet intrigue.

'What is this, Jana?' said smiling Fr. Durant. Jana took it in his hand and rolled it on the table. He looked at his Dad and smiled. He shouted excitedly: 'It's Vigi Mama's Austin Cambridge. Classic English car. The name come from England. It's also a famous university in England. Another Austin make is Somerset Gray, father. I have seen it in Kurunagar, haven't you? Yes that's where I saw it,' Jana repeated. 'I have sat in this red, white and silver car with soft leather seats. I have a picture of this car in my house,' he said as he rolled it slowly in front of the Principal and smiled.

Mr. Prahash remembered when he was at Suruvil, Jana had spent all day with Uncle Vijay and he did not want to leave that car. He would not allow anyone to touch it either. He was asking all sorts of questions and irritated Vijay, but

Vijay persevered with him because of his enthusiasm. Jana also told everybody not to touch that car unless they asked permission from Uncle Vijay or him. He was only four years old at the time.

What a day he had, Mr. Prahash, at the Principal's office at St. Peter's.

The Principal said: 'Congratulations. You have answered well and won this little contest.' He called the secretary to take Jana and show him the main college hall... 'Just for a few minutes as I need to speak with your dad privately. Thank you.'

Jana left with the lady secretary, smiling happily.

'You have a very interesting and bright son, sir,' said Fr. Durant with excitement. His observation and imagination have no limits. He is a story teller ahhh.' He called the clerk: 'Type a letter of acceptance for Mr. Prahash.' He smiled and shook the hand of Mr. Prahash who said he was grateful for this opportunity.

Fr. Durant said: 'You are the first one to get our decision turned, sir. We like to treat everybody equal here. Very few passionately contest against our decisions. I have to hand it to you for that effort. Kids see that, and they do well. I hope you understand the commitment, sir. There are costly term fees. Books, uniform and the extracurricular activities, all part of a child's education, sir. You've got to stand by all this remember.' He smiled. 'I am sure you are aware of all this.'

The letter came quickly from the offices. Jana returned just then.

'Here you are. This is to confirm in writing that Jana is accepted in the class of 1969 among the brightest of that year's annual intake.' He asked: 'Jana, you like blue?'

'Yes, father.'

'You are in the blue house of Bonaventure.'

'Thank you and god bless you, father,' said Jana.

While they were leaving the office, the Principal laughed to himself: 'I did not even think about that.'

He asked Mr. Prahash: 'Can you pick this up next door, because he have to enter a few more details in the register.'

Mr. Prahash said: 'Of course, father. Thanks for listening.'

'It's a pleasure to help a Delft boy, sir. I have been to that rest house. I know your father, too. He is a good man.'

Mr. Prahash was surprised and speechless.

'I hope to see you again sometime,' said Fr. Durant.

Mr. Prahash realized he had been trying to outrun the clergy in his younger days at St. Antony's and Henry's, but they always had the trump cards at the end.

In the waiting room, Mr. Prahash said to Jana: 'Kavanam, be careful with this father, do your studies, otherwise he will call me to let me know my son is not doing the work, ok son?' Jana was by now sitting in the waiting room, swinging his legs smiling. He had overheard all the conversations. He asked his dad: 'What is imagination, Dad?'

'Who knows, son. Come on now, you seem to know all the answers,' he said, grabbing him. 'You are in, son. You are in, my boy. You did me proud today. Really, you did me proud.' They walked away quickly after picking up the letter.

They were on the bike, it was about twelve before the school lunch break. Mr. Prahash wanted to get out without getting chopped by the kids in their hurry to have their lunch break at home. Jana asked gently: 'Can I go and tell the good news to grandma, then you can buy me a big ice choc.'

Mr. Prahash took his tie off and started to cycle towards grandma's house. He waited outside on the bike while Jana ran inside: 'Come back quick. We have to go and see your mum.'

'Mama, I have passed the test. I am in... I am in... I am going to school at St. Peter's.

A very proud Mr. Prahash had followed him inside after all. 'Yes, he did well with his verbal test and Austin Cambridge,' said Mr. Prahash.

'Austin what?' asked Grandma Joan.

'Ask him. He was at the Principal's office doing a verbal general knowledge test.'

'Really? In front of those fathers can be very nervous, right? I am proud of you my grandson, you clever boy. So when you become a big man one day, will you look after your Grandma?'

'Yes,' said Jana, 'yes I will buy you a new house and kitchen like Vigi Mama's place, then you can make me lots of cakes, without any problem. Then you will be rich, too.'

Grandma Joan gave him a hug. Jana sat and swung his legs.

'Ok Jana, let's go,' said his father. 'He wanted to tell the good news to you first,' said Mr. Prahash. 'If only the boys in this house had spirit and respect like the little ones, we wouldn't have any trouble, ahhh.'

Madam Joan did not say anything as she knew Mr. Prahash meant the unemployed uncles of Jana. He did not want the influence of the main road in Jana's life, except for Madam Joan. He hated group drinking, street fights, anonymous girl friends, singing Tamil Bollywood love songs while staying up all night, was delinquent behavior according to Mr. Prahash. He was almost like a colonial uniformed officer with the discipline and punctuality of one.

Mr. Prahash would be back in Jaffna in a few months' time

from Vanni, with his transfer to Vadamaratchi Achuveli-agriculture department. He will point the finger at everyone who is sitting at home doing nothing wasting their precious youth. He will offer advice for jobs and ideas for their prospective careers. All of them would have to start to listen and try their best to keep Marie Joyce happy at Bankshall Street.

Jana quickly made friends at St. Peter's amidst the interesting mixture of kids from all walks of life. Miss Xavier was his class teacher. Miss Eve took English, Mr. Pillai took science and sports, and Sister Alexandra took Christianity. Finally, math was taught by Anthony the headmaster. Jana was noted as a happy and enthusiastic child. But he showed real interest in outdoor activities, liked running, throwing balls and cricket at this early age. Mr. Prahash did not like that Jana showed more interest in sports. He thought that it would interrupt his studies.

Jana worked hard with the help of his mum at home, passed his yearly exams and moved into the middle school 6th grade as a ten year old. Jana was a flag bearer of the small group of ten year olds, somersaulting when St. Peter's won matches in football and cricket. Sometimes he would sit alone in the corner of the grounds and would ceremoniously watch the cricket match from beginning to end.

Jana and his friends had begun to gather in the corner of the chapel side of the field near the scoreboard end. It was quite visible to all the spectators. The college supporters were always in early and well organized. They would start the cheering early to get everybody behind the college team in competitive mood. Jana would lead, shouting: 'WHAT ARE THE COLOURS OTHERS WILL FOLLOW? BLUE AND GOLD!' Jana will lead again shouting: 'WHO ARE THE WINNERS? EVERYBODY SAYS WE ARE THE

WINNERS.' All would jump up and bang the small drums, and shake their crushed soda tops. All would become a great percussion of rhythmic cheer, bringing college kids and participants sky high with adrenaline. Everybody was happy to join in, but the match would not have even started yet. Still the Peterite passion and the fanatic loyalty was noted by the seniors and teachers at the balconies. There was also Principal Durant on the balcony of the first floor watching little Jana of Austin Cambridge fame. He had been right about Jana.

Jana was excited about sports, growing up listening to the radio, reading magazines and talking about it with great interest with everybody.

The seventies was undoubtedly the greatest time for sports. It was the post Vietnam era of freedom and revolution. Among the champions were Juanterano, Seb Coe, Steve Ovett - the middle distance kings. Athletics was the greatest entertainment of that time. Jana became obsessed with running and would listen to races on the radio and become emotional and tearful if his favorite athlete failed to cross the line, either win or lose. He became philosophical as he reflected on these with regard to his own life. The struggle, hard work, hope and ecstasy. He understood about taking part. He understood the alma mater which he took to his heart at St. Peter's. He listened when the champion read the college athletic regulations.

Like Jesse Owens at the Berlin Olympics while Hitler had his days during Nazi Germany. Owens' records stood unbroken for years. Four golds in one Olympic tournament. Like the great Mark Spitz, took 7 gold during the Munich massacre of Israeli athletes. Jana loved the history of sports. Spitz was a Jewish New Yorker. He went to the Olympics to support his family and educate himself through sports, came back a Hero of the United States of America in the middle of the German crises. These stories impressed Jana. He thoroughly enjoyed sports as an important part of his life. He listened to the coaches while standing near the college grounds at the age of nine while they talked of how competitiveness will carry you through all your lives.

As Mr. Prahash predicted, his studies began to drop standards. Jana faced angry parents with constant groundings and lock ups. Whenever he had a chance, he and Indhiran would set up competition around the lanes of Bankshall Street. There was no limit to participants. Bankshall boys Ivan, Judesh, Andrew, Joshua, Fernando, David, Mathews, all lived nearby the miracle of Mary Church. The races would start at St. James' church grounds, then turn right at Main Road passed Dr. Phill's, cut through the Bankshall Street all the way to Beach Road, passed the Kurunagar Singing Fish Gymnasium, along the goods train railway track, then turn at the fourth cross street, passed the small market stalls and the Kurunagar butchers, and finish at near Main Road near Grandma's photo studios. The idea was that the organizer who collected the money would sneak in through the back door and steal some cakes at Pedro's bakery and give it to the winning boy. If they got caught they paid the money.

Indhiran would start the race: 'Get on your marks and 10 cents to join the race everybody. So money now, please!' he would shout. Then he gave instructions to Jana like a coach: 'Don't rush until you pass the gym. Most of the boys will run out of fuel halfway after sprinting earlier on. Keep your distance fairy constant. Get your rhythm.'

Jana stayed steady in the distance, then moved gently into the corners, catching up with the leaders like the great Seb Coe for a late and fast finish. Jana was excited and listened seriously like a pro to his coach. Jana would pass everybody as they approached the Bankshall Street, its small market fairly empty now except for a few crows picking the leftover fish, and the odd drunken stall holder who had had a good day, drunk in front of it. At day's end, the stalls would be washed by the municipal water trucks spraying water from the street. Jana and friends would run through the powerful sprays from the water tank. Then Jana would be wet like a real marathon runner. He would finish at Main Street stopping the traffic for a moment. Everybody in the street looked seriously at the boys, saying to one another, *good running, good running boys.* Some old man at the bookies screamed, *careful you bloody fools from Kurunagar, you going to get killed by the ever speeding Route Master bus.* He also screamed at the driver, *careful you fool, you going to kill the kids.*

When Jana won, Indhiran got to keep his money for late night snacks. Jana couldn't keep money. His father never gave him pocket money. Jana never understood the value of money.

The Bankshall Street boys finally worked out Jana's tricks and began to beat him at his own game. The prizes ranged from cakes, sugar cream buns and ice choc and later changed to rubber bands, marbles and fire crackers, weapons of desperation. It depended on the season. Indhiran worked out the prices, Jana worked out the routes and distances.

Rubber bands became catapults, made with bicycle inner tubes. Stray dogs, squirrels, cats, birds, all got their childish torture from their minute weapons. They also drew wickets on the walls and played cricket without a keeper. They played in lanes, broke a few windows, their arguments about leg before wicket often delayed the game for long periods, sometimes even walking off frustratedly. They cheated sometimes by dropping the catches at critical times, letting it fall in the dirt canal nearby which was covered by dark black gunk, just to annoy serious players like Nixon. But they were all a good natured bunch of local close school friends. When the sun set at St. James', they would have to be out of the churchyards. Then they would move into the well lit wide lanes. When they broke the window a second time, they would all have to run grabbing the bat and the tennis ball and disappear into the darkness. Game over for all of them. No games for another few days.

They pursued other interests in the late evening in various venues and shop fronts, watched flickering TV without picture just for sound and songs. They were bored with home games like Karam, cards, Backgammon and Monopoly. Jana and Indhiran planned for a different kind of action.

They walked up to the town hall to see what was on at the Rio Cinema where they showed English films. Then they'd go to the Sea of Park Straight to see if anybody was kissing behind the cropped trees. Then the ice factory to get a cheap palm ice lolly on a stick. Onwards to climb the pole behind the Rio Cinema while holding the lolly in their mouths. Then walk above the roofs, climb down to another section to a cozy corner of the roof top and watch the sunset or an adult movie for free. Sometimes the town hall caretaker would grease the poles, thinking the scratches were all the work of wild cats and crows. But Jana and Indhiran found a way to get in every time. It was their town and they were not afraid of anyone. They could clearly see the Jaffna Police Station, office and detention rooms. The other main attraction was the officers' quarters back of the station, where they entertained their girlfriends and mistresses. The Sinhalese officers knew how to party. They had no shame. With clothes or without, in public view kissing and cuddling. It had never been seen in Jaffna before. Jana and Indhiran loved watching while they had their little afternoon snacks. It was like a live reality cop sex show of the 70's. And it was a free full 3D version. *Just don't get caught*, said both of them to each other.

Indhiran became the biggest influence of Jana's social life. He studied at Central College. His family was struggling after losing his dad to illness. Indhiran wanted to get work and not follow the route of university. He would try anything to make some pocket money. He was only thirteen but had begun to hire push bikes for 50 cents per hour at Main Road. He did chores for Grandma Joan and funeral houses to make that extra money. He understood that Jana was crazy about sports. He also began to influence Jana with regard to Tamil freedom and possible arms revolution.

At first it all sounded like the movies for Jana. But they had a deal, political meeting then watch a game of football or cricket. They moved political meeting to meeting and to the cricket ground to keep both interests alive.

The annual Thinakaran Villa was the biggest sporting occasion of the Jaffna celebratory calendar. The Thinakaran newspaper organized the biggest Tour de Jaffna bicycle race, marathon, junior marathon, and a fancy dress parade like a carnival. The final curtain raiser during the sunset, the chariot race of horn cows, near the clock tower in front of the Jaffna fort on an uneven ground, was spectacular at all times. This amazing famous Tamil cultural event was never seen anywhere in the world. Numerous trial runs would take place to give the carts, cows and the handlers all the possibilities for fair play. Lives were lost sometimes due to a loss of a wheel with disastrous stampedes. Some would pull out minutes before the race if the conditions were not right. The crowd was asked to stay well behind, to keep the animals calm and to avoid injury. People were on top of trees, on top of the fort, on top of the roofs of all the buildings nearby - it was quite amazing to watch. The ground was hard and uneven. Finally everybody would be ready for a flag start. The event had serious cultural importance. The farmers and breeders took pride, the rearing of their cow being secret. Some of the cows were fed on rich rice starch, millet protein, or kurakan thavedu to get that ultimate fitness level. Sometimes even the family could be starving but the cow would get his rich diet without fail. The lives of these amazing rare breeds of cow could be threatened by the immense acceleration of the race. It was always won by the chavakatcheri / kodikamam farmers of traditional cow breeding posts.

The cycle race was won consecutively for three years by a Kurunagar mechanic and prolific rider, Quinton. The race ended with the final climax behind the library being a finishing sprint in front of the town hall near the stadium. Runners collapsed unable to finish the marathon due to the extreme heat conditions. Kokuvil boy, Visva, took the marathon gold. He looked half conscious and dying of dehydration. Urumpurai Tharma took the silver. Bronze went to a Jaffna boy, Selvin. The junior race was won by Jana's distant cousin, Suren. Jana and his Uncle Raffa ran next to him on a bike with buckets of water pouring on him at every junction to keep him in the competition. Some were disqualified for cheating while riding on the back of a bicycle in unpopulated areas. Jana ran next to Suren for a few miles, encouraging him to go on, shouting, come *on you can do it, you can do it.* He won the race with a minute advantage from the second runner. He received the gold medal and 200 rupees and a certificate.

The show would end at the open theatre stadium with operatic drama and a comedy from the Colombo TV stars. A Singer called Manekar sang Sinhalese Southern Byla and also Tamil songs for all out late night public entertainment. He was famous because he appeared in the first x-rated Tamil movie made in the studios at Colombo. The Tamil public felt humiliated and he became a box office turkey. They all said, *oh my god, she took the sari completely off, unbelievable, no shame whatsoever.* They waited for a creative filmmaker to step in and start a cinematic revolution in Jaffna, reflecting Tamil Jaffna lives.

Jana had drifted away from home and got a severe punishment from his dad with the bamboo cane.

Mr. Prahash made a big move, buying a land near Chundikuli, to take his family out of Kurunagar and Main Road activities. He wanted to move out of Bankshall Street completely. He understood the violent street culture, drunkenness, sex, drugs, and political instigators all lurking around the corner to spoil the young minds. He wanted the kids to finish advance level before they embarked on any free spirited adventures. He wanted to move near the Old Park, tree-lined suburban area of Cundukuli postal district. He also wanted to work closely with the government offices nearby for personal and professional reasons. It was a much better choice compared to a busy, loud and brash Bankshall Street. After obtaining a plan from a draftsman, he wanted to build his house in stages.

First he wanted to complete the foundation. So he hired a mason and a handyman. He took a week off work and joined in as a third person. They laid the ropes for lines and started digging a three foot ditch all around. Prior to starting, it was blessed by an old friend from St. Anthony's Kytes, Fr. T. Sundar. Tractors brought the red rocks from the quarry and tipped them in front of the land, causing red dust and a crumbling noise. Some big rocks accidently mixed in had to be broken with a heavy hammer (suthyiyal). Jana would bring food for everybody from Main Street for the lunch time. Sometimes he would join in with his father in clearing the dug out soil, carrying rocks or materials to the masons to make way for easy access. Cement bags were stacked under the tree on a wooden board covered by a heavy rubber mat in case the monsoon came early. Two weeks had gone by and all the foundation digs were over. The rocks were ready to be laid.

Mr. Prahash prepared a dinner feast for all the workers that day with beers and spirits. Mr. Prahash managed the site well, travelling there on his old BSA motorbike. He now had his promotion to an Agricultural Instructor. Jana did help his father as much as he could. He had begun to get excited about this new project of learning about building a house by hand with no electric tools but with traditional ancient tools and Tamil craftsmanship. At the side of the house, in the middle of the old coconut tree line, the deep water well dig was also in progress. They had to dig until they got to the natural streams at least 50 feet down. Then, with water pouring out, they had to build around blocking the streams temporarily. It was a skilled but dangerous job deep down, with unpredictable water and sliding clay sometimes covering the people. At least five men would manually pull out all water and soil by rope and bucket on this special day. Everybody would be asking, *have they seen the waters, have they seen the waters? Yes, we have*, said Mr. Prahash loudly. He wanted all the neighbors to hear it, too. They worked against time. Without the water supply, house building had to wait. When Mr. Prahash was not around, Jana looked after the staff, and gave feedback to Mr. Prahash when he came back from work. Mr. Prahash's plan was, as soon as the well was done, he wanted to build a temporary house with cheap old lamppost timber columns, affordable aluminum curved metal all around, and with coconut leaves weaved thatched roof laid on top of hand-shaved Palmyra beams, which would be adequate.

Jana and his father took a trip to Pallai region, where the strong dark beams were perfected. They moved inland on a tractor, after looking at a few timber yards. Mr. Prahash finally made the deal with a Palmyra specialist. It took all day and by the time they arrived back at Chundikuli it was dark. The tractor driver by then had lost his concentration and did not manoeuvre along the lanes without touching the next door fences. The owner in anger pushed the fence forward to stop the loaded tractor making any further damage. Mr. Prahash took control of the tractor in order to drive through. The angry neighbor gave in.

Mr. Prahash took the tractor to his place leaving behind a few damaged fences. Then with his bare hands he ripped the damaged fence piece by piece creating an argument that lasted for hours. He really did not mind about his bleeding hands.

Mr. Prahash shouted: 'I spent the whole day in a desperate heat to find the timber in drastic conditions in the countryside, not eaten nor had a drink, and this guy gives me grief just before I get home in one piece.'

The locals laughed with the excitement of a fight. The families concerned stayed back and watched the men go through with the motion.

The following morning both went to church and took Holy Communion standing next to each other like nothing had happened. Mr. Prahash wanted to build a wall around his house to avoid further skirmishes. So he built all around with a blue gate to finish. Using the cutting and sticking method, he planted all his trees from all around the country in the house. Mangoes, two types all on one tree, lemons, bananas, coconuts of different kind with red coconut at the front of the house for fortune, jasmine and bougainvillea, crotons and mani valai, roses, papaw, murunkai, guava, avocado, mangustan and rumbuttan, he tried everything to keep the kids interested in home produce. He raised vegetable patches and gave them seasonal crops with chili, tomato, broad beans, squash, yams and onions for soups and sauces.

The water well was dug and finished with a weight balance (Thula) mechanism. It was a long, light, and strong tree stem shaved and polished, placed in a H shape, balanced with weights on the back, on the front with heavy thick coconut fiber rope which held a bucket so they could pull water with ease manually from the well. The toilet was built with a pit system.

The partially finished coconut leaf thatched roof was enough to live in. They moved in and boiled the milk in a pot and let it overflow to represent happiness and success at the housewarming ceremony with friends and relatives. The old lamp-post painted with black anti corrosion (solikanam) looked great and showed Mr. Prahash as an agricultural enthusiast with great recycling skills. Everybody thought Mr. Prahash would relax now after all this hard work was done. He saw his family coming together. Even his son was getting interested in the house rather than spending his nights at the town.

Mr. Prahash wanted to begin the second phase immediately. The mason, Basil, told him the amount of stones he needed. The joiner, *Asthiriyar*, advised him on timber for roofing, window ledges and doors. The roofer gave the estimate for red terracotta tiles and labor. The cost of timber had gone sky high. He would have to come up with a master plan. He decided to buy margosa trees that were going to be cut down for highway and agricultural development. He called the specialist in the ancient art of slicing a tree with a ten foot sword while standing in a deep square hole in the ground, laying the tree across above safely, one man down, one man up with pure manual manpower. They worked on all the doors, panels and windows with the fresh smell of (vembuu) margosa everywhere. He made benches, stools and bed frames. Even the saw dust became pillows to relieve certain head stress after a hard day's work. The most rigorous pain he went through was when he decided to make all the walls cement stones by hand with the help of only one handyman. The mixture was high grade homemade KKS cement with river gravel well known to be mixed with sapphires. This was added to the crushed heavy red rocks. Also added was the fine white sand. All mixed by hand and shovel, Jaffna style. One little pyramid to another. Mix and mix and mix until it became one. They added just enough water to handle. Together they put the mixture in a steel three stone mould. Three by three, Mr. Prahash and the handy man made 7000 stones in 4 months. Jana's job was to come in in the morning and re stack the stones without breaking them and water the stones prior to going to school. He just could not believe the pain his father had gone through with that stone making process. The water kept the strong mixture together and bonded even harder. So every time the rain came Jana would dance around the cement stones.

The tough and difficult job of stone and materials was done. The joiner would now work on the roof at his own timber yard near Temple Road.

Months later, Mr. Prahash organized an interim move to a small flat with his family on Temple Road. Their neighbours were some Valvetithurai (VVT) University students – this was during the uprising of the rebels. Mr. Prahash not really did know much about the boys activities. Everybody feared when they heard the name of that town, VVT. They were just university students who believed in equality and who were also brilliant in mathematics, physics and chemistry.

Jana took tuition whenever he got stuck with his algebra and calculus. Mr. Prahash succeeded in keeping Jana away from town activities and making study a little better. It worked. Indhiran also came home and studied together with Jana.

Jana missed his friends at Bankshall Street. Mainly, they all still studied at St. Peter's together, and were also growing up with different interests. He just loved that freedom of movement at nights in Kurunagar. They were also becoming teenagers.

Jana's interest suddenly shifted to his beloved trains, as he lived near the tracks, shunting stations and mini yards near the courts. Banana farm gardens and low bridges above the canals were also interesting, because they could climb up there and sit next to a fast moving train to feel the G force.

Romanticism of the Yarl Devi (Jaffna girl) began to get to the boys of Temple Road. The new gang was Jana with his young band of followers. Rani Aunty's family lived near Hospital Road too so he had his distant cousins and Bonny.

Grandma Joan's cousin Nichola's grandchildren were also part of it. They were naughty, waved and streaked at the Colombo Yarl Devi traveler's regularly. Dino squirted his water from pistols, sitting on top of a canal bridge. Bonny's homemade cracker gun, made ingeniously with cycle spokes, bolt nail and a string while a tree branch as a handle gave it grip and the finish. The fast moving train would blast the horn and shake the grounds as it passed. As the train passed over him on the bridge, Bonny would bang the gun on the walls making a sound of an underground thunder. When people looked out, Dino would squirt them with the water pistol. The people laughed at the antics and threw bread at them. One day, Jana heard the scream of Marie Joyce, to *get off the railway tracks*. It was quite far away, nobody really heard anything, but somebody heard something. She saw Bonny and Dino a little closer to the track. They were busy laying large nails and soda tops on the tracks. Bonny and Dino converted them cleverly into small knives and musical instruments for college cricket matches. The fast moving diesel train was safe to stand by, but not when the train was approaching them head on.

Marie Joyce also missed her mum and sisters in Main Road. She continuously complained about this double move prior to the house build. House building pressure begin to show at home with several moves one after the other.

'We should have stayed there until all this was over,' Mr. Prahash said, 'calm down, they are crazy enough to do some silly things like putting a nail on the track, but not foolish enough to derail the train or stand in front of it.'

'It's all Jana's fault, he has to do some sort of crazy thing one after the other,' Marie Joyce said irritably. 'I am tired and can't cope with all this, the girls gone on their bikes wherever they please. You deal with them, ok? Especially Jana.'

'That's right, I married someone else,' said Mr. Prahash. 'Let them learn a lesson,' said Mr. Prahash. 'The driver will blow the horn loudly. They are not going to hear each other for a few days.'

The train went by. Mr. and Mrs. Prahash watched from their back garden.

The three boys tried to block their ears as the horn blasted like an air raid siren. When the train passed they started to pick the things on the track, and saw they had been watched. They started to walk back towards the house, hands on the ears to try and unblock the deaf ear unbalance. The three boys rigorously shook their heads in discomfort. Mr. and Mrs. Prahash looked at each other and laughed.

The following day Jana and his mates were locked in the room during the train times. They heard the sisters outside singing train songs laughing their heads off: *Choo… choo… choo…*

Marie Joyce remembered when Jana as a child had suffered from convulsions and asthma. He had visited Dr. Abraham quite often to get his injections and inoculations. Nurse Hilary always asked Jana to scream Trrrrrain. While Jana was busy with the matchbox toy train and screaming, trrrrain, trrrrain, Nurse Hilary gently administered the injections. Jana's tears came out as he realized something had pricked his arm. Nurse Hilary quickly took out the needle after pushing the fluids in. Jana screamed, trrrrain, trr..ahhh…train, then cried in pain. The cotton wool massage soon settled his pain. Dr. Abraham would drop his bifocals, smile at Jana and say, *you fool, let the girls take advantage of you like this.* Everybody would laugh in the children's ward. Nurse Hilary always preferred antibiotics intravenously or subcutaneously. That was the preferred treatment of that time. Not enough capsules or plastic disposable needles to go around in the community. Stainless steel needles were boiled in high temperature and re-used. Nurse Hilary showed Jana all the process in the treatment room. That was the time Jana began to get interested in hospital and nursing care. It made a special impression on Jana. Nurse Hilary became a close friend as Jana grew up. Whenever he had to go to hospital, she would say trrrain. Jana would say train and smile.

So he loved the Yarl Devi and the train travel. The Yarl Devi in the morning, lunch time slow goods train, evening mail train, go all night through the dark and dangerous jungle to Colombo, was an ideal travel for Jana. He watched the railway workers replacing sleepers, darkened with oil and dirt and decaying through the years. He also visited the signal room away from the station, talked with the railway workers, asked questions about signal systems and the timing and importance of their skills and craft. Pure physical ability and darkened clothes dirty with oil and diesel stains also on the face and hands, with worn off leather shoes with holes – a sight of interest and sadness. At home Jana began to get punishment in the form of caning, for not concentrating on his studies, drifting in lanes daydreaming or walking along the railway tracks of Chundikuli. Jana was not listening to anybody. He became stubborn. A runaway from the house in the late evening. Mr. Prahash sometimes had to go and look for him. Mostly he could not be found at Main Road. He would sneak back in late at night and then be prompted by his waiting mother to go have a wash. Then he would fall asleep studying on the table. He was unhappy and humiliated in front of people by being caned by a frustrated Mr. Prahash. Angry Jana began to adopt pain and humiliation.

One day he screamed, when his father approached him:

'Come on! I am even ready for the Ray fish tail or a cycle chain. Come on! Give me all you got. It won't hurt me. I am learning to adopt pain and suffering,' screamed Jana with tears in his eyes. Then he would run away, further and further and faster and faster. He felt the relief in running; he felt the pain of the muscles and the cramps. The exhaustion and the breathlessness when he reached the end of the line. He would stop at Indhiran's for water and a rest at their coconut-leaf thatched little mud house. That was paradise for Jana away from home. Indhiran received strict orders from Mr. Prahash not to take him on his trips or to allow him to enter their house. Mr. Prahash also blamed Aunty Rohini for not disciplining her son. They had their daily problems of survival without their father. They were not really interested in his advice or intervention. Jana was welcome at anytime at 6th Cross Street. They were not just good friends, but also brothers. They learned to keep secrets. Indhiran began to notice the emerging talent of a middle distance prospect. He thought Jana could compete in the inter schools quadrangular athletic meet. Jana really wanted to win the college senior 1500 and 3000 meters. The college did not have an under seventeen middle distance competition.

Sometimes, while he sat at his cousin's porch, the monsoon rain would come to Jaffna with thunder and lightning. Water would rush like a river on the roads and lanes shifting sand and stones. Some holes in the Indhiran house would start to leak. Pots would fill up with water, making a different kind of noise according to each pot.

'It was really calm just before an hour ago,' said Jana.

Kids would leave their paper boats to float away. Some would get swallowed, some would get stuck between the tree trunks. This is the time Jana would find his sensibility increase and he had a moment to talk to his mum.

'How about going to Colombo on a weekend, to see Vigi Uncle? Your cousins, mum? We have got the family railway warrant to travel. It will allow us to travel. I would love to take the slow train that stops at every single station. Maybe take Indhiran with us. I want to take a picture of every station,' said Jana. 'The Maho Junction, the biggest junction in the country. It will be great to explore the whole country,' he said philosophically.

Marie Joyce looked at Jana and did not say anything.

'Mum, you know the trains bring flour, sugar, kerosene oil, petrol, diesel and take away cement, salt, rice, animals, gravel, fine sand and quarry red rocks. Jaffna trains took materials and labor that contributed to that great old parliament building in Colombo, in the style of the Parthenon with grand columns, built by the British in the early years,' said Jana. He was a keen social studies student. Social studies in srilanka was about history. He was also pro British, everybody knew that. St. Peter's gave him that foundation.

The Yarl Devi would arrive at Colombo on time for a lunch at the Y.M.C.A. about 13.00 hours. The well organized tasty retreat was at the Colombo YMCA canteen with affordable prices. That was a local civil servants' lounge bar restaurant at Colombo Fort. They served quality food of southern specialty all day: malu bun filled with tuna, mountain goat in rolls, mulligatawny soup with rumba, seeni sambol with roti, green lentil thosai and uppuma idli with hot sambar, king prawn and buriyani, stir fried noodles Singapore style, were some of the few regular specials at that large canteen. Afterwards, a brief stroll through the roads of Pettah and a look at the cheap imitation watches from the Far East. For quality clothing everybody shopped at Hydramani at Colombo Fort, in front of the Kandyan and Georgian architecture. Then it was routine to take a moped ride to the Tamil Union Cricket Club, to watch the premier cricket batsman of the country stay on the front foot, steady on the crease. That was top class cricket free of charge. Back at the Galle Face Hotel front garden with an easterly breeze, drinking pineapple rum punch, was a most happiest time spent for the travelling friends or couple. After visiting family and friends, late night cinema at the Regal Theatre was the closest to the station to get back home after the cinema. This enabled them to catch the early morning Yarl Devi back to Jaffna, and was an ideal quick break spent in the city of Colombo.

The cinema was also run by the Tamil upper class that selected the great box office hits from the world cinema market and distributed them throughout the country. Films like The Dirty Dozen, Dirty Mary Crazy Larry, Dirty Harry, Dogs of War, Deer Hunter, Wild Geese, Where Eagles Dare, Guns of Navarone, A Bridge Too Far, Cross of Iron, were some of the films which showed us the apocalypse now and before around the world. Jana loved the war films, then the series of westerns like She Wore A Yellow Ribbon, Searchers, High Noon, 40 Guns, Who shot Liberty Valance, Pat Garret and Billy the Kid, The wild Bunch and Ulzanas Raid, showed them the violent nature of the Wild West. Then came The Man with No Name, The Good, The Bad, The Ugly, The Magnificent 7, Sabata, Blood Money, Take a Hard Ride, 100 Rifles, El Condor, and The Professionals. That gave Jana enormous pleasure watching the different countries, prairies, and savannas and also gave him an education on the lifestyles of Indians, bluecoats, grey coats, Iron Cross, SS, and the beans-eating dirty cowboys. Black man, white man, Chinese man.

Most of all, an American born Chinese student of philosophy with his ultimate style and speed, hypnotized everyone with discipline and fearsome physical presence and with his fist of fury he was the big boss. Bruce Lee showed Jana and his friends how to get near the game of death. They allowed the dragon to enter the walls of their bedroom. They also cut their hair like him and called it the Bruce Lee Cut and wore Chinese clothes and shoes and bows on street like Master Ce Fu. Karate classes sprang up on every corner of the street. Clubs were formed. On their chopper bike they went to classes to compete for their belts.

The great caliber of actors like Wayne, Stewart, Mitchum, Marvin, McQueen, just couldn't compete with Lee's star quality in his prime. He also took the Far East, Sri Lanka and India. The Chinese began to make more films for world audiences dubbed in English. Invincible Armour, Chinese Boxer, Shallion Temple, Drunken Monkey Kung Fu, are some of the Asian influenced movies. Fights broke out in every cinema like never before. Just like the early days in the 50's for Mr. Prahash. Now, it was Jana's turn. Even the Hollywood stars wanted to learn Kung Fu from the once studio-neglected Jeet Kun Do Master of the Secrets. Hollywood also began to change with road movies.

Jana on his bike, in great excitement, asked Indhiran: 'Are you ready, machann? Guess what's the film in Srithar, opening today? Let me give you a few clues. The man with the slim cigar.'

Indhiran replied: 'Eastwood. No, no...'

Jana's eyes would wander left to right like he knew the actor personally. 'He is black and dark like you.'

'I know, said Indhiran. 'I know. Sidney Poitier don't smoke in films.'

'No, no, no, man got to keep his reputation,' said Jana. Then disappointed he gave a few clues to Indhiran: 'Taller, handsome, stylish. Ladies man. Like you.'

'Me? I am more like a James Bond, Jana.'

'Well, he can't be a Bond… he is black,' Jana said.

'He could be the first black James Bond, Jim Brown,' said Indhiran.

'Getting close, sonny,' said Jana.

'Yes, I know. It's Freddy… oh yeah, Fred Williamson.' The man with great swagger and confidence, modern king of black cinema, the new wave of many waves to come. There is bound to be a fight today, it's the area of the *Ariyaculam* [deep river] boys turf, nobody else has a chance, even the police work with them. I thought Uncle Raffa knows a few, from the fights that he was involved with some of the boys there.'

'I thought he plays both sides whenever he likes,' said Jana. 'He can't even teach us self defense, call himself a Chandian? He said we are too young to know all the killing details.'

Indhiran said nothing. He also did not get on with the man.

'It will be double the price, that is if you got that kind of money, Indhiran. Today, I just have enough for a 2nd class or gallery,' said Jana. 'Gallery in the Srithar. You are going to get suffocated in that tunnel on the way to buy a ticket.'

It was quite narrow to avoid the queue jumping. Sometimes they had to hose the people down to keep them alive while they waited for two hours prior to the first show. Jaffna cinema seats were segregated like people and classes. Cheap gallery was near the screen up front, then the second class with wooden chairs, followed by red leather 1st class, then reserve 20 seats. But the most important well-upholstered seats were in the balcony near the projector beams circled by the smoke from down below. They all smelled of tobacco after the show except the air conditioned balcony. The police held that area for the first week for their girlfriends to suck on their complimentary ice chocs.

Jana said: 'You know, Indhiran, the police get all the complimentary these days.'

'They will run out of choc ices, all been sucked dry,' said Indhiran.

They both laughed hysterically.

'Apparently this film has the first full black body sex scene ever shown in this country. The sensors are trying to cut it all off, as they do with all movies on the first week of release. That's why all these characters are here. The diehard fans of sex and violence.'

'How about you, Jana?' asked Indhiran.

Jana said: 'Listen, unlike you, I am an intelligent moviegoer.'

'That is a good excuse for your daddy, Jana, have you ever tried that?' said Indhiran.

Jana said nothing. They suddenly saw a massive canvas hand-painted poster which had dropped from the roof: Fred Williamson holding two girls in both his arms, one black, the other oriental. One of his arms was cuffed to his suitcase. There were also other pictures of him in a karate suit holding a gun. It said, this man got it all. Big bad and beautiful, that man Bolt. They looked at each other in excitement. It was like a world cup match for them. Movies took time to come to Jaffna, mostly after a few years running in the capital. Copies were well used and damaged, sometimes they saw the reel melt on the screen while they were watching the movie. They watched with good anticipation. If it was a bad show then cinema chairs would be broken. Sometimes the theatre would be bombed with petrol cocktails. Managers got beaten. Sometimes a release of a snake in the darkened cinema caused chaos and a stampede. The first week of a show was full of events like this from rivaling ticket touts. One day some drunken individual put a hand on a young boy, he was beaten until unconscious.

Jana and Indhiran would always be glued to the screen concentrating on language, accent and slangs. It was unheard of for anybody to cry or mourn during the show, until when they were leaving the cinema, they saw a pool of blood outside of the second class. They used to cope with all the crazy incidents in the cinema hall, it was mad but great life. They cheered, clapped their hands, shed a few tears during emotional films like Dr. Zhivago.

Operation Daybreak, the story about the assassination of Hitler's right-hand man who had succeeded with difficulties but was pinned down under a church betrayed by his colleague to save his own family. They fight on but eventually they shoot each other with a final hug. Amazingly shot by English Director, Lewis Gilbert, it was a hit in Jaffna RANI Theatre and ran for six months. That is a record for an English film in Jaffna. The Tamils loved the story of sacrifice and martyrdom. Jana and Indhiran began to truant school to watch English language films. Jana's relationship at home was all interrupted. With his father, Jana was always making excuses. His grades began to fall.

One evening Jana came home late. Mr. and Mrs. Prahash were up. Mr. Prahash said: 'Hey, son, come here,' as he saw Jana trying to sneak into his front office room. 'Come here for a minute. As a family it is nice to talk sometimes, ha?' He looked at his watch: 'You are late and where have you been?'

Jana tried to say something but was interrupted by his

father, while his mum sat not happy and looking away at the front gate.

'There was no cricket practice today, right?' Mr. Prahash smiled and raised his voice.

Earlier, Jana's father had to cycle past Jana's college to go and see his doctor. He looked at the ground flooded with the overnight downpour. The cricket matting was unusable and needed to be changed. It was drenched in water, play couldn't happen for another two days. Talk about the cricket grounds surprised Jana. He realized he was in trouble.

Mr. Prahash said: 'Only sport you can play there is Turkish wrestling. You look fairly clean. So there is no wrestling, too.' Mr. Prahash got up from the chair, come near Jana and looked around him and sniffed him real close. Jana realized he was in trouble. Mr. Prahash continued: 'No ball shine on your trouser, sweat, or a dive in the grass mark either. So what net practice today, Jana, or any indoor knock about huh? And you smell of cigarettes. I hope you did not start on that Main Street culture, did you ? Did you now?' he shouted.

Jana shook his head with embarrassment. Mr. Prahash asked his wife: 'Mum, why don't you ask your son to say the truth. Please, I am tired with this boy,' said Mr. Prahash.

'Jana, tell your dad the truth. Who did you go with? And what was it?' said Marie Joyce calmly. Jana lifted his head, opened his eyes and said: 'Chinatown. The Chinatown movie.'

Mr. Prahash said 'It's an 18 rated movie.'

Jana defended himself: 'No. It's not, it's 15.'

'Great ladies huh?' said Mr. Prahash. 'Dunaway. Faye Dunaway. Bonnie and Clyde fame, Dunaway. Mum, your son got good taste in ladies. He likes them slim and beautiful.

Slim and beautiful,' he repeated. Then he shouted: 'slim, beautiful and naked, that's what he likes, your son, mum. We brought up boys who like to get involved in different kinds of interests. I think I have failed him. Failed on my only son.'

He looked disappointed and was overreacting, according to Jana. Marie Joyce was biting her teeth, mumbling: 'Look at you, trouble maker. You should know better.' She got up from the chair and walked away. "

Mr. Prahash asked: 'Where did you get the money, Jana?'

'I borrowed it from a classmate.'

Mr. Prahash went crazy. He came close and intimidated Jana and said: 'You are only 15, you borrowing money. You don't borrow from nobody. Be a man and ask me for it, if that is so important, in your life. Mum!' Mr. Prahash called. 'Moreover, this is a movie about incest.'

Jana said: 'What's incest?'

'You don't know?' screamed Mr. Prahash.

Jana replied: 'I know but nothing to do with this movie.'

'So you did not even understand the bloody film.'

Jana recalled a part of the film he hadn't understood: *I know, he said, she is also mine, you know, and she said, she is never going to know that.* Jana just realized what that really meant.

'So you just realized, huh. He is a great actor, mum. Your son. Oscar fucking winning, did not even understand the plot. I heard about the film in the office, it is about the water board, farm land and corruption. Typical story of Sri Lanka, stealing water from the Vanni farmer and diverting it towards upcountry. Mountain region. Just don't need any more water than it got already. It is a wet zone for Christ's sake. I thought, I will take my son and watch it together. But changed my mind due to the incest issue. But our loving son lied to us, borrowed money from somebody, sneaked behind us and stabbed us in the backs. Shame on you. You will learn your lesson. Go away. I don't want to see you or speak to you. Go on. Go on, do whatever you like. Enjoy your freedom. I won't be here for long anyway. You can do whatever you like with your mum.'

Jana hesitantly and foolishly took out his purse, and said: 'I have two tickets, thought about you two, being your field, thought you might like it. I did not realize you will take this incest so seriously, after all it's only a fictional story. I did not watch this movie for the reasons you have talked about. It had a good cast, good writer, and a good director. That's the reason I watched this movie.'

Mr. Prahash looked at his mother: 'Please deal with him. Maybe you go with him and explain the meaning of incest to this intelligent moviegoer. Fool trying to tell me about movie business. Self obsessed megalomaniacs, just can't get enough publicity or money to waste on plastic surgery.'

Marie Joyce calmly approached her son and gave him a slap: 'When you are down, you stay down. Don't you try to take everybody with you, don't you ever. Run your own marathon, run your own laps. Don't take me with you. Run me with your clever laps without honor. You think you going to win?'

Mr. Prahash was in the garden continuing his attack: 'Ask your Uncle Reggie, he will take your ticket. They all live in that house in Main street, so they must have come real close to gaining the glory. The losers.' He poured water from the well on his head.

Jana looked down with anger and embarrassment. Mum said: 'Look at me while I am talking to you, take your tickets, give them back to your friends. Go on, enjoy yourself. Forget about us. This movie business will destroy your life and your future. You understand, do you?'

Calmly, Jana said: 'Yes', shaking his head.

Mum said: 'If you understand all this, that's ok. Can't say more. You've done enough damage for one day.'

Chinatown became Jana's all time favorite movie. He never forgot that day.

His father did not speak to anybody that day except his dog Broon. Mr. Prahash decided not to go to work, collected dried leaves and food waste around Old Park and Y.M.C.A in sacks. He also went to the churchyard and sat under the Banyan tree with his dog, said hello to the passing churchgoers. Then he cleaned up the churchyard, picking all the leaves of the Banyan and the Mahogany, while Broon sat and watched his master work with some mission in mind. Then he took it all and put it next to his trees in the garden. He asked for some water then started digging a hole around the trees about three feet deep. Broon joined him, shifting sand with his back leg, while happily running around him. He dropped those organic wastes around all his trees especially the banana trees. Then covered the ground using his bare feet to level all the area. He started singing: 'If the tree don't give fruit or flowers, cut it to the ground and burn it to ashes.' He meant his family, his son.

His banana gave great results from his agricultural artwork. There were three types, kuppal, kathali, itharai in his garden and they all came out as he expected with full size and shape. People used to ripen them quickly by smoking them under the ground or putting a very hot metal through the stem making them ready for shops or ceremonies. Mr. Prahash liked to hang it in the kitchen and let it ripen naturally. He would also give a share to his best friends. He would say, 'whenever the family eats the bananas, I will provide you all, but you switch your tails, when I turn my

147

back, just be careful when I am gone. None of you will survive. Everyone around you will try to con you and take everything from you. Especially your mum, she will give away like a charity.' He took the machete, saying, *that's right, just wait and see*. He began to trim the bougainvillea trees with giant spikes sticking out, with his all-conquering multipurpose razor sharp machete, going left and right with rhythm. He diverted the water to the vegetable patch, then to the lemon and the mangoes. Finally, he carried a bucket full of water in both hands, all the way to the front, a further 100 yards away, and watered the flower beds, crotons, ever-spreading Jasmine along the porch all the way to the roof giving fresh smell all around the year. He took the dead leaves of papaw and weeded all with his bare hands. That was his therapy whenever he felt stressed by his family. When it was all done, a quick check on the gate then back to his room for a nap. It was the turn of the little sister, Jenine, to pull his grey hair, while he slept. He bought digestive biscuits with chocolate topping for that. The family was addicted to those biscuits. Mr. Broon would take care of the local miniskirts when his master was away. He disliked all the individuals that Mr. Prahash did not have time for. He showed real respect and obedience, teaching a lesson or two scaring the hell out of all Mr. Prahash's enemies, making Mr. Prahash very happy, with his relentless stamina and swinging tale. Mr. Prahash made him a special broth of lamb bones and root vegetables with a little beer. He was a hunting dog. Jumping up to the top of the six foot wall petrifying all the visiting neighbors. The next door neighbor, Soosai, sold the house due to the arguments. That was a sweet revenge for Soosai. All eight of them cycled through the lanes making Broon crazy. Mr. Prahash argued with the teenagers. Sometimes he let Broon out, and he would chase them down the lane until they fell off their bikes in fear. Broon never bit anybody, unless you were physically violent against him. The neighbors all screamed at hot tempered Mr. Prahash.

Jana and the rest of his family stayed away from all the feuds with the neighbors.

He would give Broon a bath and spend more time with the dog than his family. Sometimes he got drunk in the house, then Broon also looked unsteady on his feet after doing his soup a little over the top. This time he had it with a little brandy instead of beer. He loved his guard dog Broon who slept outside his master's bedroom guarding him day or night.

Dogs were treated badly in Jaffna. Neglect, physical abuse, and caging them for long periods was most notable around town. Most of them ran away when they got the chance. Plaster of Paris was expensive in Jaffna. The mixture was modified with crushed shells to make it cheaper. It was only available for Jaffna hospital orthopedic department. Most common injuries were to knees and ankles due to football and police brutality. But the hospital provided the dog-catcher a removable arm of plaster of Paris for extra protection from a mad Alsatian bite. The stray dog was a frightening sight for the Jaffna residents. Usually the domestic dog would recognize the stray. The kids would use their catapults with stones to strike at them. That would make the stray go wild and crazy. Some managed to bite and created a rabies fear all around the town. The less everybody understood the worst their fears became. But the old ladies with their arthritic legs walking really slowly with sticks to aide them, they were not scared of the dog. They screamed: *she nayah*, meaning you dirty dog, freezing them like magic. It was the shock of the sudden sound that stunned the dog. The kids around said: *old lady has magical powers, be careful.* She spoke the language of the animals. Especially the dogs. The kids never understood or were taught about animal behavior. So it gripped the town in fear. The beaten guard dog policed the house well and never discriminated against anybody. If you saw a sign that said, guard dog beware, it meant what it said on the board. Do not enter.

The period during the Suez Crises, then followed by the stricken 70's rations of S.L.F.P. Government, forced people to live on the bare minimum. People did not have enough to eat. The dogs only got the leftovers and the bones and rotten flesh. Broon did not have any famine or recession. Mr. Prahash made sure, with his ability to improvise, that Broon was well looked after. He loved everybody in the family. Most favorite was Jana's little sister. If anybody was unfair to her in the house, he would be there next to her and sit there murmuring and stare at anyone. He was a sensitive, clever, and protective hound dog. But his least favorite was Jana who chased him for fun in the lanes, then jumped on him to wrestle him to the floor and then walk away. He had never bitten anybody. If you were gone down the road for more than a few minutes he would come back and lick you to make sure you were ok. Jana liked to play this game with him. That was Broon. He was also Jana's dog. He was his running partner around the Old Park.

Since the time Jana had moved to Chundikuli he had not receive a good welcome at the local parish. The locals did not know him well, except his college mates. They never gave him a chance to be in the local parish cricket or football teams. Moreover Jana always talked about Sebastian Coe and Jeffrey Boycott. It did not go well in St. John's Church yard.

The teenagers there wanted to talk about Bruce Lee, M.G.R., Sivagi, Kung Fu, stick fights, kalari and sword fights and rebel revolution. They were more interested in the Bollywood heroes of the Asian silver screen.

M.G.R is a south Indian actor who masterplanned a great propaganda machine behind his acting career, following in the footsteps of the previous Indian actor, Rao, taking the actor-politician route. He cleverly worked with producers and writers to spread his political message. He had elite Tamil poets, songwriters, singers, and filmmakers of tamil nadu India work around his political persuasion and image. His followers were fanatical and would have given their lives for the cause. He also did work against the corruption in the movies playing the villain and the hero at the same time. He would wear the distinctive Ray-Ban sunglasses and Nehru style woollen hat at all times in public. But he would come out in movies with make-up, modern hair wigs and pink and red lycra, imitating Errol Flynn. He was a Robin Hood in real life. He was the Robin Hood of Tamil Nadu, he did take from the rich and gave it to the poor. Being a trained fencing-master, stick fighter, and a wrestler, kept him in shape in his fifties and gave him a lot of popularity around the globe. His films were seen in India, Sri Lanka, Singapore, Malaysia, Indonesia, Hong Kong, Fiji, Philippines, North Africa, Iran, Iraq, Pakistan, Afghanistan, Arabia - that's a lot of international audience of a different kind. His fights were choreographed by his full-time martial arts masters who also appeared in his films on the villain side. They were well ahead of their time. A younger generation was hooked. He did have style, charisma and attraction. Moreover, he chose younger Miss World type beauties to co-star as heroines, usually thirty years younger. Nobody minded as a fictional film, but culturally a lot of Tamils did not like his films due to his sexual explicitness. M.G.R wanted to break barriers , sexual taboo moralities and succeeded. In the late seventies, after producing over 100 hit films, and becoming a multibillionaire, he reached his ambition since he was an orphan child, to be the first minister to govern Tamil Nadu along Indira Ghandhi. Whatever good and bad was said about him, he did more than anybody for the poor Tamils of India and Sri Lanka. As a chief minister he crushed extortion, bribery, child labor and poverty and built schools for the underprivileged, and brought a positive outlook and prosperity for Tamil Nadu.

Jana argued that the politics in India had no effect on the lives of Sri Lankans. It was just a movie business. Just entertainment. His stand on western interests attracted bullies in the local churchyard and they often waited for him in the evenings.

'Hey you! Sebastian!' shouted a youth while smoking a cigarette and passing it to his gang behind the church bells. That was the gathering corner of the St. John's church bullies.

'Hey Sebastian! Where are your arrows? How did you take those out while your hand was tied to your back?' They laughed.

Rumor spread easily about Jana's father's reputation in Chundikuli. People found out that Jana had been tied up a few times. They compared him to San Sebastian the saint who was killed with arrows while tied against a tree. They laughed again at Jana.

'You know, this fool is the biggest fan of Sebastian Coe,' said one youth. 'He also said Sebastian Coe has Indian blood!'

Everybody laughed: *Indian blood.*

'Pardon me, sir, he is also come from the slums of Madras and collects wood for his mum's mud oven.' Everybody laughed again.

'Give us a break, you Kurunagar boy. Who you trying to kid?'

Jana ignored it and walked passed. They surrounded him: 'Why don't you support a good Sinhalese Sri Lankan cricketer instead of Geoffrey Boycott? The Sinhalese did less harm to us than the British! Hah!' Well other than they tortured a little and murdered a few, that surly they learned from the brits. The legacy. They would throw their cigarette butts at him. 'Is that because the Tamils can't get into the national teams or is it because of the standardization? No, it's because you people are no good. People like you in college cricket, we have got no chance. Don't blame the Sinhalavan for everything.' Traitors.

Another one said: 'What about our Kumar Anandan? He broke the Guinness Book of Records by swimming across the park straight from Jaffna to India. Yeh, yeh… why don't you support him? Go on, you can't talk. Hey, have you got an egg in your mouth? We heard your father is a big talker. Somebody said he is a public speaker. Ha ha… public speaker.'

Jana had heard enough: 'Don't bring my father into this. If he comes with the machete you won't have a chance. I tell you, he will cut you down, he is from Delft, they don't worry about doing time. Go on, try to hit me.' Jana made a move. Jana shouted: 'The only reason we don't do well as the Sinhalese, our families don't encourage sports. Moreover, we don't have facilities - where is the public tennis court, a public swimming pool, coaching camps, equipment? We are all alike - jealousy, hatred, violence (errichal, porramai). We don't like new faces, we don't like somebody doing well, our

153

family decides everything for us. You watch too much M.G.R. films, that's why we are not free today,' as he mumbled and was about to cry. 'That's why we don't have a world champion. So you tell me who do I look up to? A real record breaker or politician like M.G.R.?'

Suddenly, a youth called Mohan, an M.G.R. fanatic, said: 'What did you say?'

Jana was walking away leaving it alone. Mohan followed him and landed a heavy punch right on his face. Jana did not have time to react, he hit the ground as light as a leaf, swirling in the air in slow motion. Everybody shouted, *get him*. Jana's cunning forward talk had not worked, he had to try something else. He got up and started to look for something like as if he had lost a ring or chain on the ground. Everybody was waiting in confusion, some began to walk away saying he can't fight. Jana said: 'I dropped my liver.' Everybody laughed. In hysterics, Mohan dropped his guard. Then Jana dropped him with a heavy hook with the elbow. He was down bleeding. Everybody jumped on Jana and kicked and punched. A churchgoer intervened: 'I will see all your parents and make sure they know all about your activities in the bell tower.' He kicked them and slapped them: 'Go on… kicking one boy all of you.'

'NO! He hit Mohan first,' they tried to lie. Jana and Mohan went home with bloody noses and their clothes all full of dirt and muck. Jana tried to sneak into the house while covering his face. Jana was not a brawler, he never got in a fight. Indhiran did all the fighting in Bankshall Street. For the first time, he really missed his cousin. Mr. Prahash noticed the out of the ordinary dirt-filled clothes of Jana: 'Hey you! Jana!' called Mr. Prahash. Jana tried to ignore Mr. Prahash who went to him and turned his face to see it. He saw the bloody face of Jana. The first time in his life.

He asked: 'Who did this?'

'All of them,' said Jana.

'I mean, who punched you?'

'I don't know,' said Jana.

'Who did it? Otherwise, I will go to every single house in this neighborhood and find out myself,' he said as he grabbed Jana's collar. 'Who did this?'

Jana looked at his eyes filled with a madness and said: 'Mohan.'

'Who? The master's son. Let's go. Come on,' said Mr. Prahash as quickly he put on a vest. 'Ok, let's go.'

Jana did not know what to expect. He knew there would be arguments and it would be embarrassing. He realized there was no going back, he had made a mistake by giving Mohan's name.

They approached Mohan's house. Mr. Prahash grasped a Poovarsu[flower-king] tree branch along the lane and removed the leaves. Jana feared what he was going to do with it. His brain was working like a clockwork: shall I run away now or stay? Shall I face the music? No, he won't hit anybody in their house, it's going to be…

Mr. Prahash called: 'Master! Master! Walk to the gate. Your son and my son have been being fighting at the church, he came home with a bloody nose.' He quickly grabbed Jana and hit him below the knees with the tree branch in front of everybody. Mr. Prahash shouted: 'You will never play with these people again, you will never join these people in the yard again, you will never fight with anybody in this church, you understand that, do you hear me?'

Jana said *yes* with tears. Then he also did not know whether to laugh or cry. He ran away back to the deserted churchyard, and sat under the crucifix alone.

'Leave the fights to us adults. That's it!' screamed Mr. Prahash in the middle of the road. 'Sir, you are a teacher, you do the same to your son. I will appreciate that. I don't want these kids to play or fight again.'

The master called Mohan: 'Is that true? Did you hit him?' He gave him a wild slap on the face as Mr. Prahash walked away, mission accomplished. Mohan's father continued: 'You worthless shit, you will apologize to him when you see him again, you understand? Now, kneel down in the middle of the garden until your loving mum comes and gives you a cold and comfortable wash, because you are going to get burned like a dry bush. Then you will tell me about what really happened in that yard. You will tell me all the names otherwise I will go to the police and give those names myself, including yours. I know what's going around the bell tower. It's enough, ok… it's enough,' said the master with angry loudness in shame with disgust. 'Nobody ever came to my house and created a scene like this. Ever! Ever! It's all because of you, you worthless shit. You and your M.G.R. movies. It is going to destroy your life!' he screamed even louder.

Ever since that day, nobody called Jana names. They never fought. Mostly they did not want Jana getting punished at home as well, knowing the temper of Mr. Prahash, mainly his reverse psychology disciplining that amazed Jana. That day when Jana came home, Mr. Prahash said: 'I did not hit you that hard. So why did you cry?'

'I was embarrassed in front of the whole street, that's why,' said Jana.

'You were not embarrassed when you lost a fight were you?' said Mr. Prahash.

'No, I never lost the fight. Never. I fought back angrily,' said Jana. 'Yes I did, until they all jumped on me.'

'All right, calm down. You must have made them all angry with some silly notion of yours, I am sure. All right, you won.'

All the girls and some visitors in the house laughed. Jana also laughed at the insanity of it all and went around the house to get a wash from the well, giving a smile to his sisters and telling them, I will get you all later.

"A PETERITE IS A NOBLE MAN"

UPPER COLLEGE

St Alcuins Bombed Roof... 90's

Public Cannings in the 70's

ST. PETER'S

CHAPTER FIVE

KILLING OF THE BRAVE

Jana was lying in the front room during one of his house arrests by his father at their Chundikuli residence. He looked out through the welded design handmade metal window grill, thinking about Bankshall Street friends and his beloved cousin Indhiran. He just couldn't forget, even though it all seemed to be a distant past. The day, while they were looking for action in Kurunagar, had changed both cousins. He just wanted to close his eyes and begin to see the colorful picture moments of the Jaffna main street nightlife to bring back the happy days.

The road still had the resemblance of old Dutch/Portuguese architecture. The decaying and less maintained buildings did give the effect of present day communist Cuba. It looked like a European filmmaker's paradise for location and weather. The personalities of that street varied from photographic studio creatives, funeral parlor embalmers, radio mechanics, members of the gambling clubs, skilled gold merchants, bakeries, grocery storekeepers, night café owners, and the hotel bars. All had interesting regulars of addictions. *What is the news of the last wedding photo shoot in the Lyla studio? Who was that? That must be the bride's mate and the page boy. Who died when? Who shot who? Who won the Derby? How much the current gold price on the market?* Meanwhile, in view, they melted it by hand holding the miniature pieces. Voice of America, BBC World Service was constantly interrupted by the radio mechanics looking under the heavy magnifying glass, working on those large hand-built TV sized wooden antique radios. In the bakery, the man behind the large oven the size of a huge garage, baked bread and cakes which gave a great fresh smell all around the main street. It was the place to be to get the good and the bad news. They all loved their drinks, shop holders and the customers. This was their social corner. Sport fans got the updates from the short wave radio fixed outside, especially with races and cricket reports all night.

The bookies stayed open all night due to the time difference. They would try to work out the Ceylon Racing Board printed copy of Sporting Life, all bonded up on a heavy board put up on a huge table at a slanted position with the high stool nearby, to help the punters study the history of the handicaps in detail in a comfortable position. The old boys would sit there with their Gandhi glasses and work out the weights, ground, course, age, fillies, colts, trainer statistics, jockey statistics, track advantage, draw advantage, ground advantage, good, soft, firm, heavy, claiming jockey (claiming advantage), apprenticeships, winning jockeys, sprint trainers, middle distance trainers, jump jockeys, jump trainers, fences, hurdles, Grand National, death of a horse, injury to the jockey, Lester Piggott, Bob Champion, Sea Biscuit, Red Rum, Shergar, all had the mysteries to interest.

The politics, the thieves, rebels, rich and poor, also the

king and the sheikhs: that's what made the horse racing interesting as a king's sport.

Jana, who loved horses from a younger age, asked his uncle Thass for a few details about racing while standing behind him in the bookies.

Uncle Thass warned: 'You two never come here again. Ok? I will explain but if you come back your daddy will be here behind you.' He shouted: 'Look! He is over there.'

We were both stunned for a minute. Then he laughed. 'Then I will have to explain to him about his son's interests.' He smiled. He had the gambler's sense of humor, even when he had lost a few rupees from his wages. He always smiled, unlucky fool. They all liked a little flutter on the local elections and in the classics. Some of them did not take the losing very well. They went straight to the hotel bars and drank on credit. Then went home and took it out on their wives and kids with physical violence.

Jana vividly remembered when they decided to move on to the funeral parlor house back through the door entrance. There were a few corpses being embalmed, some identifiable, some not. The angle they could see from when they sneaked up was a side profile of a fat bloated obese old man who had died of heart failure. The embalmer, Malcolm, was always drunk on jobs to avoid the gory details of the decaying body. As rigor mortis set in, the hardening body needed careful handling with sharp surgical instruments and gallons of formaldehyde to make the body presentable for the grieving families.

He asked his assistant for another glass of that good stuff please. While the glass was being filled with brandy, the embalmer pumped the fluid from the dead body. Then another small incision with the scalpel, three more litres of fluid in the suction bottle. After drying the whole body from his suction, he cleared the last with tubal suction to the unreachable areas, and then he opened the abdomen all the way up to the sternum. Like open heart surgery with laparotomy. *He was always a little too ambitious*, said the boss. But the man was with years of experience including a year in Vietnam. He swabbed all the ill fated body and also pointed out the myocardial infarction of the heart. This caused the death of this old man. His knowledge of anatomy was quite remarkable. After cleaning the body extensively, he would begin to stuff the formalin soaked cotton swabs to create a balanced body all over. Turned the bloated body into a well presented one by quickly clipping and sawing along the incision so as to make it accommodate the space in the allocated coffin chosen by the relatives along with suit and shoes. White gloves for the hands, nylon socks, tight collar shirt and tie with adequate support inside leg to keep the trousers balanced with shoes. It was some experience for Jana and Indhiran.

The embalmer said: 'Assistant. Can you put a bandage above the head? Come around and down and tie under the chin tight please. The chin is dropping, making the mouth wide open. We may have to work with some staples if it's difficult to keep it together. The relatives insisted on no visible metal and they wanted a smile too. So we really have to get it right this time, until it's all perfect for viewing,' said the man with the knife. Everybody agreed.

Jana and Indhiran had already rubbed the wicks on their noses, while pinching and breathing through the mouth and tasted the formalin in their tonsils.

Indhiran felt sick and said: 'It's time to get out. Let's get out, you wanted to see it. You have done it. You don't want it any more do you?'

Jana shakes his head and said: 'No, no, no. Let's get out. Let's go to Rio perhaps. We need to get some fresh air, on the roof?'

Jana and Indhiran as usual find a way in via their pole to their secret place without any trouble. It was their biggest secret and life's major discovery at that time for the cousins. They kept it that way for a long time.

Every Friday when the sun set at Pannai sea front, some groups of old bikers, on their BSA or Triumph, still looking for speed through the Beach Road, pass the police quarters slowly then increase the speed when they turn under the Jaffna Fort, where the road separated to Kytes Island and the other to the right back to the town centre at the beginning of the Pannai Road south. The Pannai Road separated east of Jaffna and the west of Kytes waters. The road had four circle sections of 200 yards apart of the mile long road cutting the gulf of Pannai. It had had half a circle on each side, allowing the vehicles to move in, and let the oncoming big lorry or bus to move past easily, while the heavy wind blew from both sides. Amazingly, rarely had there been any turnovers at Pannai Road. Speed was maximum of 25mph.

Right under this circle bridge water, the boats and trawlers to Kytes journeyed from one side to other, and the returning boats from the both sides avoided any collision under the road bridge. Boat trips under the bridge was a regular sight, due to the calm and shallow waters of Pannai. Some half naked local slum boys with their huge poles pushed deep and walked down the canoes slowly on the waters to catch the surfacing fish in the moonlight near Karainagar. The southern tip of Jaffna Gulf facing the Arabian Sea and Indian Ocean was lit with no clouds as the orange globe sank in the distance into the blue ocean. Everybody watched the sun set at Pannai, especially while looking forward to the full moon Poya holiday weekend. Ice cream vans would park at the half circle and do good business. Passing small cars and motorbikes would pull up and watch the still ocean in the distance while they devoured a chocolate cream.

Jana and Indhiran sat on the roof and watched the moment with great pleasure. Unlike anybody else, they had the upper deck hospitality suite in Kurunagar.

Jana pointed to Indhiran: 'Look over there. Our college senior math master Dr. Rance with his pipe. He rides his motorbike everyday to the beach like a ritual and smokes the pipe on the half circle. He must love the ocean. I also heard he is a tough teacher to study with. I don't want to do math when I pass my O level, said Jana.

'I know who you are talking about,' said Indhiran, 'you heard it wrong. Don't worry, you've got a few more years to worry about that.'

Jana quickly worked that out and said: 'Hmmm. Two years and two months.'

'There you are, you are good at your math,' said Indhiran promptly. Both smiled and moved in to hide as the darkness set on the lagoon. They moved behind the minute burial oven-like grills above the town hall roof, lined up in hundreds, which looked great from a distance all around the building roof grill work. Jana and Indhiran decided to lie flat and watch the sky. Some clouds from the north moved downwards and looked as if they were swirling around on the roof. Jana and Indhiran felt tired as the cinema crowd down below gathered momentum for the late night show at the Rio Cinema. Both fell asleep for a moment, and were awoken up by the screaming black crows from the beach with small fish in their mouths as they landed on the roof next to the boys. They also seemed to want a quiet corner like Jana and Indhiran to enjoy their catch. Jana and Indhiran gently squeezed into the window away from the prying eyes. That window could not be locked. But it could be opened from inside and outside. It was for the roof dorm repair and for the monthly cleaning inspector to take care of. Jana and Indhiran never left any food, wrappings of chocolate or monkey nuts shells on the roof. Jana also squeezed a few drops of singer sewing machine oil, from Aunty Ruby's table, on the window mechanism to avoid the creaking noise. The intermission was over now. Now it was the newsreel and film trailers. That was the best part of their free show. Jana's favorite newsreel during the seventies was the function of Peterborough Railway Junction and the development of the Cambridgeshire Countryside. That day they also watched a documentary on the building and completion of the London BT Tower. That was a landmark building of the seventies. It looked like the handle of Obi Wan Kanobi's green ray-sword in Star Wars. They watched that with real interest. It had a revolving restaurant on top of the tower to enjoy the view of London all around while you were having your luxury meal. Jaffna's maximum highest floors at that time were just four floors. The boys just could not imagine how it would look from the top of the BT Tower or the Empire State building in New York City. But they did realize one day if they got a chance to see that, that would be their dream. The ultimate dream comes true being on top of the world.

The crowd came back in slowly after the break inside the cinema hall after the intermission. Jana and Indhiran moved back out to the open carefully overlooking the police quarters to the west. Opposite the notorious holding rooms and offices of the Jaffna Police, to the right side, the Jaffna Stadium foundation were just being built near the park and the library. There was no security in the town hall, due to the close proximity of the police station. The council workers' south gate closed at seven in the evening. Only the police station side west gate opened for the cinema audience and staff. Mayor Fred Dee was a big fan of the Sri Lankan Freedom Party (S.L.F.P.) government. There were a few attempts to assassinate him. According to the government, some Marxist students burned his office because of his popularity. But the real reason was Fred Dee's lack of responsibility regarding the dead and injured Tamils during the Tamil Cultural Research Conference earlier that year and which had forced him to go underground and play hide and seek. He had been warned by the opposition parties in Jaffna, to resign immediately or leave the country. One morning, around 10.30 a.m., while the Mayor was having breakfast with his friend at 2nd Cross Street, which was near the Portuguese quarter among all the cafes and bars, a bomb exploded in a car. Everybody was stunned by the sound. It was Fred Dee's car. Apparently he was saved by a passing graduate who stopped the mayor and begged him for a job. The Mayor promised the youth a lift (elevator) operator/receptionist job in one of the newly built minister's halls of residence near a sea front, where he entertained the Colombo Government officials with Jaffna hospitality. That's how Fred Dee created job and opportunities for everyone including the hookers. Fred Dee pulled all the strings in the S.L.F.P government ministries. Madam Prime Minister delivered at all times.

Informing traitors pointed the finger at a college youth called Rajah Kumaran. He was arrested that evening as a suspect bomb maker.

When Jana and Indhiran were on that roof of Rio cinema, the off duty policemen with sweaty vests and trousers were kissing their girlfriends and dancing in the holding rooms. Jana and Indhiran looked at the fat boys and laughed, because they lacked rhythm in their moves.

Indhiran said: 'Quiet. Quiet. Look there. Just quietly ok? Otherwise we will be in a big kaka today, Jana. Quiet please.'

Jana ignored Indhiran and said: 'Look at those degenerates, enjoying total freedom away from complaints and internal affairs. I feel like joining them, joining the good life.'

'You will join anybody just for the girls, Jana,' said Indhiran.

'Look at their lifestyle, total freedom and if you are a sadist, you get to beat and rape prisoners. Free cinemas, drinks, travel, good wages with bribes and retirement abroad somewhere nice and rich.'

Indhiran said: 'Just shut up, will you.' He looked nervously at Jana with a little fear in his eyes. 'Look at this, stop preaching and watch this. Something heavy going on here tonight.' He pointed to the police station. While all the off duty police were outside watching and laughing with girls, the Assistant Superintendent of Police (ASP), came out and said: 'Come on everybody, off you go, all of you now, off you go to your quarters.' Everybody staggered slowly and walked away. Jana looked at the three brand new green Jeeps. One big truck drove into the yard. There were a few civil officers with guns.

'That's the fourth floor crew,' said Indhiran. 'I think they are very excited about the capture of the car bomb suspect. They have got their first political prisoner. He also could be a leader of the new Youth Tamil Movement. They want to crush it all from the beginning, so they send a team from Colombo. I am sure some Tamil traitors are in there too, disgustingly,' said the politically clued up Indhiran. 'Who is about to strike the first blow?'

Jana said: 'We had better go now, come on.'

'No way,' said Indhiran, 'maybe this is the last time we are going to come here, Jana, but I am going to see what they are going to do to this poor guy.'

Jana calmed down for a minute. 'Let's think about it all right. What happens if the student movement arrives here in a crowd and there's rioting? Let's say the police order a curfew and block all the roads. Are you going to sleep here all night? Think about it you fool. Ok. Half an hour then we will go. Ok. Half an hour,' said Jana and looked above at the clock tower above the park.

Indhiran said: 'Sit down, you fool. Half an hour,' he pointed at the clock tower. He was unusually angry. By now, the suspect was tied upside down by the ankles. Somebody quickly worked on his heels as Jana and Indhiran heard the cracking noise fifty yards away from the station walls.

'Torturing bastards! My god, he is bleeding from his legs all the way down,' said Jana.

Rajah Kumaran screamed: 'Amma... aa... Mother.'

Blood came pouring from his heels all the way down to his head dripping from his thick dark hair.

'What's your name?'

He replied: 'Raj... k... ku... ma...' Then he did not say anything afterwards. He hung unconscious upside down. One officer lifted his and said, *he is out. Yeah, that was quick,* said another. Someone came with a bucket of water and poured it on his head. He suddenly woke up and asked for water. They cut him down and he fell to the ground with broken angles, screaming *Ahhhhhh… amma…*

Jana and Indhiran saw all from the roof top. A blue VW Beetle car pulled up in front of the police station. He looked like a lawyer for Rajakumarn. He argued with the ASP pointing out that he wanted to see his client.

The ASP said it was *a national security issue. It's out of our jurisdiction. We have no power. Colombo security officers are here in charge.* The lawyer pointed out, *I know what you are doing. He will have to go to court tomorrow, if you are keeping him here. He better be in good shape. Any scratch on him, you are all finished, sir. It will be in all the papers. You will have youth revolt in Jaffna. You will have no case, so be careful,* he said as he smiled and looked confident as the crowding torturers begin to rush him.

The lawyer got back in his car and screamed, *no evidence, no evidence, sir,* and drove out, having failed to see his client. Somebody wrote down his car number plate as he drove away. *The mayor is responsible for this,* said the lawyer on the way out. *Call him tomorrow,* said the police. He walked back and said, *he tried to kill the bloody mayor. What happens if he does die? Who you going to call then,* said the police chief. He went straight back to his room. Made a phone call. Laughed while talking. Put the phone down and went down to see Rajah Kumaran's state. *What happened?* He looked at Rajah Kumaran who was blood everywhere, shivering on the floor with the shock. *Ok, clean him up, I mean clean him up, not clean him to death,* said the ASP. *He has to be in court looking all healthy tomorrow. After that you can do whatever you please. Take him to Colombo. I don't want him here giving us all the trouble. We like Jaffna the way it is.* After the ASP left the room, they gave him a cup of water then slapped Rajah on the back of his head and said, *you will be dead in a few days, so enjoy your last days and your meals.* Rajah- Kumaran said nothing as the tears came. He tried to drink the water.

Jana and Indhiran had seen enough, with their wet palms and frozen in fear and shock, they just couldn't even look up or outside. The pole down below looked very far and looked hard to climb down. Indhiran shook Jana's body while they climbed down. Jana was scared and shaking from the experience.

'Hey listen, Jana. Are you ok? Hey, you don't tell this to nobody, I mean nobody. We are not coming here anymore. Just have a last look at this as a bad dream.'

Jana felt like he had just woken from a nightmare. He shook his head in acknowledgement and fear, hardly holding on to the pole.

'The times are changing around here,' said Indhiran. He stood up without fear and started to smell his hand. Jana pulled him down and said *let's go.* They climbed down and this time they never looked for anything, they just wanted to get down from the top, it looked so high above the ground. They walked out casually, then ran hard down the main road without looking back.

The movie, The Passage, was showing then in Rio and also a film about SS Nazi torture. The Jaffna police officers did it better than the SS with no regrets. All the youth who were near the colleges were randomly stopped and searched, arrested and beaten that week. Jana and Indhiran did not speak for days and both fell sick and did not go out for a week. Later that week Rajah- Kumaran appeared in court accused of the attempted murder of Mayor Fred Dee. The mayor had friends in the legal system and they had their own plan. The authorities really wanted Rajah -Kumaran dead and buried. Tamil human rights lawyers fought hard with the evidence of torture and asked the case to be moved to a different court inland, almost switching judge and jury at the same time. It worked. The degree of torture and the broken ankles, missing teeth, severe and internal bleeding exposed after the first independent medical examination was enough for the judge. The case was thrown out of court with no evidence. Rajah-Kumaran was free. There was a big student movement waiting outside to greet Rajah's exit. He came out of the courts, spoke to the students, with great difficulty, taking deep breaths in between movements. His hands were all swollen and looked as if they had been crushed by a hammer.

He looked up and said: 'There is a major torturing squad in Jaffna, all the way from the fourth floor Colombo. The notorious interrogation department, renowned for their torture, needles in nails and skin graft without anesthetic, are some of their known trade mark sadist activities.' He continued: 'I don't want anybody to get hurt, there are lots of traitors amongst us, some of them right here, right now.' Everyone looked at each other. 'I want to be alone, to fight my freedom alone, and I will never get caught alive again.' He promised on his mother's soul. 'This is my promise to you all. Don't trust anyone, fight your own wars, your own way. Our dream is equality and freedom for Tamils. If everything fails we have no choice but to take up arms, fight until our last breath for our mother land. Go on, go on. Look after yourself,' he said.

The students were confused. But Rajah- Kumaran had begun to think like the police. There were lots of plainclothes officers watching every movement of Rajah and his friends. The students dispersed on their bicycles and drove away in different directions, through the narrow lanes. Rajah-Kumaran was picked up in an Austin Somerset v8 which sped via the crossroads and blew red earth dust everywhere, the police following them for a few miles. Then they just could not keep up with the local jungle knowledge of the getaway driver. Rajah- Kumaran jumped off in a busy market and left the wheelchair on the road. With old fashioned wooden crutches of solid mahogany under his arm, he hobbled through the market vegetables stalls. Then a small hut opened at the fish shop full of nasty smells of fish waste, and Rajah passed the crutches and then squeezed through and he was gone. The workers covered the hole with dirt, fish fins and waste. The police ran all over the market and looked for him and smashed all the stalls.

'The bastard is gone', one said. 'No way, he can't be with those broken ankles.' He kicked the wheelchair with his foot. 'He can't be.'

Rajah stayed under that fish shop for two months. He received morphine for pain and anti-inflammatories stuffed in fish. The doctor dressed like a fishmonger and treated his leg. All this was organised by the students.

Then one day, dressed like an old lady carrying a pot of water on his head, he walked out of that market village.

Rajah-Kumaran went into his rebellion operational duties alone.

His later attempt to assassinate the chief of police failed due to his gun misfiring in front of the torturer. Officers jumped out of the Jeep in panic. Rajah- Kumaran jumped into the deep lily pond along the river and swam away with the motor cycle inner tube while everybody cheered and booed at the police. None of the officers took the chance of jumping and getting tangled in the dark green algae with the Lotus reed roots. The chief was disgusted with his crew and himself.

He later took it out on his own men saying: 'You cowards. No one jumped in the river. Not a single one, call yourself officers! Look at you, all unfit, overweight, can't even run a mile. Tomorrow I want everyone at the central grounds at 5 a.m. We are going to work on some of your fitness levels with miskin. Do you understand?'

'Yes sir, said everyone.

'Come on, get in, let's go,' said the Chief of Police to the Jeep driver.

Later that week, Rajah -Kumaran lay in wait at the bridge in the northern peninsula. Then he jumped in front of Fred Dee's car. The driver slammed on the brakes on the Hillman Minx. Rajah- Kumaran fired the first shot, it ricochet on the driver's side, the second misfired, the third one fired as the driver accelerated away. Rajah- Kumaran stayed on the ground on his knees firing his gun in vain at the passing car windows. Nobody was hurt. Fred Dee escaped without a single shrapnel wound. The driver was given 100 rupees for his bravery.

Rajah- Kumaran screamed: 'Muruha, the Hindu god, help me. Help me to kill these torturers and murderers. Help me,' he cried lying in the middle of the road, banging in anger the homemade gun on the ground. Then he threw the gun under the bridge. Some kids ran down to get it.

He shouted: 'Don't! Don't get hurt. It is no good. It is no good,' shaking his head.

The kids stopped for a minute. Then ran down in a hurry to look under the bridge. It was full of dried bushes and chemical sludge green waste, with dark black sandy mud. The kids still jumped inside to look for the gun while getting covered in the dark mud. Rajah looked at kids down below him, like dark statues, and felt for their future.

The police announced it on the radio, giving details about the most wanted assassin of all Jaffna for murder and attempted murder. They reported that one police officer was hurt during that attempt to kill the Chief of Police. The S.L.F.P Government bloated with laughter about how disorganized the rebel movement was. They also arrested all locksmiths and metal workers around a five mile radius of the incident and burned all their workshops and homes, destroying the ancient tools and handmade machinery which had passed down the generations. All went up in smoke as a warning to workers to avoid any collaboration with the radical youth of Jaffna. The Tamil politicians would not support Rajah-Kumaran's fight against police brutality. They made that clear publicly. At that time, apart from Father Selva, all Tamil politicians were opportunistic and corrupt. All were power hungry, collaborating with the government behind the scenes. It was well known to the public.

Now the police branded Rajah-Kumaran as a thief and a killer. He was broke and helpless, most wanted and was hiding in the forests without food for weeks sometimes. He borrowed money from his close relatives, bought an ex-police Bulldog revolver, British made, with six chambers. He tied that around his neck on a hard thin rope. He would cycle down in disguise onto all the main roads to observe police routine and presence. One morning Rajah came on his bike dressed like a priest with glasses and a hat with a nun next to him, gave some fireworks to a youth who was playing around.

He said: 'There is a wedding at 10.00 a.m. Can you put those big ones on a tree. Then ask the other kids to ring the church bells at the same time. It's an open church, anybody can alert anybody by ringing the bell.'

He gave them a few rupees for their help. The kids said

thank you father and god bless you. An hour later about, 9.50 a.m. he walked into a bank in broad daylight. The kids rang the bell. They were 10 minutes early. The fireworks started. Rajah-Kumaran shot the knees of the first policeman to take the long rifle in his hands. He shot the officer inside in the hands when he attempted to reach for the gun. The staff and customers dropped to the floor without any prompting. While the fireworks crackled and the bells rang, Kumaran looked up and smiled at the standing manager.

'Come on, you know who I am. I rob banks and kill police according to the papers. That's why I am here, and you know what to do. Otherwise I will kill you,' said Rajah. 'Don't waste my time, can you hear the bells and the fireworks. I have got no time, I have got a wedding to go to. It is a poor church wedding, no ceremonies. It is my daughter Chandra. Not mine, like my daughter I mean.I am the parish priest in charge of the ceremonies. I want them to live happily ever after,' he smiled at the manager who quickly topped the table with notes without any hesitance. Rajah- Kumaran looked at him and wondered why the manager was so eager to give it all to him.

He said: 'That's enough! I don't need a lot, you keep some. You love money, don't you? It is only a small ceremony.'

He shot up in the air with the police rifle as he came out. Nobody was outside. Very quite. Dead silence.

The kids came out of the churchyard after ringing the bell. They were chased by the real priests. The kids saw the father on a bicycle, carrying guns and 100 rupee notes flying in the air with a Prime Minister's face and the Buddhist Wheel of Peace design. Rajah threw a few rupees in the air for the kids. Suddenly the kids realized it was Rajah- Kumaran.

They screamed: 'Police! Police are behind the church waiting for you. Run Rajah! Run.'

Rajah -Kumaran threw the big gun away and rode down the green paddy field walking path. The Jeeps couldn't go there. The kids ran the other way, climbed the trees and watched it all from the distance.

In numbers, the police surrounded the village and the town, blocking all roads. They wanted to catch him with evidence. They had advised all the banks in the area knowing that Kumaran had no money. That it was inevitable he would be robbing a bank sooner or later. The tip had come from the politicians trying to make a deal with the government. This time the police waited in line, on the muddy paddy field moving the paddy side to side looking for their prey. They fired the gun randomly all around. The kids could see it all from the tree.

Rajah-Kumaran was shot. Rajah- Kumaran fired back. Then his gun was empty. He had run out of ammunition. He was bleeding on his thigh. He fell in the middle of the red earth of purple weed flowers surrounded by the rice paddy field.   The chief looked at his face close and said: 'Son, you are not leaving my sight this time. You belong to me now. You are my promotion. This time I will take special care of you.'

They dragged Rajah-Kumaran by the legs, face down through the mud. The kids watched the whole event with sadness and tears. They took him in the Jeep and pressed on his gunshot wound with boots. Rajah-Kumaran looked at everybody, smiled and spat at them without fear and said:

'You dirty sons of bitches. You will never have me. Never.' He spat again at the officers. One officer tried to jump on him. Another one pulled him off and said *calm down.*

Rajah- Kumaran looked at everybody for the last time and

closed his eyes and said: 'Mother, forgive me.' Those were his last words. When Rajah-Kumaran lay there wounded with bullets, he had taken a capsule of cyanide and swallowed it. As he had promised, he would never again be caught alive. He was dead in the Jeep on the way to Jaffna hospital. All the officers looked shell-shocked. They quickly took the 100 rupees from his pocket and shared it among themselves, keeping some of it for the chief in front and said: 'Sir, the evidence.'

He looked at it with anger and disgust. Then he put the money in the glove compartment. The driver also looked at the greedy police stealing. The ASP told the driver to turn his head front.

'Shame all that money in that paddy field somewhere, may be in the deep well. The farmer is going to have a good harvest this year,' said the Chief and looked at the dead body. Holding the phone close to his mouth, he spoke on the radio to headquarters: 'No need for surgery. No need for surgery. Get ready with the medical officer and the coroner. No officers hurt apart from the two reserves in the bank. Inform the papers Rajah Kumaran died while robbing a bank, shot by a hero police officer.'

Jaffna was in a high tension alert. A few minutes later the Ceylon Broadcasting Corporation announced the news:

'We interrupt this program for a special government security announcement. Rajah- Kumaran, the so called Tamil bandit and bank robber, was gunned down in Jaffna during a shootout with police. Two officers were hurt but are doing well at Jaffna Central Hospital. Kumaran's body was found in a paddy field with the sum of 2000 rupees, a further 46,000 still missing from the people's bank. The government is delighted with the news of Kumaran's capture and death. A firefight of this kind taken by our government officials shows the beginning of eradicating extremism in this country hiding behind the name of freedom fighting. This achievement belongs to our nation's police officers and the Special Task Intelligence Unit of Colombo. Also tonight a curfew will be in place in Jaffna City between 6 p.m. and 6 a.m.

Jana, Indhiran, Grandma Joan and all the family stood next to the radio shops and listened to the news.

Grandma said: 'There were a few robberies recently in the news. I don't know who and why all these happened. Now they say he was shot. Is that what really happened? Who knows the truth. Only God will have the answer for all our troubles. He has closed his eyes for a long time.' She breathed heavily.

'They tortured him so he decided to take revenge,' said Indhiran.

'Who tortured who? Were you there?'

'It's blood for blood, grandma,' said Indhiran.

'Hey! You come here.' Grandma was angry towards Indhiran. 'You study your maths and English that's all. No politics and revolution for you now. You are too young to understand any of it. Half of it we hear from the radio, it's not true. So don't get fooled by the papers and rumors. Jana, you don't speak about this to anybody, especially to your father. He will be here for arguments sake with me,' said grandma.

'No, I won't say anything,' said Jana quietly. 'It's a promise. What's your opinion about Rajah- Kumaran, grandma?' asked Jana seriously.

She walked around the house quietly cleaning and tidying, then washed her hands and came back and sat on her chair. Asked us all to *come here, everybody come.* She looked at everybody. Took a moment.

'Today, one mother is crying for her son. Nobody is going to understand her pain and suffering. No man or politician is going to understand that. She is the only one who knows how bad it feels to lose a child. Kumaran took his chances, made up his mind, made his decisions. Maybe some others interfered with his decisions and did it for him wrongly. Now she has to live with that loss all of her miserable life, all the time thinking about her brave son and fighter. Her baby son, she carried for 10 months, given birth, washed and bathed, ran to the doctors when he was sick, her only baby is gone. She had a dream for her son to be a doctor, engineer, lawyer, even a bank cashier. He was a clever boy. Brave but it all ended before he became a man. Before he became a father. Stopping the generation with a poison, a full stop. For that poor woman the bereavement is going to be hard and long. So all of you ask yourself, has he done the right thing? For her sake, has he? Politics is tough, not for everybody. Not if you are emotional and spiritual. Politics involve corruption, crossing the line, doing what you promised not to do. Lots of do-gooders nowadays want to serve the people. But they all had agendas behind their political game. Power, greed and popularity are the main cause of all our downfall. Most of them don't know how to even talk politely. You can see them when they say their condolences with real sadness. Who are they trying to fool. They can't even speak the truth to their own mothers. How can we trust them? Rajah Kumuran could have been a good, passionate leader of the Tamil cause. His sacrifice was brave, but ended with humiliation of his soul. God will rest his soul in heaven. What do we know about right and wrong? Is there right and wrong in this world? The very hideous immoral inhuman beings, who put him through this WILL PAY! God will look after them, not

179

today, not tomorrow but when the time comes, we will all have to answer for our sins. That's all, we are not going to talk about this any further. This is a sad day for the Tamils,' she finished. 'And stay quiet for a moment.'

We all sat and listened like dolls in a china shop. Grandma mumbled: 'It is really bad for us, bad for every Tamil, bad for business, bad for food on the plate. Poor boy got tortured and died like this. Not good. It's not going to finish here, oh no. It's just a beginning.' She took a deep breath and said: 'There are going to be more Rajah Kumurans who will come out fighting. The papers are going to be full of news. I can't even read properly, only the big letters. You two be careful, watch yourself, stay out of it. I know you two are peeping through the key holes.'

Jana and Indhiran looked at each other and mimed - not me, I never said nothing. Indhiran was fuming.

'People told me that you have been hiding and watching it all. Trying to put your noses where they do not belong. Shame on you, Jana. I am surprised at you. Watching dead girls embalmed.'

Both boys sighed relief and looked at each other.

'I don't want you two to go anywhere near that funeral parlor. Indhiran, if you are doing any wreathes, once it is done I want you here or home. If I ever hear that you are buying cigarettes for Malcolm, that will be it, you will never come here or talk to me. If you ever had a love for your grandma, stay out of that trouble. Go on now, that's enough action for one day.'

'What do you think?' said grandma sometime later. 'Always researching everything and dreaming.'

'Go on, who?' asked Aunty Ruby.

'Who else? Jana,' said grandma. Everybody in the house laughed.

Outside the house, the boys laughed at each other... dead girl's body... they repeated... dead girl's body ha ha...

'She was no girl, she was 65!' said Jana.

Some students rode past Indhiran and Jana on bikes which had black flags.

'Come on, let's go!' said Jana and Indhiran together. 'Let's hire a bike'.'

They followed the flags all the way to Jaffna Hospital. They all learned the real truth behind the death of Rajah-Kumaran. Some cut their palms and marked their heads saying they will take revenge. They gave flags to the shops to fly above the door. The angry youth black-flagged all the government buildings during the curfew under the noses of the army and police. The police began to take the flags down in the morning. The Student movement requested the schools, colleges and the university to be closed to pay respect for Rajah.

The only school open that day with armed guards was Sinhala Maha Vidyalaya at Hospital Road. The Buddhist Vikarai was also guarded by the police for 24 hours. The Tamils never, never in their history of struggle, did anything to other peoples' religious shrines. They gave respect to all while their own were bulldozed by everyone who entered their land. They understood how it felt when your town temple crumbled in front of your eyes. It was really hurtful to a religious Tamil. There was always some self-immolation with that loss. Self-sacrifice is the highest reward at the laps of the gods according to Hindu scripture. Even St. Jude in the early biblical times made a self-sacrifice for Christianity and was also the guardian of the Jaffna Gulf.

Our college father rector, with regret, cancelled the public caning for a youth who tried to leak the college English test paper. We understood he entered the clerk's office and stole from a sealed envelope. He just couldn't get the stolen envelope back. The teacher adjoining the class of the rector's office noticed the youth suspiciously coming out of the office, and reported it to the father rector. It was foolish, they were all well prepared with past papers and techniques to tackle an extended essay. Some did not get the help on the critical reading and writing or have extra money to go for private tuition classes. Some took it to another level. It is also turned out to be the exam of the advance level economics paper. So that made it even worse. The government papers arrived on the day of the exam in the early morning, dropped off by a rider escorted by the motorcycle police, just as a deterrent. Exam phobia gripped the nation. Our teachers were obsessed with exams every six months. The country had stories of the leaked paper. Some sold to the highest bidding TV news companies. The schools rated each student every year giving prefectships. Personal gallantry badges were unpopular but students were afraid to speak out. They were in the grip of the priests. The teaching methods lacked in practical explanation and application towards what they were learning. They did lots of homework without knowing why they were doing it. They were fed like ducks with the rich corn through a tube, for a rich liver meat. Some did not like the methods of the priests. They drifted with their own plans unable to talk about their worries to anybody. Public caning was a disgrace but still being practiced. It was unacceptable. Public humiliation followed them outside the school. They were powerless. Because of Kumaran's death, a student was just named and shamed, not caned, only just managing to avoid the six lashes. The people behind this corrupt comedy were mostly trouble-making well loved high achievers, liked by all the teachers and rector. Their names never got mentioned or grassed by the accused during this humiliation. Jana and Indhiran did not care about their exams or the principal. They didn't even play their cricket and football. They all stood at the junction on their bikes holding on to each other and talked about Kumaran. It really affected their outlook on life. It was the early days of revolution.

It all started during the Tamil Research Conference in 1973. That night people gathered in thousands, after the week full of Tamil cultural celebrations, the music, temple events, church blessings, peaceful marches and sporting events like Thinakaran Villah. That evening, after a mass Tamil media alert that a foreign speaker with the credentials of a revolutionary was going to deliver a speech, that was going to wake all the peoples' spirits. People were excited, they all began to trickle through the four main roads: the Clock Tower Road, KKS Road, Police Station Road, and the town lane in between the pond and Regal Cinema. The mass gathering in front of the Old Jaffna Fort worried the police. The gathering was at the exact spot where the secret cow chariot race finished in front of the Brave Lion Hall, during the Thinakaran Villah. All roads were blocked by Marshalls of the volunteer senior students from universities and colleges. Mayor Fred Dee was not involved in the celebrations due to his S.L.F.P. commitments. This was disappointing. There were a lot of political games behind the closed doors. Different larger venues were requested by the student union. Point blankly refused by the authority thereby forcing the people to gather in front of the fort. Madam Prime Minister under pressure from the opposition leader, Fred Dee, was reported as having a spiritual holiday in India. There were so many rumors, no one knew the real story. The

Chief of Police wanted to take matters into his own hands. A few motorcycle officers drove around and reported the estimated crowd and the situation. He ordered the police constables to get into riot gear, with wicker style bamboo shields, helmets and long heavy batons. The police came very close to the event stage which was put up outside the hall temporarily.

The speech was amazing. People learned about their brave history while standing among friends and family. It was quite a moment in Jaffna people's lives. The volunteers begged them to leave it alone. The chief insisted that they had not gotten permission to block the roads, creating chaos around the streets.

'I am going to stop this meeting immediately. Or you stop it now, we can all go home happily,' said the police chief. The students pleaded that they were trying to contact the mayor and he was not available.

'This is not my problem. You and your mayor. I have orders from the top to put a stop to this meeting immediately.' He said to a youth: 'Move out of the way or you are going to get hurt.'

'Attention and march forward. CHARGE!' said the chief. 'CHARGE!' he screamed. More Jeeps joined with more police. They beat everyone. Women and children peacefully listening to the speech were beaten by batons. The people did not understand what was happening. They all ran with their bikes in their hands holding them above their heads, some fell under the stampede, lost children cried alone in the middle of the ground. Some fell in the reeds around the pond full of dark green algae, behind the clock tower. It looked like no other event of nightmare. The people in front of the stage stayed put. The police shot above randomly with their rifles.

The chief said: 'Fire! Fire at the high voltage wires above the crowd near the road!'

The wire came down like a swirling big snake with its tale on fire. Sparks and elements created fire, which landed near the stage on top of innocent civilians.

Nine died on the road, hundreds were injured. Jaffna Hospital could not handle the casualties. The burned bodies were unrecognizable. Completely blackened body parts fell apart. A lot more horrific third degree burns victims were treated in hospital. People ran everywhere in town in fear. They lost possessions: scarves, shoes, slippers, bags, and cycles littered the fort front. Some kids lay unconscious and were helped by the volunteers. Some jumped in the deep canals of the Jaffna fort and had to be lifted by ropes. People were half naked and in shock and sat in the middle of the road. Some gasped for breath and collapsed on the street.

By ten o'clock some youths had bought some petrol, burned a few government building including the S.L.F.P. party office. They broke windows of cars parked on that street. Some were burned. The police did not come out alone that night. They patrolled the street in high numbers in big trucks with weapons. Kumaran wanted justice, said student volunteers who witnessed that massacre.

The Police Chief was promoted and transferred to Colombo. A Public Inquiry found no one guilty but came up with accidental death as a verdict. Families of the victims' were angry at the government. Opposition politicians blamed Fred Dee saying he should take responsibility for the crime. They said he should have been there to make clear passage for his own people first at the Tamil Research Conference. The Tamils also blamed him for letting them down when everybody needed him most. Kumaran had been the only one brave enough to give his life as a first sacrifice.

His funeral was held at his home town and was attended by the Tamil scholars, businessman, poets, artists, students, and some politicians, particularly one who still managed to criticize his methods and also praise him for his sacrifice. The politicians had no shame. They were and are opportunists. Most of them refused to take advice. They acted on their instinct, not knowing the consequences.

In the meantime, a young student from an educated middleclass background of Cutting Port district north, took the torch of Rajah -Kumaran and carried the flame. He detonated bombs around the town when the Prime Minister visited the peninsula. As usual black flags were up on government buildings. The unfit police officers tried to get the flags down but kept on sliding down from the millennium dome. Students had applied cycle grease all around to make any climb impossible. The students watched that mishap from a distant ground and laughed with joy. Someone said *the fools are always slipping down from the top*. The students marched the streets wearing bloodied shirts and red bandanas. Screaming slogans like, *there is no justice, there is no human rights, stop the killing, stop the abductions, stop the standardization* (Tamils had to get 4 A's to get into university whereas the Sinhalese did not have to). Flags of Amnesty were flying high. They marched all the way to Jaffna Fort to pay respect to the nine dead. Flowers were laid, prayers said. Someone shouted: 'TAMIL KINGDOM IS THE ONLY ANSWER!' Everybody joined in the chant. The Opposition Leader sent cameras and photographers from Colombo to show the hatred of the Tamils against the present government. The police followed them everywhere. This time they were up against the well-organized youths on a

186

mission who slipped through the nets with ease. The police officers had egg on their faces.

In 1975 after successfully forming a group, the leader took a trip with two other comrades, to a temple deep north in the jungle region. After being blessed by the Hindu priest who put their holy ashes on their head, and with their blessed flowers and leaves in their hands, they sat by the Banyan Tree and started to enjoy their temple breakfast of holy Saiva, religious food filled with temple flavors and aroma. In the distance, two miles away on a lone street with a few farmers walking with their animals, a car passed them with dust coming out both side of the front tire creating a clear view of the moving vehicle from the distance. All the people at the temple were seriously in prayers but kids ran around, pointing at the car and saying: 'He is coming, he is coming!' The Hillman Minx pulled up near the temple. Three youths moved towards the car. One kid asked: 'Who is he?' Another one said: 'Don't you know? He is the Jaffna Mayor.'

Two men at the front of the car greeted Fred Dee. The leader came in between them and the men fired at him at point blank range, saying this is for the killing and torture of our brothers. Fred Dee fell to the ground. One other official was also hurt. The youths took the driver out of the car. He was frozen with fear and told him he was not getting any money today.

'We are taking your car. You don't mind, do you?' They pointed the gun and said: 'Not a word, ok?

The driver shook the head.

'Not a word. We know all about you and your mechanical and driving skills. Keep your life and get another job. Not a word.'

There was no opposition. Dee had no bodyguards or

police protection. He had been on his usual Friday prayers, away from the city, unprotected. The assassins abandoned the car ten miles from the incident, and walked away. Disappeared into thin air. Even though his popularity had been marred by the death of the nine and Rajah-Kumaran, Dee had still been the most popular mayor of Jaffna in the early years but had made some wrong decisions against the Tamils.

His funeral was held at the stadium he had been building for the city. It appeared half completed in front of thousands of mourners. Jana, Indhiran, grandma and all the family joined in the cremating ceremony of the mayor's body. He left a wife and daughters. They soon became exiles in the Far East.

Since that day Mr. Prahash talked with friends and family whenever he got a chance. *Is he a good man or bad man?* Even at the toddy huts he would bring some loud accusations and there would be a few punch ups. Then all would buy another round of drinks until they become legless, cycling on a road left and right managing to reach home just before the curfew.

Nicknamed Croc face, the Opposition Leader, J.R. Jayawardene, won the election with a landslide. Closer to the election he created anti-Tamil national sentiments with long walks giving speeches about the mishandling of the Tamil issues becoming a national security issue. He created fear in the Sinhalese communities. Fear created hatred and violence.

In 1977 Tamils were massacred again in Colombo and up-countries. Thousands were made homeless. Sinhalese thugs robbed the happiness of the hard working Tamils at every opportunity. It became a routine. '*PARRA THELMU!* they screamed and kicked while killing the innocents Tamils away from their heartland Jaffna.All the news were banned.We did not know the real truth until we hear it from close relatives.Jaffna always picked up the pieces and moved on with normal life.That was the tradition. Tamils Never fall fools for the discrimination and ill treatement. Jaffna fought with continuous normality and galantry. House build continued and completed at chundikuli.

CHAPTER SIX

OLD SILVER HAIR LAUGHS AT SRI LANKAN POLITICS

It was a house-warming party at Chundikuli for a change in August 1978. Mr. Prahash and his family had finally moved into the new house after years of hard labor. Mr. Prahash named the house after the Suruvil family who loaned part of the money very generously which kept his dream alive. Especially for his beloved daughters. He came from a humble background in Delft and achieved a house in Jaffna Chundikuli at a tender age of 43 with his government job and three kids. He had proved the point to everybody in the extended family to be positive and fight vigorously for their goals. The house was named GEMSTONE and was blessed by the Hindu and Christian priests. In good traditional style, a big copper pot full of milk boiled in the middle of the house on the floor with the margosa wood fire. The milk overflowed and put the fire out. At that moment everybody clapped and cheered. That represented that the future of that house would be happy and in the lap of luxury. Mum and the girls prepared all the food all day with the help of Grandma

Joan. The taste was unbelievable. The combination of culinary knowledge of the family reflected hospitality of the highest caliber. The female cousins all dressed in traditional Tamil dance costume and served the food and drinks on the silver trays with the sound of the bells on their ankles tinkling as they moved. All the honorable guests were blessed with fire and flower petals on a tray. The blessing began by holding both sides of the double neem (vermbu) door when they stepped into the house. Mr. Prahash lit the front and back garden with florescent light and covered the deep well with metal wire. He just didn't want anybody under the influence of Scotch whisky to fall into the deep well. Even the dog, Mr. Broon, quietly enjoyed the crowd in the corner, whilst sitting on his cushion shaking his tale. Plenty of chicken bones for him tonight. Mr. Prahash also promised Broon he would make a goat broth on the day after the party. He had bought a well matured goat, kept him for a month well fed with rich iron wheat grass and massaged the poor soul for a kill on the day of the house warming celebration. Bananas from his own garden trees ripened just on time. The goat blood breakfast for the overnight sleepers was all planned to every detail. The house was dressed from the home grown mango Thoranum. Banana leaves full of food rituals were displayed with scented oil lambs, coconut shavings, harvested rice, santhanam, kungumum, spices and fire crackers and all went according to the customary order of Hindu and Tamil cultures. A five foot brass floor oil lamp stood in the middle of the house, and the three sections of light with soft oiled cotton represented the unity of the extended family. Hand-woven bamboo chairs with red varnished mahogany frames were a hall seat and gave the classic minimal look. The red terracotta colored cement floor, polished by hand with coconut dust, shined with the reflection of the happy crowd in their multi colored saris with gold jewelry. Everybody had waited for this time to really show and share their jewelry collection.

They waited for Ranga and Vijay Uncles from Colombo as chief guest. Mr. Prahash sat down and held off all the ceremony and eating and drinking until they arrived. The house was very still and quiet.

'Officers and gentleman of punctuality,' said Mr. Prahash when he heard the car noise in the lane and looked at the other guests and smiled. Everybody continued talking and drinking their soft drinks. First Ranga came in his car and pulled up near the porch. His driver got out and picked the bags from the back boot. Mr. Prahash quickly started helping as usual, saying you should not have, politely.

Uncle Ranga looked up at the house and was impressed with his friend's efforts.

'You did all this? Quite amazing.'

'Stone by stone, annai,' said Mr. Prahash. Ranga Uncle shook the hands of Marie Joyce and Grandma Joan with humble Tamil greeting: *Vannakam.*

'Thanks for making the effort to come here and see us during your busy schedule,' said Marie Joyce.

'No, not at all. I wouldn't have missed it for the world. It's a pleasure to see you all together as a family finally, huh. Where is the cricketer?'

'He is standing behind you,' said Mr. Prahash.

'Hey, how are you, all grown up huh? My God. I heard you are an opening bat,' said Uncle Ranga.

'Only on under-seventeens,' said Jana.

'That's ok. Next year for the first eleven my man. Prahash, we must go and watch him play one day, huh?' said Ranga Uncle to Mr. Prahash.

'Well sure, if you wish,' said Mr. Prahash unenthusiastic-ally. 'Ah… Vijayan is here mum…'

Uncle Vijay had moved on from his Austin to a Nissan pickup truck traveler converted to take the extended family on long trips. The blue Nissan came into the house all modified with jade green. Smart Uncle Vijay, with his silk ceremonial westi, Golden Nehru top, heavy gold chain with tiger teeth fixed into it, bent down up to his belly when he walk forward like an injured footballer. He smiled. He sat down and said: 'Murugha,' meaning thank the Hindu god for this house.

Jana was in his element. He called Indhiran and introduced him to Vigi mama.

'He is my cousin.'

Vigi Uncle quickly asked: 'Do you play cricket?'

Indhiran said: 'Jana plays. I just watch. Uncle Vijay, you built the scoreboard at St. Johns right?' said Indhiran. I study at Central. That's at the opposite side.'

Uncle Vijay joked: 'I am not talking to you no more.' Then he smiled coolly: 'What's your name? Chandran?'

'No, Indhiran.'

'It means the same, right? Chandran and Indhiran.'

Mr. Prahash quickly moved in between the boys and said: 'Come on you two, move on and help the ladies. Go. Go.' He quickly introduced Uncle Vijay to Ranga. The two heavy hitters in the Colombo Tamil business had heard of each other but had never met before. They had handled Sinhalese thugs, the army, the police and the politicians very well. The Colombo trade ministry needed worldwide business expertise. These two gentlemen kept their dignity at all times without greed. They were never threatened or blackmailed by anybody in Colombo. Both employed hundreds of

Sinhalese and Tamils without discriminating and with equal opportunities.

The party was in full swing. The food was served. Marie Joyce had made boxes of food to take home for the families who were unable to attend due to the long distances. That was Mr. Prahash's priority. Fresh fruit from the trees, ceremonial sweets and cakes all made for vegetarian Hindu dietary requests. Vijay, Ranga, Aunty Mary in Delft, all families and kids would get their house-warming food one way or another.

Jana's uncles never came. Except Uncle Babe who came late to show his respect to his brother-in-law. Jana asked about Jeyanthi from Granddad Arul. He quickly replied that she also asked about him and gave you the love to be safe until a few more years. Then come and ask her parents to take her away from Delft.

Jana said: 'You are not serious. You are joking, Granddad.'

Granddad had already started on the good stuff in the front room alone behind the scenes. Everybody addressed the whisky as 'good stuff' in Jaffna.

Mr. Prahash came an hour later rushing: 'Come Dad, come, they are leaving, say good will and goodbye. Here is the man. Still in great shape.'

Granddad with a smile approached Uncle Vijay who said: 'I will come and see you with the family one day.'

Granddad replied: 'You are welcome, stay the night, ride the horses on the beach. Your son will love it.'

'The girls will, too,' said Uncle Vijay. 'Ranga, respectfully thank you sir and goodbye. Thanks Marie Joyce and Mum for all the great food for the kids. I am sure they are going to love it.'

On the way out both sneaked an envelope from everybody and gave them to Mr. Prahash.

'I told you, Ranga, no gifts from you. You've done enough in the past for me.'

'No, no. This is something useful. You will appreciate it, come on. You will like it.' He tapped his back. 'You are like the brother I never had,' said Ranga.

Mr. Prahash became very emotional.

'Come on, there are girls,' said Ranga.

Uncle Vijay said: 'Come and stay in Colombo for a week at least. Love to have your family.' He had a big house in Alfred House Avenue, Kollpitya, Colombo 7. Off Galle Road, minutes from the beach. His farms in the Kikaduwa wet zone along the rivers produced meat and rice and had a great harvest for that season. His shipping business was also doing really well. His most recent venture was exporting handmade ceramics to Europe. His family were the first Tamils to export and import to the west on their own ships. He was then working with the Ceylon Ceramics Corporation to make a deal on hand-painted pots, tea sets, plates and display pottery, and museum pieces of Sri Lankan art history.

Uncle Vijay said to Jana: 'Again, if you want to join St. John's let me know.'

Jana dropped his head and smiled.

'I guess that's a no, then,' said Uncle Vijay disappointed. 'Anyway, Jana, come to Colombo, go with Mena Devi Aunty and get all the kit you want. This is your chance. Nice grey Nicholas bat, some proper Gunn and more gloves. Nice pads.'

Jana said: 'Sure, I am coming, soon as I can. I haven't seen Aunty Mena Devi and Rajan for a long time. He must have grown up by now. Is he playing cricket?

Well, he is not that keen or interested in cricket, Jana.'

'I will come and show him some strokes. Get him interested. Sure, I will come.'

'Thanks, Jana, for your enthusiasm.'

'Thanks Uncle Vijay,' he said and smiled with respect.

Jana showed his Uncle that he still had his radio.

As he drove away, Uncle Vijay shook his head in disbelief. He slowed down the car and put his head out and said: 'You remember the day in the hospital with your skirt?' To Mr. Prahash he said: 'He still has the radio. Well done, Jana.'

Mr. Prahash said: 'He sleeps with that…'

'Go on, give us a commentary,' said Uncle Vijay. 'Come on, do it for me… I love it.'

Mr. Prahash said: 'Do it Jana… do it.'

Jana mimicked the radio commentator: 'Kapil Dev from the pavilion begins his run faced by the unbreakable Viv Richard, still chewing his gum, with his swagger with the SS bat, and the Roman nose shined by the hot sun, put that away with ease and effortless stroke. Wow, nobody can stop that. That is a beautiful signal for a four from umpire. A dickie-bird. Why he needed to fall against the fence like that. It was totally unnecessary, he is not going to stop that ever.'

Uncle shook his head: 'What a man, your son. Jana, bye for now. Bye everybody!' and he drove off. He still had the musical horn in the car for fun and he pressed that button. He must have taken it out from the Austin Cambridge and put it in the Nissan.

'Cool,' said Jana with a surprise on his face.

With a house full of home and kitchen presents, Mr. & Mrs. Prahash's family felt as if they had gotten married again. Uncle Vijay had given a voucher for a fridge along with some cash. That was a luxury in Jaffna in the seventies. Ranga Uncle had given a water pump voucher and accessories at his Navatkuli branch for Mr. Prahash's new venture with his brother in Vanni Visvamadu - a chili farm along the river.

Both girls got Adidas sports gear. Jana got a cricket jumper and boots. Marie Joyce got saris from everybody. She was already planning whom she could give them to as Christmas presents. She would of course keep the Kanchipuram from Mrs. Vijayan, the purple and green with liberty aubergine and silver thread edges with peacocks design.

'It's surely a ceremonial piece,' said Marie Joyce, 'bless her.'

Jana was jumping up and down. 'I am going to Colombo! I am going to Colombo!'

Mr. Prahash said: 'First you have to pass the G.C.E. O/L. Then we will see.'

Jana said: 'No problems. The results are out in December. I guess by Christmas we are all in Colombo,' said Jana confidently.

Arul began to laugh again.

'Ok dad, let's settle down. He gave me a bag full of foreign good stuff. Let's look: Martell, Scotch Red, Highland Black, Remy Martin, Courvoisier, Jack Daniels and the best of all come in small packages, Woodford and Grange. Dad, have you tried this, I am sure you did. The best stuff for travelling. Flat bottle, deep dark taste. That man is a saint. Vijayan was really happy for that family name in the front. He is a proud guy. Oh yes. Least I can do for that great family of the north.'

Arul shook his head and lifted his glass: 'Go on, pour, pour.'

Mr. Prahash filled the glass well with Johnny Walker Red.

'Just remembered. Just wait. I got a big ice block in a sack. Need to crush that down with the hammer. Here is to Ranga and the family.' Both men raised their glasses.

They both loved the garden. The Jasmine trees had all come out at the right time.

'Lovely smell,' said Arul.

'I need to go to Colombo personally to thank their wives,' said Mr. Prahash. 'The whole set up for Thomas's farm - who will do that huh? God bless his family and his children.' He looked at Jana: 'So you are coming to Colombo?'

'Yeah, let's go dad, I would not miss that. Vigi Mama promised me cricket gear. Yeah the whole set,' Jana said with excitement. 'You can't afford that with your bank balance, sub zero,' said Jana.

Mr. Prahash said: 'Who is drunk here? Go on son, go to bed. It's getting late. We talk about Colombo tomorrow.'

Grandfather Arul looked great in his late seventies, and still managed his drinks. As he became more and more drunk the time would come when he would come up with great stories. Normally he hardly ever spoke, just laughed. His inside knowledge of politics, with experience of dealing with ministers on the Delft coast, was quite remarkable. He still had some genuine contacts in Colombo when he wanted to find out about political tensions. He valued these contacts with utmost respect. He then advised his friends and family in time to get to safety before the troubles.

So he started talking about the then Prime Minister. He called him the 'croc head'. The 'croc head JRJ'. There would be a lot of character assassinations, all in the name of political satire and fabricated assumptions in regard to the popular news. Jana looked forward to this long night.

'Come here, Jana,' said Granddad Arul.

'Yes, Granddad,' said Jana.

'Come here. Do you know,' and here he lowered his voice, 'who is the leader of the Tamil Congress? I mean who formed it in the first place, Jana?'

'G.G. Ponnambalam,' said Jana.

'Very good, Jana. He is the first one to fight for equal rights. He wanted one half for the Sinhalese, the other half for all the minorities,' said Granddad.

'Muslims, Malays, Indians, Europeans and the Tamils. I don't think that was a good deal for the Tamils, dad. Father Selva put up the best proposal I guess,' said Mr. Prahash.

Granddad said: 'Ok. Listen. Soon after independence, with the complete Sinhalese government,' as he laughed at his son, 'it could have turned out to be a good deal for us. It could have been a good one. Croc face was a hat turner with his mixed Muslim background. He would change his policies day to day.'

Granddad and Mr. Prahash talked at the same time: 'Yes liar, liar, liar. He is green liar.'

'Years earlier he was the do-gooder asking for a multi language media rights from the British. Hypocrite,' said Mr. Prahash.

'He had a big agenda to take the country for the majority Sinhalese. Destroy the Tamils. Pretty much take over the country, greedy fool.'

'Bastard changed so quick with the times while the country was still run by the British and we were still at war with the Japanese. While our business-minded Indian cousins remained neutral. The British did not like that croc face in the ruling party, gagging for power. They did not trust him. They wanted to give it to the educated Senanayake family. Their hunches were always right. Islanders know about the inbred mountain men. They always fought with the Scots, don't you forget. Poor Scots never forgave the English for that bad history.'

'Ha ha. Senanyake. He is the good one. He resigned after the general strike. Poor bastard, blaming himself for the damage,' said Mr. Prahash.

'The post went to his uncle or cousin, I am not sure,' said Granddad.

'Uncle, sir, John Kottewella, caretaker leader.'

Jana interrupted the conversation: 'Is it like your caretaker of rest house Granddad?'

'That's right, Jana. Independence. I don't know what happened in the in-between period.'

"There was a new girl in town: burlesque parties, ceremonies and matchmaking games. Organized by the Kandyan ladies and the Colombo 7 celebrity set with gem dealers.'

'She was no good. Oh yes, no good,' said Granddad.

'Ok, Jana. It's late and time for you to go to bed. Go on, son. Don't get me angry on a good day' (nalla nall and a periya naal).

'It's Saturday tomorrow. I am going to be in the next room anyway. I will hear all your talks,' said Jana.

'No you won't. You will be in asleep in seconds, dreaming cricket. Go on, don't argue on a good day like this son. Like a good boy, go on now. Otherwise someone will get hurt on a good day. That's not a good omen you are crying on the new house. Don't make me mad. I also had some drinks. Think about it.'

'Alright, alright. If it makes you happy I will go. I am sixteen years old now, dad,' said Jana disappointed. That was interesting. Mr. Prahash wanted to talk about the female issues in politics. There would be a lot of swearing and sexually explicit talk. Bad enough three generations sitting in front of alcohol, also talking sex was a little too much and they were getting carried away with the homecoming. One thing though, he knew when to stop even in front of rare good stuff.

Even still, Jana listened through his vented window as the dreamy night talk continued.

Granddad continued: 'So, she met him at the parties. She was young and beautiful. He was much older and clever, Oxford educated with the convent girl barely finished O levels, and who read Mills and Boon day and night. A dreamer.'

'Convinced him about her love. He also planned, with all the Sinhalese Kandyan roots behind him, that he could use her to get the country poor vote. He just did not give a damn about his Tamil Temple Priest background. Who is Tamil?' said Mr. Prahash.

'He just did not know what he was getting into. He went and asked her father for her hand in marriage. Yep, he did that with tradition.'

'She convinced him again to defect and set up his own party. Knowing the croc face was lurking in the party for power playing cat and mouse game with alternative policies. New country is allowed to make a few mistakes, right? We got the brunt of it. Just a few more Tamils got killed. Every time they did that,' said Mr. Prahash. 'They both wanted great policies for the majority Sinhalese. Now she really changed all the equal rights for the minority into no rights at all. Perfect strategy for winning the election. Attack the minority. Bring out the color and race issues and religion and tell the majority we are not going to let the minority take over. Scare the shit out of them with a few isolated incidents in the minority area. The beating of a Sinhalese police officer, that will be enough. Or burning the bakery, more than enough.'

'She drew the map. That convent girl had good family behind her to support her, that's the key. Not to mention the gangster friends. He won the election with the new S.L.F.P party standing next to a pretty girl of culture and sexuality. The man was gone in submission. She played the political cards. The fifties were high times for the ruling family. Fresh from independence. Croc face in opposition. It was real politics all right. The country was in motion. Was he trying to be like Nehru and Ginna?'

'I don't know. It was not his original idea,' said Granddad.

'The Premier wanted to give something back for the Tamils. He was friends with G.G.P. and Selva, I mean the Prime Minister.'

Granddad said: 'First she knelt down and persuaded him to wear the traditional Sri Lankan ruling costume. He really did not like that. The man loved his St. Michael, T.M. Lewin and Saville Row Tailors in London. I think you are right about her doing the kneeling down routine and saying Mathaya, while stroking his legs and looking up at him did the work.'

Mr. Prahash and Granddad both laughed and poured more whisky into their glasses, little by little. Both were quite drunk by then.

Granddad shifted his thin scarf from shoulder to shoulder, while sipping his drink. 'So, croc face, come on let's go for a fight. He did not want the second term go to the new family again. He really brought the shit out, with ethnic cleansing speeches. Sinhalese rights had been taken away by a Tamil background Prime Minister. He accused him of being a traitor, that his family was also full of it and had betrayed the old Sinhalese kingdom, favoring the British.

'Working class Sinhalese believed everything he said. The political podium is a gospel in Sri Lanka. If you can convincingly deliver a good speech with a sweat, you are a fucking saint. Aaah, people wanted a change.'

Granddad shook his head, choking on the strong stuff.

'Careful, dad. Slow down... here, drink some water. Here, some taste of goat.' Marie Joyce had left finger licking food on the table flavored with ginger to ease any abdominal discomforts.

Granddad said: 'S.L.F.P wanted the Tamil votes and in return he wanted to give the Sinhalese a lesson in equality. The Tamil will get to speak their language in the east and the north. That would have been a great start for the Tamils. He was about to sign it. I think he signed it. Then the bitch made him rip it all up. That was it.'

'Croc face turned it around all right. We will never give up the Sinhalese language from the national agenda. Bastard turned the hat again. She probably preferred that policy too. I am sure he was having problems at home with her. He must have a few fights at home with the First Lady. Buddhist monks putting pressure from all angles. The Mahavamsa story tellers feared that he would give it all back to the Tamils, all that the British took.

'The premier marriage was in turmoil. I am one hundred percent sure, a retired police chief used to be a regular to Delft. He still comes once a year. He hated that circle of power and money family politics. Real working class Sinhalese loved the Tamil people. He told me the Prime Minister used to beat up the First Lady with the bamboo cane. That includes the servants, too.'

Mr. Prahash shook his head: 'No. It cannot be true. You cannot be serious. I heard that but I thought it was just a usual Tamil rumor.'

'I am pretty sure. What reason would he have to lie to me? I know the liars. He also beat up the servants with the whips. The youngest in the family was under pressure and wetted the bed. I mean the son. Oh yeah, there were troubles in the family. She made threats, the kids lives would be in danger with your political decisions. He wasn't afraid. At night, loud screams were heard at the Prime Minister's residence in Colombo. She had left the house a few times with her two children leaving the eldest daughter at home as she was the closest to her father. Because the mother blackmailed her husband, saying she was depressed since the birth of her son. He also felt the pain and anguish. I will kill myself etc.'

Mr. Prahash said: 'The daughter, well she understood the father was under pressure from her crazy mother. She was the oldest, right? So the First Lady had left the Prime Minister's residence.'

They both laughed.

'The papers did not get close. Her uncle was an army commander and he had control of the senior police and the intelligence unit. The news would jeopardize his future. Became a national security issue, election was on the horizon.

The monks wanted to muscle in. What was his name? The son? Ruarua. That's it. Ruarua,' said Mr. Prahash.

'Since Ruarua's birth, she dominated on every decision and refused treatment for depression.'

'He couldn't go against her because of the kids. Where did she go?' asked Mr. Prahash.

'Good question. The army commander uncle had all the protection for her family. Then she went alone to see a senior clergy in regard to her depression. It showed her lack of education and knowledge, to talk about family problems to a gossip hungry clergy. Now they really knew what was going on at the Prime Minister's residence.'

'Pretty much gave all the government secrets to

untrustworthy monks. Foolish, very foolish. Never let the women into your business. That's the downfall.'

'She really needed help,' said Granddad. 'She got no help, nowhere else to go. The Prime Minister's wife was nuts - great story. Perfect for the croc face in opposition. She sacrificed for her people with madness, hallucinations, nightmares, sleepless nights. Lost a lot of weight in the process. The people were afraid for her. The people closest to her needed a radical change in their plans.'

'The children were divided and the eldest was with her father while the boy was always with his mum,' said Mr. Prahash. 'What happened to the fat one in the middle? What was her name...? Kacha. Yeah, some name. Who knows Kacha? Oh yes, she was like her mum. Buddhist girl who went to convent to party and play tennis with nuns, movie premiers, hotel bars, and music shows with the upper class. Reading Harold Robins, not Mills and Boon. She was hot to go, one better than her mum. She really did not care what happened at home or in the country, she was in party land, with actors and musicians, frequently travelling abroad to France for trying some Class A drugs. She really did everything. She is the one to watch,' said Mr. Prahash. 'She will massacre all the Tamils one day.'

Granddad interrupted: 'Listen. The monks wanted to have regular meetings at home and in the parliament. They were in and out of the house like ants in a biscuit tin. The Prime Minister would have none of it. He instructed security, don't allow anybody in. I've had enough.'

'So, how did they?'

'The following morning somebody was ill in the servants' quarters. Security called up to say there was a young Buddhist monk at the gate. Thinking it was something to do with the servant, he said *let him in*. There were some fake police officers with hand guns, on motor bikes, also standing at the gates. The monk passed the security gate, then went straight to the verandah where the Prime Minster was sitting down relaxing, not at all worried about security. The Prime Minister asked him had he *come to see Jeyasiri the gardener? No*, was the answer he got. The Prime Minister then looked up in surprise. *Hang on, who are you? I never seen you before*, he said. He told the Monk: *listen, I have already torn the agreement apart, the deal is all gone against the Tamils and in favor of the Sinhalese, are you happy now?* He wrongly thought the young monk was the representative of the Buddhist clergy. Then he saw the security officers rushing from the gates. The motorbike policeman got swiftly away from the gate, picked up the young monk and disappeared. Shots were fired. The Prime Minister said: *I agreed for the Sinhalese language as the national language only. Oh God! You are going to destroy this country.* Shots were fired again. Security fired a few shots. The assassin was gone. It was then a matter of urgency to get the Prime Minster to hospital. His eldest daughter came running out and found her blood-stained father, his hands covering his stomach wounds. *You be a good girl. I love you.* Those were his last words. The First Lady was not at the residence, during the killing. Later she would lie and say that he had died in front of her, in her arms. Screams had been heard the night before at the house.

The Prime Minister had been ranting: *you are going to destroy the country. All the educated and the cultured will leave, you will be left with jungle devils. (Kattu Mirandi) Tamils are going to leave, and they will come back with vengeance one day. Or more economically, they will buy back the companies abroad, who you do business with? They will rule this country from abroad. How is that for a nation building speech? You uneducated fools.* He must have given his last speech to the servants while they shook like leaves behind the kitchen walls. Poor bastards.'

Both men laughed and then paused to think about the Prime Minister dying like that in front of his daughter.

'Come on, let's eat some. My goat will taste good with some string hoppers. You have drunk a lot,' said Mr. Prahash.

'Yeah, I don't feel it, though, because we took our time. Is Jana eating well? He looked thin. I was like that when I had a fever,' said Granddad.

Mr. Prahash said: 'He eats well, maybe a little quickly, and he runs all the time, he must burn it. He runs, plays cricket all day. They are not going to pay him wages for playing cricket in this country. The madness of running. I don't encourage that kind of time wasting.'

Granddad said: 'Just go along with him, he will make his choices when the time comes. Let him do the things he loves. He must have seen people getting jobs in Colombo, doing well. He's still very young, leave him alone. Give him a little independence.'

Jana, half asleep, had heard all the political history and it went into his mind like a great story. He also appreciated Granddad's good words. He had completely forgotten about the presents. Despite his drowsiness, he tried the jumpers, then the shoes. Perfect. The colors and the shoe size were just right.

He looked up in the small mirror, jumping up, jumping up. Granddad and father heard the noise.

'And here we go, he is dreaming cricket now. I don't know what to do with this sports fanatic,' said Mr. Prahash.

Granddad said while eating: 'To finish the story, in 1959 the Prime Minister was dead on arrival at the hospital. More

Tamils died, one Hindu priest was torched alive. In the wake of this troubled time, thousands were beaten on the train if they smelled of gingly oil. As predicted, all the intellectuals, skilled engineers, and doctors left the country. Tamils did not feel safe in Sri Lanka anymore. They caught the alleged monk and hanged him in Velikadai Prison in Colombo. He never spoke. Somebody said they cut his tongue to avoid further damage to the ruling party. He wasn't allowed any lawyer. He was convicted one morning and hanged the next day. The case was shut and closed. It was completely covered up by the ruling family.

'The world media came to Colombo in the wake of our first female Prime Minster, first female such in the world: CNN, AB, NBC, BBC, Channel 4, ITV, Reuters, AIR, RTL, CIA, FBI, MI6, Interpol, all asked questions:

Was he a real monk? Is he a previously convicted criminal close to the Buddhist clergy? Was the Prime Minister killed because he favored the Tamils? Where was the First Lady during the shooting? Was it a coup or inside job? Why Army Uncle did not like the Prime Minister? Why the case never got represented by a human rights lawyer? Is that true, the killer from the same village as his wife? Was the First Lady suffering from depression? Was this the biggest conspiracy in Sri Lanka's short history? A few months later, she was wearing a white sari, with baggy eyes, like a real widow mourning the Prime Minister with a soft smile. Far East friends gave her a Memorial Hall for the Prime Minister. The Sinhalese saw her as a savior of Mahavamsa. The temple priest gave her the blessing to lead the Sinhalese nation. She took on the mighty Sennayke family, with the croc face J.J. as a spokesperson. The S.L.F.P. won the landslide election in 1960. She broke records and history. A great accolade for a girl from a quiet Kandyan background from Ambalangoda.

'She began to put all the knowledge gained from her husband into practice. She nationalized all the schools. She made Sinhala as the administrative language of the country. Anuradapura became the secret city for the Buddhist, demolished all Hindu temples near the vicinity of the Kingdom of Pollanaruva, where the old Tamil Chola Kingdom stood, all bulldozed to make way to build a new Buddhist shrine with gold roof and fences. Promises to the Sinhalese nation were all delivered within the year. Then armed with modern weapons, the Sinhalese army moved into the northern and eastern regions without any opposition from the civilians. The Tamils realized this was a beginning of bad times to come. Indhira Ghandi, next door in India, reformed with compulsory family planning, crushed Sikh separatists at all angles raiding their golden temples, ignored southern India like another country. The Sri Lankan Nationalist Che Guevara Group was crushed by a joint operation with the Indian Army, during the attempted coup d'état against the First Lady. She killed over a thousand Sinhalese youths. The woman was hysterical and had a relapse into her manic depression. She brought the dreaded bill of standardization. That was a final nail in the coffin for the Tamils.'

Mr. Prahash had listened with patience to all the knowledge from Old Silver Hair, his loving term for his father.

They poured more rich whiskey. This had been the longest they had stayed and talked. It was good to continue. They may not have another good occasion like this, so they did.

'These assassinations changed our lives,' said Granddad.

'Now, when you look at it, Fred Dee was probably the

right thing to do, looking at the history of S.L.F.P. Why did he collaborate with this bitch? It's all your fault. Your generation let it happen. She fooled you all. It's our forefather's insanity that we are in this situation.'

'What about your generation, could you have done anything different? What's wrong with you people? You people never see beyond a certain point.' Granddad was getting animated for the first time with politics. Jana heard that and was behind him all the way.

'Let me tell you, how many of you kick a ball with your kids in the playgrounds? How many of you hug and kiss your children once in a while? They just don't know love, you fools. We did not know, because we did not know it. You should have learned it by now. How many of you show your love to your wife with respect like a human being? How many of you think you're better than your in-laws? Nobody is better than anybody. The whole world and all the lives are parallel. We all have the same lives, similar patterns and feelings. Rich or poor. We also create the illusion, with the help of newspapers and TV, that materials and greed make us complete? Rich from what? Poor why not? Jealousy, bitterness, unnecessary competition, and loneliness, created a breakdown in society. Everybody wants to work alone and enjoy lurid details until they bring down the family name to ludicrousness. It all begins in our home. Preserve it at home. We really have to love one another with a little more respect.

Mr. Prahash did not say anything, but took in what his father had said, seeing it almost as an apology – don't do what I have done to you, do it differently. It's not just giving home, education and clothes that matters but most important, the inner happiness, love and affection. Some of us did know

211

how to show it in the old days. We failed to grasp it but your generation have no excuse. Not a thing.

Jana listened to everything lying in his front room, eyes wide open looking through the metal grilles at the red coconut tree leaves as their shadows looked like a moving Venetian blind through the light of the moon.

Marie Joyce came out of her room: 'Dad, it's 3 a.m. Why don't you two eat now. It's late enough for talking please,' she said kindly.

'Ok, Marie. Come on, son, its three o'clock, let's eat. I am starving. Don't wait. Let me warm up those curries, it will take few minutes. We still got some fire on the stove.

Mr. Prahash quickly warm up the dishes for his father, and brought some water to the table.

'Remember those days, the queue at the bakeries in main road, Pedro bakery, Leona Stores at Bankshall Street, all rationed during our lady's government? American flour, kerosene oil, sugar, even candles, all in short supply. We really relied on small lamps and petrol max, the old pressure lamp with kerosene oil. Candles left smoke marks on our walls. The power supply to Jaffna was cut. The food tickets under the 1973 government was unforgettable. We pulled through with palmers sugar, purple yam, king silver yam, that was a good exercise she put us through,' said Granddad.

Mr. Prahash supported his statement: 'We know what to do if it happened again.'

Both laughed.

'We suffered badly because of the bitch. Some children died of malnutrition related illnesses. Some of our great horses became sick and boney. Some of them did not pull through. We suffered badly in Delft. Anyway, I don't want to think about all that today. Today is good day. Let's enjoy this

212

good food. The smell is making my mouth water. I need another drink,' said Granddad.

'No, no, Dad. Let's eat. You can have another one tomorrow.'

'Sure, son. I am proud of your achievement. You've done better than me and proved me wrong.'

'Go on, Dad, eat. Don't be shy. Let's eat. Let's eat the gods' food.'

Jana laughed in his room.

'Who's that?' asked Granddad. 'What, somebody got your mother's illness?' said Granddad.

'It's Jana, probably dreaming of his sports. He must have just hit a six or a boundary in his cricketing dreams.'

Jana kept quiet. Jana remembered those days of rations, he had been only ten years old then. His dad had asked him to go to Main Street and queue up early for bread. They had been living in Bankshall Street. The bread ran out pretty quick. Jana used to have an upset stomach with alternative Palmers sugar (chatkarai) diet. One day he realized he should have gone to the toilet prior to standing in the Pedro bakery queue. If he left the queue, there was no way he was going to get back in, which meant no bread and trouble at home. People are not nice when they are starving. They don't think of manners. He could not hold it any longer. He ran to Grandma's holding hands in between, taking little steps. He made a terrible noise in the toilet. Water taps were not working in the toilets that day. He did not bring any water from the well either. No toilet rolls in the third world yet. Now he had to go back to the water well, holding his pants in front of his prized possession. Everyone young and old laughed at him, called him kaka Jana, kaka Jana. Grandma said that's enough. He went back after washing himself to join the queue. The bread had almost run out. He was too embarrassed to tell anybody why he'd left the queue.

He came back to grandma. At the same time, Mr. Prahash was also there on his bicycle to pick him up. All hell broke loose among the in-laws. Grandma went behind the bakery to talk to the worker and bought two loaves.

'Thanks,' said Mr. Prahash.

He turned and looked at the others: 'So all of you laughed at him. I am going to laugh at you all one day. That day will soon be here,' he screamed without embarrassment. 'Come on, you fool, you national embarrassment. Defecating everywhere. You have no shame? Get on the bike.'

Jana was embarrassed, then disappointed for having creating all the argument. Somebody said in the house, when Jana was leaving: *whenever that boy comes here, the trouble follows him*. Jana heard that. He was sensitive about comments like that. For the next few months, he never went there without his parents or Indhiran. They said *he is only a kid, when he grows up he will understand. Leave him alone, it's not his fault. Just eaten too much Palmyra sugar.* Everybody laughed. Grandma's house was full of comedians. It was a happy and lazy comedy stage full of amateur dramatics.

That's what Jana was thinking lying in that room, that night, unable to sleep. Need to change, need to grow up. He did grow up away from Bankshall Street. He switched on the radio and put the volume really low: the BBC World Service Daily Sports brief.

He also tried to remember that day of the 'blood on the silk skirt'. He preferred to forget that painful day. Jana was rushed to hospital, after passing blood with urine. Then he was operated on for a penile obstruction. His foreskin was removed. Some minor urethral obstruction of some unbalance in nature. None of the family members had any idea of the condition. He was swollen badly and screamed every time he passed water. He was asked to wear a soft silk skirt to avoid contact with the clotted wound. No dressing at all, after all they were in the late sixties which were full of medical negligence. After a day he was discharged. Jana refused to leave the hospital without his shorts. He boycotted his discharge with heavy screams and grabbing the receptionist saying *I am not leaving*. They scared him with the police, saying *if you don't go, they will give you injections*.

He said: 'Never mind, I will scream train, it won't hurt,' said Jana. 'That's what Nurse Hillary told me. We should have gone to Dr Abraham, I don't like this hospital,' he said to the passing doctors and nurses. 'You are not good.' He really made a stand. Mr. and Mrs. Prahash took their time and stayed with him in the reception area.

He finally got a little tired and said: 'Call Vigi Mama. I will go home in his car.'

Both looked at each other and smiled. His sister's inner skirt was full of blood by now. Mr. Prahash asked to use the phone. He explained the situation. Vijay Uncle said to pass the phone to Jana. 'Can you pick me up, Vigi Mama?' he cried. Then he passed the phone to his dad and told him that *Vigi Mama had said yes no problem*. Mr. Prahash asked Vigi Uncle: 'Did you hear that? He is gone a little insane today in the casualty. He is so proud about his body image at this age. He is a little disturbed. Really, can you help? You should come and see the racket he is making. He said until he get picked up in the Austin Cambridge, he won't leave.'

They waited about 20 minutes. The Austin pulled up in

front of the hospital reception. Jana smiled for the first time that day. Despite his pain, he put on a brave front and walked manfully to his uncle and gripped his hand.

Uncle Vijay asked in all the confusion: 'What happened to you?'

Mr. Prahash explained.

Uncle Vijay said: 'Still, it looks a bad job. Not dressed properly.'

Jana sat in the front of the car, his skirt not much different to the red leather seat.

'Is it still bleeding?' asked Vijay Uncle. 'What's this on his hand?'

Mum explained: 'He scratched that earlier while itching. I checked the wound and it's ok now, Vijay,' and shook her head. 'That's why I put the bandages on the hand.'

Jana listened to everything.

Uncle Vijay said: 'What is all this, Jana? What they have done to you? You come to my place huh?'

Jana replied: 'They cut my saman,' meaning his possession. Everybody laughed. Jana looked back and laughed with a little embarrassment, head down, swinging his legs, while sitting on the front seat.

'Ok, Jana, maybe you go rest. Come another time to play with Rajan huh?'

Everybody agreed in the back.

'But before you go, let's do a little shopping. You can have anything you want,' said Uncle Vijay.

'Really?' said Jana and looked back at his parents.

'Don't worry about your parents, you can have anything you want,' said Uncle Vijay. He had already settled Jana back to normality. Jana wiped his tears, slightly recovering from his hours of cries.

'Ok… you know Vigi Mama, I love sports. I like cricket and athletics.'

'Good. I love football more than cricket. Go on. I know you are not shy.' Everybody in the back laughed.

'Vigi Mama… how about a transistor radio, a small one, not very expensive. I can listen to the sports' commentaries,' said Jana and smiled persuasively.

Mr. Prahash said: 'Jana, don't be rude.'

'No, the boy asked for something you all can use, can keep. Not a throwaway toy. It's a good choice. That is not rude at all. So Jana can listen to cricket. Good choice, Jana, good choice.'

'That's it, good choice,' Jana repeated and smiled. Then he shouted: *'Here comes Botham from the pavilion end ball, a real screamer. That was an out winger I guess. It passed Gordon Greenidge, he was trying to hook that outside the off-stomp out winger. That's not good, Gordon, play straight. The weather is good for an out winger, there is a cool breeze in the air. Good stroke, Jeffrey, perfect textbook drive. Any young cricketer watching, that's the way do it between the extra cover.'*

Everyone in the car laughed. His knowledge of cricket at that age was quite remarkable.

Jana and Uncle Vijay walked into the Phillips shop.

'Can you give this young man a good worldwide coverage transistor radio?'

'No problem, sir. Phillips is ok. Phillips is more than ok. Leather cover and a shoulder strap would be nice.'

Jana had completely forgotten his wound by now.

One salesman asked: 'Is he ok?'

Uncle Vijay signaled *don't*, with his head. Jana gave a big hug and a kiss to Vigi Mama and also to his parents, much to their surprise.

'That's ok, Jana. That's ok. You are the man,' said Uncle Vijay.

He knew there was something different about this boy. They had a special connection. He loved him like his own son. They would become good friends.

Jana also remembered as a little boy of about three or four, he was visiting Uncle Vijay's parents in Suruvil. Uncle Vijay was in pins and full plaster covering a compound fracture. He had been playing the first eleven football in St. Johns. His cousin, Thulasi, had said his incompetent tackles had caused that situation. An argument erupted about football. Vigi Uncle was not happy at all with his cousin. Jana came to his support. 'Stop it! Stop it now!' he said to Thulasi. 'I will break your legs. Don't speak to my uncle like that. Ok?' He pointed the finger and stood next to Vigi Mama.

Everybody asked who this little devil was. Vigi Mama's mum came down and said: 'That's my grandson. He likes to sit in my lap. He said it is very soft. My little grandson,' and she gave a kiss to Jana.

'Vigi Mama, when will you play football again,' asked Jana.

'Soon, Jana. Don't worry. Six months.'

Jana counted on his fingers: 'That's a long time, Uncle Vijay.'

Thulasi interrupted: 'Maybe more.'

'Excuse me. I did not ask you, thank you,' said Jana. 'I asked my favorite uncle who has a good car. Have YOU got a car? I don't think so. An Austin Cambridge British car. The red one, with a musical horn.' He shouted like a horn: 'Bam babam poo,' as best he could and walked off.

In the house, Jana complained to Mannikappa the senior: 'Mannikappa, that man is asking for trouble.' He pointed out

218

Thulasi, and then jumped and sat on the lap of Mannikappa. Mannikappa said: 'They just playing, son. I am the only one allowed to give trouble to anybody here.'

'Shall I go and tell them that?' asked Jana.

Everybody laughed.

'No, don't worry, son. They all know that already.'

Mr. Prahash laughed at Jana's antics: 'Everybody knows Jana in Suruvil by now. At the age of four, the first one to threaten tough guy Thulasi.'

Mr. Prahash apologized to the boys, then said: 'Come on now, who is trying to fight my son here? Take me on now.' He took up a boxing stance. Everybody had a good laugh that evening.

'Hey, that is Jana's personality. Everybody knows that in Jaffna,' laughed Mr. Prahash.

Mr. Prakash Little Paradise. 26 3/5
HANDBUILD STONE BY STONE!

CHAPTER SEVEN

PASSION OF SPORTING COLOURS
For the sporting martyrs

Even though Mr. Prahash did not show any enthusiasm for Jana's sporting interests, Uncle Vijay kept an eye on Jana's cricket and athletic progress. He also asked Jana again and again would he like to play cricket at John's, his old school near Old Park in Chundikuli. It was much better cricket there, with a lot of coaching camps and support for the players. Jana did not want to disappoint his favorite uncle but he did say:

'Sorry, uncle, I like St Peter's. I am a Peterite through and through. You are a Johnian. I will make sure and put extra effort when I am on the crease. I hope you will come and watch one of those matches.'

Uncle Vijay really appreciated Jana's honesty. Jana loved his college and the history behind it. Also he didn't want to leave his childhood classmates. His uncle always said to him: 'You are always invited to live or work in Colombo when you are finished your studies.'

That made Jana very happy.

That was one thing in the back of Jana's mind, how to get work straightaway after completing his advance level. That offer from his uncle was a safety net for him. *If everything fails I can always get a job in a firm or ask a job from my uncle.*

Jana played at St. John's and he always did well as soon as he saw his Uncle Vijay build the college scoreboard. He did keep his good average as an opening bat with a decent double figure. He would talk about his uncle to his friends about how successful he was in Colombo. His pet deer, the Lovebirds' nests, the peacock garden, the open marine aquarium display and the German Shepherd guard dogs, all were kept in his house and farm in the country's most luscious area in the wet zone near Kikaduva along the river.

He also employed hundreds of villagers around the region and supported their families. His business was breeding farm animals of the highest caliber: horses, bulls, cows, pigs and goats. He also caught the so-called crazy elephants and tamed and cared for them with the specialist elephant charmers from India. He made huge profits from his scientifically well-managed farm. He was well ahead of his time.

Jana said: 'I am going to Colombo soon to get a full cricket kit. I am looking forward to meeting Uncle Vijay's kids who are also grown up and playing cricket in St. Thomas's.'

Jana's interests and talking about his uncle made him friends and enemies on the school cricket pitch. He would channel his knowledge and have a verbal cricket knowledge competition among friends with topics like the best cricket team in the world made of players from different countries, the planet earth cricket team. The best of the best. It would create a great debate and argument about team selection. It also opened up great insight for the cricket enthusiast.

His close friends would sit together and listen to matches on Jana's radio at Chundikuli. There were some great pairs in the 70's: Haynes and Grinedge, Gooch and Boycott, Gavaskar and Mangeskar, Lille and Thompson, Garner and Holding, Khan and Miandad, Kapil Dev and Srikanth, Begit Singh Bedi and Engat, Viv and Clive Lloyd, Asantha de Mel and Sudath Vettimuny of Sri Lanka. All were Jana's favorites. Jana never forgot his little followers as they sat at the St. Peter's boundary line watching the football selection.

Jana was age 15 then. He was getting a good idea of his limitations. He was thin and an average 5 foot 6 inches. He told his friend Bonny: 'All the tall boys get to ball fast, all the bendy legged ones get to play football, all the fat boys get to be centre backs, throw a put shot and pull the tug of war. The skinny and tall will get to jump high and also to throw the javelin. Average sized like us, need to really fight hard for our positions. You know Guna – Kundan - he was selected for the second eleven football team. He strikes the ball with the point of the boot. He is also very quick and can run fast like sprinter. He is all muscles, not clumsy at all I am sure. He also has a good punch, too.'

Bonny said: One day he wanted to fight with me. I was ready for the fat boy. Hey Jana, he is in the Dunkan house. Jana, listen. You know the tall boy Ramesh? I saw him throw a javelin. I heard he broke the college record. Serious force to be reckoned with when it comes to throwing a ball. He is bowling for the first eleven under-19s already. He is only just 17. How about that? Can you face him when you get to bat? Ask Bonny.'

Jana said: 'No worries. With the sea breeze from the Beach Road behind him, he could be a little handful if you are scared of the red rock cork ball. He has his advantages and disadvantages, too, Bonny,' said Jana.

'He is a tall bird and can see the length a little easier. Swing a little, too, to both sides. You know, Jana, when they practice, he balls with just a middle stomp for accuracy. Bang! The wicket somersaults all the way to the wicket keeper. Serious bowler, Jana,' Bonny explained while imitating his bowling action.

Jana responded: 'With the fast bowling action, long and skinny legs need a lot of energy, tiring ahhh. After a little spell he will be back with fine legs warming up for the second spell. If he has taken the crucial wickets, yeah the team is in good momentum. Otherwise, medium pacers have to come to keep it in the length. Some bendy leg footballers can ball a decent first change swing, too, you know. Like Titus. He hardly puts a loose ball, always twisting and turning, keeping the batsman guessing. He will be in the under 17 selection.'

Bonny said: 'Watch that gap between the pad and the bat, Jana.'

Jana screamed in excitement: 'Come on! Let's have it! My baby! The heavy non-oil grey Nicholas won't let me down. I am not afraid of the fast bowlers or the medium teasers. I shall put myself to open the bat for St. Peter's. What do you think, Bonny?'

'That's a good strategy, Jana. Go to the front early and face the music. Where are you going to field?'

Jana said: 'Slips, gully or silly mid-on. It's not my choice, Bonny. I got to go where they put me. Got to be closer to the action.'

Bonny said: 'Throw the ball above in the ground, I can't do silly mid-on, silly mid-off. As the name itself, it is quite silly really, don't you think? And, I like my face, Jana. And I love it. I like to look and smile from it.'

'No, no, Bonny. Listen,' said Jana getting excited and he

started to talk strategy. 'To catch a ball from an opening steady bat hitting with their Gunn and Moore coming at you at 60mph will stick in your hands like glue if you are in a right position and watching the ball and the bat. Knowing your bowler and understanding his pattern helps a little, too. When you catch that ball man, everybody thinks you are a miracle fielder, Bonny. Some ballers purposely put a loose ball if they don't like the fielder on the silly mid-on. Just think about that, too.'

Bonny points the finger at the bullies. 'Just don't forget to put on a hat or chin guard, back at the centre of your waist. Just stick it in tight. Protect your spine and your coccyx. Careful, Jana, you don't want to leave the pitch paralyzed on a stretcher, do you? Then it will be all over for you. Think about it man.'

Jana looked at him and said nothing, and started to feel his back a little anxiously.

Bonny said: 'Did I scare you?'

Jana said: 'No, just thinking of how life would be without the back/hip for sports, that's what's worrying. I would go insane.'

'Don't worry, you won't. You already are!' laughed Bonny.

They chased each other around the sports ground. Bonny did keep Jana busy with his cricket at the Chundikuli lanes.

Years went quickly with all the house-building with Mr. Prahash. Jana ran every morning and hit the ball in the socks hanging on the mango tree, speaking to himself about ground strokes and positions which he read from an Indian cricket magazine Sportstar. He moved around the moving ball in a sock like a boxer around the heavy bag. He was trying to receive the ball in different angles emulating the bouncers and beamers. That was his religion. He tried this, he tried that, all kind of positions and imaginative strokes.

He began to philosophize cricket and play with patience and style. As a batsman first, he worked on the stance, grip hold and the swings of the bat. He believed there were the four big principles: read, react, readjust and adjust and finally, the follow through. You only have one hundredth of a second to do it all and if you missed one of the above three, people behind you were going to scream good ball, good ball. But if you leave it alone, you have done your effort. Jana meant the screaming and cheering from the wicket keeper, for the bowler. Concentrate with total obedience to the law of batting straight down the line.

When he played with his younger friends, Jana said personality has to change with your cricket: if you are angry, over confident or hot tempered, be a fast bowler. But when you finally get your line and length, you will probably change yourself and calm down anyway. With batting, first you got to find the rhythm of your strokes, then you find your stance and the angle of the bat. The perfect grip that suits your play, shoulder and chin totally parallel, your cap in line with your nose and shoulder. Have a good look for the last time at the field set, wait, blink your eye for the last time, too. You are facing the ball and thinking of the gaps, gully and the slips. You are aware of the extra cover and the deep mid-on. Drives would be a slant bat in between. Head down and knees bent to follow through with the middle of the bat, feel it in the thickness, which will go along the straight line, all the way to the ball boys outside the ground. Your life will begin to change.

Jana would talk like this, forever. Indhiran would come on his bike and stand alone under the college trees to see Jana playing cricket, even though he wanted to take Jana to the revolutionary speeches and meetings of the Tamil Youth gatherings. He felt the time had come for him to join the struggle alone and to leave Jana with his sporting colors. He appreciated that was where his talent lay, at the college grounds in front of a watching public. Jana had always said he was a performer not an audience.

As soon as Indhiran arrived, Jana would update scores and news regarding the world athletics and cricket. Indhiran would pretend to listen with enthusiasm.

Jana said that day: 'Indi, can we get to a television somewhere? I heard a competition on the radio today. Marylebone Cricket Club (MCC) are organizing and want to find the fastest bowler in the world.' Jana looked at Indhiran. 'Quite a few bowlers are taking part, Indhi. It's a once in a lifetime fight to the stumps. Just the stumps. It is all going to be taking place in London. All from different countries. Amazing! Come on, it will never happen again, I am sure,' said Jana with excitement, eyes wide open, trying to convince Indhiran. 'They are going to film and measure the bowling speed electronically all in slow motion,' he continued, doing a slow moving action. 'Just like that.'

'The bowling speed experiment. Another experiment,' said Indhiran. 'I am going home, Jana, I need to go.'

Jana started running along: 'Wait! Wait! What did I say? What happened to you?'

Indhiran said: 'I am tired of listening about cricket and athletics from you all the time. Sorry, I am really tired, Jana.'

'Come on, Indhiran, you just want to talk about fighting, guns, protests, war and you think that is the only answer?' Indhiran begin to pedal hard as he tried to pull away. Jana kept running alongside.

He shouted: 'The bowlers are chosen. Listen, listen for one minute.' He was gasping for breath by now. 'Croft,

Holding, Garner the Big Bird, Roberts, Kapil Dev, Imran Khan, Safarz Narfaz, Lillie, Hadlee and Thompson are all competing in one fast bowling arena. It's fucking brilliant, man! All the amazing bowlers with the occasional invincible speed. Who do you think will win the competition?'

'I don't know, Jana, I am not interested, ok?' said Indhiran his face creased in irritation.

Jana looked at him: 'Ok, forget it.' Jana jumped onto his cousin's bike and Indhiran let him.

'Let's talk about the girls ahhh.' He saw Indhiran's face begin to change with a smile.

That evening both attended a meeting near Jaffna central behind the chapel. It was all about raising arms and the struggle. Some older men had weapons. They looked serious and no nonsense. They all sat and listened not knowing the politics really well. They were only just sixteen and about to leave school in two years. But at that time in Jaffna, boys talked only about movies, cricket, football, athletics and girls. Unlike Jana's cousin, Indhiran, who did love all the above but he also wanted to be a serious freedom fighter, too. He understood the importance of it. He read the history books. He talked about the old kingdom. He really hated the colonialists. He wasn't interested in foreign travel or fancy cars. He loved his country and the people. Jana appreciated his interests and fully supported him. They all sat and listened to the local leader's speech. Indhiran had helped out with the printed materials. After the speech only a few remained. Finally, the missions began to surface for the dedicated: the plan, policies and the ultimatums. 'I feel quite stressful hearing about war and killing. I am a little scared, man. I just can't see you getting hurt, you, my only friend. I know the day will come you will all fight,' said Jana. He had read the leader's statement on the notice.

We will take control of the majority Tamil area. I have already got support from various government officials abroad including the First Minister of Tamil Nadu. There are overseas students, too, helping the cause. All I am asking is commitment from you and your friends to join and be ready to give your life for the people's struggle of Tamil Ellam. We will never forgive now or ever. They will pay for all the crimes they have committed against the Tamil people. We will never. We are a righteous generation, with a lot of pain and suffering passing through our genes. Yes, to all the women, too. You will also accept and contribute for the sisters are going to play a key role in our destiny. The destiny of our own nation. We will have it sooner rather than later.

Everybody had shouted: *TAMIL ELLAM!* (TAMIL SEPARATE STATE!)

Jana had come early that weekend for the cricket field. He was selected to open for the First Team, on the back of getting the best batsman award: the match was against the unbeaten tough Jaffna Central College. Jana and Titus took the Champions Shield in 1977 as Captain and Vice Captain. Jana also took the cup as the best batsman. There was a young kid who tried to help Jana padding up by providing his equipment.

Jana said: 'Thank you, fellow. What is your name and how old are you?'

'Alfie. I am playing in the under fifteens.'

Jana smiled and said: 'Very good. Oh you are that leg spinner! Best of luck. If you want any help don't hesitate to ask me.'

Alfie shook his hand. Jana sat back for a moment and thought about his first day practice for the first team as a young fifteen year old. That had been the best day of his life. He hadn't been able to sleep the night before: ironing all his kit, polishing his shoes with white chalk. Jana walked up to the grounds very early that day with his stylish kit: clean socks, haircut, jumpers, Adidas track suit and Dunlop tennis shoes, English style blue cricket hat, wrist band of red blue and white. He began to warm up by pulling his knees to his chest, then a few head and neck turning exercises, and moved around the ground enjoying the run of 800m warm-up before the cricket practice. The coach saw Jana and said: 'That's the sprit, let's all go for a gentle stroll.' Everybody looked at Jana and said *wait until we get you making us run before even we start our cricket practice today.*

When Jana got closer to other seniors, one approached and said: 'You are a good runner eh?' and tapped him on his back. As Jana smiled and relaxed, the senior pinched him hard on his neck and said: 'Don't you ever fucking do that, ever ok?' Jana took the pain, and said: 'Ok. Ok. All right.'

'You will never play in the first eleven, if you try to get to be a fit smart ass.' Then he smiled and tapped Jana's back and walked away. The coach sensed something and asked Jana if everything was ok.

'Nothing, sir', said Jana but tears were in his eyes.

That bullying senior went back to his group and laughed at Jana; others joined in. Jana wanted to prove anybody who laughed that day wrong in that cricket field by showing his talent. The coach started hitting the ball from the centre of the pitch with the keeper standing next to him.

He said: 'I want a fast quick throw to the keeper, there is nobody to cover the throw. If you throw a bad one, you have to go and pick it up, ok? Come on, let's go. Come on. Everybody play it safe, and throw slowly to the keeper.'

Jana ran fast, picked up fast through to the keeper with a great follow through. The coach said: 'You see that, what is your name son?'

'Janarth,' said Jana.

'I want everybody to show some energy. Like Jana here. I want the ball to travel fast through the air parallel to the ground cutting the single.' He called another youth: 'Can you stand on the baller's end with the bat please. When I hit the ball to the field, I want you to run to the keeper end, ok?' He looked at the field: 'Here is the single, you got to cut it down by throwing to the keeper. Come on. Let's see. The commitment is in the practice. That is very important chaps.'

That was the kind of real life situation type of cricket training Bernard had planned for the boys. He was respected due to his credentials as a player with the air force then for his mercantile premiership captaincy with a top rubber company at Colombo. He gave it all up after a messy divorce turned him into an alcoholic. Fr. Durant gave him a coach position, a job for an old boy. He still loved his cricket and was top of his bowling skills. He was specially brought in to improve the St. Peter's bowling talents. Apart from a few, most of them did not have any discipline or real interest to do well. It was just great for Jana to be in the cricket team those days, have jokes about teachers, students' gossips, get to the cricket team somehow. Get to travel with the rude boys singing and joking in the only school bus which still managed to stay on the road without the MOT. Moreover, all of the boys also talked about the female talent in the local convent girls' school. Bernard put a stop to all that: 'If you are here just for fun, go home now. Otherwise I will find you and send you home. You will not play cricket in this field while I am here. Not in this college. Real officer style discipline. No one is going to waste my time or anybody's time.' He looked at Jana and said: 'I look at that kid over there, on time for practice, asking me every day - can you give me a chance to pad up - that's the sprit I want all of you to be. Matter of fact, Jana, you're going to pad up and bat today.'

Jana started to run to the pavilion.

'No… no, not now, sorry, Jana.' Everybody laughed. 'No laughing, please. No laughing, no teasing, no bullying in the cricket team. It is a gentleman's game. Everybody try to understand that properly. It is not a football or a boxing match. It is a non-contact intelligent sport for the intelligent people. Do you understand? I am saying all this because I want to get the team first together, I mean together. Looking out for each other, creating the team spirit. Then we work on our weaknesses, which are the easiest part. Believe me, really that's easy. With the bowlers I can perfect your actions, swings, bouncers and you will surprise yourself. But you've got to help me with your fitness levels. I want you to run a mile every morning around your streets. Fitness is the real key of winning long matches. For the batsman I've got a top batsman from Colombo, old boy of St. John's. He is doing me a favor, going to take the top five batsmen and give you extra coaching on the weekend in front of the Jaffna fort, free of charge. He is promoting Jaffna cricket to encourage people to realize their dream to play for the country. He is only here in Jaffna for a month. He is on the national squad as a coaching assistant to the senior national cricket coach. So this is your chance to ask questions about anything relating to batting, bowling, field setting, how to turn the losing match into a winning one. He has the answers and the experience. Then I want you to share that knowledge with your teammates.'

Jana heard all this, he was already planning to go with Indhiran and watch the coaching at the fort. He was looking forward to telling him the story about the coach from Colombo. So Jana was in his element. Best day of his life. He ran and fielded catching the balls diving side to side. The ball was hit at the midwicket, he ran, dove front and caught a catch to everybody's amazement. As a fifteen year old in the first team he cruised through the practice session and was selected in the first sixteen college senior first team. Lots of bullying seniors did not get in. Jana was the youngest. He was fit from his running: he chased the ball around, threw good and always walked with the bowler.

As a young player with such discipline he was soon picked up by coaches. They soon realized this kid was not going to miss a training session. He was brought closer to the action after two weeks in the outfield. Soon he was in the slips, watching the good batsmen, learning all the time, listening to the coach about bowling and field setting. He cheered the bowlers, batsmen and the fielders: *good ball, sir, well played, sir, well fielded, great catch,* to the keeper. He was learning from a great bowler called Mohan, left arm swinger, how the batsman's hope was the unpredictable out swing. In the first two weeks all who had been selected were given the chance to bat except Jana. Knowing they had the 12th man/waterboy, they just did not need to. But Jana went up and asked the captain, then the coach. They agreed. Jana was padding up front of the school to face the senior bowlers. He warned his friends - I will be batting this week, but I don't know when, you better come and cheer for me. They did not want to miss that, all were waiting with Bonny and the crew. Indhiran came twice, but did not make it on the third day. Jana was disappointed about that. Jana looked around to see once more, looked for his beloved cousin anywhere.

Jana put on those gigantic cricket pads - they almost came up to his hips. He also managed to push that plastic balls guard into the box. Rubber green spikey, inner-leather hand glove to keep those knuckles safe. He finally checked his shoelaces and double tied them. Put his little invention, chin guard, in the trouser pockets. Adjusted his hat, did a final check on the pad straps. Chose an old heavy non-oil Gray Nicholas bat with dark maroon stripes, and walked down to the cricket pitch. Yes, that was his moment, the moment he had dreamed of all these years, to play good cricket in the college at bat. He heard the cheers near the scoreboard: 'Come on, Jana, this is your chance. Show them, show the bullies,' shouted Bonny. Even some of the seniors said: 'Go on, Jana. This is it.'

Coach Bernard said: 'Told the bowlers, keep it down, he hasn't got a helmet, poor guy.'

Jehan, the captain, asked: 'Jana, have you got your box guard?' he asked pointing to his balls.

Jana said: 'Yes.'

'Is it the pink one?' somebody said from the slips.

Jana smiled.

'Did you wash it? You know who wore it before you? That's it, you gonna catch something.' Everybody laughed. 'Come on, don't scare the boy,' said the coach 'and quiet in the slips, please. Come on, get in your positions,' said the coach.

'Where you want leg stump?'

'That's your leg', said coach Bernard.

Jana marked it with the chalk on a matting. He looked around, took his stance, blinked his eyes.

There was a good length ball from Jehan. Jana played it with textbook forward defensive stroke. Everybody cheered. Jana's confidence increased. Jana played that on his back foot with quick foot work, and kept the ball down. Again a big cheer. The rector watched this new kid from the first floor balcony. He wondered what was all the excitement. Jana played a beautiful leg glance from Jehan coming around the wicket. That became his first boundary and a signature stroke in his early days as his confidence grew. Jana produced some clean forward drives with follow through, assessing the loose balls well. Coach Bernard and Captain Mohan talked quietly about the new kid: *cheering stopped in the slips: they're worrying about their place in the team by now. The kids in the boundary hit their drums especially for Jana. He is their 12th man: if somebody did not do well he gets the first change. He's not afraid of a fast ball and he's got a good eye.* Jana lip-read the whole thing from the distance.

Jana soon impressed everybody, even Fr. Durant. Some did not like his presence, knowing their team place was in jeopardy. Certain bullying took place in the changing room: someone asked him to clean the plastic ball guards, to pack the equipment, while they threw things at him. Some landed on Jana's head, grabbed him from behind, squeezed his balls. They said it was the 12th man's job and asked nobody to help Jana. Jana did it all with interest, did not complain. He put all the plastic guards and straps in the soapy water. Yes, they all used the same guards. They did not have any individual cricket equipment. He cleaned and organized the kits. Jana would come early and organize the kit, put the stumps and helped the grounds man, George. Jana would sit in the corner like a ghost without getting noticed by anybody, while the seniors talked about the current alleged relationships between the teachers. That also included some nuns and priests. The conversations were full of hardcore sex, homosexuality, girlfriends etc. The boys knew all the school scandals, some of them were prefects involved in college conferences and meetings. Some of the younger teachers had affairs with the attractive sporting captains. Jana quickly learned the mood in the changing room. He totally avoided getting involved in any conversations. He kept the changing room talks in the changing room. Most of the senior players began to like Jana's attitude and began to appreciate his commitment. Some also talked of him being captain one day. He had the talent to do it, but it was all up to the priests. Someone asked: 'Is Jana's father rich?' Another replied: 'Government servant.' 'Well, no chance then.'

Day by day Jana would wait for his turn to bat: usually on a bad light just before the finish of the practice session Jana would get his chance. He did not mind, by this time he had mastered all the weaknesses of the bowlers. The well-used practice ball without a swing or shine did not bother Jana's risky shots. He began to go for the strokes at the end of the day. His natural instinct and critical observation began to pay off. His major influence of that time was Jeffery Boycott and Gavaskar who opened for their countries and stayed on the crease no matter what. He wanted to emulate the great opening batsmen of all time. He decided he wanted to be an opening batsman. He began to develop confidence slowly but surely. He was the first fifteen year old who faced the full force of Coach Bernard's 110 mph fast ball without fear. The faster the bowler, the easier he guided them along the field. He said : 'Just have to feel the ball on the bat, then you know, it hardly needed any power to hit it.' He was learning the full toss, the beamers, the bouncers. His favorite defensive stroke with text book accuracy and follow through with style gave him the nickname 'the Block Master.'

Soon Bernard asked Jana to pad up for failing length bowlers. Jana would come and put the front foot and play beautiful ground strokes to frustrate the bowlers. He was even good enough to be open for the college first eleven at fifteen.

They said he was too young to play in the team, the usual red tape private Catholic school bureaucracy. Jana accepted the 12th man job wholeheartedly. Whenever Jana entered the pitch with water and towels there was a big cheer from the scoreboard end. He would take messages from coach Bernard to the batsman on the crease. He would encourage them to *stay there; don't be in a hurry, you got all day to bat.* He would signal the cheering boys, *cheer on the batsman.* He was learning from everybody all the time. He turned the bullies around with his commitment and patience. They began to respect Jana but occasionally pulled his trousers down in the changing room.

St. Peter's did ok that year. Their greater opponents, like Jaffna Central and St. John's, did dominate the late seventies. Jaffna cricket produced some great players who would eventually play in Colombo premier clubs and the mercantile tournament with full time jobs, cars and decent wages.

The following year, Jana was selected as vice captain for the under fifteens. His commitment was rewarded as he was open batsman for the college team. He averaged 60-70 in his first season. That was a good average for an opening season. He set the field with captain and changed bowlers. He quickly recognized the weakness of the batsman, and he prompted alternative field sets. As a team player, it would pay off with great catches in the slip field. He stayed in the crease and batted for hours whenever he opened the bat, taking the shine off the ball, scoring very few runs and giving the opponent a chance. He would give a chance to low order the sweepers, heavy hitters, the ones who take the ball from the outside the off stomp and turn it to the mid wicket. They only had a five steady batsman, the rest of them were bowlers. Jana took the responsibility to brink the score to 50-100, every time he went to bat. He shouted, complimented, he made clear whose call when it was time to come to take a run. He would say, *WAIT THERE, WAIT THERE*. He never wanted to get run out. That was his principle; he followed that throughout his career. He also got respect from other colleges, they all talked about his commitment.

He believed to run out was a bad omen, especially when they were in the process of saving the match from losing. Therefore, it was always repeated to them and they were reminded whenever they met their prefect of games prior to our match.

The prefect was always warning them: *'DON'T, DON'T EVER get run out. NEVER, THAT'S THE LAZY CRICKETER'S EASY WAY OUT. Speak observe, assess the throwing time and distance in practice all the time. That's why you practice day and day out. Some of you, like our Richard here, who can't turn up for practice on time, will be a little late getting to the wicket, too.'*

They would all looked at each other and cover their mouths.

'But catches win matches, remember that. I say this again and again. Don't come and see me again if you drop a catch please. That really makes me angry. You have to be alert in the field. Slips, midwicket, fine leg or anywhere, expect a catch anytime. You're only going to get one chance in the whole match. That will change the game. Don't panic, calm down and take your time judging it.'

He asked Jana: 'What is the main principle of catching the ball from a fine leg? Let's say a high ball coming at you on the line.'

Jana took a moment and said: 'Watching the batsman and the bowler while walking up from a set field from the boundary line. Anticipating the sunlight trying to blind you while you move, judge whether the ball will swing to deep fine leg, get under the ball, both hands against the chest.'

'Well done, Jana,' said the prefect of games. 'Why against the chest? You, sleepy head,' he said to the wicket keeper. 'I don't want no byes today.'

Startled, the wicket keeper said: 'So that you may have a second chance, if it did catch you by surprise with the outward turn. It will act as a third hand or a shield.'

'Great! That's all there is to it. There you are, all of you know it now, how it works. Now put it into practice. Simple, right? Go on, good luck!'

That was their prefect of games, a real drill master. They listened. He would also encourage them with his after match speech at his home with some snacks and drinks. They were unbeaten that year and they got to maintain that record. 'I think you are better than them. Better than anybody, so, come on, let's show them where the real talent lies,' he said.

Jana's childhood friend, Andrew from Bankshall Street, was a wicket keeper. He came from a family of keepers. His elder brother a great goalkeeper. Jana opened with Andrew with the early spirit of Bankshall Street, for the under fifteen. They settled well and pushed for singles. St. Peter's kept the unbeaten record that year.

The most important match of their under fifteen calendar was the game against the visiting Sinhalese boys from the upcountry. St. Anthony's Kandy was a private Catholic school for the upper class Kandyan society boys. Sport was their high priority. They had sport scholarships and boarding school with top education in the misty mountains at the high altitude. They had a mixture of students from all backgrounds, Europeans, Buddhists and Catholics, even some Tamils to Jana's surprise. Some of the cricketers and athletes went on to take part on the national team.

St. Anthony's won the toss and elected to bat. Their opening batsman Marlon V.H. looked a difficult bat to break down initially. The breakthrough came as the bowlers began to find the gaps. Jana was in a competitive mood to show the Kandyan boys that the Jaffna boys were not a pushover. As a vice captain, he took charge when the captain began to ball from the Beach Road cemetery end. He caught two amazing catches in the leg slip.

'Collapse is on,' he shouted, 'come on, boys.'

Marlon was out, clean bowled. That changed the match completely. It was limited overs and they were ready to bat chasing a reasonable score of 178. Jana quickly padded up, asked his little followers to throw balls at the nets near the chapel. He asked Bonny and Dino to throw a few balls hard between his legs. Dino put a full toss.

'Come on, Dino. Right here, I want it here in front of my legs,' said Jana. He wanted to do well like no other time. He bent down to get that forward defensive stroke right. He felt comfortable with his small white hat, bent down, got up and warmed up his knees. Jumped up and down for the battle of the counter culture.

Jana and Andrew were ready to bat. They came out with a great cheer from the full house pavilion. Anton Raj swung the ball both sides in line and length. After four overs, he stopped for a moment and looked at Jana. Jana understood, he was beginning to frustrate the bowlers. Jana believed in give respect and get respect from the bowlers. When they were balling well, Jana would play steady and straight. Field set was tight. He spoke with Andrew well, he warned with the sentiment of the coach: no silly run outs. They were also picking and throwing well, waited for the loose balls. Both began to settle down. Jana and Andrew took a few singles, then came the gaps and the loose balls.

Andrew came and said to Jana: 'Mr. Boycott would have been proud of you. You are unbreakable.'

Jana did impress everybody that day. He batted for two hours and scored the 100 for the team without a fall of a wicket. Andrew began to take the risky shots to reach his unbeaten 50. Runs were coming up, they were in a great position to pass their score. Jana showed the southern boys how to put Jaffna on the Sri Lankan cricket agenda. They couldn't be beaten. The match was drawn. Jana carried the bat with captain after losing a few wickets. He was the man of the match and St. Peter's gained great respect from the visiting St. Anthony's Team. Their middle school records officer, Singha, a quiet man, personally came and wished and congratulated Jana. That rarely happened at the school. He was an old boy with a great cricketing record at St. Peter's in the 1950's. His opinion was respected by the school sporting committee. Jana also heard that he fought for Jana's captaincy during the selection process. That was one of the moments Jana cherished after he took off the pads, walked out of the changing room, cheered on by all the players and staff and visiting staff. Jana was speechless.

He had just turned fifteen.

Then he was approached by the team coach of Kandy and offered a sports scholarship and studies at the upcountry St.

Anthony's. Just like his father got a scholarship, the miracle of St. Anthony was trying to repeat history.

Jana looked around; there was no one from his family. There was no one to appreciate his cricket and to decide his future. He always looked around to see whether his father was there to watch his matches. Unlike his father in those Delft days. Jana loved his family and friends and most importantly his cousin Indhiran. He just couldn't leave, even when it was the proposition that couldn't be refused. It could have been life-changing for Jana that would surely have taken him for national trials. The dream of playing for his country. No, he couldn't leave Jaffna.

Up country, to live there and study at the boarding school playing cricket and running in the mountains. The beauty of Wella, Temple of the Tooth, Kandy lakeside, Nuwerellya, Matala, misty lower cloud in front of your garden, streams of mini rainforest, and the clean fresh air would have been great. The British built colleges and colonial estates and gardens in Peredenya and Bandarawella. The mountain trains would go through the hill country like no other tropics in the world. The Royal Botanical Gardens, with long hanging and lush fruit from the old trees: pears, rumbuttan, mangustan, starfruit and jackfruit, fresh cinnamon aroma all around, rich tea from your own garden, while the rubber dripped from the trees into a container up. The ancient art of Sinhalese filled the caves with colors ranging from brilliant red to bright yellow, and carbon black gave the ultimate contrast that would be sobering to watch alone. Bronze sculptures, rock sculptures, ancient carvings and staircases, walls and pillars and rivers built in time of Parakiramabaku, would have reminded of the country's rich but violent history. People walked from the stone pedestals of the Sigriyan rock cave beauty. The dams, large reservoirs, irrigation canals, some of them built in the early years of Parakirmabahu, would have been gigantic and a shock to look at and digest. Some of the buildings were majestic compared to the size of the country.

Jana really dreamed these options and said: 'I will speak to my dad and get back to you sir, thanks.' He was too young to know all this, too young to appreciate the southern hospitality. He said to his close friends: 'Would you like to join me in Kandy, boys? I am moving there soon with upcountry's Sinhalese beauties. I am going to play first class cricket with a scholarship among the lion bees of Sinhala kingdom. They are going to give me a bitemark under my neck and take my juice away.'

Everyone laughed: *you gone crazy Jana, you staying too long in that heat, you fool*, and poured water on his head. *You smell Jana, boo. Bite in your back. Go and have a shower before you see your beauties.*

Two weeks later, Jana got a picture of both teams sitting together in front of St. Peter's. It had been posted to Jana by the teacher from Kandy, who asked him to come and join the SAC Kandy. Jana looked at that photo with great interest: he was sitting in the front on the floor with his white hat on, among the future champions of Sri Lankan cricket. He showed that to everybody.

In his home, nobody was really interested in Jana's photo or his scholarship story.

Somebody said in the house: *we can't even see you properly in this picture with your hat on*. Jana would quickly have an argument with the family.

'Unlike any of you, at least I understand the endurance and dedication of sportsmanship. If all of us loved cricket in Jaffna, we could have resolved our grievances against our enemies with sportsmanlike conduct and saved a lot of pain and suffering.'

At this moment in time, Jana's best place was his college grounds.

He was popular at school. But he did not pay any attention to anything else but sports. During the absence of a class teacher, the class monitor was asked to point the finger at the eccentric intellectuals. The champion storyteller, Jana, would get the class all excited. The intellectual bookworm types, with their prefect badges, were advised to kneel any individuals outside the class room if they found them disruptive. That was on the long shiny corridors. Corridors full of past masters of sports, intellectuals, principals, group photos of the champions of 40's and 50's hanging because of their greatness. Jana was to take the first kneeling place and he looked at those photos real close. He was about to take three lashes below the knees on behalf of class 9a just outside in the middle school shiny corridors.

Moses Joseph walked up quickly from the office. His shoe noise and sound of the heel coming from the distance would tell how angry he was. He looked like Lee Marvin when he sought out The Dirty Dozen. He looked at Jana: 'You! Three lashes hard.'

Jana took it, squinting his eyes and then got up and walked back. All the kids from the other classes flinched and shrunk when the cane split into threads. Jana took it like a man. He went back to the classroom. Everybody felt bad, except the fools in the back row who laughed at everything.

Jana, just about to finish the middle school, handed in his English essay expecting a great review of the hard work he had put in in the last months of grade 9a. Now he would be moving to upper school wearing all white. He had chosen science and math as subjects to keep his father happy. Jana made good progress as he prepared for his G.C.E O/L. His favorite subjects were English, geometrical drawing and health science.

He also made continuous progress as a solid opening bat and began to receive respect from coaches and colleagues. He would continue his vice captaincy in the year 1978 and his friend Titus deservedly took the captaincy. That year both the captain and vice captain created a certain bond spending time in each other's houses watching Monkey Kung Fu and became friends for life.

That showed in the pitch: they were unbeaten and became the Jaffna champions. In the final decider against the tough central college, Jana and Titus would put up a partnership and break the college record for the junior team. Jana would receive the best batsman accolade. The winning was the shield carried by the team all the way to the college, with screaming college students following them with flags: *who are the winners, we are the winners.* It was an unforgettable moment for Jana. The group photo was taken and hung in the corridors among past champions with Jana and Titus sitting either side of their prefect of games, their beloved chemistry professor, Sam Fredrick. He was very proud of that photo on the corridor. He understood that it would hang there for another 50 years.

Jana and his teammates wanted to celebrate that in style. They had known about their free travel vouchers. The boys from the business background did not worry about the money. Their cricket was first class: they were going to go to Colombo in first class sleepers, too. They took the quiet night mail train. None of that jumping on the fast moving train to catch seats for the relatives - the crazy activities practiced by the adrenaline junkies. They used to bribe the station platform policeman with a packet of Bristol cigarettes. Then from the far end of the station past the barriers, the train would come to a slow speed while approaching the station. Seat catchers would jump on the 40 mph. train, quickly move along the corridors and corner a whole row of seats for their family or friends for a small fee, going away good will and pocket money, to bring luck for the travelers, as they journeyed in search for jobs and marriage at the capital. The train was usually pretty badly overcrowded up to Anuradhapura. The train meant hope, foreign travel, romance, honeymoon, holidays and even an entertainment-filled celebration. They loved the mysteries of the Colombo stories: robberies at gem jewelers, hijacks and demands, sex shops and working girls, peep shows, strip clubs, adult cinema and the lifestyle of the rich and famous at the casinos Galle beachfront Ritz. Titus took care of the upgrade from 2nd to 1st class sleepers. They also made sure a good supply of Necto and Fanta, Kothu roti with lamb from the main road in a brown paper oil-stained parcels. Some of the seniors who joined them had a bottle of Martell. The cricket fanatic ticket-checking guard also got a bottle of Arrack and food from them. Martell drinkers took the room near the toilet. Their team member, a half-Tamil half-Sinhalese boy call Guntelke, was a left bent arm swinging bowler who took a lot of wickets. In Sri Lanka, he had a calcium deficiency. Kids were born with bent elbows, cleft lips and pallets, and bad teeth malformations. In cricket it worked to the advantage with the spin ball when it came to bent elbows. They couldn't break a rule with the deformed elbow. No umpire was going to waste time calling no ball. Unless he had an issue with the players. Guntelake could become hysterical with a shot of Martell, even if it was for medicinal purposes in egg coffee.

They sang Sinhalese byla songs, totally out of tune with their portable musical instruments. It was all mixed up with Tamil lyrics with Jaffna jokes. There were few comic geniuses in the group, like the scorer and former leg spinner, Xavi. One who would never say no to a party. He had a light hearted but perverted sense of humor. If you didn't get the joke, you might think he was being rude and obnoxious. A few of our good-looking light skinned boys flirted in the buffet carriages. Some were on the corridors, waiting to bump in the night and give a surprise. It was all in good spirit of St. Peter with a little chaos. By this time half of Guntilake's body was outside the train. Jana had to keep order and pull him inside and put a wet towel over his sweating body. He had just had a few more than he could handle.

The train screamed through the lion jungle. The monkeys on the trees gibbered, some birds' shining eyes could be seen in the dark. Elephants trumpeted in the distant jungle, wild animals howled, river frogs chorus lined and screamed for miles. They all took turns to keep the rhythm of the Vanni jungle when the train passed through.

A few hours later, early morning birds squawked and cocks sung to give the signal of the dawn break. Jana quickly woke up all the tired cricketers to brush their teeth and enjoy the beauty of the real countryside. Sunlight flashed in between as they passed the giant wild trees and the small huts began to disappear. They began to see the bungalows and farms. Their eyes were like a speed camera capturing all in small motion for a second, registering it all in their minds forever. There were river dwellings, some living in the adjoining slums deep below as they approached the Kalani

Bridge. The train slowed down from the musical feast sound to a little clutter of rolling wheels blowing diesel smoke. Then a loud blowing of his horn. That was the alarm for the locals at 6 a.m. The bridge made noises of a weight bearing a heavy crane, cranking and tightening bolts and rivets as they slowly moved above the heavy morning tide down below. They arrived on time at Colombo: still slightly dark with street lights which made it look amazing. Some of them were adults but this was their first trip to Colombo. They were amazed by the speed of movement, the street cleaners, water pumping and washing all sides of the station and in and out of the station. The train also began its full service and wash prior to its trip back that night to KKS Jaffna. The mail was picked up quickly by the Royal Mail vans from the mail compartment, and the vans pulled real close to the platforms.

Jana promised his teammates breakfast in Colombo Port Harbor Café overlooking the shipping business district. Uncle Cecil was there to show the Jaffna boys how the harbor system worked. He had already arranged the security clearance. Jokingly: 'The Tamil boys are here to take your jobs, fools. No shooting here alright,' said some of the colleagues.

Uncle Cecil replied quickly: 'Don't get confused, it's only a cricket bat.' He was a senior wharf officer, with fifteen years of experience in sea freights. 'Say hello to Jaffna Champions,' said cricketing fan Uncle Cecil. He quickly ordered breakfast in Sinhala and spoke to us in English to explain the harbor systems. He was not afraid of anybody and was outspoken. They told him to be careful. He said: 'Don't worry, none of these fools understand good English. He is in charge here. Totally controlled by the trade ministry and the union gangsters. There is no coast guard, just Navy Patrol to avoid smugglers and thieves. The Navy does all the jobs here along with the police. They get their cut from the shipping magnates of rice and tea barons. After that, rich tea gets swapped in warehouses prior to departure for a local builder's brew. Dollars and gold get to be exchanged in large amounts. They ran all this operation from the slave island city. The city was run from the port authority profits in millions. That was the people's money. Everybody is making money except us honest civil servants who have to put in long hours to cut out Parker Pen bureaucrats who can't even change their refills,' said Uncle Cecil.

They walked around and got some hostile stares, then decided to leave. That was a quite a dangerous place for new faces. Everybody watched everybody's back except Uncle Cecil, who did not really care. Like Mr. Prahash, he also was a man of taste and hard work. Loved and trusted by his friends for his taste in foreign liqueur. Jana gave him a bottle and some message from Aunty Ruby for the time he gave us. Like his father, he was learning quickly to please people. He was very happy. After a small bus ride, they walked down to the market to reach the Galle face seaside. Silingo House Insurance complex imitated the World Trade Centre. The twelfth floor view of the city and the port all around was quite amazing. They took a swim at the Y.M.C.A, prior to lunch. Then they watched the American film at the Majestic Theatre called The 'Taking of Pelham 123', played by Robert Shaw and Walter Matthau. It was also a train film. That was a fantastic story of desperate ex-army individuals.

Then they took the 155 bus to Marathanai, walked down to All Saints Church, Borella. They met some old Peterites at Kittyakara, the poor man's medical halls of residence where they were told to stay away from the Wellikadai prison area if they don't know Sinhala. The cricketers said they were only there to watch the Ananda and Nalanda cricket teams doing their daily practice. That was all.

So they walked down and sat on the grass and watched the game. If any thugs come their way, they were to enter the church in the next block, the Church of Our Lady of Perpetual Help, as Guntilake would do the talking. Some of the boys were already on the nets, it was only 1 p.m. on a bank holiday poya. In Buddhist tradition, no work or play on that day. One batsman started to bat. He had a full kit and bowlers and a band of supporters. More joined in, each had a spare cricket bat.

Back in their college, they used three or four bats for the whole college team on a first come, first served basis, or may the rich come first basis. The complete kit was kept and repaired under the first floor stair box room and kit storage room. The genius of the groundsman, George, kept all the sports equipment under that small space reconditioned and also saved money for the college. He was thin and frail in his 60's; his son helped him out on his holidays and evenings. He was the master in seasoning the cricket bat with oil and hammer. He also cleverly twined the bat with nylon fish wire to give extra strength and compact protection.

Sometimes the loose nylon confused the umpires with the out swing. A loud appeal from the wicket keeper was enough to confuse everybody. Their captain always said, *please, please don't join in the appeal from the fine leg position. Moreover no silly appeals. If you do, it must be followed by the apology to the umpire with sincerity, thank you.*

'Now pass that sauce,' said Titus at the dinner table at the Galle beachfront after a good cricket watching time. They also managed to talk to some cricketers. Most of them were friendly and looked forward to coming to Jaffna on next year's senior tour. That was the time they also met the Nalanda captain, Arjun. Titus reflected the sentiment: *don't upset the umpires, remember. Well, in this case I will tip the waiters, and ask for some more noodles. Then we will have that hotel specialty, the rum punch.* Everybody agreed and took out their notes. They all said: *Gaba to Patrol, Gaba to Patrol* – a quote from the Pelham 123 movie. Another one said: *Who wants to know?*

During the night they had good security escort from a Kotchikadai Tamil business men, who showed them around the town: the peep shows, adults book shops, and also talked to some working girls, all in good nature with good manners, just for the experience and knowledge. One or two wanted to take it to another level, but they had been warned by the locals. Security Escort informed them, *these are clip joints, and you will lose everything if you enter those places, including your foreskin.* They laughed and joked all the way to the Y.M.C.A. They stayed there overnight and took the lunchtime train back to Jaffna.

That was a real bonding trip which made them come even closer in college as a team. They all loved each other like brothers; some of them were emotional about where they were going to be, they wanted the group to continue even after their college lives. Some already knew they would be leaving the country for fear of abduction and torture.

That same year they were surprisingly invited by the upcountry Matala and Kandy under-seventeen cricketing circuit. After all, everybody wanted to test the Jaffna Champions. The idea had been to bring the Catholic schools together all around the country in brotherhood and harmony while all the anti-Tamil propaganda gripped the nation. They stayed in seminary halls and played Matale Catholic colleges.

Then Jana met his under-fifteen friends from St Anthony's whom he had met two years earlier, after he refused to take that invaluable scholarship to play in Kandy which had been a foolish decision and he regretted it when the captaincy did not came his way.

Two train trips in the same year, covering all breathtaking locations and views of the Island. Jana could not believe it was happening. Xavi also couldn't say no to this opportunity. His beautiful left hand writing, and well kept scorebook, his motivational humor unlike any other cricketing seniors, always attracted the teachers and students. He also tied up all the sarongs during the night, pulled it all together and took a photo of us all naked on a Polaroid camera.

The following morning, all in good humor, they started to score big scores on the cool swinging cricket turfs. They won the first match. Then the second one. News spread: the Tamil boys are in town winning matches. They attracted lots of female attention which gave them a lot of support. But it also created a little rift among the locals.

They would wave their machetes at the end of the match. The Jaffna boys did not take it seriously: *come on, it is only a cricket game. We just happen to be playing a little better than you up country boys. I can see why, all this beautiful distraction of sensuality. It's begun to support us. Anybody wants to settle in up country, look what you got boys for the audience. I am not leaving this place.*

Jana gave a few smiles to the girls. They were young and stupid, *jack fruit (pila palam) slicer won't frighten us,* they joked at the farming character, gestured back with fingers without fear. This was a goodwill tour among the Catholic brotherhood, not a competition.

St. Peter's did lose a match with a science college due to all the excitement. Jana played the last match at Kandy, just to impress the old Anton Raj crew. Jana played the most amazing innings of his life, scoring an unbeaten century and declared. He was so pleased with his performance he even got a few numbers and addresses in Kandy. He kept in touch with the boys and girls as pen pals.

Their trip contributed to great relationships with southern colleges. They also looked at the Adam's Peak and the surrounding mountains after the match. Suddenly, from nowhere, they were traveling the whole country. That was unforgettable.

Jana also traveled to the college charitable interact club event in Colombo, where he met some of the Kandy college boys.

That brought the senior years. Jana expected the captaincy this time after the consistent service to the college cricket. The new influential opening batsman would arrive to take the leadership. Jana would again take on the responsibility as vice captain. Runs were not coming as usual. A friend from Jaffna Hindu College Cricket Team, called Balan, talked about joining the movement in Jaffna. Jana introduced Indhiran to him. Both found each other interesting. He was a soft spoken and good cricketer.

At this time Jana was really confused about his life; his interest in cricket began to diminish when he understood the hardships of Tamils around the country. The only thing he wanted to do now was concentrate on his running to take the college senior 1500 and 3000 meters.

This time Jana read all about Sebastian Coe. His training regime by his father Peter Coe was published in one of the international athletic magazines. He pinned that on the wall. Seb Coe was training for his Moscow Olympics, and there was a lot of pressure on boycotting the games, with Steve

Ovett right in front of him. Jana also planned to leave the country and applied to colleges in California and Texas. He wanted to be with the horses. He needed the sponsors. He asked Uncle Ranga to help. He was prepared to do that. With that good news he concentrated back on cricket and athletics full time.

The United States boycotted the Moscow Olympics due to the Russian invasion of Afghanistan. The British left the athletes to decide. Sebastian Coe decided when he broke the world record.

'He will go for the Olympic gold,' said Jana to his friends.

Peter Coe trained him to perfection. Some of their parents did not even come to the sports field to encourage their kids. Everybody was supporting the working class Steve Ovett. He did take the 800m with total surprise to Coe. Jana was disappointed and went into hiding until the 1500 final. Seb Coe wouldn't let Jana down this time. The energy and the determined look and the timing and the devastating finish with number 254 on his vest, it made the hair stand on end when Seb Coe won the 1500. Breathless, he knelt down and kissed the Moscow grounds with tears of joy, completely out of energy. It was on all the front covers of the newspaper around the world. The whole world praised the Coe as magnificent, the English middle distance runner. Jana would go to the shop front to watch the clips on his bike. Jaffna did not have TV yet. Not in all houses, anyway. With that long awaited inspiration, Jana would run and run, in the cold morning on the college grounds, alone, in the darkness before the sunrise. Some priests looked at his dedication from the dormitory balcony.

He thought about the days that he had been punished for his mischievous behavior. Jana somehow never got caught with that kind of misfortune in his final year.

He understood the time had come for him to leave the school. He wanted to leave with honor and good memories.

The boy who ran barefoot down the street to avoid the police, the army, had set up tournaments in the lane and church yards, had run behind the cycles, run everywhere like a lunatic, whenever he was physically beaten down, would finally take the gold medals in front of the full house audience in the college athletic meet celebration for 1500, 3000m ,400 X 400 and silver in the 800, just missing out on the four timer. Jana would also go and take the Inter Jaffna colleges quadrangular meet awards in middle distance. He would make all the bullies and the unfair selectors take notice of the champion sporting colors.

Finally came the long-awaited day in Jana's senior final year cricketing life. The big championship match against Jaffna College. Jana was a little disappointed the match was played away in the countryside in and around the paddy field. He wanted a home game. He wanted the party of success in front of his friends. He wanted his name to be announced on the college loud speaker when he entered the pitch, like the old greats of the college past. That was every little kid's dream when they sat next to the scoreboard and somersaulted for the boundaries. Some of the big names rang in his ears from the unforgettable two and half days of high class cricket during the early seventies big matches.

It was not meant to be. They even spelled his name wrong on the big match souvenir. Moses Joseph even joked at Jana's expense in front of the team: 'Maybe that's your lucky charm. It might change that not-so-high scoring season.' He was not one of Jana's favorite rectors. He had recently been promoted from the middle school. He really tried hard to gain his authority with his unorthodox methods. Jana preferred the constructive criticism from the prefect of games Sam Fredrick, which was without any indirect victimization. He preferred the straight talking of a tall man. It was a quite a sad occasion when he passed away that year with illness.

Jana played his most important innings, saving St. Peter's collapse and batted for five hours scoring 168 and carried the bat. He dedicated his best batsman award to Sam Fredrick and earned his name in the college cricket record books in regard to the big match with the college greats.

Jana saw the face of Moses Joseph when he was handed the cricket cup as a visiting principal. His joke at the rectory turned out to be a reality. Jana looked at him with a locked eye and said: 'Thank you very much. Thank you very much for overlooking the captaincy twice. Thank you very much for the cricket colors and thank you very much for the athletic championship shield.' All this Jana had missed out due to Moses Joseph.

Moses Joseph favored students according to the class and status in the college. He liked the power with aggression. He also mis-organized a few events in St. Peter's which would cause trouble and violence for students they would all like to forget. Particularly the school carnival for cancer fund: bringing police and violence inside the college grounds was a black mark for any priest of that college stature.

To make matters worse, when Jana approached him to get his Leaving Certificate, which was drafted by the senior English teacher on behalf of the students, the rector got all animated in his office, saying, *I can't accept anybody's draft. We will do the letters ourselves.* He shouted and lost his cool, on somebody who had served the school well for 12 years.

Later that year their beloved senior English master was tragically gunned down in front of the house by the army, while being questioned by an officer on the mistreatment of an innocent female bystander. Even in his last minute, he was trying to help somebody unlike some of the beloved Catholic priests at St Peter's. Jana left the school and never forgave them for all the mistreatment and physical violence by the priests and he hated everything St. Peter's stood for.

Moses Joseph made a lot of typing errors, blemishes, bad grammar and listed all Jana's achievement in the college like a cooperative store bill. His letter also contained patronizing comments with the dreadful final statement. If you had made your contribution, and had been nice to the college clergy you would sure gain any certificate you liked on your leaving day. They really did not like the free spirited outspoken youths. If the boys can't do that – speak out - in their own school, how could they fight for their rights in their torturing dictatorial country.

That was the stance Jana took, face to face with the rector when he said goodbye for the last time, with a lot of emotion. He said: 'Rector, when I came to this college first time, in front of Fr. Durant I shed a few tears for my inclusion in this great college. Today, I have achieved quite a bit as a Peterite, starting from a humble but educated background from Delft. I had no support from anybody regarding my sporting achievement. My family had no sports background or understood it. I had nobody come and see my participation. My greatest achievement apart from my studies was hard work and tenacity towards my athletics. Father, that is really God's gift. Nobody can take that away from me. I am looking forward to continuing my struggle elsewhere and looking into my positive future. Thanks for your contribution. Especially with your bamboo cane.'

Moses was not happy at all, tapped his pencil on the table

and said: 'Listen, I got a lot to do today. Shall we talk about this next week? You got a friendly match coming next week against the Colombo St. Benedict's, you are staying to play, aren't you? Well, you don't want to miss that, if you are going to Colombo to get a job,' he said patronizingly. 'Before you leave, Jana, just don't take it too serious and get into all this conspiracy mood, thinking everybody is against you. No, you are a good person, you did better in sports than in your studies. I wish you all the best in your future. Come and see me before you leave next week. Ok, Jana, speak to you later. Shut the door when you leave, will you, thanks.'

Jana walked out disappointed and confused. He was really beginning to hate nic named casanova, the rector. Yes every priest in St peter's had a nic name.

He would stay and face the speed king of Colombo, St. Benedict's champion bowler, Ratnayake, when he opened bat for St. Peter's. Jana did not see the first two balls, there was not even a background white board. It was a zinging noise with a swing. No time to read, react and re-adjust but Jana managed to lift that heavy grey Nicholas to put the third ball to the chapel end under the scoreboard. That meant a good follow through, between the midwicket and the fine leg. A few youngsters somersaulted to put the metal numbers on the board. Jana had a big cheer from the pavilion, too including from his nemeses, Fr. Moses Joseph. Ratnayake was a key fast bowler in the Sri Lankan college eleven. He was also guaranteed a place in the test team. Jana stayed on the crease as usual, but without runs this time. After two hours, he had only scored twelve runs. Wickets were collapsing on the other end. Jana pleaded with everybody to stay there without going for the big shots. Unlike other colleges, St. Benedict's were all out for 120 against St. Peter's. They thought that was an easy target to reach. But it was not meant to be. Benedict's got them out at 95. They lost the match by 25 runs. Jana was the not-out batsman scoring the highest 27 runs.

Their heads drooped as the Colombo boys put out their byla songs in the changing rooms. They came and thanked Jana for his patience and said *well batted.*

It turned out to be a great trip for them. Some of their girlfriends and teenage sweethearts also toured from Colombo, and they came to their changing rooms making all of the St. Peter's Catholic boys all shy and horny. They cuddled and kissed in public in the college corridors and made Moses Joseph a little uneasy but he could not do anything. Jana loved it, started chatting to the ladies *whether they enjoyed the trip? Were they going to look at some romantic spots in Jaffna? We have some of the best, cleanest beaches in the country,* he boasted.

Well, you have that in Colombo, too, I guess. They really looked sexy with their tight miniskirts.

In Jaffna they were completely repressed about talking or expressing sexuality before marriage. It was taboo. The girls came from the capital, all adults and it was a vocational cricket tour. They were allowed to do what they pleased. It was a quite a sight in the night quarters. They invited the boys to join them later in their top floor rooms overlooking the Beach Road. A few of the boys did go to that party. But a few of their well-mannered friends had to leave early, due to the lack of direction the party was leading to. They were really confused at the full orgies which the girls planned for them at the top floor of St. Peter's above the priest's dormitories.

'What an excellent idea,' said Jana.

One of the boys came and said: 'Come on, come and join

man. It's ok, it is all paid for. They are our close girl friends, Colombo 7, raunchy set. Not to worry. Come on, don't be shy, you hard working Tamil boys.'

A few of us did kiss the girls and enjoyed that they managed to annoy Moses Joseph. Jana did not go home that night. He got drunk for the first time in his life. Then slept at Indhiran's place. He really did not want to leave that final party at St. Peter's. It was almost a send off for Jana. Nobody remembered anything about the girls and the alcohol. They smuggled a lot of bottles from the back of the college cemetery end, in the middle of the night. They really scored the double century and won the match that night.

They said cheers to St. Peter's! Cheers Moses Joseph! Cheers to St. Benedict's for giving them all the best time of their lives! They said cheers to Ratnayake! Cheers to Ranatunge! Cheers to Mendis! Cheers to Asantha de Mel! All the cricketing greats of that time.cheers to all the beautiful teachers, cheers to all the class mates, all of you good bye. Cheers to Fr. Durant!

Goodbye.

CRICKET-CLOSE FIELD SETUP.
1978 LINDEY 1st CHAMPIONSHIP
AT JAFFNA CENTRAL

CLOCK TOWER
OPEN THEATRE

CHAPTER EIGHT

KISSING THE GIRLS WHEN LONELY

Jana woke up with a heavy head. He muttered: 'I need to see her. I need to see Priyanka. I don't want to give any details to you, Indhiran, just take me to her will you? Then you will understand. She is a Colombo beauty came with the cricketers.'

Everybody laughed at the Indhiran's house. They all slept in the same room on the mud floor, lying on a reed mat. There was one bed in the corner taken by the most tired worker in the house. They were happy with their mats. It was the most comfortable mat for any back pain but did impress all the marks of the woven reed onto the skin. Jana rolled side to side. He looked quite insane and funny. Nobody had ever seen him like that, ever. Jana continued sleep talking: 'I don't know what it will be, just nice to see you again, touch you, speak to you, perhaps. Let's say curiosity will not kill the heartache.'

'Hey, Jana! Hey, Jana. You dreaming… go back to sleep,' said Indhiran. He pinched his ears and said: 'It's only 6 a.m. and it's a Saturday, so you can sleep a little longer. I will wake you up later, ok?' No more school for you. You are out. Clean bowled.'

Jana looked up, eyes wide open and said *sorry* and went

back to sleep. He kept on turning left and right on the matt trying to get comfortable. The alcohol did not go well with him, that was the first drink he had ever taken. Indhiran woke him about 10 a.m. Jana still smelled of alcohol.

Indhiran said: 'Let's have a shower and enjoy your freedom. You are leaving the college, aren't you?'

Jana shook his head and said *yes*. They both had a quick shower in the outdoor well, bringing the water from deep below on a bucket and rope on a rolling wheel.

Indhiran said: 'You want to go and see a lady?'

Jana looked up and smiled: 'Why not?' Everbody laughed in the house.

They dressed and left quickly without even having any breakfast.

Jana said to his Aunty Rohini: 'I am ok for breakfast.' He just didn't want to take the portion of another cousin, after all there were five boys and girls having to manage a couple of loaves of bread and some seeni sombol. Four slices each, with plain tea. Times were hard in Jaffna during the early eighties.

It was a beautiful Saturday morning as Jana and Indhiran cycled passed the Hospital Road on their way to Windsor Theatre, then turned left on a five face junction famous for all the Muslim Chefs who specialized in south Indian food. The mosque stood above the buildings and they heard the Imam praying the Saturday morning Kerath through the loudspeaker. The vibrant Muslim Tamils came through the trades from Middle East via India from the Arabian Sea. They have contributed wonderful color and culture to the Tamil nation. Textiles, sculptures, culinary, gold and silver workers, joiners, slaughter houses - all lined up near this junction. Indhiran knew about this place. This was where all the political gatherings and recruitment took place during the late seventies.

The gold workers also brought the women to the area. Girls would come and see the varieties of jewelries: some were costume; some were very expensive with gold with diamonds pressed in. All were made by hand in front of the client. Pipe blowing on a live fire made of burned dark coconut slates looked an intricate ancient art, and was still carried on by the gold crafting Pathan generation. So the police and the military were there too; unofficially, in plain clothes.

This was the area where the north suburb and south of Jaffna City meet. It was a speaker's corner of the seventies. You could have a great meal, hear the speeches, and then it was up to you to participate in further gatherings elsewhere with short notice. It was a light-hearted debating area where they first heard about human rights. Especially the Right to Peaceful Protest. But Indhiran did not bring Jana there for any debates or meetings that morning. He came to see a working girl. Indhiran had finished school a year earlier, and was still looking for a job. Jana just finished and didn't know what to do, as his father was away, and his mother was not well from a tragic accident and his sisters were growing up so he had to make his mind up what to do with his life while he waited for his A/L results. Indhiran had to find a job quickly; his younger brother had started work in the glass factory blowing glasses at heavy temperatures for low wages. He was a year younger than Jana but looked ill and thin from malnutrition. He would come home with burn scars. Sometimes he had collapsed at work with exhaustion. But he persevered to help the family in some way. Jana asked Indhiran: 'How is your elder brother? I don't see him much nowadays.'

Indhiran said: 'He is working in a textile firm doing sales. Even I don't see him much. He comes in at an odd time and works seven days a week. He loves French clothes and style.

His dream is to work and live there. He really wants a black Peugeot 504.'

Jana said: 'The one like the police chief drives. Yep, he likes it. He thinks French means reliable. Ask anything French, he would love to talk to you for hours nonstop. He loves the French movies: Aliean Delon, Belmondo, Bardot, Trufout, Melwille, Depardue, Deveraa. You know what his favorite French film is?' asked Indhiran.

Jana said: 'Let's say, he likes Delon and Mellwille. How about Le Samurai?'

'Yes, he likes that too but his all time favorite is Lavelsus. He went to Colombo to watch that film, twice. If you can find a video he will pay 200 rupees. No Beta Max though. He's got the American version of a poster called Going Places, on his wall. Just don't even go close to that, he will go mad. He likes the French girls, too. He really wants to go to certain places.'

Jana said: 'You know, Indhiran, I'd like to marry a European girl, too, you know.'

'What's wrong with the girls here, Jana? Dirty, loose knickers? The European girls like a mean machine, machann (cousin), they can suppress their emotions whenever they feel liked it. Change and swap relationships with quiet calm. Getting over it, they say? Getting over? The divorce is quite normal, all agreed in advance, some plan it before the marriage with the thing call pre nupt, pre napt - I don't know. It is all worked out by the lawyers. Yeah, all worked out. Yeah I read all about it in the Reader's Digest. Hah.'

Jana looked surprised: 'What? Please don't put me off. Don't say that. You are destroying my fantasy, Indhiran. No wonder being a lawyer is big business in Europe.'

'They have lawyers for everything they do. Marry one of

them, fall in love, do whatever you want, you will be set for life with beautiful mixed race kids. Marriage lawyer, business lawyer, house lawyer, you know for selling and buying, divorce lawyer, music lawyer, film lawyer, litigation lawyer, meaning big corporate firms like to fight it out for their millions. These guys like to laugh loudly at the parties and state their presence. Like to read big folders full of small print and like to speak in public with prompting cards. Ha ha ha… I like the criminal and the public defendants, immigration lawyers, human rights, most of all I admire the death row lawyers. Why don't you study law, Jana, like our famous G.G.P. who won the case with two elephants in the matchbox? Even a cook, the thief, the killer, the child molester gets a lawyer in Europe. You don't have to say anything until you get your lawyer.'

'Yeah,' said Jana, 'I have seen it in the films, they always talk the fifth. That's an American right.'

'In England it's all brown files and pink lace knots. Pays well. It is not all standing in front of the judge delivering your argument. You know, my dad used to take me to courts. He was a courts official,' said Indhiran. 'What do you think? That I read it all in the Reader's Digest? Anyway, the girls in Europe like to marry a few times. Another day, another wedding dress. Another child with another guy.'

Jana was disappointed: 'You are exaggerating, Indhiran. The British are not like the other ones in Europe especially as the country is made up of different cultures like Irish, Jewish, Scottish, Welsh and Italians. The mother is the leader of the family. They like to keep the extended family traditions, like us. Come on, you are lying, making it up as you go along. How about do they have caste system? The Queen must be the highest caste because the Royals also have arranged marriages among other Royals. The British Queen Elizabeth married a Greek-German prince, right?' said Jana.

'I thought the British didn't like the Germans after fighting two great wars. I guess after the seventies' flower period and rock and roll, Mercedes, BMW, Porsche, no choice with its all free love now ah?' replied Indhiran sarcastically. He did not like the British because of the past colonial history, by breaking the kingdoms of Sri Lanka against the minority Tamils

They were still cycling as they approached their destination. Jana said: 'I think love, romance, relationship, marriage - all are similar wherever you go. Everywhere all the same. If you really love someone let them go free, if they come back, they are yours and you will find satisfaction and happiness. Anyway, what do I know about satisfaction, ah Indhiran?' said Jana. 'Running and cricket give me a lot of satisfaction. The rest of it maybe. I had a little taste of it last night. Delicious.'

'Very good baby, now you are talking my language. Satisfaction. That's what we are here for,' said Indhiran while looking at Jana with a smile. 'You did not even go home last night. You drank, kissed a Sinhalese beauty. Your mum was looking for you. Don't worry, I lied on your behalf. my brother is doing some shopping with your sisters and lying for you that you have taken the Colombo boys on a tour of Jaffna. Nice and believable lie for your sick mum, on your behalf. So, don't worry but if you talk about this to anybody, when your dad comes back from his high seas adventure, he will drop us both in the deep well, seriously man. Prepare for a long dark isolation in cold water. I know you, with all the excitement you will slip up a few times. Even at your school remember? I heard you had a little face to face incident with Father Nesam. He gave you a few slaps in front of the class.'

Jana had tried to forget that embarrassing violent moment

with the upper school priest, and did not say anything. Indhiran continued: 'Not even to your cricket mates. Don't be scared ok, you are a big man now. You don't need to take that kind of abuse from the priests.' Indhiran was a little angry about the violent beating by the priests that went on in Jaffna schools. 'Believe me, all good Catholic boys dip their little dogs somewhere, but nobody talks to anybody, except the lovely Rosita, of this town's sexual kingdom. She will give you a few clues about the regular customers but it's a secret. It is business, Jana, don't be so truthful. It is painful to watch you being so honest. Lie a little, keep a few secrets. It's all a sign of growing up. Somebody close might betray you. Imagine that, hah? There goes your lovely character references, cricket colors, final Leaving Certificates to get your dream job in Colombo's top mercantile firm, opening bat, Colombo Athletic competitions, all the beauties from Kollpity Colombo Seven to Mount Lavania. Big dowry. Come on, you love it all. What's happened to your face, it's all gone black? What's happened, Jana?' said Indhiran. 'You look like you've seen the Muni ghost. Have I scared you? Just made you think about your morals and honesty, that's all. Come on, you fool. We were just doing it for fun. It is not going to destroy your future and your sensibilities. Jesus Christ, relax. What have you become, Jana?' Where is that guy who said one time, I will try anything once. It is a business to someone. It is a Police business. It is a relief and experience to another one. You will look at the girl in another light. Be sure about it. It was a liberation for me. So you can forget all this nonsense of no sex before marriage crap. You will find out after all it's not what everybody makes it out to be. It is a simple bodily function. You don't marry somebody for this, you marry someone because you like them, trust them, you're going to have a friendship that's going to be long and non judgmental, a partnership that leads to parenthood. Just don't break your moral marbles because our elders preach this. Just do it.'

Indhiran appeared restless, thinking Jana might change his mind. He began to smell his right arm. Jana pulled his hand down and said: 'Ok you bastard, zip up, not a word anymore.' He smiled: 'Let's say the rabbit's going to bust the dust. Let's do it like Randall McMurphy in One Flew Over the Cuckoo's Nest. *Rosita is going to feel it like a pinball machine.* Shit we have to pay, right?'

'Don't worry, I have got that all covered, for today at least.'

Jana and Indhiran parked their bikes, put the locks on and took the keys, looked left and right keeping their cricket hats well low to cover their faces, and walked through the alleyway. Water dripped from a low pipeline: some crack on the large sewer pipes emitted a stench. There was also a yellow slime of dead algae mixed with urine on every corner. Water trickled down the pavement slabs which were also broken and repaired recently with cement which looked quite obvious with finger marks. Incense sticks were burning and the aromatic poor man cooking with basic ingredients, diverted the thoughts. Kids were playing among the street dogs in the adjoining derelict area.

They took a sharp turn left. Indhiran paused. An old lady sat on a low stool, smoking a homemade tobacco pipe with spices. She smiled at Indhiran when he dropped something in her hand. Her tobacco-blackened mouth had a few teeth and looked like something in a horror film. She did not smile at Jana until he passed her. Then she turned around and looked at his back side, then she laughed loudly, insanely. The whole shanty town probably heard that wild laugh.

Indhiran smiled cheekily at Jana and said: 'She likes you.

I never made her happy like this ever before. Hey, Jana, you devil, how do you do it? Even to the old ladies.'

A little kid came with an English book and asked *what is this grandma?* The old lady very reluctantly said: 'Let's see, my dear. Which one did you not understand?' The kid in the school uniform spoke English well with perfect grammar. The old lady sent her grandson to the top school in town. Even though they lived a simple life, they made sure the kids got all their education. The clothes were all drying in the middle of the hall, it looked clean and well kept with cooking eating and sleeping all in one room.

Jana watched all this detail as he climbed the old derelict stairwell then down from another to get to the small annexed flat. If a heavy person climbed on that stairwell it would have come down without a doubt. Jana and Indhiran tip-toed one by one. The kids on the other side below gestured with palm and fingers mimicking intercourse, closing one hand and porking with the other. Jana was embarrassed. Indhiran kept a straight face, pointed a finger over his mouth and said: 'Quiet, shhhh. The army are patrolling the streets. You know what happens if they come here! Go on get some ice (lolly) palam, go on,' he said and gave them a few rupees. 'For all of you, ok?' They ran quickly on the loose stairwell. Indhiran cringed: 'Oh careful. You suckers. If I don't do that they will be here peaking through and wasting our time, with Rosita making a scene of it all. Even with all this disruptiveness you just have to get on with the job in hand, so you got to look after everybody. It is hard work, Jana. Too many middle men. But we always pay!'

Indhiran turned around, and said: 'Everybody call her Pinky, some call her Rosita. She was the well-known police hooker in her glory days a few years ago. The police also protected her and the army had a cut in the business too. I knew a copper who likes grandma's hoppers. He recommended Rosita to me. She used to be a nurse before, then she got struck off for having sex with the patients in the middle of the ward.' Both laughed loud. 'That's why she is clean and healthy. She really understands the risks involved. Now she is into sex education and therapy. She will teach you everything a man needs to know in half an hour. The things you can't even ask your parents or do with your wife. Here is your rubber, you are the opening bat, go and face the pair of full blooded body, tossed straight to your almost broken face. It is not a test match. You just got twenty minutes, then I do the rest in ten. It's not research or a social gathering for talking and asking silly questions. She is clean and highly recommended. Guess who she looks like? Great Indian movie star Sharmili. Oh baby, oh baby, oh baby Sharmili,' Indhiran sang an old Boolwood song.

Jana looked at Indhiran: 'You go first.'

Indhiran paused for a minute, did not argue. He said: 'Can you please read that paper and cover your face? There are a few windows open in this area.'

Jana looked around anxiously, then sat down and said quietly: 'I haven't done anything yet to worry about anyway.' He smiled. He looked above the windows around and said: 'So what. Have a good look.'

Indhiran said: 'Now you are shaking the legs in panic. I will be quiet inside, she won't be.' Indhiran went inside.

Jana squeezed his hands. After a few minutes he began to hear a moaning noise from both of them. Jana quietly moved away from the door. *Hah… haa…* the female noise got a little heavier. Jana took the paper up, nervously sung a Tamil song (ulakam prenthathu ennakkaca), an old M.G.R. song about somebody enjoying their life in this world.

Ten minutes went by. Indhiran came out with a smile: 'Yes, I am done. It's your time, big boy. Go on!' He pretended to grab Jana's pants.

Jana said: 'You ponce. Gay fool. I heard you going huh, huh, huh, like a baby screaming for the milk.'

Indhiran said: 'You heard! Ah she loved it. Go on, let's see what you can do. Big mouth.'

Indhiran knew Jana always liked a challenge. He pushed him in.

Jana went rushing with a kind smile, quite shy. Pinky lay flat with a small Chinese paper fan swinging it close to her lips. Her body looked slightly sweated and swollen up. Her olive-like skin with the dark erected chest looked a great contrast. Jana was feeling the heat of seeing a woman in real flesh. He began to keep his hand down. He looked up. There were boxes everywhere, even up to the ceiling. Jana always looked around to ease the tension.

Pinky smiled and said: 'Your name is Jana. I heard you are a running man. So you going to disappoint me?' She smiled. 'I am really looking forward to this.'

Jana could not believe her frankness.

She laughed. 'Come here, you dirty boy, don't be shy.' Jana came close. 'I have a few regular sprinters and spinners,' said Rosita.

Eighteen year old Jana sat close and looked at her with sympathy like a little boy. Outside, Indhiran looked at the time anxiously. Jana began to ask Pinky personal questions about her life, like *where are you from? What's your village? How many in your family?* They were all anxious questions of a man under pressure. She began to get bored and began to lose interest. She lifted her skirt up gently, while talking. She really had a swollen stomach. Jana fell back in shock. 'What is this? You are pregnant?' Jana felt angry and annoyed with Indhiran. 'He never told me this. Where is your husband? Are you married?' he asked with a scared face. He asked her this while standing naked in front of her in fear. Pinky said: 'Come here and calm down. Come. Come,' she called him in a soft voice. Jana approached her in small steps. 'Calm down, you silly fool. I don't know what you all learn in the private schools.' She grabbed him closer to her chest. 'Bury your face and your curly hair in here, stupid boy. You fool. I don't know who the father is.' Jana interrupted and said: 'I don't want sleep with someone else's wife. That's all. I am not a home wrecker. I don't want the trouble. Shit, shit!' he screamed like a good Catholic-Tamil boy.

She told Jana: 'Kiss me. Go on, do you like what you see' Jana said quietly: 'Yes.'

She smiled and said we all are someone else's wife, brother. Do you want to make love to me or not?' And she kissed him on the lips. 'Say yes, don't waste my time. I am very busy today. It's a Saturday.'

'Ok, I will be gentle,' said Jana.

'Don't you worry about that, I will be all right.'

She stroked his sharpened arrow and put on the latex. Jana was so uncomfortable by now, still he began to relax a little.

'There you go, big boy. You are not Jewish, nor Muslim, why?' she said as she pointed at his circumcision.

'It was a mistake,' said Jana. 'Let's not talk about that, please. First I was pissing fine, second thing I knew, I couldn't do it at all. That's the result, I have to wear my sister's silk skirt wet with blood for two weeks.'

'Silk skirt? Blood?' asked Rosita.

'Well, it looks good and clean,' said Pinky. She took Jana's hand, asking: 'You don't have nails, do you?'

Jana began vigorously kissing her all over.

She said: 'Be gentle, it's quite tender, as you know. But I like it.' She took Jana's hand and gently controlled his movement.

She said: 'Come closer to me, closer,' and she pulled Jana towards her. She said: 'That's good.'

Indhiran begin to hear the moans. The noises increased: aaah… ah… ah… aha…

By this time Jana was in love with Pinky and said: 'I love you. Aahh ahh! I love you! I love you!'

Indhiran laughed hysterically outside, making all kinds of hysteric emotions like a joker with a painted face. Pinky also screamed: 'Yeah, yeah, good.' There was a lot of heavy breathing. 'Oh, Jana, that's good.' Then she got up quietly and washed quickly, paused for a few minutes and said: 'See you, sometime,' and kept a straight face like she was meeting Jana all over again. Jana slowly pulled his pants up, all the while looking at her amazing change of character in just a few minutes. Then he went and washed his hands. She gave him a hug. Jana gave her a kiss with a tight hug and said: 'Thank you, thank you very much. I will never forget you and said goodbye.'

She said: 'Thank you. You are a good kisser, Jana. You gonna make a nice girl screaming happy.' Then she pulled that Chinese fan in front of her lips. She put on the water taps to fill the bucket for a shower.

He said 'I guess I will see you again,' he paused, 'no probably not, why lie, Pinky. God bless you, take care of the baby and yourself.' He walked out slowly.

Indhiran said: 'Come on you preacher. Did you organize a social worker for Pinky? Get on with your job in hand you time wasting block master.' This was insulting his cricket. 'Time is money in this town.'

Jana shouted: 'Hey!' and angrily grabbed Indhiran for the first time ever in a rage and put him against the fence. 'Why did you never say anything about her pregnancy? What if something happened to the baby eh?' he said squeezing his neck. 'Complications, miscarriages. I can't take that kind of shit and suffering on my conscience.'

'You fool!' said Indhiran. 'I did not know nothing about this until today. Seriously, Jana. It was the honest truth,' said Indhiran. 'I don't come here every month to know her well being.'

Jana let go of the grip. Indhiran said quickly: 'But you loved it. You enjoyed it, hah? Say thank you, you fool.' Then he smiled and said: 'Hey, did you enjoy it or not? Was it all natural?'

Jana shook his head.

Indhiran said: 'Ok then. Who will do this for you? Say a big fucking thank you. Rushing me like that. You fucker. It is safe to have sex with a pregnant lady, you fool. You know that, don't you? Unless you are a devout Catholic and don't know much about the human anatomy and evolution. As long as you are gentle with her it is ok. I don't want to talk about this anymore, ok? I am exhausted. Man, you owe me twenty five big ones.'

Jana gave fifteen and said: 'I'll give you the rest later and I will buy you lunch at Shubass café.'

'Have you got any change?' asked Indhiran.

Jana took out the few coins he had. Indhiran added some from his pocket and gave it to the old lady on the way out and said she is the boss madam.

'Appearances can be deceptive, Jana, don't be fooled. These people are not well off. Well educated, forced to do these things by the police and the army. Just business, Jana, survival of the brave and the unconcerned. Even the ball kicking against the fence was a signal for the time is up. When you hear a loud knock a few times, the police are on their way for their cut. They like to keep an eye on their investment.'

Jana did not speak for half an hour. He sat in front of a cool glass of pink sherbet with tropical fruits with the floating vanilla ice cream, the pink knickerbocker glory that tasted so good. He sipped the drink like a different person, with Indhiran looking at him strangely. First words he said: 'I felt sorry for her, sorry for the girls who are in that position without any choice. I am sorry for the men who put the women in that position. I am really saddened by our society who let this happen. She was a beautiful woman. Yes, I am touched by the whole experience, Indhiran. Thank you. I want a family more than ever. I want to marry a nice Tamil girl,' said Jana to Indhiran's surprise. Then he said: 'Thank you for doing this for me. I love you for this forever.' He also almost cried with emotion.

'You fucking fool, you going to make me cry too. Stop it!' said Indhiran. 'I must also say to you that it made me realize the importance of the family too, Jana. I never thought it would hit me like this, but it did. What an experience being with a woman for the first time. This is mesmerising.'

Indhiran called the waiter and said *can you please bring the bill*? Jana said: 'My hard earned pocket money from my dad was running for soda mix for his alcohol for miles and then not finding the brand that he wanted. At the end he taught me a lesson saying, the brand never existed. All he wanted to see was my tenacity to find that particular brand. How long I pushed and tried to do that. I came home two hours and ten miles later in the melting tarry heat, having walked bare foot all around the town looking for it. My dad had almost finished the drink and said, I did not want to you to see me getting drunk and you have earned your first twenty rupees' pocket money. That was I think when I was 14. Well, this is the best pocket money I ever spent and also the biggest lesson I have ever learned.'

Indhiran said: 'You never said that story to me. What happened?'

'My dad was fed up with me. I am always asking him to time my runs to the shops. So he had this old classic Swiss watch with a stop watch on it. It's a diver's watch, somebody gave it to him in the 60's in Delft. He sent me on a wild goose chase, I ran and ran up to the town centre from Chundikuli, fearing if I bought anything else he would go mad at me and mum. Because he was about to drink. I got blistered badly that day. Then moved to the side from the road and got cooked in the hot soil. I came back with a heavy sweat, money and in pain having failed to find the soda. My body odor dried and smelled like old blood. My father looked at his watch and said, you've been gone a few hours. You are well out of the target. You must have covered a few miles. You are fit, Jana. I got to hand it to you. You looked hard for it too, I guess. You could not find it. Never bought any cheap imitations, genuinely looked for something for your dad, that's the sprit, Jana. That is commendable. You have earned your first pocket money. It is all yours. My father was slightly drunk. He said, don't use it on watching any x-rated movies. They will destroy your life, son. Those movies. I said, dad the film is about the body, it is not porn. It is a sex education documentary. He paused and said, sex education.'

Indhiran smiled and said: 'Your dad is crazy, you know that. What did he say to that?'

'Well, for once he did not say anything.'

'But I like him, he is hilarious. He is not afraid of anyone. He will talk to anybody if he's got something to say. We all get it from the insane generation I guess,' said Indhiran with his head down.

Both laughed.

'Insanity of our fathers,' said Jana quietly.

CHAPTER NINE

TERMINAL RELIEF AT THE BELOVED OCEAN

At the agriculture department, a few staff talked about Mr. Prahash like never before.

Someone said: 'Look at that man keeping the seat warm looking at the horizon. The man is a cycling champion all the way from Jaffna to Athcuvelli. That's some distance to cover every day. Sometimes when he gets tired he will put the bike on the bus. He loves to cycle through the paddy fields, instructing and overseeing the farmers and friends whenever he had time. Yes, he had time for everybody, helping them with their personal loans to avoid the local Vatti man with high interest trying to take the harvest.'

'How about bribes? Has he ever,' one officer asked. 'Did he take?'

One jumped in the middle and said: 'Don't you ever say that. Ever. He has given to the ministers to get the work done quickly on some occasions. No, no, no. Never, never took it. Never took a penny from anybody. The man is strong Catholic.'

'I thought he was a Hindu,' said another officer.

'He was, he converted. His mother is a Christian and his father is a Thaninayaka Muthaliyar Vamsa Hindu two strike Vellalan,' said the caste conscious officer proudly, while fingering his solid gold chain.

278

'Maybe a bunch of onions or some chilies from the farmers. He loved his cooking you see, he cooked here a few times. This place used to smell great in the afternoons. He had stayed over during the curfew. The man loved his loneliness in the countryside. The tranquility of isolation he used to say, and smile. St. Anthony's, St. Henry's, he was well so well behaved. They made him the Halls of Residence Supervisor.'

Some one laughed in the back.

'No. Nothing. It's true,' he insisted. 'But he was not a saint either. The priests made him the head of the halls because, if you make the troublemaker the chief, then there won't be no troubles eh?' Everybody laughed. 'The man gave a hard time to those strict Catholic Oblates of Mary Immaculate priests. He is not a saint either. Some of them are too crazy hitting the young boarding students with belt and cane after stripping them naked, stroking their cheeks gently and yanking their bollocks before they put them through the pain barrier.'

Someone said: 'You are exaggerating. Come on, some of them got away with abuse to the boys. It was an awful affair. I am sure he has a few old marks too. How about all those speeches in the schools about agriculture? The man likes to do something good all the time.'

'Do gooder, one clerk said at the back.'

'In return he wanted nothing but gratitude.'

'He likes the power though,' said one officer. 'Who doesn't? These days, if don't have that kind of attitude, you can't get anywhere, can't get anything done, man. How about when our minister from Colombo came here, every one of you hanging at the background. But the man took over. Oh yes, he spoke in Sinhala and English. The minister was impressed with him and had a drink with him in that office like an old friend. Go and look at his cabinet, there is an unopened Scotch that is always ready for a special occasion. He never drank alone. Never. He would never touch it. I heard they went hunting in Vanni later that weekend. After the Kundasli graduation, he was posted in Vanni. His wife was pregnant with their second child. He used to walk with his Rosary beads and Enfield rifle, rolling his cycle alone with his distinctive khaki trousers and sandals. He hunted and loved the forest, it was in his blood. He was good with his knives, too. He can camp out quickly in the middle of the jungle, set up fire, roast his catch on a stick. He will become an ancient Verdan in the conditions of Madu to Mangulam.

'Listen, he used to say the monkey brain is good for asthma. Monkey brain is good for srimavo, too, ahh, ahh. He used to roll up his khaki, get his hands dirty with the farmers shoveling shit, that's right, shoveling shit. You should watch him, when the water pump waters, he will move fast, row to row, with mambati, directing water just the right amount to the crops, moving swiftly filling all the gaps irrigating well, showing the farmers. He used to say love it while you are doing it.

'He's married fifteen years, he loved his women. No, no, no, he don't go for that ladies business. I mean his ladies are his wife and daughters. Built his house, oh yes, stone by stone. How many stones?'

Someone in the back said: '7000.'

'Three lovely children. The eldest is cricket captain in Jaffna.'

'Vice captain,' said the other.

'Some sort of captain, I don't know the difference. I don't even understand the game, let alone knowing captain, vice president, I don't know. I heard he was talented. Mr. Prahash was not interested in sports, he loved politics, congress man, G.G.P. K.B. Ratnayke, that time Minister of Agriculture. Remember the great elephant march at the Vanni Tamil Congress? He was there next to Fr. Selva and G.G.P. Fr. Selva, yes, he was in the congress before, don't you know that he formed the federal party?'

The thing I admire about Mr. Prahash,' said one officer, 'he used to help poor families by getting them nanny jobs in the well-to-do houses in the city. Room and board, some went to schools, too.'

'Yeah, but how about all the stories we hear about the servants in the politicians' houses being abused.'

'Some do, some don't. We can't change some of the nasty people in our society. The good cultured and obedient Tamil worker always gave the respect to his elders even though it came with sufferings. Girls and boys, even some old cooks, improved their lives, got their girls married in the process. But the European families did really give them a lot of opportunities. Even travel abroad to work. You know he never did anything to his close family. You know what they say, do it to others, your children will grow naturally. That was his motto.

'I remember one day he took a smoke out of my mouth, I was just about to ride away on my motor bike. He took it out, pulled a thumb for himself, I was saying, bro you only need to ask. He said, how can you smoke this heavy tar and then he started to cough violently. I saw some blood coming out on his handkerchief. I got off the bike and said, sir, what's wrong. He said, that's what smoking does to you, sir, makes your wife a widow and your children fatherless. Give it up, sir. But you never smoked, said the colleague, why is there blood. That's the mystery, nobody knows. Well, he wasn't finished. He said to me, two places you don't smoke, one is in your bed and the other is in your vehicle. Both situations, you may wake up in a hospital after a fire in the house or a road traffic accident on your way home. Because the smoke, it makes you go to sleep. These are deadly on these occasions. I never smoked for three months, then my dreaded habit came back to haunt me again. I need to stop that now, at least for Mr. Prahash's sake. He worked on those big Vellanai tobacco fields, Kytes to Punkuduthevu. He covered all Tamil farming areas but he never smoked. He probably tried for aroma and quality control. That's about it.

'He was never late for work. Twenty years of service without a single day of sickness. I tell you, if he was sick, he would be here doing something in the office, drinking all the brandy remedies with the

boiled bush herbs (kudineer). Have a container full of lime water,
drinking it to keep him hydrated in the heat conditions. He was a
strong man. It's going to be difficult to replace someone like him. One
of a kind.' .

    'Let's do a card and a collection for him,' said one officer. 'Who
knows, he probably could use it for his treatment.'

    'He would not accept it. He would not. He will say you all tried
to put me away quickly, aah. Sooner than I thought. Yeh, that's what
he will say. I know him, he is so proud. So proud.'

    'Hey, we will do it anyway, huh,' said the departmental head.

    One officer was punching the pedal of his motor bike with anger
while starting it: 'We will give it to the missus, ok? Just not yet to him
please.'

    That was the talk of the Agricultural Department that morning.

Mr. Prahash sat and watched the sunset with glassy eyes. He
couldn't swallow the tea properly. His cough was very horsy
and painful. His eyes would turn red with pain and tears. He
choked while he talked. He was taking a day off tomorrow to
see the family doctor, Dr. Abraham, who was also a close
friend for more than fifteen years. To get the final second
opinion. Second opinion. Everyone needs that nowadays
with all the negligence, even the third opinion

    Mr. Prahash managed to cycle from home to the doctor's
the following morning. Dr. Abraham had a busy pediatric day.
It was all inoculations, mainly the MMR and BCG so it was
screaming kids all around the wards, all with toys, and it
brought memories of Jana doing the same in front of the
Jaffna Hospital after his emergency operation. He smiled as he
remembered the train screams. Nurse Hilary walked passed
looking busy with relatives and patients. Mr. Prahash usually
came up with the joke about the streets, neighborhood

improvements, politicians and would tell them with a dry humor. This time he sat among the outpatients and watched the swirling poovarsu (kingdom flower) leaves on a wind-filled Beach Road. Passing locals slowed as he scrutinized the patients, while patients looked at a fixed point. He wasn't looking at anybody, just his eyes fixed to a point without a blink thinking something or nothing, away in another zone. Mr. Prahash's thoughts were miles away, too. Every time he sat down he thought about his funeral. His wife and children still did not know anything about it. He had just started to pay up for the house loans. He feared for his kids and wife, which made him even more unwell. He sat helpless thinking what he would do next to overcome this obstacle. He needed a miracle. A miracle of St. Anthony. He had the Rosary in his hand at all times. He believed the miracle of Mary would save his children and really prayed for it day and night. Whatever disagreements he had with the clergy, he was a strong believer in god and the country.

He could not sit on the chair anymore, so he walked and mumbled the Our Father and Hail Mary. His face looked tired and resigned.

Suddenly, Dr. Abraham tapped on his shoulder:

'You are not in a hurry?'

Mr. Prahash shook his head.

'Ok. Ok. Don't worry, you will be Ok.'

Mr. Prahash grabbed his hands and looked at him. He was almost at breaking point.

He said to the doctor: 'I am not a sinner. Like everybody I made a few mistakes but I am not a sinner, doctor. But I have done nothing to nobody, always tried to do the right thing. Why me? Why did God let me down?' His tears came out.

'I am sorry, Prahash, I am really sorry about the misfortune.' Dr. Abraham kept his face like a professional. He went back quickly to the wards.

Mr. Prahash went back and sat in the only available chair, next to a patient, an old man with less hair and it all grey, all facial muscles sucked in against the bones like a gaunt heavy smoker with lung cancer. His eyes looked jaundiced and protruded outside. He looked very ill. Mr. Prahash asked *what water*? meaning drinks and alcohol.

'What?' the old man asked, he did not hear it well, then he said gently in Mr. Prahash's ears: 'Cancer in the liver. I have a few months to go. I hope he will take me real quick. I had my life. Done everything, it is up to him now.' He smiled and said: 'I am finished, I am happy about that. I don't want to be a hindrance to anybody. What about you? You are too young to have something like that.'

'Same thing in the throat,' said Mr. Prahash.

'Oh, sorry to hear that. Oh, that's painful, eating and drinking I mean. Don't worry when that happens, they will put a tube in you, you won't feel a thing,' he said holding Mr. Prahash's hand. 'Don't be scared, carry on with your life as usual. You will do everything before it all ends. Cancer is bad and painful, but it gives you a little time to fight and play with you, hide and seek. You look like a fighter to me, so be strong.'

'Thank you, sir. What's your name, sir?'

'Anthony.'

Mr. Prahash grabbed his hands and said: 'Be in peace. God will take care of you.'

'Eat well, rest well, don't stress yourself, love your children. I can see you as a strict disciplinarian type. Kids have grown up, they know what's best for them. Stop the shiny liquid in the glass. Occasional glass of wine does no harm. You will get plenty of pills and medicines and,' he laughed hysterically, 'don't take any electrocution therapy. Chemo! What chemo? Just a waste of time, giving false hope for few more days. I may be wrong. I am not a doctor, just a drinker,' he laughed hysterically. It made him cough until he had red eyes and cramps in the stomach. Mr. Prahash called a nurse and said, *sorry* and walked away in tears.

Nurse Hilary came out asked Mr. Prahash to come in. It was quite a big office and treatment room. It even had a small operating theatre adjoining the glass consulting room. The room was mostly black marble which showed his popularity and efficiency. He sat with his grey Littman stethoscope around the neck, the bifocals dropped from his face a little. Mr. Prahash looked at the Resus equipment in the emergency area. He said: 'It's been long since I have been here. You have achieved a very successful hospital, with lots of praise from all the people in this town. You have done really well, and I am proud about that, sir.'

Nurse Hilary wiped her tears, walked and sat at the nurse's table in the room. The doctor kept his cool. The big boiler full of stainless steel injections cleaned in high temperatures, made a little noise.

'So, tell me, doctor, give it to me straight.'

'Sit down, sit down. We've got plenty of time, unless there's an emergency. I have looked at all the patients,' the doctor continued, taking his time. 'We will do more tests to verify the severity. It could go into regression. You might feel a bit better for a while. The damage was done by the poisonous agricultural chemicals. You have got throat cancer. The government failed to protect the field workers from the exposure. There wasn't enough warning. Total negligence.

You should sue the Sinhalese Agricultural Ministry for lack of information. Awareness, information and most importantly, health and safety education. We are still learning about the agricultural chemicals and pesticides. It can be quite dangerous, yes, quite a bit,' he said as he dropped his glasses. He looked at Mr. Prahash, paused for a moment: 'You could buy a few more years. Another five years if you do the right thing. It's all in your hands, Mr. Prahash.'

He quietly answered the doctor: 'All I want to make sure is that my family can keep their house, and have enough for the girls to do a decent wedding. That's all. That crazy boy with his sports, I don't know what he will do. I think he will be all right. I have to get him out of this place. He will get involved, I know, he is passionate about this country. I don't want my children to kill anybody or be killed by someone before they become an adult. He has tried all kind of games in front of my eyes. What he will do to his mum if I am gone. I don't know. I want my children to serve the Tamil society. Even if I have to sell everything, I have to send him away. But I have got to think about the girls.'

He looked helpless.

The doctor raised his voice: 'Now calm down. I have been a doctor for your family for fifteen years.' He looked at Nurse Hilary. 'Train.' She smiled. 'Your son and the train. To be honest with you, have your last drink with your friend Ranga and say goodbye to the bottle. Your lifestyle, food, should be good and healthy. You need a good rest. Stress-free working environment. So for you, it's a total dramatic life change. Can you handle that? You will be receiving chemotherapy. You will lose all this lovely hair, slightly graying anyway. Saving you the dye money. But if you don't comply, it will be insanely bad with morphine, with difficulty in eating, fluids only, unable to walk with lack of strength, these are the worst case scenarios you will put yourself in. Tube fed fluids with loose bowels can be difficult. I have given you all the worst painful truth. There is surgery available.' The doctor looked at Mr. Prahash.

'You mean I have to talk like a robot with the machine?' asked Mr. Prahash.

'You are in your late 40's. I would suggest buying another 10 years with surgery. Otherwise, three to four years at the most.'

Mr. Prahash sat back with heavy breath. He was relieved with the doctor's honesty. He was that kind of person, liked the truth to his face. He might not like it but he will take it.

The doctor said: 'If you want any sponsorship or a recommendation letter to the embassies, I will help your son's education abroad. Even, you can borrow some money from me. I am prepared to help you.'

'I couldn't do that, doctor. No, no, no, you also have children. I can't do that.'

The doctor interrupted: 'I've known you for fifteen years, you are a good man. I know you will pay me back in this life or in your next. Feel free to ask anything I can do, I will do it. But wait, wait. I have the final jack in my sack. I haven't put it on the table yet. It is not a medical suggestion. It's more of a social, practical and occupational solution.' He paused with a smile. He was a genius among the best in the city.

Mr. Prahash was smiling for the first time. He said: 'Treatment abroad.'

'Wait, wait. Hear me out. There are a few agents around doing good business in Jaffna. Taking people to work on the ships. You are a natural with the sea and the salty water hah! You love your deep sea diving and rescue boat actions. There is plenty of opportunity for you in Greece. They are recruiting Tamils due to their hard work and the experience of sea as islanders. You have still got some fire in you. While you are working you can get treatment at arriving ports for free as an employee. Some have good occupational medical plans. It might give you a break, fresh air, something that you like to do. Healthy lifestyle at sea. Choice of good food and fruits. You have money coming in, paying your debts, it will give you more time than you will realize. I will give you a letter for no pay leave for a year. The Agricultural Department owes you a big favor. You deserve another chance; you have done well, built your house, educated the kids. I heard your son is a great cricketer, opening bat, little devil. Don't stress, shy away from the Agricultural Department. General Medical Council will write to the Agricultural Ministry to avoid such incidents happening in the work place again. We need more protection for the workers. God knows how many there are like you in the country. So go and have a think about it, we will talk more. Take a break with your kids in Delft for a few days away from here. I got some painkillers, if you are in any trouble. But come and see me anytime.'

Mr. Prahash asked: 'How much for today, doc?'

'No, no, I did nothing today. We just had a chat. You have got no more than advice today, sir. Thank you and God bless you.'

Mr. Prahash smiled and said: 'Ah… you don't like the dead man's money doctor? Ok, you don't like my money.'

'Now that's what I like to hear you say. You and your sarcastic jokes. We want our old Prahash back, a little less louder when you talk perhaps.'

He smiled and said thank you to Nurse Hilary for the

painkillers. His sprit was lifted. He thanked them for that wholeheartedly. 'You know, doc, they said to me go to the cancer specialist in Colombo. I said to them, I know a man who knows a bit more than a specialist. You proved me right again, sir. You saved my disturbed soul, thank you. You are good, doctor. We are very lucky to have you here in this town. Very lucky. Very lucky.' Then he coughed and said: 'Sorry,' and shook his head, swallowed his saliva. He gave a smile and went out of the hospital like a new man, smiling.

Mr. Prahash took a break with his father for two weeks in his beloved Delft. He cooked and ate well. All his paperwork came as predicted along with a letter of sympathy from the head of his department. Mr. Prahash told his family he had a mild form of ulcer, maybe he was going for treatment in Europe. Marie Joyce feared the worse and began to cry alone, and started to do pilgrims to St. Anthony by walking every Tuesday nearly five miles after work to the church in Jaffna Pashauur. Every Tuesday St. Anthony was worshipped by all the communities, including the Hindus. Ten thousand people moved in and out of the area to receive the blessing of the miracle of St. Anthony. Sometimes friends and family picked up Marie Joyce on their cycle during the tiring walk, she would be almost on the verge of collapse. For once Mr. Prahash was laughing, he understood his fate. Knowing your fate is something of a blessing in disguise in Srilankan Tamil tradition. He went to see Ranga Anna at Colombo and explained the situation. He took Mr. Prahash to the top throat specialist, who said pretty much the same thing as Dr. Abraham.

He did all the bribing at the passport offices in Colombo to get the adequate rubber stamps to make his journey quicker. He bought some fisherman's clothes, rubber walking boots, no goodbyes, no relatives at the airports.

Mr. Prahash had gone to Europe.

Still his plans were disrupted by the lying agents who left him stranded at the borders of Greece in the middle of nowhere. He blamed his in-laws; Reggie's contact was a rogue agent and scam merchant. There were thousands of so-called agents who took money from vulnerable Tamils running for their life after selling their lands and avoiding persecution from the Srilankan Army. He was aware of those downfalls so he prepared for the worst. He walked alone in the deserted land with his Rosary thinking of his family, whether he would make it to the port. He walked two days eating raw vegetables from the farms. Someone gave him a lift to the closest city. He crossed the border in an agricultural tractor after working on the farm for two weeks for some money. He gave some expert advice on agriculture for European farm conditions. He walked up to the house and the first thing he saw was St. Anthony in the front hall of the farmhouse. The person that gave him a job was a Catholic. When they dropped him at the borders, he walked another ten miles with a smile. He was inside Greece, able to see the sea and smell the fresh air. There was a Dominican monk with a bald head who appeared on his route and told him to go to a hotel in a particular city near the port, that he would find his job. People were helpful all the way to his destination.

When he reached there, he saw his relative Antonypillai at the hotel reception with Uncle Babe, his loving in-law, sitting and waiting for him. Mr. Prahash always believed that his trust in St. Anthony had guided him to this place and it was a miracle. He asked the receptionist: 'Where is the closest church?'

The first thing he did was to light a few candles for all the people he loved in his life and said a few prayers kneeling down in the middle of the church's open arms. The family would work together and get a job for Mr. Prahash on a Greek cargo ship mini-lines. Mini Lido was his new home.

He was sitting on the deck fully kitted, breathing fresh air. A cloud was moving in; he said to the crew to get in, we're going to have a sudden downpour. He went back inside and lay in his room thinking what Dr. Abraham had said about his family, especially his son. He had said: 'You must have encouraged him to play cricket.'

Mr. Prahash had replied: 'No, I did nothing, did not even go to see him play.'

'How about you must have bought all the kit, and took him to the practices surely?'

'No,' Mr. Prahash had replied.

'What do you mean?'

'It was all his own personal effort and plans. He self-taught all his sports including his training regimes. We don't have anybody in our families who knows about cricket. He got a lot of gifts from his favorite uncles, especially Vigiyan. I did not do anything at all. I wish I did get involved. I was too busy with my work and the house building. He really has the ability to work alone to get his things done. He always set his standards high. He used to annoy me with his hitting a ball in a sock for hours. He said he was getting an eye. I felt like taking one out. He came home with cups and certificates all the time. I was also surprised when he passed the G.C.E O/L with distinction for English and Christianity. He hardly studied at home. If only he could channel his energy and ingenuity on his advance level. He could be a winner.'

But Mr. Prahash was not worrying about his son anymore. He wanted to get back in one piece to his loved ones after his first year away from home. He pinned the picture of St. Anthony and Our Lady of Perpetual Help on the cabin wall. He remembered what the doctor had said, that the kids grow up faster than us. Times are changing. Let them find their own feet on the ground. Some do it earlier, some take their time. Just can't force them to do anything. Encourage the things they do better.

Mr. Prahash's throat gave very little trouble. He was coping well with no further spreading of the cancer. The affected area had responded well to the treatment. He talked to the staff about his son's stories and his sporting achievements - for the first time. He became a popular crew member and was asked by the captain to accompany him during the rough sea voyages. He talked about weather conditions in the Arabian and Indian Seas.

Mr. Prahash saved a crew member who had gone overboard during a heavy storm. He jumped into the swirling deep waves to pull out the young man while risking his own life. He cooked Tamil Sri Lankan dishes to impress the captain. He did a lot of overtime, taking a few hours to rest, as he loved the sea. The captain commented on his natural instincts. When the pain came back after overworking, he had to take morphine in secret. He hallucinated with creepy crawlies and chameleons appearing in his cabin. He also dreamed of a massacre of innocents in Jaffna. He was scared for his family. He acquired more morphine in an Italian port black market. He showed his medical letter, which made things easier for the Milano gangsters.

He visited the Vatican and got the blessing from the bishops, and drank the holy water. Later he found out that his cancer showed some remissions. He lit the candle on every port he landed for every single one he loved, especially Dr.

Abraham's family. His pain and suffering managed to stay below the threshold. He drank the occasional wine with the crew.

Ranga contacted a few friends in London to organize a quick chemotherapy. His ship docked in Harwich for a week. He took the train to London. Then got treated at a Harley Street physician's with his prognosis and report. He took a walk around London BT tower and took some college prospectus and post for his son and visited the Royal Botanical Gardens at Kew. The man never liked the camera or any fancy equipment. He wrote it all in detail with sketches and posted things from London. He looked at London Bridge and the docks around the city. He really loved the dock workers lifestyle. He was looking for clues to develop Delft as a great port of Jaffna. He bought some reading materials at Charring Cross Road classic book shops: meteorology, cultivation, development, irrigation, farm management, great ports and agriculture were his favorite subjects. At Foyles, he also bought a medical book Living with Throat Cancer. He mastered meteorology with his natural knowledge after reading nonstop for months. He cut down on rich food, lost a bit of weight and increased eating fruit and vegetables. He began to smile every time he was on the deck. Now, knowing his situation, everybody was amazed at his positive outlook in life.

He began to enjoy the job on the ship; it had become so natural now he had a year's experience. A lot of the staff jumped ship for better pay, but Mr. Prahash showed loyalty for his crew and stayed and worked another seven months before he planned to go back home. He would send all the money he earned to pay all the debt off in one year and six months. He worked an extra month for himself, for maybe a nice motorbike when he got home.

Jana fully enjoyed the freedom, played cricket and ran the races, and took the notes in the advance level without revisions or studying for exams. He did not listen to anybody, he was free at last. He and Indhiran enjoyed the teenage years in total rebellion chasing girls on their bikes. Marie Joyce punished Jana one day with utter disgrace because of his behavior. She hit him with the rubber slippers. Kneeling down. That was the most degrading punishment ever in Tamil society. That practice was common when the Tamils were forced to slavery during the occupations. Hitting them with boots and slippers. Somebody informed Mrs. Prahash, now the Vice Principal of St. James' girls' school, that Jana was seen in the notorious red light district with another boy. Jana ran away from home for a week in shame, living in Hindu Temple shrines, eating and living with the meditating gurus in a monastery twenty five miles away. He ran for two days barefoot in tears and finally found this place and refused to come home.

Indhiran told his mum: 'We were there just looking around, just voyeurism, nothing like you are worrying about.'

Marie Joyce was worried and said: 'Find him quick, otherwise I need to call the police.'

Indhiran warned her not to do that: 'they might think he has joined the movement and will get a good beating in the station. They will break his legs and that will send him into a suicidal mood knowing he can't run anymore or play cricket. I know where to find him,' he said confidently.

Two days later Jana sat in front of a cinema for the opening of Live and Let Die. He had no money. Somebody tapped him on both shoulders. Two cousins on both sides grappled him in case he ran away again.

Indhiran said: 'I know you, bloody fool, will be here for

the opening of your long awaited favorite Bond movie. I got sick of hearing from you all the details about this movie for the prior month. Roger Moore, your favorite Bond. The Saint, The Persuader.'

They sang the John Barry tune together: *tang ta tang, tang ta tang.*

'I knew you would be here.'

Jana loved Live and Let Die, it was his ultimate entertainment: New York, black villains, funky music, Caribbean, New Orleans, boat races, crocodiles, Jane Seymour, speeding route master double-decker, snakes and black magic and the final scene in the train with the flute man's laugh. Most importantly, the Paul McCartney hit song and the music was fantastic. For Jana, that was the real black exploitation movie.

Indhiran asked: 'Where you been?'

Jana said: 'Hindu Temple in Mallaham.'

'Mallaham, why? You going to become a Hindu priest?' The cousins laughed at Jana. 'You are a Catholic.'

'I don't believe in Christianity. It is all lies. It is all business. She hit me with slippers on my face, on my face! I can't love her or live with her anymore.' Jana looked a little disturbed.

'Come and live with us. Your dad is coming in a few months. You don't want him to start to have a fight with your mum. Come on, let's go home, my place. We talk later. We will see this tomorrow. It's a full house, anyway. Uncle babe is getting married; they want you as best man. Come on, there are plenty of girls on that side of the family. Go on, you love it all, the suit and the group photos.'

'No.'

'Why not?'

'You know I don't let anybody take a picture of me.'

'You are crazy,' said Indhiran. 'Why, you afraid they might take you smelling your arm. Your mum is going away to Delft to give the wedding card personally to your father's family. Why don't you go with her?'

'No. I can't be bothered anymore,' said Jana. 'When he comes back we're going to have a real fight, you watch. Heads are going to roll in Chudikuli, man. Get ready. We will join the movement soon, run away from this madness.

'Shut up! Not in front of my little brother you fool.'

Marie Joyce was in the hospital two days later, due to the navy thug saboteur who caused an accident on the way back from Delft. The bus rolled off the road. A few died, many were injured. Marie Joyce suffered a crush injury to her neck and was paralyzed from below the waist - a spinal injury. That was a big blow for the Prahash family, the father with cancer away over the seas, the mother in hospital receiving rehabilitation.

Indhiran did the hospital runs. Jana was there a few times. But he was drifting away with all the pressure of suffering and uncertainty around his teenage life. Nobody was there to cook at home, his eldest sister Joselyn began to take the responsibility of the house, doing a better job than Jana. She also loved her mum more than anybody in the family.

Dr. Abraham came to see her in the hospital and wondered why all this suffering for this family. Grandpa Arul came to Jaffna to give the girls company.

Jana would sit in a corner in the ward with his head down, looking at this once fit lady who walked for miles on religious pilgrims, now paralyzed. This was how God respected his devotees.

He began to hate religion and God. He was also accused

of not having love for his mum. She began to improve and sit up, and then managed to take a few steps.

Jana did nothing wrong except he did not know how to say, *I love you, mum.* Expressions were all suppressed deep down in the Prahash family. They were a close family, but they all seemed so far away when it came to love and affection.

In Jaffna, abductions and torture were becoming daily news. The poverty was also visible all around especially with his cousins. Indhiran was forced to work as flower arranger/wreath maker. He helped the embalmers for a small fee. He was now a part-time worker in the funeral parlor.

Mr. Prahash came home a month earlier than he planned due to his wife's accident. For once Jana was happy to see him, but still a little afraid. Mr. Prahash brought a lot of sports magazines and cricket books to the total surprise of Jana.

Marie Joyce was discharged after three months in hospital. They sat together on the chair for the first time, feeling happy to see each other after a year and a half.

Mr. Prahash said to Jana: 'I am sorry I wasn't there when you needed me. I am very proud that you achieved all the best batsman accolades. I was there on two occasions that you weren't aware of, one was your athletic meet, you should have taken the 800 Gold, just missed out on the timing on the bend. Your hero Seb Coe also made that error at the Moscow Olympics. But I was impressed with your fitness level. Everybody collapsed after that race; you picked up your kit and walked to your house hut proudly. Yes, I was there. Again I was there for the final match in Central when you won the Best Batsman Cup as Jaffna Champions.'

Jana's tears rolled down like a baby's. He could not believe what he was hearing.

'Well, you want to talk to us what that's all about?'

Both of them were worried thinking different things, mum worrying about girls maybe, dad worrying about Jana going to join the boys, sisters thinking let's hope he doesn't bring up all the fight stories, complaining about mum. Everybody wondered what the dreaded bad news was.

'Don't worry, not that kind of bad news,' said Jana and looked at his mum. She looked away.

'You two have done everything for me, bought me fire crackers during the Christmas; my favorite Hanuman brand. Chocolates on weekends. Digestive biscuits. My cricket outfits from Taylor Deva. Looked after me when I had asthma and convulsions. I thank you for all that. I did manage to do ok on my O Levels: choosing math for A Levels was a mistake. I am not an engineer, engineering is not for me. I prefer the biology and medicine. I am behind in my studies. I am not an academic,' he repeated. 'I want to go abroad and work with people, maybe nursing, something I can learn while studying a skill. There is no future for me in this country. Not for a young frightened Tamil like me. I will come here every few years when they kill a few more Tamils during the election riots. I just have to run for my life instead of for prices and certificates. They are arresting randomly, some to the fourth floor (torture room) for going for a meeting. I am scared. I don't want to die young. I want to do something before that. I don't want to waste your money on tuition classes. It's just a waste of money,' Jana said irritably.

Dad looked at mum with disappointment and shook his head.

'I want to help the people, do nursing, and eventually work in the Red Cross or something. That's it, I have said it. I am sorry if I have let you down.'

Mr. Prahash got the shock of his life. He was speechless. Mum was relieved, she had expected that anyway.

'So movies finally got to you, son,' said Mr. Prahash.

Mum said: 'More than that got to him.' She looked at him angrily.

Prahash said: 'No, no. I like the way you came clean, like a man. Your son is a real man today in front of his father.'

Jana walked out slowly. The girls came and sat next to their parents, laughing.

'I will do well in the A/L, dad,' said the little one.

He said: 'You are *my* daughter, that's why. All the others, we found them in the canals. The eldest said he fooled us with all the running and the cricket. Bloody stone-hearted fool (kalnengan), he has no feelings for his family. Just leave it alone, let him go for another run, that will do him good,' said Mr. Prahash.

The household looked fed up with Jana but he had a sense of relief. People did not talk to each other for a few days. Everybody did their routine.

Mr. and Mrs. Prahash lay on their bed looking at the roof.

'All the hard work, the house. You think, is it all worth it?' asked Mr. Prahash, 'did we do the right thing with Jana? It's my fault. I did not talk to him properly during his crucial age between fourteen and seventeen. That's the year for the boys. We were not late with the girls. I wasn't here. It was my fault. You were in hospital. I was too busy concentrating on my job, house building, did not pay enough interest to his interests. He is hardworking, intelligent, managed to do it all by himself. Did you ever go and see him playing? He was also a leader of the Catholic Students Federation, Interact Club, won prizes for the English day competitions for acting and singing. He represented the college in conferences. So they must have found something special in him. Just we did not nurture that. His strength lies in social and political, I did not see that. He did not know. He was too young to know. Well, he is still finding himself. It is my fault, beating the hell out of him like a dog at times. Insanity, insanity,' he said disappointedly. 'I am going to suffer for that.'

Marie Joyce saw a little low shift in Mr. Prahash's mood and turned around and looked at him: 'Are you all right?'

'Why?' asked Mr. Prahash.

'You are talking like a dying man. Forget him. He will find the way out.'

Mr. Prahash did not know what to say. Sooner or later he would have to say something about his illness to his family. He only had a few more years to live.

Marie Joyce said: 'You know the teacher Sam Fredrick died? I took Jana once to his house. When he played up with his home work. He was his class teacher. Because he liked his chemistry, and he was also the prefect of games. That's why he did ok in the chemistry, to keep him happy. Everybody feared that master. Jana was very friendly with him, to everybody's surprise. He loved his cricket and the athletics boys. He was one of the best chemistry lecturers in the country. He died of diabetes, loved his drinks. A secret drinker. Boys went to see him in the hospital, he looked frail and had lost a lot of weight. Jana said he spoke like a man who knew his consequences, still regal even when he was with his debilitating illness. He got better, but then went downhill.'

Mr. Prahash could not speak a word, he was all choked up wondering whether Marie Joyce knew about his fate.

'That teacher gave me a lot of respect as a fellow teacher and listened to my worries about Jana. Poor man died in his sleep. Peacefully. That's how I'd like to go as well,' said Mr.

Prahash. 'They decorated the street all the way from his house to the college. He was the last class teacher of Jana's batch in the eighties. Lots of students all around the country came to pay last respects. The mass was held at the college chapel. His son is tall like his father at 6'4", played cricket with Jana. Fast bowler, I heard. That was the end for the chemistry lab, I guess. He was a strict teacher, everybody feared him you know but he hardly hit anybody. Just a few strong words. Are you trying to say something?' asked Mr. Prahash. 'Look, I am not going to raise a hand anymore. You can take over that job, then he gave his wife a long awaited hug.

Both smiled in harmony after such a long time.

CHAPTER TEN

WAR OF THE INNOCENTS: THE CONFLICT

Once J.R. Jay came to power, the Tamils started dying everywhere in the country. Young students in Jaffna really felt the pinch with the 'stop and search'. The police moved in to a busy shopping centre at a rural busy market in the north of Jaffna called Chunagam where grandpa's cousin had a banana export business.

The police beat up everybody in the market stalls - like Jesus of Nazareth – as collaborators and burned the historical hand carved shopping centre. J.R. Jay called the student movement militants, radicalized, poisoned rebels against the Sinhalese people and government. He declared war against Jaffna people and set up an army camp in the middle of the fishing village Kurunagar. The daily fish market and the Beach Road were deserted. Night life, volley ball, the punthi man with honey corns and roasted chick peas were all gone. The army arrested everybody; anybody who looked suspicious. The kids' playground was wiped out by the police. If you walked by, with fear in your eyes, you were deemed to be looking suspicious.

Jana would cycle down to the funeral parlor via small lanes, avoiding the Beach Road, to get the news of the dead and wounded. Even the funeral parlor workers like Malcolm were not saying a lot those days.

Indhiran said: 'Don't ask random questions of anybody. You just speak to me, ok? Dead bodies are coming every day, some identifiable, some not,' he said quietly into Jana's ears. Jana was confused and angry; he saw Indhiran's personality change into a vengeance state. There was recklessness, no freedom for the students; all confined to schools and home.

Daily curfew under martial law did not stop Jana. He worked out a route that the Jeep or armored truck would not get through. It also included an underground unused and dried waste canal with passages. He also made sure his bike was fully serviced. He worked out how to hide in gardens and parks and used well-known college friends' houses en route. He also had a quick get in and out if he saw an army truck in the distance. He was taking a high risk assuming the army would not hurt him. He thought he would find a way out if he was caught. Mr. Prahash couldn't go this time and look for him. Marie Joyce said, *let him learn a lesson, you stay here.*

The coffin business brought night carpenters to work late, so the late night chats in the coffin workshop behind Grandma Joan's house were quite interesting. Dias, the coffin maker, would make all the intricate cutting of the silk with all the soft cotton cushioned inlaid. The bronze clips and handles were all struck in strongly with sharp tiny nails. He had a biting mouth full of nails, taking out one by one quickly and finishing it off. Golden ropes were ready to hang with thistles. It was already painted and hand finished with French polishing, imitating the zebra and sable wood lines. Everybody wanted this coffin to look great for somebody whom they'd known very close to home on Main Road. A close friend of Jana's and Uncle Raffa, Yamal. He was stopped and searched, humiliated at the junction. He came from Kurunagar. He decided to fight hand to hand combat at the roadside with the armed men. Knowing the end was near, he kept his family name - he did not want to go to any detention camp. He strangled a soldier with his bare hands. His body was laid out - a large open chest wound. His heart was taken out and was missing. He had been a softly spoken martial arts teacher from the Kurunagar. Young boys were trained by him since the Bruce Lee craze gripped the nation. They trained in derelict shops and warehouses.

A month later, a Delft native, Wannan, also a martial arts teacher, was found dead in the street near Chundikuli. He also fought the army hard on the street refusing to get tortured in unsavory conditions. He was shot at close range but not before he broke the neck of a soldier with Jeet Kune-Do. His last words were to the other soldier, *did you see the way your friend died, you fucking Sinhalese pig.* The gun fired three times, he lay in a pool of blood with his head blown off. The trucks took the dead soldier and left Wannan's body for stray dogs along the dead dog canal. Locals watched all this behind the closed fences of their homes, unable to go near the stray dogs. Finally, the dog catchers came out and took care of the body until the family arrived from Delft and the students came with the hearse. Cries were heard for long distances when the cars arrived with relatives. Jaffna people were helpless. There was nobody to defend their human rights. The army was trigger happy; they also burnt landmark buildings like the Jaffna Library which contained ancient scriptures of Tamil history: rare first editions of poetry and philosophical masterpieces. That was a heavy loss for the

Tamils. The only great Jaffna reference library had been a sanctuary for the young and old students. That really created hatred towards the mindless Sinhalese government in Jaffna.

1982 began the rise of the armed Tamils: the time had come, enough was enough. There were various groups fighting the Sri Lankan army in different sectors and districts. There were heavy losses on both sides. There was real street warfare on the roads and lanes in Jaffna City.

One Friday evening in the month of July 1983, four Tamil girls were cycling home from their school when they were abducted. They were forced to perform unbearable sexual acts in front of the army-police combined intelligence operations. They were also gang raped and thrown from the army truck onto the roadside. When the public found the innocent school girls with ripped and blood-stained clothes, their faces bruised, they went first into shock and then revenge. Later that evening, one of the victims committed suicide. The other three girls disappeared into the jungle away from public scrutiny. The Tamil culture looked on at this terrible event with helplessness. Young girls in this situation did not have any support from the professionals. Some never came out in public to complain. Only the student movement gave any shelter or hope. One parent also attempted to commit suicide because of family pride. The news spread like wildfire. Schools were closed the following day in Jaffna and stayed shut for two weeks. A mood of anger and revenge was in the air. Some of the students realized it had gone on long enough.

The mayor was powerless. The student movement organized marches and held a meeting in regard to the recent killings and rape. The main topic of discussion was how to deal with it immediately without wasting time.

Now well armed, help was also coming from overseas. It would become an historical ambush of torturing criminals. The young leader's favorite weapon was a German Heckler and Koch G3 fitted with a long lens. With all the comrades armed with sub machine guns, they looked well-organized, according to eyewitnesses, all dressed in army uniform, like engineers working on electrical sabotage, after cutting off the electrical supply. They laid the Claymore mines in the dark with pen torches attached to their heads. There were a lot of traitors and informers, forced and blackmailed by the police. The police also threatened to bulldoze the whole village if not they were not co-operated with.

This was an operation the students wanted to really succeed without failure.

Switching and changing the location of the firefight, they finally chose the site of ambush.

The day arrived; years of running and hiding, protesting against the inhumanity, learning more about revolution, the history. They'd done the drills in the jungles of Tamil Nadu in South India. The endurance training included carrying a sack full of rice on their bare backs and running for five to ten miles in the scorching heat which gave them a special strength: the strength of immortals. All weapons were checked; for water and sand protection.

'This is it. This is it,' said the young leader.

They took the money from the torturers who took the lives of the innocence. It looked desperate at times, but they had no choice but to take up arms. Some of them got caught in the Indian Ocean while smuggling but this attack would avenge all the misfortune of the past ten years of suffering. How do you stop a movement based on revenge for loved ones, families of the victims?

Every minute, every chilling detail was timed well to the second tick. The drills all went well. Things were all kept secret. Nobody knew who was in the group, who was involved. It was impossible to know, impossible to cut down or obstruct a just cause.

All predicted tests went perfect. The escape route all checked and verified. The minibus and Austin Somerset v8 fully serviced were on standby along with a doctor. All diversions were in place. They were ready and would take their masks off after the victory - that was the leader's plan. That was the order they received from their leader. If anybody was injured or dead, they would be carried out of the battle.

'We do not leave any bodies on the street like the pigs we are going to kill today. This is our great beginning. We will hand the fallen to their brave mothers. Praise the Lord. The Lord help Tamil Freedom. Help this seed to grow with a heavy trunk and spread leaves of lives. We had our kingdom. We will take it back from the illiterate inhuman race,' said a movement comrade.

The clock ticked: a landmine exploded, Jeeps and trucks of the Sri Lankan Army (SLA) flew up in the air and fell to the ground. Craters appeared for the first time on the roads of Jaffna. SMG and Heckler and Koch blasted and flickered with a rapid noise: shick, shick, shick, shick. Some soldiers jumped off the fallen truck and shot in any direction with fear and shock on their faces. One soldier managed to get under the truck. He fired indiscriminately at the houses nearby. The residents were by now under their beds; saw the holes appearing in the verandah furniture. Ten minutes later, it was all over. The SLA lost eleven soldiers; the student movement lost one member. Another SLO soldier died in the hospital. People had never seen or heard such an event, did not really know what to do or say. They were initially happy for the revenge, then thought about the consequences.

The following day a government-organized Sinhalese mob massacred 50,000 Tamils all around the country. Thousands were made homeless and would sleep in the Hindu Temples and Churches. In the capital riots broke out, burning every Tamil business and home. The government and dock workers were beaten naked in the streets and burned alive with cheap kerosene oil. The whole world saw the savagery of the Sinhalese brutality in British Ceylon.

The politicians fueled the fire, scaremongering that the Tamils were going to take over the country with arms. That same day, a mass of Sinhalese shoppers near the temple would run along the Galle Road in Colombo, miles away from the incident, saying (kottiya avva) the movement is coming, the movement is coming. The innocent Sinhalese people ran and fell on top of each other in a mass stampede. The Tamils lost their faith in the government, police and the army, who stood and watched the Tamils losing their life.

The events following this day would change Jana's and Indhiran's lives. Jana's beloved cousin sister, Jeyanthi and her friends, had been travelling on the Delft Ferry and were massacred by the plain clothes navy militia who killed every person, young and old, who was on that boat. She was only fifteen and had over six machete wounds to her body. At the same time, Uncle Cecil would also lose his life in Colombo Port. He was robbed of his wages, beaten and thrown in front of the train at Colombo and this was reported as a train accident. Some recognized in the passport photograph the spotted St. Michael's shirt he was wearing that Mr. Prahash had given him as a wedding present. He had always carried his identity card.

The picture was advertised on the national paper asking: 'Do you know this man?'

Jana's family was faced with a double funeral. Now somebody had to go through this troubled time to bring the body home. Tamils did not want to go past Vanni via Vavuniya. The Sinhalese did want to come past Anuradapura. Mr. Prahash quickly hired a few individuals who were fluent in Sinhala, Tamil and English. That included the embalmer, Malcolm. They also took an empty coffin from Jaffna all packed full of cigarettes and liquor including some Scotch Red Label from his own old supply.

Marie Joyce said: 'What is this?'

'It's not for me. I don't drink anymore,' said Mr. Prahash. 'It is for the police to bring the body home safely. Malcolm is also coming with us.'

After a whole day of driving they reached Colombo Central Hospital and saw the aftermath of the riots. The beauty of the capital was covered by ash and smoking buildings. It looked like a bombsite after the war. Mr. Prahash called a few friends to get some support in Colombo. He spoke fluent Sinhalese to the hospital staff and learned that the body had been moved to the medical students' theatre, after lying in the mortuary for two weeks. It was too late. Mr. Prahash persisted in calling the university chancellor's office to gain access to the body. He also called his friend's daughter, who was a lecturer in anatomy /physiology at Colombo University, to give him support.

After pushing a few buttons, Mr. Prahash approached a part-opened body. The train had done a fair bit of damage. The medical students did more and worse and had made it look unrecognizable. It was cut, sliced, dissected, even pierced in the skull and leaked body fluids. They would not release the body fearing revenge from the relatives. First he had to get permission to get Malcolm to do a decent job to cover and make proper Uncle Cecil. Crush injuries from the train had smashed all the bones. Finally, he called the Agricultural Minister and the Tamil shipping magnate, who had access to the wharf, to find out who had done this hideous crime. He had all the staff arrested that day regarding the murder of Uncle Cecil.

With all the information in hand, he juggled and threatened authorities with major consequences if they persisted in their pretend innocent existence. While all the paperwork was going through to get the body released, he worked hard and bribed the lower echelon of the hospital workers and eventually took the body out of the Colombo University Hospital, while the troubles continued. Then he had to take the body back from the violent south to the north.

He hired another car and crew from the Banana Garden mafia with the help from a local MP. He had an escort with the funeral hearse through Ranga up to Mangulam Vanni. From there they diverted through his old stomping ground, the jungles of Madu and Mannar, via the elephant pass, to avoid the main roads in and out of Colombo as they were checked constantly by the army and the police. He bought more bottles and Rothmans cigarettes, which were put next to Uncle Cecil's body from head to toe along with roses to keep down the stench of formaldehyde.

He drove up to every city police station, gave drinks and cigarettes to the police officers, sweet talked with his English and fluent Sinhalese. Some of them even escorted them to the city borders for a safe journey. Some phoned the other station and said, *listen I am sending you some drinks and cigarettes with a dead man*, and laughed while drinking Mr. Prahash's good stuff. By the time they arrived at Vvavuniya all the paperwork had arrived from the Colombo office which was clearance to show to the northern army.

Mr. Prahash said to himself, *I am afraid of no one, I've only got few years to live anyway. I am only afraid of my wife and St. Anthony.*

The boys from Pettah said, *goodbye sir, Mathaya.* Mr. Prahash gave them all the leftover Bristol cigarette packets and some bottles. He said, don't drink it all or smoke while driving, enjoy it when you get home.

As he promised, all the wages of fright were settled. He took the travelling crew to his old agricultural post first for a long rest after their nonstop morning drive all the way to Jaffna. He had a shower at a river pump after a glass of hot coffee, and started to talk about Uncle Cecil.

'Poor guy has two beautiful children. The boy beautiful with yellowish cat eyes, the girl with brown eyes, both have very fair skin. The wife is still young and beautiful. It's going to destroy their lives. I don't know how they are going to cope.'

Mr. Prahash was tired and went to sleep in one of the rooms. He said to the boys: 'There are some parcels of rice and curry, help yourselves. I don't feel hungry, I ate a few fruits.'

'You sure?' asked Malcolm for formality.

Mr. Prahash slept for hours. He was woken up by something moving and shaking. The boys in the front laughed and said: 'We did not want to wake you up.'

Mr. Prahash was lying next to the coffin in the back of the hearse.

Mr. Prahash had a serious meeting with his mates and clowning Malcolm. He talked about how the coffin display and the relatives needed to be handled in Jaffna. The grief of the close ones was going to be unbearable to watch.

The Jaffna army and the police never stopped the hearse.

They finally reached the main road. Everybody cried saying, *the body has arrived, the body has arrived.* The people comforted Aunty Ruby and the kids. Malcolm quickly settled into the funeral parlor and began to work on the dismembered body of Uncle Cecil. He advised the family to have the coffin closed with a glass square showing the face only. An accidental glimpse of the scarred and battered body was a tremendous shock and horror for Grandma Joan and the extended family; all the aunts joined arm in arm and cried and screamed.

Jana and Indhiran watched from a distance. Jeyanthi's funeral would take place in Chundikuli two days later. They were waiting for her elder brother, Raguram, to come from Thelthenya Campus. While he prepared to leave the university, someone spread the rumor that his sister was a student activist killed by the forces. He was ambushed by the Sinhalese boys, killed and thrown in the river. The police found only his shoes. He had been about to take a job as the government agent of Jaffna in Old Park near Chundikuli near his uncle's house. His Aunt Arulmalar had prepared all the suitcases and was ready to move in with him in Jaffna staff quarters. All would end in tears.

This was the first time Mr. Prahash shed a few tears for his own family. He had had a high regard for Raguram and had even asked Jana's sister to marry him, her own cousin, because he was his eldest nephew with excellent first class grades in economics at the Jaffna university. He had been very proud of him.

His death really brought the truth home to Mr. Prahash.

The police and army questioned all the family about the death and arrested all relatives for further questioning - as a precaution.

Helicopters flew above monitoring the funerals all the way to the cemetery. Every young relative was arrested and detained to avoid further reprisals.

Jana and Indhiran with Jayanyhi's younger brother, were all armed up and were ready to join the movement. They hid in the jungle of Ariyalai. They swam the deep lake full of lotus flowers. Their destination was a banyan tree where they would meet the contact and make their life choices. One of the party climbed by grabbing the swing roots of a banyan tree, on top of which a cache of ammunition and weapons had been left for the newcomers. He slowly brought the sacks down one by one and began distribution without saying a word. He put two grenades in his top pockets, pistols on both sides. He signaled them to follow. Then he attached the silencer, lay flat on the ground and started shooting the lotus stems one by one. Each flower bent in half with not a single petal lost. A few more youths from the far side of the river came through. Some of them were young females. The group stopped firing at the lotus. The senior recruit looked at his Casio watch and said, *sisters, you are an hour late. Sorry brothers, the funeral helicopters are everywhere looking for us. We were hiding in the fishing boats for two hours, Pandiyan drop port.*

In the meantime, thousands were returning on the cargo ships from Colombo and Kandy as refugees. Most of them lost their jobs and belongings; some lost their friends and relatives. Some would like to take their chances and go back in a few months after the dust has settled in Colombo. Most wanted to leave the country for good.

'The Tamils in Sri Lanka would never live happily again with the murdering Sinhalese,' said an old lady.

Everybody took their jewelry, land deeds, and savings from their banks. Their main aim was to send the boys and girls out of the country.

Mr. Prahash looked for Jana after the funerals. He asked some of his friends to look for Jana. Moreover he met up with the student movement and asked them not to take his son, he was the only boy in the family and he himself was suffering from a terminal illness that would leave the family without any help.

Marie Joyce was now partially paralyzed. Mr. Prahash began to cough blood, due to the stress he was going through. He shouted: 'My family will not fight for anybody, not for J.R.J. or any movement. My son will only fight for his people's wellbeing in a non violent manner. That kind of discipline I brought him up with and sent him to study in private catholic school.'

At the Ariyali jungle, the student leader began to explain the rules and regulations of the movement.

'If you are in, you are in. You are in for at least five years. No smoking, no drinking, no relationships. It's a hard and lonely journey. Sometimes we have to go without food for days. After five years we will give you the option, to go away or stay and continue the fight. If the authorities know your identity it will make it difficult for you to get out of the jungle. For us, it will be difficult to maintain security if any of you get caught. They will torture you and your families. We can't just let people come and go whenever they feel like it. It is a security nightmare and your families all will be in danger from the army, too. It is going to be a hard road to freedom.' He looked at everybody for a moment.

Indhiran looked at Jana for a moment: 'Listen Jana, you are the only son in the family, you can't join the movement. Your mum is sick and they need you there. You go abroad and do something with your running and cricket. Get out of this place. You can't manage this lifestyle anyway. It's not you. It is ruthlessly lonely. You are not a lonely type. I won't be with you all the time. We might be in a different group. I know you from a small age.

Indhiran took him to the corner to shelter as the monsoon rains were coming down again on the funeral day. They all ran under the Banyan tree for cover and began to shiver in the wet and cold.

Indhiran said: 'You do me a favor. I may not see you again for long time.'

Tears came for the first time in Indhiran's eyes. 'You go and say to my family that I am gone to join the struggle. Apologize to grandma for letting her down. Tell my elder brother to take care of my family. You go now.' Tears were in his eyes like never before. That was the only time Jana saw Indhiran cry.

'God willing, I will see you in the free world. I want you to do well, do what you really want. You are very passionate and the only friend and relative I ever had. I am going to miss you.'

Water came through the Banyan tree and fell on their heads and trickled down their faces to mingle with their tears. Lotus flower leaves, being waterproof, created hundreds of little circles of water balls which glistened even in the dark.

Darkness was approaching.

'You will be a great man one day, I am sure. Whatever you decide to do, you will be fine.'

Jana's other cousin also gave him a hug and said goodbye.

Jana said: 'You two look after each other.'

Jana removed the weapons and grenades from his pockets and loops, handed them to Indhiran and walked alone through the Ariyalai jungle, to a tiny mud walkway which led through a paddy field. Jana walked further and further until he could only see the shadows under the Banyan tree in the distance, then saw an arm go up to the face of a youth. It was Indhiran smelling his right hand. Jana also smelled his right hand and waved goodbye. He had just left the only friend he ever had in his life. He felt he might not see him again. The boys and girls with their rubber bata slippers and check polyester shirts, began to walk away from the Banyan tree hand in hand like brothers and sisters. They had found their new family.

Jana stood and watched and felt annoyed and angry he could not join them. The winds began to increase. The coconut and the charismas trees made a strange noise. It looked very dramatic with grey skies, rain and thunder. The music of storm and light of thunder reflected the loneliness of the boy who wanted to run away from everybody. Run away from the sadness. Run away from the deaths. Run away from his disappointment at not being able to fight for his people.

Jana ripped his trousers into shorts after walking a few yards, wrapped his shirt around his head like a hat. He began to run barefoot holding his slippers in his hands. The rain helped to keep his body cool. The heat of the road gave a roasting smell for a few minutes then begin to cool down with chill winds. Water ran like a mini river along the road. Jana began a clean nine mile run all the way to Main Street. Every mile he covered another step towards his and his cousin's freedom. He said to himself: *come on, give me the strength to fight this war, help me. Help me fight this war without weapons.* He wanted peace in Jaffna, he wanted his mother to walk again, and he wanted his sisters to have a good life. He wanted a good relationship with his father. He wanted to run somewhere where he would be cheered for his ability. After all, he was the best middle distance runner in the year of 1982 in Jaffna. He wasn't afraid of the army or the police. All Jeeps and police vehicles went past him looking at him like - this guy running, from what? Jana kept the face of a runner's concentration, of an athlete. Not somebody running from fear of something. Jana had found the rhythm, he was not tired anymore, he felt like he could run another few miles but he had reached the Chundikuli area.

He continued towards Indhiran's house in Main Street. The rain had stopped. Somebody recognized the champion and cheered him: *go on you boy! Keep on running! Keep on running whatever happens in the world. You just keep on running.*

He reached the finish line of the race, somebody said: *Jana is coming, he is running barefoot with slippers in his hands.*

He had some cuts from the street stones which bled while he stood in front of everybody like a madman. He never felt any pain. His mind had been set on reaching home safely. The rain had protected him all the way. Somebody gave him a towel. He sat down in front of the house. Some people were still there after the funeral. People thought he had been running from the army.

Jana said: 'He is gone. He is gone, Grandma. Indhiran is gone. He has joined the movement. I also went there to join. I just could not do it. I just could not join. He would not allow me to. Maybe he is right. I am selfish and a coward. He asked me to go home only because I never had a brother. I LISTENED TO HIM! I had to come back here, leaving my

317

only brother there. He is the only brother I ever had. Now he is gone.' Jana screamed and cried: 'I don't know whether I did the right thing but I am not happy.'

Mr. Prahash, who was sitting in the corner behind the main hall, said. 'Ok, calm down. You made the right decision. You did the right thing. You will find out sooner or later.' He coughed hard. 'Indhiran also did the right thing sending you home. You are leaving this place. Leaving this country tomorrow. Say your goodbyes. I will look out for Indhiran and Ruban's safety. You are going to Colombo. I will tell you what to do and you will listen for once in your life. Say your goodbyes.'

Grandma Joan gave him a hug and said: 'Keep this rosary in your hands until you reach your destination. I will pray for you.'

Jana said: 'I want a tea from you, from your own hand. I am going to miss you and your love, your food and your smile. I am sorry.'

The aunts gave him a last kiss. He looked at everybody in the house, *the troublemaker was finally leaving the town,* and cried.

His mum had helped to pack his bag. He took his school certificates, his running record book, two jeans, two shirts, and a few bits of underwear.

Mr. Prahash said: 'Don't pack too much. You're not going to stay too long in Colombo, just a day.'

Jana hungrily ate the food and looked at the family in the aftermath of the funeral. They all sat there, frozen, nothing to talk about. Everybody knew the risks and consequences. Jana began to feel the love for everybody, especially for his sick mother. He still did not know anything about his father's illness. Jana could not talk to anybody or sleep that night. Gun shots and bombs were heard all night long while he lay for the last time in his house. He thought of all the good times of Jaffna life. He realized that he might not see his parents again. His grandma would not survive another ten years. Jana hoped that maybe one day he would come back to a peaceful Jaffna, married with kids. It was just not right to think about that after all the events; the funerals and sacrifices of the people. His mind was also dreaming of a peaceful future in Europe. He felt he was among the fortunate few, the few that were going to have a chance. He felt it was not fair on the people who were left in Jaffna to face the brutality. He had no other choice but to save his life for his own sake and the sake of his family.

CHAPTER ELEVEN

JOURNEY TO THE KINGDOM UNITED

The following morning Jana was escorted by his father to the Jaffna Railway Station. He would take the final journey in Sri Lanka on his beloved Yarl Devi/udereta meneka, London Electric built train, to Colombo. Finally, he was leaving Jaffna for good. He was only eighteen years old. It was hard saying goodbye to his family; they were all in bed when he left home early that morning. He peeped through the door and looked at the female members of the family sleeping peacefully together. Marie Joyce had sat and talked with Jana for a few hours the night before. She said how happy she was when he was born as a first child; how much she loved him as a baby and as her elder and only son. She said, with a few tears: *to forget the entire negative past and try to gain a qualification wherever he went. Learn and work hard; you are easily influenced by others; think twice before you make any harsh decisions; talk kindly and be nice to all the people the same way you would do it to your own family. Either at work or social life, make your decisions wisely and don't rush into anything, especially with your sex life, have protection and to avoid multiple partners. Make sure to give a better life to your kids*

320

than you received from us. We did our best with you with great difficulties and you know that.

Jana listened with such stillness, took it all in for the first time, because she had never talked to him that frankly ever. He gave her a hug and went to bed. That night Marie Joyce shed a few tears.

The Yarl Devi looked busy that morning. The news was that the Defense Minister was on that train, a key government official in regard to the policies of the north. The compartment was full of army soldiers, frightened mothers and daughters and the usual travelling Colombo city workers, so soon returning after the troubles. The soldiers ordered the 2nd class passengers to move to the 1st class. They moved the Minster to the 2nd class; they also changed their tops to civilian clothes and let their SMGs hang low. A few stood at the end of the corridors. Prior to the departure, Mr. Prahash got up and spoke to the soldiers in Sinhalese, and said to look after the people. They seemed to agree and gestured not to worry.

'We won't do anything, except if there is an attack from the jungle. That will put us and all these people in danger,' said one officer. 'I am on a holiday. I have done my twelve months in Jaffna, thank you. I am going home to see my family,' said the officer. Mr. Prahash shook the officer's hand.

When Mr. Prahash got off the train, Jana saw a tear from the big man. He had never witnessed such a moment ever before. For some reason, Jana felt he might not see him again. Jana never understood why he felt that way; something told him in his ill fated negative mind that there was a tragedy ahead. Jana disliked his father's methods, but he had learned the reasons when he left to work abroad on the ships. He had learned to love him since he came back from his hard work on the high seas. He never raised his hands again towards his children; he had been the bedrock of the family.

Mr. Prahash pulled out a cricket bat and running spikes and gave them to Jana as a surprise going-away present, appreciating his sporting achievements.

He said: 'Good luck, be good. I will pray for you.'

Jana waved his hand, the train moved slowly. He saw his father red-eyed, tearful, until his image faded in the distance.

Jana took the transistor radio and turned it on; plugged his earpiece in and sat back in his window seat.

He would sit and not even bother to look outside. That was a moment that changed Jana's life forever. He looked at that brand new grey Nicholas bat and the Puma red and white canvas spikes, and for the first time he wasn't interested in sports.

After sitting for two hours quietly thinking about all the Jaffna family, relatives and friends, he got up and started to say hello to the fellow travelers and even to the officers of the army. The topic was cricket. They all asked about Jana's cricket and the trips on the train to Colombo. Some soldiers joined in with the civilians. After all, they looked young, just out of the officer cadet school, just following the orders from the difficult government, beginning the process of ethnic dominance.

The trip turned out as planned, safe and swift without any delays. Jana reached Colombo that afternoon after making a few friends on the train. Picking up his cricket bat, and his running spikes sticking out of his holdall, Jana looked like he just coming from a cricket match. The smell of diesel and malu bun came from the Colombo Fort Station platforms. Station workers, in shorts and sarongs, looked blacked out by diesel smoke and black dust. Some buildings were still smoking from

322

the riots earlier that week. Colombo came back to life as normal. Mini buses and Toyota Hiaces were picking up people randomly from the station Fort Road, to Galle, Mountlevenia, and Kotehena Ettiyawatte as the conductors screamed the destinations while holding notes folded up in between fingers with change in their palms, hanging onto the door as they approached the pickup area. Jana saw the different sense of ill feeling of Colombo. This was not the place he had visited a year ago. Jana was quickly picked up by the rice dealers of Petah in a car. They took Jana near a Marathna safe house. The area was controlled by the Banana Garden gangsters who were working closely with the ministers. Rice dealers had the minister bribed to protect the Tamils born and bred in that area. One agent came to the house and took Jana's passport. This agent came highly recommended from the senior businessman in the city and had all the right connections. He said he would be back in an hour, after taking a few photocopies. He also asked Jana to show his traveling bags, to keep it to a minimum. Jana asked about his bat and the running spikes. The agent looked, and for a moment Jana thought he might be asked to leave that behind. After a moment's silence, the agent said: 'That's good, Jana, keep it. Do you have a cricket jumper? Put that on when traveling, too. You are leaving tomorrow. Don't speak to anybody. Stay indoors,' he warned Jana. 'I don't want you to speak to anybody until the job is done, ok?'

Jana shook his head. He was anxious.

The agent said: 'It's bad luck speaking about it before you go, even to the airport. Are you hungry? I will bring some kothu roti, ok?' he smiled. 'See you in a few hours.'

When he came back he bought a Sri Lankan Club cricket bag and said: 'Put your clothes in this bag. You are going to play cricket in London. That's your next destination.'

Money was transferred shop to shop from Jaffna to Colombo; Jana never handled or saw any money. Jana, for the first time, tried to undo the spike laces to try on his new shoes. He puts his hands inside and stretched the canvas and felt a few pieces of paper inside. When he pulled it out it was 200 dollars in a rubber band. Mr. Prahash had said nothing about this to Jana. Jana got a going away pocket money. That was the first real pocket money he had ever received from his father. That's all he would have in his pocket when he landed in England.

The following day, Jana was escorted by a few Sinhalese youths to the airport. They worked for a Tamil businessman in Colombo. In Colombo, there were many Sinhalese people who saved thousands of Tamil friends and families from the government thugs and paramilitaries during the riots. The war was not between the Tamils and Sinhalese. It has always been between Tamils and the dictatorial distant right wing politicians of Sri Lanka.

Jana took out his rosary from his top pocket. He was one of the few to safely reach the airport that day. A lot of unaccompanied Tamil people were ambushed by the militia on the way to the airport. Jana looked through the window at the world outside: cars and vans were being stopped and searched by the police and local youths holding machetes. Some were beaten as they stood on the side of the road and their passports burned. Someone in the train car said, *please don't look outside.*

Jana arrived safely at the airport. The agent said to him: 'You are going wherever he goes,' and he pointed out an insider. 'I think it is desk J. That guy with the big moustache. He is also a big cricket fan, he will ask you where the Marleybone Cricket Club is in England. I am sure you know that answer. Keep your answers to a minimum. I mean minimum even inside the plane. Enjoy the United Kingdom. You are free. Say thank you to your father. A big thank you, sir,' said the agent. Then he was gone.

Jana gave the man with the big moustache twenty dollars to buy some food for the travelling boys. He said: 'Thank you, sir. I guess I will see you at Lords.'

Jana took his transistor radio, connected to the BBC World Service, while sitting in the airport lounge. He heard: *any Tamils who fear for their lives can take shelter in the United Kingdom temporarily. You will not need a visa. Cases will be scrutinized individually. Any bogus applications will be deported immediately without hesitation.* Jana could not believe his luck. He thought about his dad: *he had pre-planned all this, from Jaffna to the airport, he had put together an elite team of professionals to help me get inside the airport so I could reach London. I was lucky - among the few hundred people travelling tonight after losing someone in the family.*

Bogus agents and train robbers, all made life miserable for so many unfortunate travelers that week. Jana was finally in the plane, travelling to Great Britain to his favorite destination in the world: London. Land of the horse races, Beatles, Seb Coe, Keegan, rugby, boat races, Oxford, Cambridge, formula one, ships, Tornados and Spitfires, Wimbledon, the Queen, Wembley Arena and the Lords Cricket Grounds.

He also loved London for films: Hitchcock, Lean, Reed, Gilbert and Sweeny. Loved the London of Alfie's. Loved the London of frenzy. Love the London for its docks and gangsters. He loved the home of James Bond.

He was about to see the English countryside and the English gardens.

Jana loved the architecture and the houses all lined up with front and back gardens with fences. The streets looked wide and clean. Traffic lights, cats eye sparkling green on the road, British Rail hooting the horns, rows of cars moving slowly in traffic, all of it colorful, sparkling like fireworks for Jana.

He looked in amazement when he looked outside the plane. Somebody tapped on his shoulder and asked, is this your first time to UK?

Jana said: 'This is my first time ever in a plane, sir.' People nearby smiled. Jana asked others: 'How about you? You travel often?' He was happy to talk to every European he saw that day. One American lawyer gave Jana his card: *if you're ever in the States give me a call.* 'Thank you, sir. Sure I will, sir,' said Jana. They saw his genuine and innocent enthusiasm.

The plane touched down at London's Heathrow Airport.

Jana followed the crowd to the waiting room where he was screened and processed.

His new life would all begin in a few hours. It was going to be a long day and night in this country.

He had arrived.

His dream had come true. He knew he was going to be happy in this country.

Late 70's over a small rock bridge... YARL DEVI - along the LOTUS RIVER, overlooking the Bandaria gardens.

327

CHAPTER TWELVE

WERE YOU BORN HERE?

All passengers on that Air Lanka flight were stranded at Charles de Gaulle Airport. The airline, agents and Ministry of Sri Lankan Transport had plans to take the money off the Tamils. Every time there was trouble in Sri Lanka, people tried to escape. So the transport machine worked with some Tamil traitors by doing an inside deal. The Tamil passengers all wondered how come they let us through the airport. Some of the children did not know anything of the dilemma they all faced, so they ran around the transit area really enjoying watching the Europeans walking around. Some mothers did not show their sorrow to their kids. They were in France and couldn't speak the language; there was fear they might be deported. Some boys planned to storm the gates and run away.

They waited and showed their tickets which clearly stated their flight and destination. The Sinhalese pilot did his best to make their lives miserable, even in Europe. He did not succeed on this occasion. Jana, and another lady called Romi, negotiated seats on two different Air France flights to

London. That was one of the first victories for the escaping Tamils. They had just exercised their first right, the right to be an airline passenger.

All the passengers eventually made it to Heathrow safe and sound. Some relatives worried for their loved ones and waited at the airport for more than ten hours.

The Heathrow waiting area was heaven for them. Some of the arrivals had already been taken by their relatives who told the others not to worry about anything: you are home safe and you can call your families tomorrow.

Jana and the remaining Tamils waited for a few hours waiting for their names to be called one by one. Everybody wondered whether there were temporary camps they would be going to or some bed and breakfast places, maybe even a detention centre. Everybody was quite anxious and sat quietly, exhausted. It was almost eighteen hours since they had left Colombo Airport.

One immigration officer shouted: 'Anybody speak English?'

Jana lifted his hand immediately and offered his services. He was excited to talk to the first British Immigration Officer. He walked up in his all-white cricket uniform.

The officer asked: 'What's the score like? Do you play cricket?'

Everybody laughed. Jana also laughed and said: 'It is obvious right? You are teasing me, right, sir?'

'No, no, no,' said the officer.

'Yes, sir,' said Jana, opening bat.

The officer said: 'Great. What's your name please?'

'Janarthanan but everybody call me Jana.'

'Ok Jana, we will do the same. We need your help, Jana. First, we need to quickly register all these people. You need to explain to them about these forms, nothing serious, don't worry too much. We are going let all of you into the country. You are all commonwealth citizens and have a genuine reason to come here. We are aware of the difficult situation you are in. We will also ask Sri Lankan Airlines to explain the 'mishap' in France. You have the right to appeal for your money back or compensation. Ok, Jana?'

Jana nodded his head and said: 'Thank you for understanding.'

'So, Jana, what made you to come to the UK?'

Jana smiled. 'First of all, you came to our country uninvited but I have come here after receiving an invitation from you, via the BBC World Service. It has been broadcast that the genuine refugees will get a chance to better their lives with adequate English language or even as qualified professionals to contribute to the British economy, such as doctors and nurses. So my father sold everything except his house, took a big risk to send me to safety, because my interest was in medicine after my A Levels. Unfortunately, my cousins, uncles, my school friends and their relatives either died or were abducted by the paramilitaries. Most of the people around us in Jaffna simply began to disappear. I was waiting to get my advance level results and planning to go abroad to do medicine. Then, miraculously, I got this opportunity to come here. We are the lucky few. Thousands will not make it to Colombo Airport.'

'Sorry to hear about that,' said the Immigration Officer.

Jana gave all the funeral documents, the letter from the local parish priest, and his letter from the college to the officer.

'So what do you like about this country apart from cricket?' asked the officer.

'I like the railway, education system, judicial system and Sebastian Coe. He is a fantastic runner.' Jana was excited, with a smile on his face: 'I like watching him run. He will take the 1500 hundred in Los Angeles, I am sure. He is the best in the world. A record breaker. I followed his career with his father from the early days.'

The officer smiled.

Jana translated for all and helped the elderly and frail. Most of the people were picked up by their relatives. Tamil organizations and community centers helped the women and children. Even though England was in crises, the charitable organizations did their best for the Sri Lankan Tamil refugees. Jana and a few boys were the last ones to leave. Jana sat and watched all the people leaving. He worried whether he would be put in a detention centre because he had no relatives. When he looked around, there were only the young Tamil men remaining. They were lined up just as they had been lined up in front of the army back home for an ID check. He was a little scared but kept a positive face, while others looked down and depressed. Jana approached the desk: 'Ok, sir. It's me now. I am ready for the real interview.'

'Ah Jana, let me look at your papers,' said the officer. 'Jana, you have more qualifications than me. Seriously, I am not joking. Your character reference from your college is excellent. Leader of Catholic Student Federation, Rotary Interact Club President, athletics, cricket. You are an all-rounder and you will have no problems in this country. We have decided to give you a temporary visa for the time being. You are free to go. Free to study and work. Thank you for all your help with the translations. You are going to be fine. Go on now, Jana.'

For a minute, Jana wanted to stay a little longer and talk.

The officer pointed out an older well-built gentleman with grey hair wearing a suit: 'You are going to go with this gentleman, Mr. Singam, a trustee of the Hindu Temple in Effra Road, Wimbledon.

Jana said: 'Wimbledon? Wow… amazing. Wimbledon.'

Jana was already thinking of Wimbledon of tennis. Borg, Macenroe, Connors, Lendel – just brought back great memories.

'Those people who have no relatives or friends in this country, Mr. Singam will help with accommodation at the Hindu Temple.'

Jana would get all the information and help. He would stay and sleep on the floors of the Hindu Temple for two weeks with his twenty other male refugees. The temple provided food, clothes and social advice. The temple's regulars would come and talk and give them gifts of advice towards education and employment.

The following morning, Jana was woken up from a bad dream by the temple staff. Jana explained the dream to his friends: *he was switching on the Sri Lankan TV while waiting to go abroad. Suddenly, a man came into the room and said to please switch off the TV. He looked afraid and was blood-stained. You are new here, we don't watch TV here. It's not allowed. It's all bad news. He continued scratching his bloody head, and picking out an animal tooth from his tangled hair. Do you realize, we are not far from the Velikadai Prison? A week ago the murderers and rapists were all let out to kill the Tamils. It's a real dirty place but surrounded by the colorful garden city of Borella among the beautiful churches and schools. They kept the Tamil prisoners, Mani and other political prisoners, in one quarter, feeding them with good buriyani as a last supper. They were hungry, they ate it all quickly, except one man, Mani, whom they tortured several times on the notorious fourth floor. He never talked. He knew*

332

they are going to kill him anyway. The case collapsed with no evidence. The legal system in Sri Lanka sometimes overrode the Presidency. Quite remarkable for a country with a terrible human rights record. Mani spat at every torturer until he collapsed in pain. They planned to kill him inside the notorious Velikadai Prison but they waited for the opportunity. Well, the July riots were a bonus for the intelligence. They put away all the enemies one by one. They were planning to pay back for the dead soldiers of the north. They opened the doors of the mass murderers and let them in to the Tamil prisoners' quarters, who were just about to finish their meal. They decapitated Mani first, then the rest of the prisoners, it was a bloodbath. Finally, they carried the heads around the town while burning the Tamil homes and businesses, looting and raping. It all happened around here said the bleeding man. They took pictures for the newspapers. My sister was one of the girls they took. He cried and screamed. Jana also cried while telling the story. I said, that's enough. I took a machete and killed one of the devils. I cut down the shoulder of the second one. I was happy then. I was happy for once. I began to enjoy the execution of a murderer. Dirty Singhalese blood flowed in some thickness. I felt somebody biting, somebody biting my head. I turned around - they let a mad Alsatian dog attack me. He took a piece out of my head, and the man turned to show the half open skull. The dog barked, blood was everywhere, Jana screamed… no… no… dog… mad… dog…

'Somebody hold him, please,' said someone in the temple. 'Calm down, calm down. It was only a dream. It was only a dream.'

The Hindu priest gave Jana some blessed lemon water to drink.

Jana switched on the TV and, with tears in his eyes, calmly said: 'That was a real dream, a real story; it's been happening right now.'

Everybody looked at him strangely and said, *he is gone loose.*

Loose was the Tamil expression for a nervous breakdown. *A Singhalese mad dog must have bitten him and given rabies,* tells another housemate. Everybody laughed.

'Shhhh… shhhh,' said an ex-navy boy, Ragu. 'Breaking news: London race riots, miners' strike, economic crises.' Jana has walked away from the nightmare right into the troubles. Now he had to fight racism, skinheads, football hooligans and, moreover, face another female prime minister who was in the mood to radicalize and destroy British traditions by creating yuppies and shoulder pads.

That was the era of strong-willed women and weak men rulers such as Indira Gandhi, Srimavo, Golda Meir, and Margret Thatcher. They did open the doors for female equality and proportional representation. They also brought troubles to their country and in the process killed thousands. Srimavo killed the Tamils, Gandhi killed the Sikhs, Golda Meir killed the Palestinians, Margaret killed her own people with starvation, race riots, strikes, poll tax and the Falklands. During this time, in the name of freedom, they created more widows than ever before.

Jana was quite unsettled in the Kingdom that was not completely united. It was such a culture shock. He had very few friends who had also come to England after the violence in Sri Lanka. Most of the young boys suffered from the trauma of violence. Arguments would erupt in the shared house in regard to politics and discrimination. Jana eventually found a box room in Palmerston Road in Wimbledon. The Y.M.C.A., Cinema, Tiffany's Night Club, 80's music and fashion, all fascinated Jana. He would stand in the road and smile at people and watch for hours just to understand the south London culture. Jana loved the London girls. To him, all the girls were beautiful. He was somebody who appreciated women of all natures; he found some attraction in every single gorgeous London girl. He was told off by a few for staring constantly. He was in love with all the girls.

Somebody gave him a part-time cashier job in the local Fina Garage.

The country was under tremendous pressure. Soup kitchens were opened up to keep the unemployed from starving. Rubbish was not collected for months and it littered the streets of London. Tamil boys were in the news, too. The immigration officers had found discrepancies in some of their paperwork; they were to be forcefully deported from Heathrow. The youths quickly dropped their pants and shirts, then stood in just their underwear on the tarmac, half-naked – person. The law says you cannot deport a naked man. This caught the media headlines. Islington MP, J. Robin, fought hard for the Tamils plight and raised the issue in the parliament. He reminded the government of the Geneva Convention, to stop all enforced evictions. The Tory Home Office Minister, Leon the Dispatcher, wanted all the Tamils out of the country. His policies were unfair and broke all the rules. He later became the European Commissioner and served all the people according to the European Law. The Tamil boys succeeded and were given indefinite leave to remain in the UK. Most of them were qualified professionals in medical and civil engineering fields.

One late evening, while working in the Fina Garage, Jana saw a few youths pushing a car towards the service station. While one remained near the car, the other three came to the counter and told Jana they wanted to purchase a petrol can. They explained what happened to their car. They were stranded. Jana's manager had insisted that under no circumstances was he to open the door at night. The camera surveillance or mobile phone technology had not yet arrived. Jana, in a helping mood, took the money, gave them the change and then took the can to them via the main door. When he opened the door to give the can, suddenly there were six of them. They had come from nowhere. They had been hiding behind the building, waiting for the signal.

One punched Jana and shouted: 'Take him in. Take him in,' he ordered the others: 'Go on, go on behind the counter. All of you hide below the glass and stay there. Shut that door and put the closed sign up.'

Jana was bleeding from his nose and lips. They dragged him down the corridor to the toilet. One of them put Jana on the toilet seat, put a knife to his face: 'Don't look up. If you look up again, you lose your fucking eye. Look the fuck down.'

Jana just could not believe the fast-organized attack. He heard noises from the store. A few minutes later, they said: 'Let's go!' They shouted back to Jana: 'You are lucky, you fucking Paki. You are a lucky motherfucker!' he said over and over.

The other one said: 'Let's go now.'

They were all gone. Or so Jana thought. He was about to look when the knife cut his ear lobe and his attacker said: 'He bleeds like a fucking virgin.' Then he left to catch up with his mates.

Jana waited for some moments until he was sure they were all gone. He pushed open the door gently, trying to stop the bleeding; there was blood everywhere.

Jana would learn about racism and hatred for foreigners very quickly. He began to be introverted and did not talk to anybody for weeks. After phoning the police, he phoned his boss. The racists took just over 70 pounds, cigarettes and

Maltesers. He never worked in the service station again. He was happy to escape with a broken nose and a cut ear lobe.

Jana phoned home every two weeks. His father would go to the nearest family house or an office to receive the call. Jana kept all the family optimistic telling them he was going to church on Sunday; he told nothing of his misfortunes, he always would tell the good and the positive of London. He would often travel far to find a vandalized BT phone booth which would take less for overseas phone calls.

They saved every penny in the eighties. They did not have a lot of money but were very proud to live near the famous Wimbledon Tennis Club, even in a box room. Jana would keep Mr. Prahash happy with small parcels which would reach him after three weeks to a month if, meantime, somebody had not tried to open it.

Jana's family told him the bad news; his father was ill and dying. The war had intensified in Jaffna. The army and air force had bombed any area that they suspected was home to the Movement of the Rebels, as they called it now. When the movement moved closer to the Kurunagar camp, they bombarded over a three mile radius of Jaffna Police Station, flattening all Jana and Indhiran's childhood hangouts: Rio Cinema, parks, courts, churches, Beach Road, Jaffna Central, and the top end of the Kurunagar. They came up to 3rd Cross Street, bulldozed shops, houses, including Granma's catering business - all went up in smoke. She fell ill, too and became bed ridden during the bombing in Jaffna. Over 2000 people died from indiscriminate shooting from the helicopters. Most of them were children on their way to school.

Indhiran stayed close to his family and fought the army. He was lucky to be alive. He lost his right arm and an eye. His hearing was also partially damaged. He was nursed with a few others in Chundikuli. Mr. Prahash was taking kids out of the camps, doing whatever he could. For a period he worked with the Sri Lankan Army as a Tamil moderator. He would shout: 'If only, if only they let the kids study the Sinhala language, without scaremongering about the Thamilarasu, we would have had a chance. We could have communicated, saved all these people from the grave. If only the bastards…' he repeated. He was always the old Congress man when it came to politics but his love for his Tamil Hindu cultural background was unlimited. The man believed in negotiation and communication. He learned that from an imminent friend and the country's best lawyer G.G.P. He was renowned for his election canvassing skills for his ministers. He said, *the young lack the knowledge how to resolve grievances without malice.*

Sri Lanka, asking or offered help from Rajive Gandhi was a big mistake. Historically, India invaded Sri Lanka for the riches, beauty and serenity. Rajive came to Sri Lanka for takes. One of the army soldiers tried to hit him with his gun during the parade inspection. It was a message he didn't grasp. It was humiliating for him, something like his mother's assassination by a Sikh soldier. He decided to send the Indian Peacekeeping force. They tested their banned chemical weapons on innocent Tamils, prior to using them on the Pakistani/Kashmir borders. The movement had been fighting just the local army. Now the Indian Peacekeeping Force was coming into Jaffna. Seeing that all the lifestyle and space was better than in India, made them greedy. They wanted to take it all. At least, they wanted some of it. They began their real damage with rape and torture and killing. The movement would *fight* at both ends: one side the Indians, the other side the SLA. The movement would *defeat* both ends, the Indian army lost on all sides, the SLA also had heavy losses. Eventually, India was kicked out of Jaffna. The Sri Lankan Government finally began talks with the Tamils.

Mr. Prahash had been imprisoned by the Indian Peacekeeping Force for two months during which time he was beaten. When he was released, he had lost weight. He looked insane and had given up. Jana's sister said: 'He will argue with his kids and with Marie Joyce.'

Mr. Prahash and injured Indhiran who had the machete, tried to defend his aunt. Marie Joyce was forced to move out of the house, unable to cope with her disability and the constant arguments. Her youngest daughter left home to follow her mother's path to become a teacher. She would train in Trinco and work in the volatile eastern regions during these conflicts, living alone with locals.

The eldest girl, Jocelyn, had to take shelter in Europe. She would marry her love and live in Germany.

Mr. Prahash was sick and alone. He was looked after by the youngest sister at home, all the time refusing treatment for his cancer.

Jana was helpless in London. He was also disturbed, unable to make sound decisions with his life. He would sit in the church alone for long hours. One day, Mr. Prahash called everybody and apologized for his behavior in recent times. He realized his end was near. Dr. Abraham had given him a few weeks to live.Uncle vijay also suddenly died of a heart attack due to worries about his hard worked fortune been decimated by the thiefs in the south.His legacy was another story and a sad one.He was a great man.He was his real uncle and a father.That was the nail on the coffin for jana's future dreams.

Jana walked into a London Soho bar and started drinking

and meeting with Bohemians in an attempt to forget his miserable life. Mr. Prahash managed to survive another six months in bed coping with his pain, unable to eat or drink, even talk, anymore. He was fed by tubes and high energy drinks. He would sleep with his Bible and Rosary Beads from Lourdes.

Later that week, after seeing a Catholic priest in Wimbledon, Jana would get a job in the Priory House as a care assistant. He would work in the acute psychiatric unit. He was good at his job. He coped with the mentally ill with a lot of patience. He was a professional, maintained confidentiality, and gained respect from the staff very quickly. The Charge Nurse, Mac from Mauritius, took a liking to Jana and gave him advice on how to apply for nurse training. Jana listened and learned from experienced Mac who handled violent patients with alertness and calmness. He was always ahead of the insane. They all thanked him when they were discharged, not remembering any of their bad episodes.

Jana was accepted to train in Queen Mary's, London.

He would run in Richmond Park, occasionally, while studying. He also worked part time as a care assistant.

With difficulties, Jana qualified as a nurse, coping with indirect discrimination in the form of over-enthusiastic students with hidden agendas. He took the hospital and health authority to the tribunal. While waiting for the tribunal Jana continued his training with great difficulties. Jana was given a job with a contract back at Priory House. He also got to live in the staff quarters.

He would enjoy his new life as a qualified nurse. In his first year of nurse training, his father passed away. Under immigration rules, Jana was not allowed to leave the country. Most of the refugees who found living in Europe too hard and who went back, were tortured on arrival, then imprisoned as movement sympathizers. Some simply disappeared. Jana was traumatized. He began to miss his father badly. Mr. Prahash had wanted all the good things for his family. He never wanted anything for himself. Such a man Jana will never see again. That devastated Jana. His father's funeral was held at St. Mary's in Jaffna. There were thousands of officials, ministers, farm workers, municipal workers, fishermen, doctors, relatives and friends all the way from Delft, Vanni, Vadamaratchi, even from the capital Colombo. The Ranga uncle and Mannikam families took care of the funeral. People were surprised as the crowd walked all the way to Jaffna Cemetery. He was always only a simple man. A simple agricultural officer with lot of charisma, integrity and belief.

After his father's death, Jana's relationship with his sisters and mum broke down. He just could not forgive all this had happened while he was away. He blamed himself. By doing that, he became secluded and did not talk to his family for at least another three years. He would sit and watch athletic meets, then he would start to cry like a baby non-stop for hours alone, thinking of his father.

His life became unbearable in London.

Jana went back to Soho, started trying hard drugs and funk rock trance and redemption.

He finally found his corner in Artistic London. Everybody loved Jana's enthusiasm and his honesty. He also had style.

Life in Soho with his Irish friend, Jess-Donny, took Jana to his new found artistic freedom as a club promoter, starting on top of a Chinese restaurant in Gerrard Street. He quickly formed DJs and bands to perform free for their own promotions and got 20% from the bar and the doors. He began to enjoy his part-time, once a week, escape from the busy mental wards.

A few months later, a bomb landed in Chundikuli and destroyed the back of the family house.

His elder sister arranged a marriage for the youngest who would immigrate to France after marrying a French Sri Lankan. Her wedding was held in Colombo, and was taken care of by her father's friends.

Marie Joyce joined her eldest daughter in Germany; she was quite ill with renal failure but would live to see her grand children. Marie Joyce always thought about her only son. She always said: 'I will never die until I see my son.'

Jana, as a qualified medical prfesional, would get his permanent residency and be allowed to travel abroad.

Jana had missed two weddings and one funeral. He really wanted to see his mother.

When he arrived, Marie Joyce saw a fit and matured young man from London.

Jana stayed in Germany for a week and spent the last days asking about his father, late Grandma Joan and Indhiran. Indhiran survived the war and left the fighting. He married a teenage sweetheart from the Holy Family Convent, moved to India and opened a café in Tamil Nadu.

One day, back working in a London hospital, Jana received a call from his sister saying *your mum wants to talk to you.* Marie Joyce would say her last words to Jana: 'I am going, my son. I am going. Your dad is calling me. Take care and marry a nice girl.' She passed away peacefully on Easter Sunday in Germany. She was one of the most generous, giving, kind-hearted, soft spoken women with inner and outer beauty. She had always spoken very little but thought about everybody and about life. Jana had learned a lot from her life, even though he had to live away from her for a long time. They all missed her tremendously. Her funeral was held at the beautiful Garden Cemetery in Stuttgart, attended by relatives from all around the world. Everybody cried for her unlimited kindness and generosity.

She was lying frozen in front of everybody. Jana touched her and felt her numbness. Even some of her young students, now grown up with kids of their own, wanted to pay respects to their beloved teacher. As usual, her brother Reggie got drunk and disorderly and caused bodily harm to a relative and was deported by the German authorities. Mr. Prahash had always been right about him; he had failed to take his chances to improve the family name of Bastian. He would become a heavy alcoholic refusing to get any help and spend his life in Jaffna sleeping his days in verandahs and hallways unnoticed by anybody. His wife and son were somewhere in Germany and they did well and had a better life than him.

Jana wrote a tribute for his parents at the funeral:

'*Two people believed in other people's happiness before their own; they were the elders and leaders among their brothers and sisters. They were not only strong but also relied upon. No one could improve their greatness. Their love was discrete and they had immense respect for each other since the day they met in 1963 at St. Anthony's Kytes. It was only their weak flesh that let them down on their death beds. Their minds were pure and simple and strong. Mother believed in the Sacred Heart and taught everyone to believe in themselves. Father loved the land and agriculture and helped everybody to grow old gracefully. At the end, they are both surely in Paradise.*'

Jana read with tears, thinking of his younger sister who could not make it due to her pregnancy. She was in labor during the funeral. A beautiful girl was born who looked very much like Marie Joyce. Everybody said, *God takes one and gives one.* She would also be the favorite of Uncle Jana.

Jana brought the ashes from Germany and buried his mother in the beautiful Richmond Cemetery, where he ran every morning. The natural wildlife, streams, the deer, ancient trees and gardens - she would have loved all of it. Jana was sure she was looking out for him. That's what Jana believed. Jana believed his parents were saints.

Jana would run in Richmond Park, and visit his mum very often. He would sit on the bench and drift away, thinking of the day when he came first to Richmond Park twelve years ago, he had been running as usual.

The deer moved together, into the wood, the sun setting on Richmond Hill. Jana had never seen a lushness like this anywhere in London. Just a mile from Hammersmith Bridge. The Thames, Barnes Pond, St. Paul's, the woods of Roehampton and Putney, all looked amazing and so near to each other. The little stream in Richmond Park with its clear water moved slowly stroking the stones gently. Jana went close and looked for black guppies. He saw a reflection of Indhiran pointing out: 'Look over there, stupid. Over there.' He looked up but there was nobody. He grabbed a stick and threw it away in the air. Walking slowly in the middle of the park he saw a shadow of a running man with grey top and blue shorts with Nike style shoes, coming towards him from the hill downwards. It was almost like the man with no name coming from the smoke of the dessert heat; the shadow of a pale runner. That was the first man he had seen running alone since he came to London in the 1983. Few cars passed through; an orange Capri, metallic blue Renault Fuego, dark blue Granada and a slow moving flower van which seemed to go forever. The old florist took his time doing the 10mph limit. His van blocked the runner but the running man began to gain ground as he went to pass the vehicles fairly quickly. Jana looked closer and closer. The action of the running looked familiar. He thought he had seen this man somewhere before. It finally came into his head. He just could not believe it! This was just a few weeks after he landed in Wimbledon. It was Jana's childhood hero, Sebastian Coe, training for the Los Angeles Olympics. The world record holder of 1.41.73. The Olympic Champion, training in Richmond Park while everybody had written him off as burned out. Jana could not believe it. He wished Indhiran was here; most of all the bullies of the churchyards. Jana looked at the stream where he saw the reflection. He saw the image of Indhiran smiling and smelling his right hand. He looked at the champion with tears in his eyes. He moved slowly like a shadow. Jana punched the air saying: 'Go on, you champ. Go on, you champ.' Then he cried for the people of Jaffna and punched the ground. He cried for the losing runners. He cried for those who could not finish the run. Jana believed the spirit, believed the talent of Seb Coe will prevail. Seb Coe ran passed with a smile. That was a great moment of Jana's life. Sometimes, if you wish for something so bad, it will come closer than you ever could imagine and scare the hell out of you. Sebastian Coe retained his 1500 hundred title and said to the world he is the number one in the middle distance. He also successfully brought the Olympics home. His campaign was the children of the world taking part in London.

Jana's little niece loved to run. She ran in the park and once a month she visited her Grandma's resting place. Jana would tell her stories. She loved running unlike anybody else in the extended Prahash family. She was also winning all the competitions in school. Somebody said, she's got God's gift. There are a lot of refugee children around the world who will take part in the London 2012 Olympics because of their athletic powers. That's the beauty of London, it is a cosmopolitan multicolored city like no other, where everybody buries their past and learns to move on. Earlier refugees have contributed to make the country a world player. That was the beauty of this present empire. This is the beauty of the Commonwealth; this is the only beauty of the past empire.

After a long time, middle-aged Jana felt like running again. Will his niece break the record and carry the flags for Tamils and Great Britain? Yes. The day she decided to take part, was the day she had already won through participation alone. She will take the lap of honor. Whatever she chooses to do, one thing Jana knows, he will be there to support her all the way to the finish line. Jana dreams for that day. Now, at least once a week, he runs with his niece in the Regents Park, London. He began to talk and remember his cousin Indhiran, now living in India. Jana promised to make a trip to India and help his cousin with his small farm.

Jana and his niece are planning to run the 10k in Hyde Park in support of Charity International and the suffering of the many in Asia under dictatorships. The first time Jana was fit and running well, the troubles in Sri Lanka escalated, more lives were lost through betrayal by the allies of the Tamils and in-fighting led to genocide. Jana wanted to do something to make people aware of the plights of the concentration camps. He cycled through London while talking to strangers on street corners. He did that for hours. He wanted them to know this is his home. He cycled through Regent's park, passing the occasional night fireworks at the BT Tower. Jana always argued for London to host the 2012 Olympics. He put a point across about how London had recovered to host the Olympics from post war ruins; people did not have food to eat, but they wanted to host the Olympics, for the glory of England and for the kingdom united, for the great British spirit. Jana argued that history repeats. London was now in modern capitalist problems, recession, wars, terrorism, floods, volcanoes, heavy winters, heat wave, oil spills, and fat cats. England will overcome and host the *greatest show in Europe in the midst of the Commonwealth of multi-cultured Stratford in east London. The people will run for love, run for the suffering, run for their dreams, run for their countries; the people of Great Britain will unite, will come and love London even more. They will also host the World Cup in a few years' time. The East London train line, Kings Cross, and St. Pancreas will show the world who started the train travel around the world.*

Jana would successfully run his last 10k for the charities. Watching at home with his family, Jana thought about why he was never lucky in love. He felt a little pain in his chest… he was soon admitted to the Accident and Emergency with myocardial infarction. Jana had no underline illness, he was fit and healthy, running and cycling in London. It was very mysterious for everybody. As he lay waiting for the open heart surgery, all he could thing of was Jaffna, the place where he was born, of his classmates, Rish, Les, Angel, his gang, and of his Dutch cycling partners all cruising past Park Lane looking at the girls of St. Johns Chundikuli. The red and black ties, plaited hair beautiful Tamil girls all walking hand in hand with a smile. Tears came from his face and dripped on his shoulder.

He said to his doctor: 'Tell her I have written it all down. I have written it for my father, I have written it for my mother,I have written it for my aunts, I have written it for my cousins and my people. I am happy to go to the theatre where you will cut my heart open, a heart of pain and suffering alone without my father. I am ready doctor.'

Jana never recovered from his operation. As soon as he was given the anesthesia, he babbled like a tortured soul in his dreams. Then he was quiet. The anesthetist put the tapes on his eyes just before 1000 watt lights gleamed over his body on the cutting table.

The surgeon's report would state that Jana had a severely damaged artery.

Jana was wheeled into the recovery room for formalities, but all the machines were shut down.

He wanted a quiet funeral and after-party at his favorite African club with dj Gower.R and Collin.P. He had even written that down.He loved the soul,funk and the African roots music.

He was buried with his mother in London.

Jana was a fighter, born on the 11th, an extrovert who had an interesting life, an ever-changing chameleon with his appearance. He looked like a young man again lying in his coffin. His family Hindu palm reader had told his father years ago when Jana was three, *when 46 years old, your son will be the king of the world.* He never stressed which world.

He was right all the time said his sisters.

In his diary he wrote so many different theories and scenarios to get back what the Tamils lost in Elam: the dignity, especially for his sisters, and for the female rebel fighters who faced the killing fields of Sri Lanka.

The next generation looks ahead to build clubs and tournaments and interschool athletic meets in London and Jaffna, looking for that next sporting protégé, the next one to carry the flag in the future Olympic Games. The flags of Ellam as a nation.Jaffna begin to rebuild the bombed railway lines and transport infurstructure.Everybody hope for Tamil gets opportunities and employment in their own land.Without being treated for slave labour in their own land by forighn contractors.That is our new and current agenda while we wait for the conclusion of this terrible conflict.

Jana lies in his grave, his niece's medal in his hands.

As the wind blows rain in over south London one person stands alone in front of the tombstone. After a few moments, she starts to run through the rain in Richmond Park. She can hear the sound of the drums and cheer of the pavilion at the Stratford Olympic Stadium.

No martyr's songs will be written about Jana. He did not take a bullet for his country but it killed him nonetheless.

They will tell of his prowess on the cricket field and his curiously smiling face and how he never married any one girl because he loved all the girls.

Some will read his story and know and understand.

Jana loved his people.

He loved his country.

Two elephants in the matchbox, the suffering of many and the celebration of a few, on a small island. Whether this is in Sri Lanka or Great Britain, the wars of the world are too painful for any mother who loses a child in any continent.

Whoever you represent, help to open those matchboxes and release the stricken souls.

"THE ONE WHO SEES THE FINAL BEND AND THE TEARS THAT CROSS THE LINE" THE GAMES 2012 LONDON.

TEARS CAME TO OUR EYES WHEN WE SAW A CHAMPION MIDDLE-DISTANCE RUNNER FLY THE FINAL BEND IN MOSCOW.

SINCE THAT DAY WHENEVER WE WATCH A MIDDLE DISTANCE RUNNER SOME OF US HAD TEARS. ONLY THING WE CAN DO IS RUN.

SO WE RAN THE HOT SANDS, TAMED THE ELEPHANTS, DIVED THE CORAL DEEP , DRANK THE TEA AND THE TODDY , PLAYED CRICKET WITHOUT STUMPS ,THOSE WERE THE GOOD TIMES BEFORE THE BAD TIMES IN THE ISLAND OF SERDIPITY NEAR INDIAN OCEAN.

BRITAIN ALSO A PROUD ISLAND OVERCAME THE WAR AND STAGED THE POST WAR OLYMPICS.NOW IT FACED WITH THE GLOBAL ECONOMIC CRISES.BUT WE SHALL OVERCOME AND FLY OUR FLAGS FOR OUR FATHERS.

SEB COE DID IT FOR PETER COE. TWICE HE KISSED THE FLOOR AND POINT THE INDEX FINGER. I AM THE NUMBER ONE IN 1984.

SPIRIT OF THE CHILDREN OF THE WORLD WILL DO IT FOR THIER NATIONS IN UNITED COLOURS .DREAMS THAT'S WON THE GAMES FOR US IN SINGAPORE.

IT WILL WIN IT FOR GREAT BRITIAN IN EAST LONDON. SOME WILL CRY WATCHING THE FINAL BEND OF A MIDDLE DIISTANCE RUNNER FROM THE STAGGERD START OF 1500M.

TEARS OF JOY WILL COME TO OUR EYES.THINKING OF THE SPORTING SPIRIT. TAKING PART, LAP OF HONOUR, MOMENT Of GLORY.CHEERING FOR THE BRAVEHEARTS, WILL CREATE AN UNFORGETABLE HISTORICAL MOMENT WITH ECHOES IN THE DISTANCE MILES.

WHILE FEELING THE FREEDOM FOR THE WOUNDED NATIONS AROUND THE WORLD.

IT WILL BECOME THE MOST EVER WATCHED EVENT OF THE EUROPEAN HISTORY.

REFUGEE CHILDREN OF THE WORLD WILL RUN FOR THEIR NEWLY ADOPTED FAMILY.MAY BE IN DIFFERENT COLORS BUT WITH A ROOTED HEART WITH RESOLVE FOR THE UNFORGETTABLE HOMELAND. KINGDOMS WILL UNITE WITH PEACE AND PROSPIERITY.

OLYMPIC SPIRIT WILL UNITE US ALL.

"THE ONE WHO SEES THE FINAL BEND AND THE TEARS THAT CROSS THE LINE"